FLAMES
of the
HEART

*The compilation of
You Were Mine For A Time and Passions And Pleasures.
Fifteen breathtaking short stories, turning sensuality into hot and
sexy nights of ecstasy. Plus, two new stories to kindle your passion
and ignite the flames of your heart.*

KATIE SANTEE

Flames of the Heart
Copyright © 2023 by Katie Santee

ISBN
978-1-959365-88-4 (Paperback)
978-1-959365-89-1 (eBook)

TABLE OF CONTENTS

ACKNOWLEDGMENTS

A lot of effort has gone into the compilation of these two hot, sexy, steamy short story books. I would be remiss if I didn't first recognize the person who talked with me for hours on end about the advantages of doing this book. Donald Anderson, my Literary Agent, was extremely patient with me, and worked through the struggles I had going on in my life as we worked for solutions to make this book possible. He is true to his words and never let me down. Thank you.

My family once again was put on the back burner as we worked to put this book together. Thank you to my husband for his kindness and understanding.

Many thanks to my fans for their support through the years. Their emails, phone calls, and purchases of my previous books have encouraged me to keep writing. It has been my goal to awaken sensuality, desire, and fantasies that lay within us. That the reader finds joy and happiness through their own pleasure.

As always: MAY ALL YOUR FANTASIES COME TRUE!!!!!

CLIMATIC FLIGHT

Our flight was leaving from LAX at five-thirty AM heading to Miami, FL with a three-hour layover and on to St. Croix, V.I. This was the first vacation Max and I had taken in nearly six years, since our son Jason was born. We were so looking forward to it. We had already received our boarding passes with our assigned seats. Max had the aisle seat and mine was the middle (between him and the window seat). We were the sixth row from the back in coach.

"I sure hope we don't get stuck sitting next to some loudmouth or snorer," I thought to myself as we boarded the plane.

To my great relief, the passenger was a pleasant looking man about six-foot-two and one-hundred-ninety pounds. Built like a brick shit house, he had sandy brown hair and was clean shaven. He nodded his head to us as we took our seats and we acknowledged him in return.

Once in the air, after refreshments were consumed, I draped a blanket over me, laid my head on my husband's shoulder and drifted off into a light slumber. I felt him lift my head, put his arm around my shoulders and put my head down on his chest.

Sometime later I felt his hand under the blanket, down on my right breast lightly rubbing it and teasing it with his fingertips through my blouse. It felt good so I made no reaction, but just sat there enjoying the feeling. I'm not sure if Max knew I was awake or not but he increased the pressure gradually and began pinching my nipple, pulling on it making it stand out.

"Oh God," I thought, "he's driving me nuts. He's got to stop this. He can't be doing this here. What if the guy next to me sees what he's doing?"

I started to lift my head up to protest but Max put his chin on the top of my head to keep me still. He turned his body a little toward me so his hand would reach my breast easier filling his whole hand. He massaged it, squeezing it and releasing it, then pinching and pulling on the nipple. I moaned quietly, but enough that Max heard me.

"Oh shit! That means the guy next to me by the window heard me too. Damn, what he must be thinking. He must think I'm some kind of slut!" These thoughts were going rampant in my brain.

The next thing I felt was a hand on my right thigh. Slowly, it started at my knee and went up to just below my hip. Then the hand went from the inside of my knee to the inside of my thigh to just below my vaginal area.

"That cannot be Max's hand as his is on my breast. So OH MY GOD!!!" Realization screamed at me.

I tried to move my leg away from the hand but it was held in place. Little did I know that Max had made eye contact with the man in the window seat and had nodded his approval when the man indicated his intentions. Max thought it would be a real turn on for me. He wanted to see how far I would let this go and if I would enjoy it or not.

The next thing I knew the hand was under the blanket and was pulling my skirt up my thigh by his fingertips. At the same time, Max was reaching inside my blouse and taking my breast out of my bra and teasing and tantalizing it.

The man on my right had turned in his seat so that he was now using his right hand and fingers.

Slowly, his hand moved back and forth from my knee to the edge of my pussy.... stopped...then went back down.... then back up again and gently moved over the edge of my white lace panties.

Meanwhile, Max had moved himself so that he now had the nipple of my right breast in his mouth and was suckling on it and driving me crazy.

Between the two of them I could not stay still in my seat.

Sandy, as I chose to refer to the man next to me, continued to move his fingers into my panties and work his magic on my labia. He whispered softly in my ear how soft my pussy felt and how he loved moving his fingers around inside my panties. He said I was getting wet and he was going to make me a lot wetter and would make me cum like I never had before. He kissed my neck, sucked on my earlobe and kept his fingers playing with my pussy lips, back and forth from front to back, over and over.

Oh, God I was so hot! My hips moved with his hand going up and down with his fingers moving to a rhythm all their own. As I moaned

Max covered my lips with his kissing me deeply, his tongue going into my mouth, circling around my lips and back into my mouth.

With my cunt getting wetter, Sandy inserted a finger into my hole and I came with a grip on his finger so tight he grinned at me.

"So, I guess you liked that, huh baby?" he asked me.

So into the climax was I that I couldn't answer him. All I could do was shake my head.

"You haven't felt anything yet darlin'." he stated matter of factly.

As he was telling me that, he inserted a second finger, reaching up to press on my spot while thumbing my clitoris. I exploded into a million pieces. Max had all he could do to keep me in my seat. My cum ran out of my pussy, all over Sandy's hand, down his arm and my legs. Holy Jesus...I came and came. I thought it would never stop. And Sandy didn't let up either. He kept pumping his fingers into my cunt, harder and harder and I came again.

"Oh My God. Oh My Gooooddddd!!!!" was all I could say muffled by Max.

Max reached over with his left hand and inserted another finger into my cunt and I really felt filled to the limit. I had slid so far down in my seat that my whole rear was off the end and Max wet his pinky finger and started rubbing my little pucker hole with it. Holy saints but that felt wonderful. Then he slid it in slowly. Pow...another orgasm hit me like a sledgehammer. Both holes tightened up and constricted several times and I felt overcome with the most extreme orgasm of a lifetime.

As I came down from the most fantastic climax ever I looked at two totally wonderful men. One I knew not at all, except that he had the most incredible fingers and the other, the best husband a woman could have.

While in the throes of my last climax, I had reached down and grabbed my husband's right thigh and held on for dear life. I had such a death grip on him that I probably left quite a bruise. As I calmed down I moved my hand and noticed that he had quite a hard on. Max was rather well endowed with a wide girth so it stood at attention proudly. I reached over and put my hand around him and caressed him, moving my hand up and down his length.

I also had grabbed Sandy's leg and noticed he had a hard on as well. Though he was a bit smaller than Max, I rubbed him in rhythm with my hand on Max. Both men were moaning and their cocks were growing with my stimulation.

Sandy undid his belt, unbuttoned and unzipped his pants pulling out his dick. He took my hand and put his hard cock in it, keeping his hand over mine as we rubbed his dick up and down while I took my finger and went over the tip. His precum was sliding over, around and down the sides. His cock was so slippery and wet. Oh, how I wanted my lips around him.

I turned sideways and bent over as Sandy raised the blanket, lifted his hips and brought his cock up to my mouth. Taking my tongue, I licked at the tip of his purple head tasting his precum and moving it around his head and down the shaft to the base by his pubic hair. I proceeded back up to the top and opened my mouth and put the head of his cock into my mouth. Sandy let out a low moan of pure lust. I circled the top of his prick with my tongue then moved my tongue down to the ridge and just below it running circles around and around. It was driving him crazy. His hips were moving back and forth, up and down, slowly pushing his dick further into my mouth. He hit the back of my throat and I started to gag but worked my way past it and swallowed him into my throat.

"Oh baby," said Sandy. "You do that so well. Suck my cock, girl. Take all of it."

That was all the encouragement I needed. I sucked him deep and hard. Keeping a steady rhythm, I moved my head up and down on him sliding his dick deep into my throat and back out to the tip again. With each up and down movement he let out a moan lower and louder than the last one.

"Ahhh....make me cum baby...I want to cum way down in your throat. Swallow me honey." Sandy pumped his cock deep and I felt his jism rising up from the bottom of his prick. I took his balls in my other hand as I held his shaft at the bottom while my lips pressed hard on him and I sucked for all I was worth.

He suddenly stiffened and I felt his warm cum hit the back of my throat. He held my head as he shot a huge load and I had all I could do to keep it in my mouth and swallow it before the next shot came and then another. Four or five in all and I didn't lose a drop.

As Sandy eased his hand off of my head I slowly pulled back up his cock, licking and sucking him clean, making sure I had gotten all of his cum off of him.

As I turned to look up at him, he had a huge smile on his face. He reached and pulled my face to him and gave me a kiss. Tasting himself on my tongue, he sucked it into his mouth and savored it. He then released it and held me close to him.

"Thank you. That was the best blow job I have ever had in my entire life," he said. "You are one hell of a woman and he is one lucky man," nodding his head toward my husband. I answered him with a giant grin on my face.

By this time Max was super hard and in need of my expert attention. He took hold of my shoulder and slowly turned me around to face him.

"Baby, you were very thoughtful to take care of Sandy over there, but I need your help here. You think you can take care of this problem before the plane decides to land?"

I took hold of his cock and gave it a squeeze and said, "Sure baby. anything in particular you had in mind?"

"Well, as a matter of fact, yes."

"Okay…what will it be? I am at your service, sir."

"Oh, sir is it? Well then, how about you place you lovely pussy over the top of this hardened pecker of mine and let me feel it in its home where it belongs."

With that said…I got up out of my seat and spread my legs so my pussy opened up and Max could slide his cock up inside me. Slowly I settled down on him until he was buried to the hilt…all the way to the hair on his balls.

"Oh my Lord…Max. you feel sooo good," I said quietly as I leaned into his chest with my back.

As Max nuzzled in my neck and kissed on my ear, shivers ran up and down my spine making my pussy quiver and want more of him. Max had me by my hips moving me up and down on his shaft as he was moving his hips back and forth. Then I felt a hand on my clit…moving in circles making it hard and making the little hood move back away from the head. God, I was getting so hot and wanted to cum so bad.

I looked over and there was Sandy looking at me and it was his hand on my clit. He kissed me hard and rammed his tongue into my mouth. He bit my bottom lip as he reached up and pinched my left breast…and he rubbed my clit harder. All of a sudden, this guy showed no mercy and pinched my clit hard and I came and came and came. My juices squirted all over Max's cock and Sandy's hand.

"Ahh, a squirter we have here," said Sandy.

Oh, God, I was coming so much…it wouldn't stop and they didn't stop…Max kept pumping his cock into me, harder and harder. Sandy wouldn't let off of my clit and I came again…more intense, more ecstatic, more erotic.

"Ahhh baby, your pussy is squeezing me so tight.. I'm going to cum so much…here it comes…ready love…it's yours."

And he did…so much. I felt him get so hard and pump after pump of his cum went into my love hole.

"Yeah baby…give me your love juice…cum in me. Fill me up lover." I cried.

It seemed like he pumped in me forever and I was filled to overflowing. His cum was running down my legs and Sandy had gotten a hand full. Lord have mercy but this was the best sex ever!!!!

Slowly, I slid back into my seat and pulled my panties back up. I laid my head back and turned to look first at Max and then at Sandy. Both had shit eating grins on their faces.

"What's so funny you two?" I asked.

"Well, baby. I would like to introduce you to Jacob Wilson. Jacob, this is my wife Sheila."

I looked at him dumbfounded.

"You see honey, Jacob and I work together. He told me one day that he thought you were one hot lady and wouldn't mind making it with you one day. So, after thinking it over I figured the only way to get you to go along was to do it this way and hope you would once we got you hot enough that you couldn't stop even if you wanted to. And baby, you were awesome!"

I didn't know whether to laugh or cry. So, this was all a big setup. How could my husband have done this to me? Although it did turn out to be pretty great.

I wanted to hit him but I reached up and laid a big lip lock on him.

"I can't believe you did this to me. But I must thank you because it turned out to be really great. Jacob…thank you. You were awesome. But next time guys…just ask me."

DOCTOR KEVIN

Today was Shannon's birthday, her 35th birthday to be exact. Long ago I had run out of ideas of what to get her and each year was getting harder and harder. This was definitely a milestone birthday and what in blue blazes was I going to get her.

"Honey don't forget that I'm going to the doctor for my yearly exam today," Shannon called to me from the master bathroom. "You'll have to pick up Cassidy (our 8-year-old daughter) from the sitters after you get off work, okay?"

"Sure doll, at Marissa's, right?" I asked her to make sure I had the right sitter.

"Yes, Kevin. She's been our only sitter for the last six months," Shannon answered me as she was walking into our master bedroom looking like a million bucks.

I was still laying on our king size bed in just my boxer shorts and my male body part immediately came to attention.

"Wow baby, you look fantastic. You always go to the doctor dressed like that?" I asked her as my cock got even harder.

"What?" she asked with a sheepish grin on her beautiful face.

Shannon had on a slim, tight fitting black stretch skirt and a vee neck pull over red and white long-sleeved sweater that showed her well-endowed chest off perfectly.

"I suppose you have on a thong too?" I asked her.

"Kevin, it's not like the doctor will care. He does these exams every day of the week, all day long. It's just another one to him. Don't get so bent out of shape about it. We go through this every year baby. Nothing to worry about. Besides, he won't see the thong because I will be completely nude. Well, except for that little paper gown I have to put on."

Oh, that made me feel a whole lot better. Shannon tried to coax me down a little but there was another man going to look at my wife's pussy!!! Oh My God...I hate this. Wonder what it does to her though?

What does it do to her?? How does she feel when he's looking around inside her and touching her there? Oh God...

Kevin decided that he needed some answers as to what exactly happened inside that room during an examination and he knew just who to ask. Janis Clayton, a nurse at another doctor's office, lived across the hall from them.

Later that morning he spotted her in the parking lot getting ready to leave for work. Kevin flew down the stairs and just made it to her car in time to stop her.

"Kevin, what is it? Are you okay?" asked Janis.

"Yeah, I'm fine but I have a huge question to ask you and please don't slap me or think I'm getting too personal. Okay?" God, this was going to be strange.

"Okay, Kevin. Whatever it is it can't be that bad. What's going on? Are Shannon and Cassidy okay?" she asked.

"Yeah, they're fine. Okay, here goes. Shannon has her yearly female exam today and I...well...I was wondering what all goes on and how it feels to her. I mean is it painful or does she get embarrassed or what? And how can the doctor look at all those pussies...I mean cunts...I mean.. you know without getting a hard-on?"

Man, I felt like my face was beet red. I hope I didn't embarrass her and/or myself too much. But damn it, I wanted to know.

Janis sat in her beige-colored Camry car seat and stared at me for what seemed like an eternity but was really only a second or two and then a smile spread across her face.

"Well, first of all, I guess the doctor is just immune to pussy. Except for his wife I suppose. Secondly, no, a woman doesn't usually enjoy it very much. I mean first, the doctor mauls her breasts looking for lumps and then has her spread her legs wide open and shoves a speculum up her twat and spreads her insides open and gawks up there. Then he takes it out... shoves his finger up there and then up her ass, tells her she is fine and leaves the room. Now, does that sound like a lot of fun to you? Have a great day Kevin and quit worrying so much." she finished with a huff.

Kevin thought a minute and as she started to pull out, he hit the car to stop her again.

"Janis, could you do me a huge favor?"

Later that night after Kevin, Shannon and Cassidy had gone out for a fantastic dinner and a surprise birthday cake at Shannon's mothers, Cassidy wanted to spend the night with her Nana.

"Great idea. Of course, you can," answered Kevin before anyone had a chance to even think about it.

Once they were home Kevin escorted Shannon up to their huge master bathroom and fixed her a relaxing hot bath. While she was in there, he prepared the bedroom for her birthday surprise. The items, which he had asked Janis to get for him were neatly lined up on the nightstand and covered with a small lavender colored hand towel.

He quickly changed into the green scrubs which Janis had also brought for him. Just as he had finished, he heard Shannon climbing out of the bathtub and let the water drain out. As she was drying off, she asked Kevin to bring her the turquoise nightgown hanging on the hook in her walk-in closet.

"Oh, you won't be needing it tonight dear. I hung a robe on the hook on the back of the bathroom door. If you would, kindly put it on and come into the bedroom please." Kevin told her with a smile on his face from ear to ear.

The white silky robe Shannon found behind the door was short sleeved and as she put it on, she noticed that it barely covered her ass cheeks and left not much hidden in the front either. As she left the bathroom to enter their bedroom, she saw Kevin waiting for her wearing a set of green scrubs.

"Kevin, why are you wearing those scrubs?" She asked.

"Well, my name is Doctor Kevin madame. Tonight, you are going to be given your yearly exam. I want you to be as comfortable as possible. Relax and find as much enjoyment as I can give you. If you are ready, please lay on the exam bed on the towels provided."

Shannon looked at her husband as if he had lost his last marble in his so-called brain. "What on earth are you doing?"

"Please madame, just recline on the bed so we can start with your exam."

Kevin assisted Shannon down into a reclined position upon the lavender towels he had laid out on the bed, putting a pillow under her head and her arms down to her sides. Picking up a clipboard with a piece of paper attached, he started.

"Well, Mrs. Abbott, it says here that today is your 35th birthday. Congratulations. How have you been feeling? Any problems with sexual intercourse, any breast pain or lumps, etc.? Okay, we will start with the breast exam. I'm going to open the left side of your robe and feel around your left breast for anything abnormal."

Kevin moved the robe aside and started massaging her left breast. Shannon was dumbfounded. Kevin started out doing it like he was actually feeling for lumps or anything out of the ordinary. But then he started going into a deeper massage and then began to rub her nipple and twirl it in between his fingers. Her nipple immediately hardened in reaction to his touch.

"Very good reaction with your breast and nipple Mrs. Abbott. Now I am going to move your right side of the robe open and do the same thing to your right breast."

And thus, he did. Shannon was almost to the point of moaning. In fact, she did stifle a couple of almost silent ones and felt tingling all the way down to her mound.

"Oh, Kevin...what are you doing? This isn't what really happens." Shannon was starting to protest but Kevin quickly quieted her back down and told her to relax.

"Both breasts seem to be quite normal. Both are very reactive to stimuli and that is very good indeed."

He could see Shannon squirming around the bed a little bit as she was getting turned on by this little exam he was doing to her. He turned and smiled to himself as he made little notations on the paper attached to the clipboard. Yup...this is going to be fun he thought to himself.

"Mrs. Abbott, it is now time for me to do the pelvic exam on you. I know this is not the most welcome part, but it is a necessity, so please place your feet on the mattress with your knees bent up. Spread your legs open so I can see and examine your pelvic area."

Kevin moved to the bottom of the bed. As Shannon placed her feet on the mattress and bent her knees, Kevin put on a pair of latex gloves and got the k-y jelly ready.

"Okay, madame, I'm going to feel around your vaginal lips and your clitoris if you are ready?"

Shannon almost wanted to laugh at the seriousness of how Kevin was trying to carry out this exam. But, God, it was feeling so damn good. How could she stop him... why would she stop him?

"Yes, doctor. I'm ready." She figured she would play along.

That said, Kevin applied a small amount of the lubricant on his gloved fingers, he didn't need much as she was already getting pretty wet on her own and started rubbing on either side of her clitoris. The lips were so warm, and she moved her hips in response to his stimulation. Purposely Kevin stayed away from her clitoris and massaged her from the top to her little pucker hole. Her hips rotated and moved up into his hand as he stimulated her. He then inserted his index finger into her and her hips rose up to meet him, wanting him even deeper into her.

"OMG," Shannon thought. it never felt like this at her doctor's office. Slowly he pulled out his finger.

"Mrs. Abbott, I must now insert the speculum so that I can look inside of your vagina to make sure you are healthy in there. Are you ready?"

"Kevin, you aren't really going to do that, are you?"

Before she could think of anything else, Kevin had the instrument already just inside her pussy and was starting to push it in. Shannon's eyes went huge and she tried to lift up to see what he was doing to her.

"Please Mrs. Abbott, remain laying down. I do not want to hurt you with this speculum inside of you. It will be over in just a moment or two."

Kevin continued opening the speculum wider inside his wife's vagina and then got down lower on the floor, so he could look inside.

"Wow...so this is what it looks like inside her," he thought to himself.

He could see her cervix, uterus, the walls of her insides...right where his cock felt so warm and at home. He saw where his seed entered going through the cervix to enter her uterus where an egg could be made into a baby...like his little Cassidy.

Kevin stared at her in awe. "My beautiful, gorgeous wife. She's breathtaking from the inside out." His thoughts went straight to his groin and his cock was so hard he thought it would break.

"You're doing just fine Mrs. Abbott. I'm going to remove the speculum now. I still have to do an internal examination with my fingers inserted into your vagina. This shouldn't be too uncomfortable."

Slowly Kevin inserted his index and middle fingers into her and Shannon felt herself stretching to accommodate him. As he was going in deeper, pushing on the little walnut at the top of her vaginal wall he reached up with his thumb and started massaging her lips on either side of her clitoris. Shannon couldn't hold her hips still and started rotating them trying to make him have contact with her clit.

"Oh God, please. I want to cum." she heard herself crying out to Kevin.

"Now, now madame, just relax. You are showing all the natural reactions of stimuli. This shows me that you are indeed a normal, healthy woman."

Shannon shook from the red-hot fire of desire she was feeling. Getting his pinky finger wet from the juices she was secreting he started rubbing her puckered hole. Shannon jumped at the contact and then it started to feel good. As he massaged it, he felt it relax a bit and inserted his finger into the hole. At the same time, he hit her clit with his thumb pushing Shannon into a climax so hard she had stars in her eyes. Kevin continued to fuck her ass as he rubbed her clit and plunged the two fingers into her pussy. Shannon's hips slammed into his hand over and over as she rode out her climax until it subsided and left her panting and breathless.

Kevin could stand it no more. He stood up, removed the latex gloves from his hands, bent over his wife and pushed his cock into her until he was deep into her cunt. He held still and relished in the feel of her as her vaginal muscles tightened around him. Then he slowly pulled back out almost leaving her warmth and pushed back in all the way again. Her moans were deeper than he had ever heard from her. He built up a rhythm of in and out until he was pounding her pussy with all he had to give. Shannon was matching him hip to hip, pubic bone to pubic bone until they both cried out together and came with a power they hadn't known or felt in a long time. Kevin ejaculated inside of her three, four, five times before he had totally emptied his balls. Shannon shook with a fervor that took several minutes to calm back down. Each had reached a pinnacle of completeness beyond their comprehension. Kevin eased off of her and rolled onto his back taking her with him and she cuddled and rested her head on his chest.

"Baby, that was the most awesome experience I have ever had in my life." stated Kevin when he had caught his breath again.

"If my real exam had been like that, believe me I would have been there more than once a year." Shannon knew he would react to that statement and here it came.

"I don't think you need to go there anymore. One Doctor looking inside you is enough, and I can do the job just fine."

They both laughed and made passionate love the rest of the night.

HOT STUFF

Taking the bus on a long-distance trip can be a real hassle. Here I am, going from Charleston, SC, to Fresno, CA., and the bus is full. Hot, sweaty people squished into rows of three seats on each side of the aisle. Yuk, this was going to be a bad trip. At least we weren't going to stop in every little dinky town along the way. This bus went farther between stops. So, I put the seat back, closed my eyes and settled in for the nightmare. The two ladies beside me did the same thing. A few hours later the bus slowed and pulled into Savannah, GA. It was right around supper time, so the driver gave us one hour to get something to eat and be back in our seats ready to leave.

When I got back to my seat, there was a gorgeous man sitting in the seat by the window. Guessing that he was in his thirties, he had dark brown hair, hazel eyes, wore a green pull-over shirt and jeans. He had sneakers on his feet. As I took my seat he looked over, said hello and turned to look back out the window. He seemed to be looking intently at or for something or someone, so I followed his gaze. Standing near the bus was a beautiful, slim blonde and she was waving at him and was signaling something to him. He nodded his head like he understood her and smiled broadly at her. Hum, just my luck. He had a girlfriend. Not just a handsome man, but I mean all out gorgeous and not available. Ugh...oh damn!! Then he looked away from the window and turned in his seat and looked right at me. Oh God. Now what do I say?

"Um, hi, my name is Dixie."

"Hi, I'm Ricky. Nice to meet you. You are very pretty." He then took my hand and held it to his lips and kissed it gently and let it go.

My face must have turned ten shades of red because he said, I'm sorry if I embarrassed you. But you are. You have the sexiest green eyes and the most luscious red hair." He reached up to touch my hair as my hand knocked it away.

"How dare you try to flirt with me after you just said goodbye to your girlfriend!"

I was completely offended by this time. The look on his face went from puzzled to humorous in the blink of an eye. His smile grew bigger and his eyes brightened.

"Wow!!! We just met and already you're jealous! I'm flattered."

"Well, don't be. I'm not jealous. I don't even know you. It's just that one minute you are waving and smiling at the blonde on the platform and now you're flirting with me. I don't get it. Nor do I like it very much. It's not very flattering for either of us, meaning her nor I." I stated flatly.

Again, Ricky's smile covered his face and I wanted so badly to reach up and slap it off.

"What the hell is so damn funny?" I asked.

"You are jealous. You wouldn't be acting like this if you weren't."

"You sir, are so full of yourself." I started to turn away from him, but he stood up and took a hold of my arms. He stood so tall that he had to duck his head to keep from hitting the ceiling of the bus. He sat me down in my seat and then returned to his own seat, turning to look straight into my eyes.

"Look Dixie, if you weren't paying attention to something that wasn't your business, you wouldn't be acting like a jealous schoolgirl. But I will let your jealous self-know that the woman on that platform is my sister, not my girlfriend. We were saying goodbye because I won't be seeing her for the next few years. She is going away to college in Massachusetts next week for medical school. And I will be clear across the country with my law practice. So, miss know it all. Are you satisfied?" With that, he turned and looked out the window as the bus pulled out of the terminal.

I sat there starring at my hands that were sitting in my lap. I had no idea what to say. Stupid didn't even begin to describe how I was feeling at the moment. We sat there in silence for a couple of hours. The lady sitting to my left was sound asleep within a half hour of us being on the road. This was really going to be a shitty trip. I pushed my backrest back and closed my eyes.

Ricky was reading a book...probably some law stuff. And I had already made enough of an ass of myself...so I chose to remain quiet.

Soon, with the rumble of the road, I was sound asleep. At some point I had turned in my seat and my head was resting on Ricky's shoulder as I slowly opened my eyes when the bus came to a stop. He leaned over and told me it was time to get off the bus and take a walk.

"The legs need to be stretched and moved around or you can develop blood clots."

"Sounds like you've done this before." I said in my sleepy voice. "Yeah, a few times. I enjoy this trip a lot. I meet interesting people and I enjoy the scenery, present company included." he answered with a grin.

As I stood up my lower back ached. I reached around to rub it. Ricky saw what I was doing and brushed my hand out of the way and proceeded to rub just above the waistband of my jeans. God that felt so good. I could have let him do that forever. But I wanted to go into the terminal restroom and freshen up and change into my sweats for the nights ride. I could sleep better being more comfortable. So, I told him thank you for the back rub and I would see him when we got back on the bus.

Little did I know that Ricky had followed me and watched to make sure I got into the restroom with no problems. I did a quick sponge bath with baby wipes and shampooed my hair and dried it under the hand blow dryer. My hair came almost to the middle of my back and wasn't quite dry, so I pulled it up in a ponytail and tied it off with a band. I put on just a dab of makeup and changed into my purple nylon/rayon, fleece lined sweat suit. Putting back on my socks and sneakers I went back out into the terminal heading toward the restaurant. I was famished, having not eaten since Savannah earlier that evening. As soon as I turned the corner, out of the ladies' room, there was Ricky.

"Hi. Wow! I didn't think you could look any better, but you look fantastic." he said with a huge grin on his face. "May I escort you to wherever it is you are going next?"

"What are you doing...following me?" I asked him. I tried to look perturbed, but I couldn't. I really was kinda glad that he was there watching over me.

Being a single woman traveling alone and all "No, I just happened to come out of the men's room and saw you coming out of the ladies' room.

So how about it? Can we go somewhere together and get something to eat? Are you hungry?"

The man could read my mind. "Sure. Where do you want to go? I'm starving."

"Well, we can grab a bite here in the terminal or we can go across the street and grab something to go and take it back and eat it on the bus. What would be your pleasure, ma'am?" Ricky still had a grin on his face.

"Well, let me see. The food in the terminal usually isn't very good. So, let's go across the street to the diner and get something to go," I answered with a smile.

"Damn baby, you sure are gorgeous when you smile," he said and leaned over and kissed me on the forehead. I was so surprised by the gesture that I stumbled as we moved toward the door. He took a hold of my arm and led me out and across the street.

We entered the diner and walked up to the counter. Looking at the menus, waiting for the waitress, I wondered what I should get that would be easy to eat on the bus.

As the waitress came over, she looked at us and said, "Well, what will it be, and you better hurry if you want to catch your bus." How did she know we were from the bus? I looked around the room and to my left sat the bus driver, finishing up his dinner and drinking his coffee.

"I'd like a cheeseburger all the way with French fries and a mountain dew in the bottle, to go, please." Ricky ordered the same.

As we waited for our food we dabbled in small talk. I discovered that he was on his way to Madeira, only a short way from Fresno. He was a lawyer in a small law firm with two other lawyers. They were primarily defense attorneys of criminal law. He was single, divorced recently with no children.

I told him I was also divorced recently, two months ago, and was on my way to my aunt's house in Fresno to restart my life. I told him that at the age of twenty-eight, I thought my life was pretty well set. But my husband had found a new "love of his life" and wanted out. So, I gave him his walking papers. I also told Ricky that I am a court stenographer, so we had a little something in common. We both know our way around a courtroom. The waitress brought us our food and Ricky insisted on paying for it, then we went back to the bus. We ate as the bus rumbled down the road.

After finishing eating, we both settled down with books and started reading. He with whatever it was he was reading and me with a good erotic romance. I noticed that every once in a while, he would slide a sideways look over at me. I would smile to myself as I kept on reading. I was into a really good part and was starting to get really warm when he reached over and took my hand in his. He kept on reading, content with holding hands. Almost two hours rolled by as we read and just held hands. It was very relaxing and with no pretensions.

Once in a while I would set my book in my lap, take a drink of soda, set the bottle between my legs and pick the book up and start reading again. The last time I did that he asked me,

"Is the book that good that you need to cool yourself off?"

"Um," (and I swallowed really hard), "it was just an easy place to put it, that's all."

"Aha," was all he said, and he went back to his book.

I couldn't stand it anymore. Between the book and this hot, gorgeous man sitting beside me I was getting so horny, so I put the book away, stood up and pulled my blanket and pillow from the over-head compartment and settled in to go to sleep. Putting the seat back, I stretched my legs out and tried my best to get comfortable in such cramped quarters.

The lady next to me was already fast asleep. She must have been in her sixties, graying hair and small in stature. Her feet barely touched the floor. I took the blanket and covered my shoulders, put my hands under the blanket to hold it in place, turned my head toward the lady and closed my eyes.

I was almost asleep when I felt Ricky's hand slip under the blanket and search for mine. He had turned in his seat and was leaning near me. As he grasped my hand, he leaned his head to my ear and kissed it. I moved my head slightly and he moved with it. He kissed it again. Then his tongue reached out and licked my neck. I turned my head slightly toward him, but he pushed it back with his head. Again, he licked my neck.

"Boy, this guy has some nerve." I thought. "We just met today, and he is already trying to neck with me."

About the time I was thinking this, Ricky let go of my hand and reached up and cupped my chin. Turning my head towards him he planted his lips on mine. At first, I was so stunned that I couldn't react. His lips were soft. So tender that I wanted them to stay there. So, I kissed him back. His tongue reached out to caress my lower lip, teasing, pressing it a little then he bit it lightly. I moaned. Oh, God. What was he doing to me? I started to put up my hand to protest. Quickly he held my head and pressed his lips to mine harder and pushed with his tongue until I opened mouth and let him in. Oh My God he tasted so good. He was ravishing my mouth. Touching my teeth, my gums, the inside of my cheeks. He was hungry for my mouth. His hand slipped down my head to my neck and on down to my shoulder and under the covers. I brought my hand up to his face and it felt soft, only a little rough where his beard was starting to have a day's growth. I held his mouth to mine and kissed him back oh, he felt so good and wonderful. I put my tongue into his mouth and explored it as he had in mine.

I felt his hand go lower down to my left breast. He was massaging it through my sweatshirt. God it felt great. It had been over a year since any man had touched me. My nipples were getting hard and I could feel the twinge in my vagina. Ricky reached down under my shirt and lifted it up so he could get to my breasts better. I had left my bra off so I could relax and be more comfortable for sleeping. Now he had full access.

He massaged my breast and then played with my nipple as he continued to kiss me fervently, feverishly. I was starting to squirm in my seat. He released our kiss and whispered in my ear to be quiet.

"Hush baby. Just enjoy this. Don't wake up our little lady over there."

I turned my body toward him. He reached around me, held me and kissed me again, hard and passionately. I reached up and put my fingers in his hair. It was soft and felt like silk in my hand. I played in it, pulled it to pull him closer to me.

I wanted him now. I wanted him to do to me whatever he wanted to. I moaned into his mouth. He returned the moan with a groan from deep in his throat. His feet tangled with mine and he was going up and down my calf with his bare foot. He must have kicked off his shoes sometime, I thought to myself. So, I kicked mine off too. We let our feet play with each other's legs while he played with first one breast and then the other.

God, I was getting so hot!!! He was turning me on so much!!!

His hand then started downward toward my stomach, down my abdomen and to my curly bush. He went under the waistband of my sweatpants. With his long slender hand and his fingers, he played in my cunt hair and moved on down to my pussy.

OH MY GOD!!!! As his fingers hit my clitoris I jumped and a slow, low moan emitted from my lips.

"Hush baby, it's ok...just take it easy. Enjoy the ride." Ricky whispered into my ear again.

That was easier said than done. He was making me burn down there. I wanted more.

"Please Ricky, take me...make me cum. Please baby..." I begged him. "I will baby, I will. Just take it easy...relax and let me take care of you, hot stuff. My God, you are so hot...your pussy is on fire darling."

Ricky was driving me crazy with desire. He let his fingers go down deeper into my slit clear back to my pucker hole. I was so wet that his fingers just slid down, so easily, and back up again. He was teasing the shit out of me. Then I felt two fingers go inside me. My hips automatically went up in the air. He put his other arm around my shoulders and pulled me into him and held me as he started pumping his fingers in and out of my pussy. I was so wet he was sliding in and out and moving his fingers around inside of me.

He pushed his fingers up on my gspot and flicked his fingers faster and faster.

He pinched my clit...

"Oh..." Ricky plunged a kiss on my lips to quiet my cry as I came with an explosion a burst of lightening going off in the sky.

Each stroke he made seemed to keep the climax going a little bit longer. I soaked his fingers and my cum ran down his hand. I was holding on to him for dear life.

Ricky didn't take his fingers out of me but kept playing. He wiggled them around, in and out and up against my gspot again. He twirled around my clit and pinched it again. As I slid down on the seat, he flicked his little finger along my pucker hole, and I exploded again. Intense, deep, cumming with so much force he had all he could do to smother my screams with his mouth.

I was cumming so hard I reached out to grab something and grabbed his cock. He was so hard. And so big. As I slowly receded from the best climax I had had in a very long time, I knew this awesome man deserved to be taken care of as well.

As I rubbed my hand back and forth his cock swelled and I knew I wanted to have him. Quickly I unbuttoned his jeans and slid down the zipper. I moved the blanket around so that some of it was covering his lap as well as mine. I then took out the most beautiful cock I had ever seen. God, it was huge, and the head was thick and moist from his precum. Oh, I love the taste of precum and couldn't wait to get my lips on his engorged meat.

I lowered my head and put out my tongue and licked the tip of his cock. Ricky let out a low groan. He buried his head in my hair and I continued to lick his stick like a mad woman. He tasted so good. I opened my mouth and put the head into it, and he moaned. His hand went into my hair as he held my head to his dick. I worked my way down his lovely shaft until I had most of it gone. I started to gag. He was too big for my mouth and throat. But again, I tried to take all of him. After several attempts, I finally was able to take him to the hilt. My nose was buried all the way into his pubic hair. He didn't hold me there though and I bobbed up and down his rod until I could feel his cum rising up from his balls. Up the shaft it came and into my mouth. I swallowed rope after rope of cum as he squirted into my throat. I sucked him until I knew that I had drained him of all his juices. Then I raised my head and looked at him.

He had that huge grin on his face, but this time I was glad to see it there. He grabbed hold of my face and kissed me deeply, tasting himself as he did. A deep groan came from down deep in his chest and came into my mouth. He bit at my lips...he sucked them and kissed me some more. Ricky's fingers had never left my cunt and he was once again playing inside of me. I was still soaking wet from my previous orgasm, so he was able to move about easily. In and out he moved his fingers. Then his thumb found my clit and he started rubbing it. Gently at first and then harder and harder while never missing a beat as he pumped me with his fingers. I knew I was going to cum again. I pushed my pants down to just below my hips, while still covered by the blanket.

Ricky turned more towards me and held me tight while he pumped my pussy like a man possessed. I bit into his shoulder as I came, and came, and came. The flow of my juices went all over his hand and wrist. Still, he didn't stop. I was so turned on I thought I was in heaven. I reached over and touched his cock and he was hard as a rock again.

"Come over here and sit on my lap. Carefully, so we don't wake up the little lady." said Ricky.

I was too far gone to argue with him...besides. I wanted his cock in my pussy so bad. So, he held up the blanket for me to move over onto his lap. He had pulled his jeans down and I pulled my sweats down to my ankles.

Although it was rather awkward, we managed to get it where I was straddling him, and I sat down with his cock aimed for my opening. He held my lips open with one hand and guided his cock with the other into my cunt.

"Oh, God, you are so big." I whispered. He was stretching me and stretching me. Even with being so wet and loosened up, he was making me so full.

We worked back and forth, in and out until he was all the way in me. God, I was stuffed. I didn't think I could take someone that big... ever. Well, tonight I found out different.

Ricky was moving ever so slowly, letting me get use to his size. He felt wonderful. We were trying to be as quiet as possible, but it was so difficult when it felt this good.

Soon we had worked out a rhythm that felt good to us and we were enjoying each other. Just then the old lady stirred and started mumbling. We held very still. Waiting...she finally settled back down and started snoring again.

Slowly Ricky started moving in and out as I moved up and down. This was ecstasy as its best. I never wanted it to end. But I was on the verge of a huge climax. Damn, he was good at doing that to me. I never got this much enjoyment in the whole eight years I was married, let alone get it now with a total stranger I've known just a few hours.

Ricky pulled me back into his chest and wrapped his arms around me. Then he started pumping his cock into me rapidly and I went off. Burst after burst of fulfillment went through me and I was propelled into another realm of reality.

I felt as his cock get stiffer and bigger and as he started squirting his cum deep up into my vagina, right into my cervix. Deeply he pumped his juices of maleness into me, over and over.

So much that it was leaking out of me. Our combined juices were creaming us. I pushed my fist into my mouth to stifle my scream of joy.

God, this man was one hell of a great lover. I kept my head on his shoulder and rested against his chest. Cuddled in his arms, he kissed me gently on my head and I smiled. I really smiled for the first time in a long time. My whole being was relaxed and happy. Within a few seconds I was sound asleep, still in Ricky's lap, his meat still inside of me. Light was just starting to come in through the window of the bus when I slowly opened my eyes. I was still on Ricky's lap and to my amazement his cock was still inside of me and was very hard. I moved slightly to see if he was awake. Oh yes, he certainly was. He gave me a jab with his cock, straight up. I jumped a little and he chuckled. "Good morning, hot stuff. I hope you slept well. I know I sure did." Ricky said with a grin.

I turned my head to look up at him and I saw a set of eyes looking straight at us. I sat straight up...forgetting to pull the blanket up with me.

"Oops, sorry." I said as I pulled it around us.

"Oh, no need to be sorry dear. I heard everything last night. I'm sure glad you enjoyed yourselves and it was me sitting here and not some snooty old biddy who would have raised a ruckus with you. But I would suggest you put yourselves back together before the other passengers start rousing from their stupor. Might be a little embarrassing if you know what I mean." The little old lady hid a giggle, excused herself and headed for the restroom.

HOT STUFF: THE TRIP CONTINUES

Dixie and Ricky spent the day's bus ride reading, watching the scenery wiz by and having small talk. The bus stopped in Colorado Springs, Colorado around four thirty that afternoon. It felt so good to get off the bus, stretch their legs and move about the terminal. Neither one was very hungry at the moment. They had messed around with each other a little bit on the bus and both were very horny. But due to the daylight hours privacy was nil.

Ricky was dying to get a taste of Dixie's hot little pussy. But it was next to impossible to do on the bus. He had to think of a place to get enough privacy where he could get his fill of her. But they were on limited time and he didn't know his way around this vast city. Where could they go? Then a light bulb went off in his head.

"Dixie, are you adventurous? Do you trust me?" God, he sure hoped so.

"Well, it depends on what you have in mind." she answered. Ricky grabbed her hand and headed for the middle of the terminal right towards the men's room. Dixie pulled back to a dead stop. "What the hell do you think you're doing?? I can't go in there."

Dixie was adamant.

"Sure you can.. just follow me and I will cover you." Ricky was grinning.

Dixie looked around and no one seemed to be paying much attention to them so she let Ricky pull her into the men's room and into the stall at the far end.

"Pull your pants off of one leg and then stand on the seat and straddle my face, baby. Let me have your pussy right on my face. I want to taste you so bad." Ricky was already seated on the stool with his pants and underwear pulled down.

Dixie thought he had lost his mind but she was excited at the same time. So, she did as he asked and pulled one leg of her jeans off her left leg and the same with her panties. Then she stepped up on the back of the stool and straddled him while holding onto his shoulders for balance.

Ricky had to slide down a little to reach her lovely pussy as he could smell her before he ever got to her. God, her scent was intoxicating. He wanted her so much.

Ricky grabbed her by her thighs and lowered her down to his face as his tongue licked the sides of her thighs, first one and then the other. Dixie's legs quivered. He held her steady as he raised his tongue and touched her outer lips, softly, licking back and forth.

Dixie's hips started to move and Ricky quickly grabbed her, holding her still as he licked and her hips moved again. She dug her fingers into his shoulders. She needed to balance; this wasn't going to be as easy as he thought it was. How could she stand here and stay in control while he drove her insane?

Ricky moved her lips apart with his tongue and dove in deeper into her cunt as he lapped up the juices that were starting to drip from Dixie. Oh, she tasted so wonderful. Just like he knew she would. He couldn't get enough. He wanted more. Driving his tongue into her hole he buried it deep inside of her. Dixie let out a moan.

"Oh…My…God." Dixie thought to herself. This man is awesome. He's going to make me go crazy. She couldn't help but grind her hips down into his face as his tongue went deep into her hole. Up and down she moved in spite of the hold he had on her hips.

Ricky pulled his tongue out of her and grabbed hold of her clit with his lips. He ran his tongue over the hard tip as he sucked it into his mouth. Dixie let out a yell and exploded into a huge climax.

Just then someone came into the men's room, walked up to the urinal and peed. Nothing was said. Dixie was still in the rapture of coming. The man flushed and left.

Ricky never missed a lick as he lapped and sucked up her cum. His face was glazed with her juices as he devoured her, relishing her taste and aroma.

Dixie had a death grip on Ricky's shoulders. Her legs gave out and she started to fall from the commode. Ricky grabbed her by the waist and lowered her down until her cunt was in line with his rock-hard cock. He was so turned on by her sweet, warm pussy…now he wanted to fuck her. Be in her and feel her tight around him. He lowered her onto him and sank deep inside of her. Dixie gasped as a moan left her lips.

"Dixie…Oh My God Woman!!! You feel so good." Ricky said as he let out a groan from his throat. He placed his hands under her butt and lifted her up and brought her back down onto him, moving his hips up and down at the same time. He was drowning in lust for her.

"Ricky…fuck me baby. Make me cum again. Please baby.. fuck me… Ahh…yes…fuck me." Dixie was beside herself.

Planting her feet solidly on the floor on either side of him she rode him steady and braced her arms around his neck. She reached up and kissed him…gently at first…tenderly…licking his lips…nipping at them…then she stuck her tongue into his mouth and his cock jerked inside her. Dixie sat on him and rotated her hips back and forth and side to side. God, she was driving them both crazy.

Ricky grabbed her by the back of the head and buried his tongue deep into her throat. Dixie gasped for breath. He kissed her hard as he buried his cock deep into her wet, juicy pussy. She was so hot inside. He loved the feel of her, so tight on his cock…so warm. Ricky held her tight to him as he started to pump into her harder and with more passion. He wanted her to know he was starting to care about her, not just sexually, but emotionally. He really liked her.

Dixie felt a change in the way Ricky was holding her. He seemed to be caressing, more like making love to her than fucking her. "Wow!! This feels so good." she thought.

Together, they moved as one, in and out…up and down. The rhythm was set and they both were totally into each other. Ricky could feel he wasn't going to last much longer. But he wanted her to cum first. He let go of her head and reached for her clit. One good pinch and off she went.

Dixie felt Ricky getting harder inside of her and knew he wasn't going to last for very much longer. She tried to rub her clit up against his groin but couldn't get it to hit enough to get her off. Ricky must have been reading her mind. He reached in between them and pinched her clit. She felt the rush and her insides burst into a million pieces. Blood rushed through her body.

Ricky had a death grip on Dixie. She screamed…she cried…she wound her arms around his neck tighter than before. Her body moved at lightning speed as she rode his cock, faster and harder than she had ever done with any man before.

Ricky felt his cock tighten like a piston as his semen rose and exploded out and into Dixie's cunt…deep, deeper. Rope after rope of semen coated her vagina and cervix. Still he couldn't stop moving and pumped her some more.

Dixie was spent. Tired. She couldn't move. Yet Ricky was pushing deep inside of her. He pushed her down onto him…then he just held her there. Contentment. Peacefulness. Joy. Elation. All of these feelings ran through Ricky's mind as he held Dixie close to him. Never had he felt like this before. What the hell was she doing to him? What was he doing to himself?

Slowly Dixie climbed off Ricky, cleaned herself as best she could and dressed. Ricky did the same. They headed for the door as the door opened. A rather portly gentleman entered, smiled and headed for the urinal. Dixie nudged Rickey to get out of there. NOW!!!

Once in the terminal they grabbed some munchies and a couple of hot dogs, drinks and ran for the bus. The bus driver was getting ready to close the door and told them to hurry up and take their seats.

Once seated, Dixie opened her drink and took a long sip. The old lady sitting beside her gave her a sideways look and said, "Your face has a glow about it my dear. Seems you and your friend had a good time, nearly costing you your ride. But I guess this ride isn't as important as the one you just had, is it?" With that the little old lady went back to her knitting, a sly smile on her face.

As the trip continued, several of those on the bus decided to get into a hot and heavy game of spades. Dixie was an avid player and Ricky knew after the first few hands that they were a team to be reckoned with. After an hour of playing, they were winning. Then came the hand from hell.

"Dixie, why did you bid that amount when you couldn't make it from your hand?" Ricky asked, feeling disgruntled.

"Because usually you can cover my back and I didn't want to under bid and go over." Answered Dixie. She was totally flustered by that hand.

"Well, next time, don't over bid, okay? I'd rather take the points back at the end than lose now. Damn." Ricky was frustrated.

"Okay, relax, it's only a card game, Ricky. Why are you getting so mad? It's not like we are losing." Dixie didn't understand the edginess in Ricky's tone.

Just as Ricky was about to answer Dixie the bus swayed and a huge bang was heard. The bus had hit something and was swaying all over the ice and snow-covered mountain road.

Ricky looked up in time to see a white van going over the side of the mountain, front first. Dixie jumped from her seat as she heard the screams of other passengers and saw the van going over the side.

"Oh My God, Ricky. Did you see that? What the hell happened? Was that a van that just went over the side of the mountain? Do something!!" Dixie was screaming, shaking and crying at the same time.

"Baby, come here. The bus has wrecked too. Sit down and let me go see what is going on. Let me see how bad things are. Stay here and sit still. Do you hear me?" Ricky warned her to stay where he had made Dixie sit. She shook her head that she understood.

A female passenger was running down the aisle toward the front of the bus yelling that she was a nurse and to let her off the bus so she could go check on the people in the van. The bus driver, being stunned, didn't seem to hear her. When she reached him, she checked him to make sure he was alright and then demanded to be let off. He obliged her and she and a male passenger ran back to the crash site. Dixie watched as the two of them disappeared over the side of the mountain.

Ricky took out his cell phone and called for help. Reaching the police dispatch he tried to describe where they were. Having been playing cards, he really hadn't been paying much attention to the road. He looked for landmarks, but with all the snow it was hard to tell. He went to the front of the bus to ask the bus driver where they were but he was of little help. Finally, dispatch came back on and said they had tracked him by his cell and knew where they were. Help would be there soon.

The road seemed pretty desolate and no cars were passing by. They were pretty much on their own until help arrived. Ricky had Dixie get blankets to keep the passengers warm and drinks to keep them hydrated. He then grabbed a couple blankets and told Dixie he was taking them down to the victims at the van.

What he saw astounded him. A woman was laying prone on the ground, a leg twisted underneath her, very apparently broken. Her left arm was also twisted and broken.

Her face was scratched and bleeding. She was unconscious.

Ricky saw a young man sitting over to the side, his head in his hands, shaking and crying. After covering the woman with a blanket, he took another one and wrapped it around the man. The nurse was busy working on the woman so he stayed with the young man.

"What's your name, man?" Ricky asked.

"James. James Simeon. I... I can't bee... belli... believe. I can't believe this has happened."

"Hey, man, it was an accident. The roads are slick.. icy ya know. Don't beat yourself up over it. Help's on its way. Who's that over there?" Ricky asked.

"That's Lillian, my mom. Is she hurt bad? God, she looks so bad.

Oh man, I'm soooo sorry." James was now crying uncontrollably.

"Sir are you hurt anywhere?" the nurse asked when she came over to check him out.

"No ma'am. How is my mom? Is she hurt bad?" James asked with tears in his brown eyes.

"Well, yes, I'm afraid she is pretty bad. I have to go back to be with her. I just came over to check you out. Are you going to be okay?" she asked.

"Yes, I'm fine. Please, take care of my mom. Don't let her die out here." James begged her.

"I'll do my best. I'll do all I can for her until help arrives. Okay? You have to stay strong for her." then she left and went back to Lillian. Ricky heard a rustling and looked up in time to see Dixie sliding down the mountainside. "Damn woman."...he muttered to himself. "I told her to stay put and safe. Should have known better."

"Dixie, I told you to stay in the bus where it was warm and safe. What are you doing here?" Ricky grabbed her as she reached where the van had stopped.

"I knew you would need these." She held up his gloves that he had forgotten in his haste.

"Damn woman. You aren't dressed to be out in this weather. You'll freeze to death." Ricky was both angry at her not listening to him and pleased that she had thought enough of him to risk herself to bring him his gloves. What a woman.

He had his hands full, that was for sure. Ricky admired Dixie. She was stubborn and tenacious. Loving, kind and hot as hell. Whatever was he going to do with her? Then he smiled inside. Oh, he knew full well what he would do with her. Oh, yes, he sure did.

Several hours later, after the ambulance had taken Lillian and James to the hospital and they had switched to another bus, Ricky and Dixie settled back to rest and cuddle in each other's arms. It had been a long and trying afternoon and evening. Nerves were still on edge and neither one of them could really relax.

They lay in each other's arms, each in their own thoughts. Dixie had her eyes closed, her head on Ricky's chest. Ricky held Dixie in his arms, looking out the window watching the stars and moon as the miles rolled by.

Ricky's thoughts went back to the accident. What if that had been him and Dixie that had gone over that mountainside? Why did it bother him so much? He really didn't know that much about her. Yes, he was enjoying his time with her since they had met. She was fun to be around. She was smart as hell. And Sexy. Damn was she sexy. The sexiest woman he had ever known. She was game for whatever he wanted from her. He'd never met a woman like her before. And he wanted her. Dixie's thoughts were confusing. She really liked Ricky. He was strong, kind, intelligent. He was great to have sex with. What was it that was drawing her to him so strongly? What was she wanting with him? This was only a bus trip. It would be over when she reached her aunt's. Then he would continue on. Damn. This sucked. What was she going to do?

Dixie finally fell into slumber. She was dreaming a most pleasant dream. She and Ricky were laying side by side looking into each other's eyes. She loved his eyes and the expressions he said in them. He touched her face. Gently, tenderly caressing her cheek, moving his finger to trace her lips. She kissed his finger. Then licked it. He moaned.

Her hand was on his chest rubbing his hair and playing with his nipples. She loved bringing them to a peak. Her hips moved into his and he reciprocated in like. Their movements were so easy, tender and slow. They just took their time loving on each other. So sensual, sexy and hot.

Ricky was sitting in his seat, still not able to sleep. He watched out the window, thoughts of not wanting to leave Dixie behind when she reached her aunt's. But how could he convince her to continue with him to his place. Lord God. Why was he thinking like this? He had never wanted a woman as much as he wanted her and had never wanted to take a woman home like he did her. What was it about Dixie that mattered so much to him? Certainly, not just the great sex. No, it was much more than that.

Just then Dixie's hand slipped from his chest to his waist. But it didn't stop there. Her hand went on down to his crotch and landed right on his maleness. She seemed to be asleep, yet her hand went right for him.

Instantly he felt himself grow. He knew this was going to get uncomfortable fast. All she had to do was look at him and he got hard. Now she had a hold of him...oh ves...he was in big trouble now. And sure enough...he was growing harder and harder. Her hand seemed to be getting tighter and tighter on him. Dixie moved slightly.. even closer to him and adjusted her hand to take a better grip of him. Damn this woman was going to drive him mad.

"She must be having one hell of a dream." Ricky thought.

"Well, maybe I can help this dream along." He smiled to himself. Ricky wrapped his arm tighter around Dixie's shoulder and reached for her breast. He lightly massaged it through her clothing and she moaned. He looked over at the older woman and saw that she was dozing. He continued to slowly massage Dixie's breast. Damn, she felt so good in his hand. He worked her nipple until he had it peaked.

Dixie was in the depths of her dream. She had rolled closer to Ricky and he had a hold of her breast and was massaging it and tweaking her nipple. It felt so real. MMM. it felt so good. She had moved her hand down his body to his male hood and took him in her hand. She had started to stroke him. They were lying so close it felt like their bodies were becoming as one. Dixie wrapped her leg over Ricky's. He leaned his head down and started suckling on her breast.

Dixie's body responded at once to the feel of Ricky's lips on her breast. Lost in the dream, it felt so real. She rolled her head on to Ricky's chest. Ricky pulled her closer to him. He knew by her movements what she was dreaming about and wanted to do to her what he knew was going on in her mind.

"Oh, God...to have that breast he had in his hand in his mouth." he thought as his mouth began to water.

Ricky began to unbutton Dixie's top as he looked again over at the older woman in the seat next to Dixie's. She was still sleeping. He undid the first few buttons and reached inside. He pulled her breast so he could hold it in his hand. Damn, she felt so good. He massaged it. rubbed it. He wanted to take it in his mouth so bad. How could he maneuver it with the little lady sitting beside Dixie?

Dixie was not in a good position for him to reach her the way he wanted to.

Dixie and Ricky were in the hot throes of love making. She wanted him between her legs. She wanted to feel his lips on her womanhood, her love button, and his tongue inside of her. She was so hot for him and needed him. She rolled over and opened herself to him.

Not realizing what she had done in her sleep, she had rolled off of Ricky's chest and back into her seat. Ricky lowered her seat as far back as it would go and turned in his seat to have better access to her. Now he could put his mouth on her breast, her nipple between his teeth. Oh, yes, this was much better indeed.

The woman in the seat beside Dixie had been watching what was happening and decided to give them a little extra privacy. She stood up and retrieved two blankets from the overhead compartment. She took one and covered Dixie with it as Rickey looked up at her, never removing his mouth from Dixie's breast. He nodded his head in thanks. Their eyes met. She smiled and returned to her seat. She then covered herself and went back to sleep. Or so it seemed.

Dixie was so hot and ready for Ricky. She spread her legs in anticipation for what he could and would give her. She wanted him so badly. Her body craved him. Needed him.

Ricky watched as Dixie spread her legs. He knew that she was still in her dream and what she wanted. As he sucked on first one breast and then the other, he reached down and cupped her between her legs. She moaned. He wanted to feel her wetness. He wanted…no needed to taste her.

Ricky unbuttoned Dixie's jeans and slid down the zipper. He reached inside her pants and panties until his fingers reached her most warm spot and he felt her warmth. Oh, God, she was so wet. He moved his finger around her clit and then to her opening and slid his finger inside of her. She was soaked. His finger went in easily and he moved with ease. In and out he stroked as she squirmed around, moving in time with his finger.

Ricky pulled his finger out and put it to his lips, smelling it as he did. He loved the aroma of her…the essence of her and then the heavenly taste of her. Dixie stirred. She rolled her head toward him.

Dixie knew she wasn't dreaming anymore as she saw Ricky licking his fingers. The site was so hot. But she wanted his fingers back where they had been. She looked up into his eyes. He looked back and saw her raw emotions.

"Please baby, don't stop. I need to cum." Dixie pleaded. I've got you baby." Ricky responded.

Ricky reached down and started to lower Dixie's jeans and she helped him get them down to below her knees. He then licked his fingers again and put them back to her clit and circled it lightly, teasing her. Dixie moaned and he hushed her with a kiss.

Ricky looked over to where the older lady was and thought he saw her looking over at them…but wasn't quite sure, so went back to playing with Dixie. But just the thought of the old lady watching them was turning him on more. He moved around her clit and let his finger extend down her slit to her opening and go inside of her. Dixie's hips rose to meet his hand. She pumped her hips in rhythm to his finger moving in and out as her moans grew louder.

He thought he heard another moan, other than Dixie's and looked up. He saw movement from the lady beside Dixie. He watched for a moment. Then the lady held still and he looked back at Dixie. He concentrated on having Dixie reach her climax. She shook as she reached the pinnacle of relief. He heard the other moan again and looked up quickly. Ricky couldn't believe his eyes. He saw the other lady as she was playing with herself under the blanket and had reached her own orgasm. He smiled to himself. Apparently, she had gotten turned on watching the two of them. Well, at least he had just satisfied two women. Wow.

"Ricky, that was awesome baby. Thank you." Dixie was saying. "AH, you're welcome baby." Ricky turned his attention back to Dixie. He smiled into her eyes.

"Let me take care of you now." Dixie said as she reached for Ricky's cock.

"Not now baby. I'm fine for right now. I just wanted you so bad. I wanted you to relax after such a hard day and to show you how much I care about you. Go to sleep for a while, okay?" Ricky really didn't want to put on more of a show for the little old lady sitting beside Dixie.

Dixie shook her head and curled up, put her head on to Ricky's chest and was soon fast asleep.

Ricky's thoughts wandered back to seeing the little old lady beside Dixie reaching her climax at the same time as Dixie did. That amazed him. He had never seen anyone get off by watching someone else reaching their climax before. That was amazing. He wondered if that was the first time she had done that during their love making sessions? Interesting to say the least.

"Wake up sleepy head. We've stopped at a restaurant. You want to clean up and get something to eat?" Ricky asked Dixie.

As Dixie roused from a deep sleep, she smiled at Ricky. She was so relaxed and didn't want to move. When she started to get up she realized that her jeans and panties were still below her knees and maneuvered to get them up without being noticed.

As the older lady had already exited the bus, Ricky folded the blankets and put them in the overhead bin and they left the bus. The two of them walked hand in hand to the restaurant and Ricky opened the door for her. It was crowded with most of the bus riders having found seats already. The old lady was sitting by herself so Ricky asked if she minded if they join her.

"Of course not. Please, have a seat. I would love to have your company." She smiled sweetly up at them.

"Oh, God, if Dixie only knew what happened last night." Ricky thought to himself.

But he smiled back and they both sat opposite the little lady. They read over the menus and when the waitress came over they all placed their orders.

Dixie excused herself and said she wanted to freshen up a bit before the food came. Ricky got up and let her out of the booth. The little lady said she needed to also. So, they went together to the ladies' room.

Ricky sat at the booth waiting for their food to arrive holding his breath until the ladies returned from the restroom. He wondered what the little old lady would say to Dixie and what her reaction would be if she found out what had happened while she was in the mists of a fantastic climax. He would just have to wait and see what her face looked like when she came back.

Dixie stood at the sink washing her hands. She had used the facilities and was cleaning herself up a bit when the little old lady came up next to her. They eyed each other for a couple minutes.

"Well, my dear, you seem to have quite a man on your hands, don't you?" the old lady said.

"What do you mean by that?" asked Dixie?

"Oh, only that he is quite handsome, well built, seems to be educated and is very sexy." stated the old lady.

"Thank you, ma'am. He is wonderful. And he is very good to me." Dixie replied as she blushed a bit.

"Yes, I can tell. He is most attentive. Especially at night. He is very attentive to your needs." The little lady gave Dixie a knowing smile.

Dixie's cheeks turned bright red. She really didn't know how to continue this conversation so she turned to leave. As she reached for the door handle the little old lady stopped her in her tracks.

"Well, I'm certainly glad my husband had been able to satisfy me like your man can satisfy you. My life sure was wonderful." The little old lady looked Dixie in the eyes.

"I'm so sorry for your loss, ma'am, but you really need to stop eaves dropping on Ricky and I." Suddenly the thought struck her that this little old lady had watched them last night. She grabbed the door handle and ran to the table where Ricky waited for her.

Ricky saw Dixie coming. No... running to the table. What the hell had happened? Oh no....he knew. That little old witch had said something to Dixie. Damn it.

Dixie quickly sat down next to Ricky.

"We have to get our food to go and get out of here. Now!!" Dixie exclaimed.

"Slow down baby. Tell me what's wrong. What happened in there? Did she upset you?" Ricky tried to calm Dixie down.

"Oh, My God. You won't believe what she told me. Ricky, I think she has been watching us make love on the bus. Come on. We have to get out of here. I can't eat in front of her knowing this. Please.." Dixie was pleading with him.

"Okay baby…we need to talk about this. Come on outside with me." Ricky took her by the arm and they headed for the door as the little old lady reappeared to the table.

"Are you leaving? Aren't you going to eat your breakfast?" she asked. "We'll be right back. Just tell them to keep our food warm, please." Ricky said. The little lady nodded as they left.

Dixie was totally confused and upset as they walked over to a bench beside the restaurant. Ricky had them sit down and he faced her and took her hands in his.

"Babe, I didn't want to talk about this until later, but I suspected that she was listening last night. I wasn't sure so I kinda watched her while I was playing with you. After a while she seemed to be sleeping so I didn't pay any attention. Then, when you were really in your climax, I heard another type of moan. I knew it wasn't yours. I looked up and I saw her playing with herself and she was in her own climax. I couldn't say anything and ruin it for her. I couldn't ruin yours either. So, I just let it go. I went with it.

She didn't say anything afterward, she just went to sleep. I rolled you into me and let you go to sleep. That's why I didn't let you take care of me last night. I just didn't know what to do." Ricky searched Dixie's eyes for some kind of response, some kind of inkling of what she was thinking.

"Oh, wow! So, she got off by watching us. She reached her climax at the same time I did?" Dixie was in total awe.

"Yes, she did. It apparently really turned her on. Who knows how long she hasn't been with a guy or had any sex at all. Maybe just hearing how happy you were, made her feel that good." Ricky was grasping for straws here. But he didn't want Dixie to feel ashamed. He wanted her to understand that someone else could get turned on by her sexuality.

"Yeah, I guess that's possible. But what do we do now? I can't keep doing that in front of her. I can't make love to you knowing that she's watching everything we do." Dixie was not going to do that.

"Okay baby. I hear you. Let's find out how much longer we have to travel with her. I'm sure there's a way to work this out. Let's just get through breakfast and we'll take care of it." Ricky needed time to think of what to do about this. They went back inside and took their seats.

"So, ma'am, I guess you really enjoyed yourself last night, huh?" Ricky said after he and Dixie sat back down at the table.

The little lady smiled slightly and her face turned a little pink. "Well, if you must know. It was rather exciting and such a turn on. My late husband was a very sexual man and I really miss what he used to do to me. Dixie, you are such a lucky young lady. Ricky here, is such a thoughtful lover." The little lady replied as she took Dixie's hand in hers.

"I'm so sorry. I really thought you were asleep and didn't know what we were doing." Dixie said as she pulled her hand away.

"Please, my name is Estelle. And I've heard you every time you've done it. You two are so sweet and romantic to one another. I just love such young, sweet, tender love. You are both so good for each other." The lady just went on and on.

"Well, thank you Estelle. But I think in the future, we will try to restrain ourselves in your presence. Making love is a private thing, ya know what I mean." stated Ricky.

"You know, what happened isn't a bad thing. What is so wrong that you gave me a little bit of pleasure out of your pleasure? You didn't touch me other than with your emotions. I felt your heat, your desire, your joy of each other." Estelle gave them a sensual grin.

They ate their meal and boarded the bus. Each stayed within their own thoughts as the miles passed. Estelle reached her destination and Ricky and Dixie wished her well.

Another passenger had boarded the bus and took up Estelle's seat, so Dixie got engrossed in her book and Ricky studied some legal files until the bus arrived in Fresno. Neither had wanted a repeat of their escapade with Estelle.

It would be two more hours before they would reach Fresno. Dixie called her aunt to make sure she would be at the bus stop waiting to pick her up. She also informed her that there would be another person joining her for a few days and asked if that would be alright.

Betty Jean was waiting for them when the bus pulled into the Fresno terminal. Dixie introduced her to Ricky, then loaded their belongings into the Ford Escape.

"Welcome to Fresno, Ricky. I hope you both had a good trip. Dixie, it's good to see you again. Your room is all ready for you and Ricky, you can have the room in the basement." Betty Jean wasn't sure what the situation was between the two of them but wasn't making assumptions.

They talked about the trip and other conversation on the way to Betty Jeans house, while watching the beautiful landscape. Dinner was ready to be put on the table after they unloaded the car. Dixie poured the wine as Betty Jean finished showing Ricky the rest of the house.

After dinner, they watched some television, then each retired to their rooms for the night. Dixie was exhausted from the trip and quickly fell to sleep. Ricky missed Dixie, having gotten used to her being beside him. It took longer for him to finally drop off into a peaceful slumber. They both woke to the smell of fresh coffee and arrived in the kitchen at the same time. Their gazes met each other with looks of longing. Betty Jean knew that look all too well. She wasn't so sure that Dixie was ready for it yet. She had just met this man on a bus trip. Had known him for only a few days. So, was it love or simply lust?

"Good morning you two. I hope you slept well. We are going to have a busy day and then we are going out to a party tonight. My company is having this huge celebration for a new contract we just secured. So, dress up nice, that means a suit for you Ricky, and we'll have a great time." Betty Jean shot Ricky a sideways look.

"No problem. I have one with me. Sounds like fun." Ricky replied with a huge grin.

"Is this a semi-formal affair, or will a party dress work?" Dixie inquired.

"We're going shopping for dresses for you and me. I want us to look simply adorable and a little sexy tonight. I want to show you off. After all, you are my favorite niece." Betty Jean saw the look of uneasiness cross Ricky's face.

The girls went and had their nails and toes done while Ricky went to get a haircut. They met for lunch before separating as the ladies went clothes shopping and Ricky scouted the city. They met back at the car, returning home with their parcels to get ready for the party.

Ricky waited in the living-room, sitting patiently on the couch. He was decked out in the black suit he had worn in court a week ago. Thankfully, it had not wrinkled in his garment bag. He wore a white shirt and a paisley tie. He checked again to make sure the little package was in his pants pocket.

Betty Jean came down the stairs wearing a red dress that sat just off her shoulders and hugged her slender body. It came to just above her knees, showing her long legs as she walked into the room wearing two- and one-half inch black heels. Her red hair was piled on top of her head into a pillow of curls. A black choker was around her neck with black dangle earrings. She looked amazing.

Ricky stood, walked up to her, took her hand and kissed it. She smiled up into his eyes. He looked so handsome, she thought, and is so much a gentleman.

Ricky heard the bedroom door close as Dixie started to come downstairs and his heart rate increased.

He saw first one long black stocking clad leg, then the other as her five-foot eight-inch body slowly appeared on the stairway. Her tight, form fitting black dress came halfway down her thighs with enough cleavage to show over half her breasts. All Ricky could do was stare, his mouth watering with desire. Her red hair hung down over her shoulders, silver earrings hung from her ear lobes. Her black three-inch heels made her a statue of exquisite beauty.

Ricky walked over to the end of the stairway. He reached out his hand taking hers. He led her into the living-room and spun her around. She was the most gorgeous woman he had ever seen. He knew in that instant he was in love with her. He would not leave this town without her. He noticed the little diamond necklace she had on. He stood behind her and unclasped it. Dixie started to protest. Ricky stood in front of her and took out the little box in his pocket.

"While I was out wandering around this great city today, I found this amazing store. While going through it I came upon this. I would be honored if you would wear it tonight. It belongs on such a beautiful woman. My gift to you Dixie." With that he opened the box.

Dixie almost fainted. It was the most beautiful necklace she had ever seen. It was an Amethyst with a diamond on each side. The stone was huge. Ricky took it from the box, went behind her and clasped it on her neck. He went back in front of her and admired how it shown lying between her breasts.

Betty Jean watched with awe. This man really did love her niece.

Did she love him??

The party was a great success and everyone had a lot of fun. Ricky danced with both women, but never left Dixie's side for very long. He knew he had a wonderful woman and wasn't taking any chances of someone else turning her head.

"Baby, I can't stand not sleeping with you. Not being able to touch you or hold you. This is killing me." Ricky said during a slow dance.

"I know. I don't like it either. But we can't go against Aunt Betty Jean. It's her house and her rules." Dixie didn't know what to do.

"Look, we only have a couple more days until I have to leave. I'm going to get a hotel room so we can have some time together. I can't leave here without spending more time with you. There are some things we need to talk about too." Ricky was determined.

"Yeah, I'd really like that too. I've missed you so much. I know she means well but I can't stand not being with you anymore either. Please, can we go somewhere tonight?" Dixie was more than ready to make love with Ricky. She needed him.

"Yes, baby. Anything for you. We'll explain things to your aunt. I'm sure she'll understand." With that they left the dance floor in search of Betty Jean.

After explaining things to her aunt, she gave them the car keys, saying she'd get her car later. They got their things and went to the hotel she had recommended. It was very plush and accommodating. There was a hot tub in the room as well as a wet bar and snacks. Dixie thought this room must cost a fortune.

Ricky took Dixie in his arms and held her close to him. She felt so good. He never wanted to let her go again. He didn't know how it happened, nor did he care. It had. He had fallen in love.

He had sworn to a life of solitude after his marriage had fallen apart more than eight years ago. She had been a gold digger, only wanting what his family had. He was determined to never let that happen to him again.

Then he met Dixie. She was so different from anyone he had ever met. She didn't ask him for anything. Hell, she told him off when they first met. She wouldn't let him pay for her meals on the trip. She was a hot little vixen. She was so sexy. And he meant to keep her...now and forever.

This man is everything I've ever wanted Dixie though as she stood comfortably in Ricky's arms. He's got a good job. He's fun to be with. He's adventurous, and sexy as hell.

She sighed contentedly.

Ricky put his finger under her chin and lifted it. Her eyes looked up into his. Heat passed between them. Raw, passionate emotion. Ricky lowered his head until his lips touched hers. Sparks...electric energy grabbed them. Zapped through them like bolts of lightning. His lips took hers in a deep kiss as her toes curled.

Lifting his head, he looked at her, "You look smoking hot tonight Dixie. You drive me crazy. I want you so much. More than you know baby." With that he pressed into her with his body letting her feel his need for her.

Dixie melted into him and she whimpered. "I need you too." Ricky wanted this night to be the most memorable of their lives.

Before he told her everything, he wanted her completely relaxed. "Dixie, let's have a drink, sit in the hot tub and relax for a while.

We have all night to enjoy each other and I want us to take our time. Are you okay with that?" Ricky said as he released her and walked toward the wet bar.

"Sure, that sounds good. I didn't bring a suit with me though." Dixie said.

Ricky smiled at her. Such a sweet little southern lady.

"Umm…I don't think we really need suits…do we? Aren't we a little bit beyond that by now? Take it easy babe. You want me to help you undress? It'd be my pleasure." Ricky said with a smirk.

"I think I can manage. You may need to unzip my dress though." Dixie replied with a slight smile.

"If I start on that zipper, I'm not going to stop there." Said Ricky as he started toward her.

Dixie giggled as she turned her back and started for the bathroom. Then she stopped and lifted her hair. Ricky got the message and reached for the zipper, slowly lowering it, as he planted kisses along her neck.

As the zipper lowered, so did the kisses. Then the licks began along her spine. Shivers traveled along her body causing tingles and aches. He knew he was driving her insane and loved it. He dropped the dress off her shoulders and down her arms. Slowly he lowered it off her body. His hands traveled, caressing her, touching her. Wrapping his arms around her he pressed his hardness into her. He heard her moans as her head came to rest on his chest.

His hands squeezed her breasts and nipples through her bra. They hardened at his touch. Ricky pulled them out and held them in his hands. So warm and soft. He pinched her nipples making them harder. She moaned louder, her butt pressing into him. His left hand roamed lower, over her abdomen, to her pantyhose. No panties underneath. Nice, he thought.

His hand massaged her through the thin material. She was damp with desire. Ricky went back to put his hand under the waistband, rolling them down so he could get to her warmth. She was on fire for him. Her body was in motion with need. His hand cupped her womanhood and held her. She was so hot and wet for him.

Kissing her neck and biting her ear lobe, he slid his finger down her slit, along her clit and into her vaginal warmth. Her muscles grabbed him and held him. Her legs wobbled, trying to hold herself up as she knew she was getting close to coming.

"Please Ricky. Make me cum baby." She cried to him.

"I will baby. I will." Ricky turned her head to him and kissed her, putting his tongue into her mouth as he put another finger into her. Fucking her mouth and her pussy at the same time drove Dixie over the edge and she came in a torrent all over Ricky's hand. He kept the pace, riding out her climax until she quieted.

Dixie's legs gave out and Ricky grabbed her, lifting her up. He cradled her in his arms as he carried her into the bathroom. He helped her finish undressing, then undressed himself. He cleaned her with a warm washcloth then walked them both out to the hot tub and assisted her to get in. After making sure she was comfortably placed, he went to the bar to make them drinks. He returned with them and got in beside her. Turning on the jets, he sat back to relax.

They played in the warm water for a while, teasing each other. Him grabbing a nipple, twisting and tweaking it. Her massaging his semi hard cock. He wanted her to relax and enjoy herself before they got into the deepest conversation they had yet had. He didn't know what her reaction would be, but he knew if he were to lose her now his life would never be the same.

A light knock on the door stopped their frolicking as Ricky left the hot tub, donned a robe and answered the door. Room service was right on time as the server set up the table in the corner of the room. Dixie hadn't known this had all been prearranged before they had arrived at the hotel.

Ricky checked the bottle of wine the waiter held out to him and nodded for him to open it. The waiter did so and poured it into the glasses. He then opened the lids to the food and set them before Dixie and Ricky as they took their seats.

"Ricky, did you know about this?" Dixie asked after the waiter left. "Ah...yeah...I did. Are you unhappy about it? I was hoping to surprise you." Ricky looked at her with a sheepish grin.

"Oh, no. I love it. This looks fantastic! How did you do it? When did you do all this?" Dixie was truly perplexed.

"Well, I must confess. Today, while we were all shopping, I decided that I needed some alone time with you. So, I kinda did this by phone when you and your aunt were busy looking at other stuff." Ricky took her hand in his.

"I'm so glad you did. But Ricky.. ummmm I know you want to make me feel good and all. But this is not a cheap hotel. And all this.. the food.. the hot tub…everything. Baby.???" Dixie couldn't get out all she was trying to say. She was tongue tied.

"Dixie. You are worth the world to me. Everything I have I would give to you. I want you to feel like the most important person in my life. And you are. Let's eat and then we are going to have a very deep and honest conversation. There is a lot I need to tell you about." Ricky had a death grip on her hand.

Dixie looked at him quizzically and in astonishment. She didn't even know what to say to him.

"Please don't look at me like that. I'm not a monster, killer or a criminal. You know I'm a lawyer. You just don't know to what extent. It's all good baby. Please trust me. I would never hurt you. I... Let's eat…then we'll talk. Okay?" Ricky needed time to get this all straight in his head. God help him.

'So, he drops a bomb shell on me like that and I'm supposed to just sit here and eat. Yeah, okay. Dixie's head was in a whirlwind. Her steak and shrimp was delicious, but her taste buds seemed not to be working right. She seemed to be going through the motions of cut and chew but didn't really taste it. Her mind was on what he had said, and of all the expense he had put out on her.

Ricky prayed that he hadn't gone too far. He hadn't meant to scare her but wanted her to know how he felt about her. He would give her anything and everything. He had fallen in love with her. Now he had to figure out a way to keep her. That wasn't going to be easy. She had had such a bad marriage, that she didn't want back into another relationship. So, what would it take to get her to come with him to his home. Certainly, not the promise of riches, wealth and never having to work again. So what??

They finished dinner and Ricky walked Dixie out onto the balcony. The air was warm with a slight breeze.

"Would you like a drink or a cup of coffee?" Ricky asked.

"A cup of coffee would be wonderful after such a filling meal. Thank you." Dixie looked up into his expressive eyes.

Ricky brought out their coffee, handed her a cup and sat beside her. Sitting up high and looking out over the city, the lights were beautiful reflecting off the clouds with a few stars peeking through. Ricky reached out and took Dixie's hand in his. Her warmth was intoxicating to him. His body reacted to her. But now wasn't the time for that. He turned his chair so he could look into her eyes.

"Dixie. There are things I need to tell you. Please, just hear me out. Then if you have questions, I will do my best to answer them. Is that okay?" His eyes were pleading with hers.

Dixie could only nod in the affirmative.

"As I told you, I am a lawyer in a small law firm. But that firm is part of a much larger one. That firm was owned by my father, until recently that is. He passed away about ten months ago. Then it was my responsibility to take over and run the firm. The whole firm. There are offices across the states. Actually, there are sixty-five offices. I kept my office in the small firm in Madeira but I also have one in Los Angeles. And one in Las Vegas. Then I travel when needed to the other firms.

When I met up with you on the bus, I had just finished up with a huge case and was on my way back to Las Vegas. But, then I met this incredible woman and wanted to be with her and know more about her. So, I didn't get off there but continued on with her to here.

Now, I know even more that I want to be with her and don't want to leave here without her. I can't see my life without her. You, Dixie, You." Ricky stopped, inhaled a deep breath and let it out slowly.

Dixie sat there staring at him, her mouth agape. She didn't know what to say to him. No wonder he could afford this room and all he had done for her. But he didn't act like he had money. Quite the opposite. He bewildered her. He wanted her. He did say that... right?

Her hands were shaking as well as the cup she held. Ricky took the cup from her and set it down on the table beside them. Then he took her hands in his and held them.

"Dixie, I travel by bus because I get tired of all the phony people on the airlines. I get tired of being around stuffy people in business suits, offices, restaurants, meetings and all the crap. I wanted to be around real people. People who feel things. Like you do. Honest people who say what they mean.

Hell, you told me off the very first time we spoke. That was so hot." They both broke out laughing as they remembered her getting mad about him flirting with her.

"Yeah, and here it was your sister. What a dumb person I was." Dixie laughed again.

"But that's my point baby. You were real. And I loved that. Babe, I'm around women all the time. In my office, the court houses, etc. But none of them can hold a candle to you. You let out what you feel and you show your emotions. I love that about you. Besides, you are a very hot lover. Your sexy as hell and you know how to please me very well." Ricky was grinning from ear to ear.

"Dixie, I want to make a proposal of sorts to you. I would like for you to come to Madeira with me. Give us one year to see if we are able to form a life together. You can work or not, that is entirely up to you. I just ask that if I need you to be at a special function with me, that you do so. We would live together and be together in every sense of the word. A full relationship. If, after that year, you do not want to stay, I will make sure you are given what you need to start a life wherever you want." Ricky held his breath. He looked deep into her eyes. They were warm and kind. No sign of coolness.

"Why would you offer to let me go after one year and pay my expenses?" Dixie thought she knew the answer but wanted to hear him say it.

"Because, deep in my heart, I believe that if you stay for one year, you won't want to leave. We will be so deeply in love, there will be no need of us to go anywhere but with each other." Ricky leaned in and kissed her lips gently.

"Ricky, the money doesn't matter to me. I have also fallen in love with you. I had asked my aunt if you could move in with us if I could talk you into moving here to be with me. So, I had already wanted to be with you before you told me all of this. But I also got her to agree to let us share a room, because I told her we were not going to sleep apart anymore." Ricky grabbed her and held her close to him. God how he loved this woman.

"My God woman, you are something else. How two minds can work together. Man, we'd be dangerous if we ever teamed up." They both chuckled.

"Seriously, I would love to stay here, but I can't. I have too many responsibilities where I'm at. And with the other offices, I really have to be in that area, at least for right now babe." Ricky studied her face.

"Maybe I can be talked into it." Dixie said with a sly grin.

"Oh yeah, and just what kind of talking did you have in mind? I can do simple, easy or torturous. Which would you prefer my lady?" Ricky's fingers started moving up her legs, under her robe toward her nether parts.

"Well, dear sir, it might take some work. So, take your pick." Dixie was now squirming in her chair as his fingers had reached their mark.

He lifted her up under her armpits, turned her around and leaned her over the balcony railing. Lifting her robe, he stooped down and brought his mouth to her buttocks. Spreading her cheeks, his tongue lapped between her lips until he reached her clit and she shuttered. He licked and licked while holding her tight against the rail. Her juices were flowing as he ministered to her, his tongue finding her opening and entering. Her moans were turning into groans.

Standing behind her, he opened his robe, grabbed his tool and held it to her. She backed up to him and aided in him entering her. She gasped as he pushed deep and hard into her till he was fully seated. He held her still as he savored the feel of her warmth.

"My God Hot Stuff!!!!.... I love you more than you could ever imagine. You have given me such joy in my life. I never want to let you go. Please, baby. Say you'll come be with me. Take my love and all of me that I have to offer you. My life I give to you." Ricky pushed hard into her again and again.

"Ahhhhh… God Ricky… yesss yessssss mmmmmmmmmm… cummmmmmming" she shouted.

Ricky pounded her as they both reached their climaxes together. He pulled her to him and held her. Dixie turned and wrapped her arms around his neck kissing him over and over.

"I love you Dixie Lee Givens." Ricky looked deep into her eyes. They were smoldering with love.

"I love you too Ricky McPatrick." Dixie saw warmth, strength, need and desire in his eyes. She walked back into the room and started to get dressed. Ricky looked at her puzzled. Dixie looked up at him and smiled.

"Well, I guess it's settled then. What other options do we have? I guess we better head back to Aunt Betty Jean's and pack our stuff for the bus ride to Madeira tomorrow. Wouldn't want to keep the bus waiting.. now would we??!!!!

JAMIE LEE AWAKENS

What was he waiting for? Could he not tell that she was more than ready for his hard dick? God!!! This guy was either dumb, crazy or stupid. Maybe a little of all three. Well, she would just have to take matters into her own hands then. Suppose she grabbed him by the hard staff in his pants and led him straight to the barn and up to the haystack. Yup... maybe then he might get the message. She had been leading him on all day long and still he wasn't getting the hang of what she wanted. She'd just show him…that's all.

So Carrie Ann told Jamie Lee to meet her in the barn in ten minutes, that she had a job that she desperately needed his help with. He said he was busy with the gardening, weeding to be exact, and the mistress of the house would be mad something awful if he left before it was finished. But Carrie Ann was persistent.

"Look, Jamie Lee, if I don't get this job done, there will surely be hell to pay, and you will be just as much to blame as me, cause I can't do it by myself. I'm just a weak female and you're a strong, virile male, and I need you desperately to make this job happen. Please, Jamie Lee? Please???"

"Carrie Ann, you don't work here, you live here and you don't have no job to do. You just want to lure me away from here to get me into trouble with the missus. Now go away with yourself and go find something to do. You're a spoiled little girl looking to get into some kind of trouble. I just know it. Now get along and leave me be to do my work. Go on.... get out of here."

Jamie Lee turned his back to her and continued to pull weeds. His six-foot three-inch frame had towered over her a minute ago and now was bent over, ignoring her. She'd just have to find some other way of getting him into the barn and up into the hayloft was all.

Most of the hired help here were black, but Jamie Lee was a white man, a good-looking man at that. Carrie Ann knew what she wanted. and she wanted Jamie Lee…and she would have him, come hell or high water. She was eighteen now and could do as she wanted. Her daddy had died a few years ago from some disease that she couldn't remember the name of and now her momma ran the plantation. She ran it with an iron hand. No one messed with Mrs. Carmichael. No one. Not even her own daughter. Carrie Ann knew the rules and was expected to obey them to the letter. One of which was not to mess with the hired hands. But damn, Jamie Lee was so well built and every woman's dream.

How could she stay away from him? She knew that she turned him on, too. She saw how he reacted to her whenever she hung around him for very long. Carrie Ann could see too that he was very well endowed. God, but she wanted some of that.

She had thought of him often when she had taken care of matters in the privacy of her bedroom at night. She knew just how well he could satisfy that hunger that drove her crazy with want night after night. While she played with her pussy, drove her fingers deep inside herself, she pictured Jamie Lee on top of her, driving his stiff rod into her, deeper and deeper until they both were spent.

"Carrie Ann, would you please tell Jamie Lee that he can come in for some refreshments. It is so hot out there today and I would hate for him to become over heated," stated her mother.

"Sure mom, would be delighted to." Wow, another chance to drive this man crazy. Of course she would go get him. Off she went to the garden at the side of the house near the side porch.

"Jamie Lee, mom says to come into the house for some refreshments. She says it's so hot out here." She fans herself as if to emphasize the point, even though she has on a cool white sundress.

"This Mississippi heat will sure get to a person if they aren't careful and stay hydrated, you know."

"Yes ma'am, I do know that. That's why I carry this cooler full of ice water with me all the time. Tell your momma thank you just the same, but I am fine. I have plenty to drink."

"Oh yes, Jamie Lee, you sure are fine. Mmmm, mmm, mmm." she thought to herself.

"Now Jamie Lee, if you don't come in as momma asked, it will be my hide she'll be after. She'll say I never gave you the message. Now hurry along and come with me into the house for the refreshments she's made for you." No way was she going to go back to the house without him. She wanted this afternoon to flirt with him and win him over.

Carrie Ann didn't know exactly how old Jamie Lee was, but she knew he was old enough to take care of her cravings. She knew he had to be at least her age, maybe a couple years older. How experienced he was in the art of sex; she had no idea. But what he didn't know, she could surely teach him. After all, her daddy had been a doctor and she had read all those medical books about the subject she could find in his library.

"Carrie Ann, would you please sit still. You're wiggling around like a little worm. Drink your lemonade and behave. Follow the conversation if you please." her mother chided.

"Yes ma'am. What were you saying?" she replied.

"I was saying that the weather has been so hot that I'm afraid that I might lose my garden before poor Jamie Lee can get all the weeding done. What we need is a good, slow, soaking rain. It would cool it off and the flowers sure would love the moisture to their petals." Momma was carrying on so.

"I know some petals that would love some attention too," Carrie Ann thought.

But I smiled at momma and then at Jamie Lee.

"Do you think there is any rain in our future, Jamie Lee. Someone once told me that you have a knack for telling when rain is coming. Is that true?" Carrie Ann was trying to keep her mind where it should be instead of where she wanted it to be. Oh, he looked so handsome and sexy sitting here. Did he even know how he affected her?

"Well, some people believe that I can tell...I'm not so sure myself. Except that I get this funny feeling along my leg bone whenever it's going to storm out. I mean really bad storms. Like hurricanes and such." Jamie Lee gave a slight smile.

"Oh, well, perhaps you should tell me when your legs start to hurt or act up, Jamie Lee. Then we can prepare for such a forceful storm." her momma was buying into this whole psychic bone theory thing.

"Awe, ma'am, I don't really think there is anything to it. Just what people say is all." Jamie Lee was a very shy and quiet person.

"Just the same, you tell me," momma said as she nodded her head.

"Yes ma'am. Now, if you'll excuse me, I really need to be getting back to the weeding in the garden. Can't seem to catch up to them this year. Thank you for the lemonade," he said as he bowed to Mrs. Carmichael.

"You may go, but don't work too late. It's better to come early in the morning when it's not so hot out." She was half hollering as he walked down the steps and off to the side of the big, white house.

Later in the afternoon Carrie Ann walked around to where Jamie Lee was working and stopped dead in her tracks. She saw the broadest bare back, muscles rippling with sweat pouring down, that she had ever seen. God, he was an Adonis. He was magnificent. He was ALL MALE!!!! He suddenly turned around. His chest muscles tweaked and she was mesmerized. She couldn't move. She was rooted to the spot. Like a weed that couldn't be pulled out…she couldn't budge, flinch or draw a breath.

"Carrie Ann, you startled me. I wasn't expecting anyone. I thought you ladies were taking your afternoon naps. Please excuse me while I put my shirt back on. I'm sorry you saw me this way." Jamie Lee was truly embarrassed. He reached down and put his button-down shirt back on.

"Please, don't be upset. It's so hot out, if I could get away with not wearing one, I wouldn't either," she said with a grin.

"You're a lady. You shouldn't say such things as that, Miss Carrie Ann." Jamie Lee replied…even though he would have loved to see her without that dress on. But he couldn't let her know that.

"Why Jamie Lee, you're not embarrassed around me are you? We are about the same age and we kinda like each other, right?" No time like the present to push him a little. She gave a look downward and noticed that his little tent was growing. It started slowly and was now growing quite a bit. OH, how she wanted to reach out and touch that tent and what was in it.

Carrie Ann finally found her feet and walked closer to Jamie Lee and touched his arm. He flinched a little and she touched him again. He held still this time. She rubbed her hand up and down his arm, feeling his hard muscles as she went.

"You are so strong, Jamie Lee. All this weed pulling and shoveling. Hoeing, raking and stuff sure keeps you in shape." She reached up to his chest. He grabbed her hand and stilled it. Carrie Ann looked into his hazel eyes with her blue ones. She didn't even blink. She massaged one side and then the other. God, he felt so good. So well built. So hot.

"Carrie Ann, you don't know what you are doing. You had better stop this now. You are begging for trouble. Trouble we both don't want." Jamie Lee took her hand off his chest and put it to her side.

"Oh, but I do know what I want. It is you that I want, Jamie Lee. I dream of you every night. I think of you all day. It is you that makes me want to be a woman. Please, Jamie Lee. Let me be your woman. Make me your woman." Carrie Ann pleaded with him, her eyes never leaving his.

"Oh, Carrie Ann. You are such a child. I cannot make you my woman. Your momma would have my hide and I would be out of a job. You are not ready to be a woman yet. You have so much to learn first. Give yourself time my little girl." He smiled at her gently.

"I am old enough to be your woman. I will make you see I am right for you. You will see." With that she turned and went back into the house.

Several nights later a storm came up from out of nowhere. The wind was howling, the barn doors had not been secured properly and needed to be re-latched. Her mother had called the bunk house but no one had answered.

Carrie Ann had come down and asked her mother if she could help. Knowing that the horses would get loose if someone didn't close the doors, Carrie Ann went out into the weather to do the task.

Just as she pushed her way through the big door of the house the rain pelted down. Carrie Ann ran as fast as she could toward the barn but the wind kept pushing her backward. She'd get two steps forward and three steps back. With a concentrated effort, she finally made it to the barn doors. Slowly, she opened the one to the right and stepped in, pulling it closed behind her. She then secured it with a board between the latches.

After trying the power switch and nothing happening, Carrie Ann turned to pick up the lantern that she knew was usually beside the door, hanging on the hook. As she reached for it, she felt a hand cover hers. She started to scream but was stopped when she recognized Jamie Lee's voice talking to her.

"Oh, thank God you are here. Mother has been trying to reach you about the doors being open. When she couldn't, I came out to secure them. Where were you, anyway?" Carrie Ann asked.

Seeing that Carrie Ann was soaked to the gills, Jamie Lee needed to get her into something dry before she caught her death of pneumonia. Lord, this was all he needed. She already had the hots for him and here he was in this predicament.

"Carrie Ann, you are soaked through. You have to get out of those wet clothes and put on this blanket. I'll go to the house and get you some dry things. Go into the stall over there and do as I tell you, girl. Hurry up. I'll be back in a few minutes." He only hoped that she would do as he told her.

"Jamie Lee, I'm too scared to stay here alone. Don't you dare leave me here by myself during this bad storm. I'm afraid." Carrie Ann then leaped into his arms and held on for dear life. She was trembling, but he doubted from fear. Probably from being cold from the wet clothing she was in.

Jamie Lee could feel himself instantly start to harden at the feel of her touch and so did she. So, she snuggled a little closer, moving her hips closer into his. Jamie Lee groaned, low in his chest. God, what this girl was doing to him. How was he going to restrain himself from her?

He grabbed her arms and lowered her down, back onto her own feet. She glowered at him. She looked down at his groin and his hard on was raging. She looked back up into his eyes. They couldn't lie. He truly wanted her. Desired her. She saw it...raw...real...needy...aching. Oh yes, he wanted her.

She moved a little bit closer and his cock jumped. Damn thing had a mind of its own. Her hand rose up and touched his face. It jumped again. Damn. Jamie Lee was beside himself. God, he wanted her.... wanted her really bad. But, oh the trouble he would be in. Her momma would skin him alive if he touched her little girl. But this was no little girl standing in front of him.

Jamie Lee saw her womanly breasts rise in front of him. They grew before his very eyes. Oh how he wanted to taste them. Suck on them. Make those little nipples hard and responsive to him. He had dreams of her. Dreams of what she would smell like, taste like, feel like lying beneath him. Oh, to awaken such lust in a man was dangerous, especially to such a little girl..no this woman. But he wanted her.. now!!!

Slowly he led her backward until he had her backed up against the stall and had his chest against hers. She was breathing hard and her chest was heaving. Her breasts moving against his chest was driving him mad. "Carrie Ann, are you sure baby? If I start, I won't be able to stop.

I want you more than life itself. Be very sure little one. There will be no turning back once we start." He wanted to give her every last opportunity to stop now.

"Jamie Lee, I have wanted you forever. It's all I have dreamed about, thought about. Every time I see you, I want you…I need you. Please, make love to me. Make me your woman. Now." She pleaded with him, again.

He reached out and touched her long blonde hair that was flat against her head from being wet and pushed it back from her neck. Jamie Lee leaned down and kissed her, gently, softly, lips barely touching. He licked her lips. He nipped at the bottom one. Carrie Ann moaned.

Jamie Lee hardened his kiss a little more and pressed his lips over hers sucking in hers. She gasped. His tongue licked and pushed, licked and pushed and finally she let his tongue into her mouth. Carrie Ann stiffened and stood very still. She had never kissed a man and this felt really strange. But a good strange. And he tasted good. He must have eaten something sweet because he tasted sweet.

Jamie Lee continued to kiss and lick her and to tongue her as his hand reached up and caressed her right breast. She had put her coat on over her night shirt and had no bra on. Oh, sweet Jesus, she felt wonderful. So soft, his hand so full of her. She was so precious. His Carrie Ann was going to be all his. Oh, dear God, how was he so lucky and so cursed at the same time.

Carrie Ann didn't realize what was going on until Jamie Lee already had her breast in his hand and was massaging her. He felt so good. So fantastic. Better than when she did it herself. Emitting a soft moan, she moved into him a little bit. Jamie Lee moved to the other breast and massaged that one too. Leaving her lips, he moved along her neck, trailing little kisses and a nip here and there as he worked his way down. As he looked at her he removed her wet jacket and lifted her night shirt. Lifting up her arms, she let him remove it. Now, she stood there in only her panties. God, she looked awesome. No, beautiful. No, gorgeous!!!...and she was his...only his.

Jamie Lee bent down onto his knees and brought Carrie Ann down with him onto the hay at the floor of the stall. She had her hands on his shoulders as he once again reached for her breasts with both hands. He lowered his head and gently placed soft kisses on first one and then the other. Carrie Ann moaned in pleasure.

Jamie Lee took her right breast into his mouth and rolled his tongue around her nipple, it instantly becoming hard. Carrie Ann was on fire. Her body was hot, burning like nothing she had ever felt before. Jamie Lee switched to the other breast and the fire built more.

As the rain pelted the roof of the barn, the storm of passion heated the barn on the inside. Jamie Lee licked his way down her belly to her belly button. As he twirled his tongue inside it he slowly leaned her backward till she lay flat on the hay bed. He worked his way down to the rectangular patch of blonde hair between her thighs. But he stopped short. He lifted his head and looked up at her.

Carrie Ann opened her eyes and saw Jamie Lee looking at her with heated passion. She had awakened in him a need so great that she didn't know the extent of what she was going to get from him. His fires were burning out of control. And hers were about to reach combustion. She just didn't know it yet. The playing she had done to herself had just been the tip of the iceberg. She would learn what real sex was, what real satisfaction was, what having a man doing that satisfying did to a woman. She was about to become a woman.. a real woman.

Jamie Lee reached his hand down to her thighs and caressed them tenderly. He rubbed first one and then the other to the top of her groin, but not going into her private womanhood. Carrie Ann moved her hips. She wanted his hand there so much. Needed his hand there. She didn't know why, but she did. God, he was driving her mad.

He took the index finger of his right hand and moved it up into her outer lips and across her clit. She jumped. He cupped her mound. He held her still. As he held her there he moved his finger again, up and down over her lips, moving them slightly, gently. Carrie Ann wiggled. She felt her temperature rising. He continued to move his finger, a little more inside of her each time. She was getting wet. A little wetter each time his finger passed. He reached in and circled her vagina. Her little hole responded and quivered. With his hand he pressed on her clit as he pressed his finger into her. She let out a moan and raised her hips to meet his hand at the same time.

"Oh, God, Jamie Lee. Please, that feels like heaven. You feel so good." she sighed as she continued to move with the rhythm of the movement of his finger going in and out of her. His finger was very wet and moved easily into her until he felt her hymen. He stopped abruptly. He wouldn't hurt her.

"Please, don't stop. Let me cum." Carrie Ann begged. Still moving her hips, moved his finger a little bit more.

Jamie Lee pulled his finger out and crawled down between her legs. He lifted her knees and looked admiringly at her sweet, pink pussy. God, she looked delicious. Eating her would be so sweet, tasty, the effervescence of her was intoxicating. He could smell her essence from where he was and couldn't wait to taste her, to savor her flavor.

Slowly he bent his head downward. Jamie Lee had waited forever for this day and was in no hurry to have it over with. He wanted to relish in taking Carrie Ann on a journey she would remember forever. As his mouth reached her pussy he touched her outer lips with the tip of his tongue. Carrie Ann moved and moaned at the same time.

"Oh, God." Carrie Ann couldn't believe the feeling going through her. The warmth of Jamie Lee's mouth on her was electrifying. She wanted more. Much more. She had waited a lifetime for him and now she wanted all of what he would give her.

Jamie Lee took his tongue and licked the length of her. Up and then down. Then back up again. She tasted exquisite. Sweet. He took a lip into his mouth a sucked on it. Then the other. He groaned in passion. Carrie Ann was squirming. Moving her hips up, tighter into his mouth. His tongue was working its way toward her center. She was moaning. That wonderful little hole that led into her. Jamie Lee pushed his tongue into that little hole and it was Carrie Ann's undoing.

She screamed out his name as he held her hips tightly.

"Jamie Lee....Oh My God....YES.... YES!!!" Carrie Ann cried out as he stroked her inside with his tongue.

Her inner muscles sucked on his tongue and pulled him in further. His nose hit her clitoris and sent her spiraling into her first true vaginal orgasm.

He held her tight…wouldn't let her move…buried his face deeper.. his face harder into her. He rode her out as her climax came and then settled down.

Carrie Ann felt her vaginal muscles contract around Jamie Lee's tongue as he sucked her and tongue fucked her. His nose was rubbing her clit, sending her into an orbit she had never reached before. Her juices were flowing over his tongue and down her backside. She was drenching everything in its path. So hard was this climax. She tried to pull back just a little but he held her tight. Tears were rolling down her cheeks as she cried in pleasure.

She felt like the climax would never end. Finally, her muscles calmed and she relaxed her legs. Jamie Lee pulled back and looked up at her, their eyes meeting. No words were needed to express what each was feeling. Jamie Lee had never had a woman respond like that to him before and Carrie Ann had never had an experience like that. Both were amazed. Both were enthralled. Both were hot as hell for each other. Jamie Lee knew that no one would stop him from having her now. Carrie Ann would be his woman now and forever. She was his.

Carrie Ann wanted Jamie Lee in the worst way. He was hot. He was all she had ever dreamed he would be…and more. Then she felt his tongue again. His hot, wet tongue was caressing her clit. Slowly, small little circles. Round and round, over and down. He tilted it, tipped it, and twirled it. She was going nuts. She loved it.

Jamie Lee was teasing her…tormenting her clit. Loving her little body with all he had in him. He wanted her to cum again like she did before. He wanted to give her so much pleasure. Slowly, he inserted his middle finger into her vagina as he tongued her clit some more. Carrie Ann jumped. Her hips came up to meet his hand. With his other hand, he pushed her hips gently back down to the mat they had made in the hay.

Carrie Ann was wreathing in delight as she felt his finger inside her. "Damn, what didn't this man know what to do to her?" she wondered as she was in total bliss. As she felt his finger moving in and out she suddenly felt a second finger being inserted. Just as that happened Jamie Lee took hold of her clit and sucked it into his mouth. Carrie Ann's hips came off the hay and her legs became rigid as she went into a strong climax. Her stomach muscles tightened and she came all over Jamie Lee's mouth and fingers. Her juices flowed and he sucked and licked as fast as he could to get every last drop.

When Jamie Lee lifted his head, Carrie Ann was laying quietly her arms on either side of her head. She was totally spent and content. Jamie Lee smiled as he watched his angel. She had the glow of an angel. Radiant. Beautiful. Sexually satisfied.

He wanted to feel her lips on his stiff, hard shaft…but not this time. All he wanted now was to feel himself buried deep inside of her sweet body. He wanted her.. all of her. She was his, would be completely his… and would complete him. Now.

As Jamie Lee moved up over her body, Carrie Ann watched him, her eyes never leaving his.

"This is your last chance to say no, sweet baby. Otherwise, you are now going to be mine…and only mine. Do you understand, Carrie Ann?" Jamie Lee gave her one last chance to save herself.

"Jamie Lee, I want you more than life itself. Please, take me. Make me yours. Make me a whole woman. Make me your woman. Please Jamie Lee." Carrie Ann said as she held his face in her hands, her eyes never leaving his. She was indeed ready to become a woman…his woman. Nothing could stop them now. This was meant to be.

The storm was still raging outside. The thunder crashed and the lightening was flashing. Rain was pelting down in buckets. But nothing compared to the blazing firestorm that was raging inside the barn.

As Jamie Lee covered Carrie Ann's body with his he held her in his arms for just a moment…savoring the feel of her. Her soft, young breasts against his chest. Their bellies touching together. His cock touching her womanly home.

"My sweet, little girl. This will hurt for a moment. I can't stop it." Jamie Lee was pushing her hair back from her face and then softly touching her face, then her lips with his fingers. "I will be as gentle as I can be. When I get all the way in you, I will stop and let you get use to me until the pain stops. Then you will enjoy our lovemaking. I promise, this will be the only time it will hurt. Do you trust me?" He was trying to be soft and gentle with her and not scare her away.

"Yes, I trust you. I know it will hurt a little. But I am ready. Just hold me tight, okay?" Carrie Ann was trying to assure him that she was ready.

"I've got you baby. You ready?" Jamie Lee took her in his arms and held her tight. Carrie Ann nodded that she was.

Jamie Lee kissed her lightly and then a little harder until he had her in a full lip into lip kiss. Tongues were on tongues and they were lost into each other's mouths. Slowly he moved his cock to her entrance and pushed until he got just inside of her pussy and stopped. Jamie Lee waited until she relaxed and then pushed some more. He continued this until he reached her barrier. He told her to relax and reached down and toyed with her clit.

Jamie Lee bent her legs up more and played with Carrie Ann's clit bringing her almost to the brink of her climax and then pushed through the barrier of her womanhood. Carrie Ann froze and let out a small cry of pain. Jamie Lee reached down and held her close. He held very still. Didn't move a muscle. A couple of tears escaped down Carrie Ann's cheeks. He licked them away. Then kissed her cheeks and then her lips. It was at that moment that he realized that he loved this woman.

"Carrie Ann, I truly love you. I thought I knew it before. But I truly know it now. I love you."

Carrie Ann burst into tears of joy. "Oh My God, Jamie Lee. I have loved you forever. I have wanted you forever. Please, my darling, make love to me now. Give me all of you. Take all of me. I love you so much."

Jamie Lee started moving inside of Carrie Ann. Slowly at first so she could get use to the movement. Then he picked up the pace little by little. In and out a bit deeper each time until he was balls deep inside of her.

"God, Carrie Ann, you feel so wonderful. So warm. So tight. I love being inside of you." Jamie Lee couldn't get enough of her. He rocked her. He was so hard inside of her. But he knew he was too close to coming and he didn't want that to happen yet. He wanted her to experience her first climax with him in there. He wanted to feel her. He wanted to feel her cunt muscles tighten and spasm against his cock. So he pulled out for a moment.

"Oh, please, don't take it out. You feel so good. Please, put it back in Jamie Lee." Carrie Ann begged him.

"I will baby. In a minute. I don't want to come yet. I want you to enjoy this. I want to feel you climax on my cock. This is what is so great between a man and a woman my darling. You are my precious angel and I want you to have it all." Jamie Lee slowly put himself back inside of her. A groan escaped his lips as he relished the feel of her.

"Oh, Jamie Lee, yes. Oh, damn. Mmmm." She didn't care about being lady like at all. This was too good to care.

Jamie Lee was ready to finish what he had started with Carrie Ann now. He was ready to bring her to her ultimate climax. Steadily he paced his strokes to reach deep inside of her as he stroked her spot. He reached down and tapped her clit and she went into a spasm of clenching muscles around his cock and her juices flowed around him. He got harder than he already was and he felt his seed rising up from his balls into his cock as he started spewing into her. Rope after rope ejected deep into her.

"Ahhh…baby girl…you are so awesome. I love you so much… take all of me." he said as he filled her completely. Jamie Lee didn't think he had ever cum so much in his life. He knew he had filled her to overflowing. He felt their combined juices flowing out of them and running down between her legs.

They held on to each other, legs entwined. Two lovers who had discovered the joys of lovemaking, far beyond their expectations.

The storm was still raging out of control outside. The one in the barn had been fulfilled. Tempered. They heard a rattling of the barn door. "Oh, shit…it must be momma. She must be in a fit with worry.

What are we going to do?" Carrie Ann was starting to panic.

"Calm down little girl. Wrap this blanket around yourself. I'll get dressed and check it out. If it's your momma, I'll just explain that you were soaked and I had to get you out of those wet clothes before you caught your death of pneumonia. She'll understand. She knows I won't let anything happen to her precious daughter." Jamie Lee said with a grin as he took and wrapped her in the blanket.

Sure enough, momma was at the barn door and Jamie Lee let her in. After the chosen explanation was given momma returned to the house to bring back dry clothes after the rain stopped. Jamie Lee assured momma that he would take care of Carrie Ann until then.

"Now, where were we before we were so rudely interrupted." Jamie Lee said as he reached for Carrie Ann. "I know I love your sweet body and I'm not through wanting you yet."

"Oh, Jamie Lee. You say the sweetest things. I really like what you did to me. It feels so much better than what I try to do to myself." Carrie Ann said while smiling up at Jamie Lee.

"Oh, so you do this to yourself, do you?" Jamie Lee asked.

"Well, not like you do, of course. But yes, in a way." Carrie Ann answered.

"Show me, little girl. I want to see what you do to yourself." Jamie Lee was intrigued that she had actually been taking care of her own needs. "I can't do that. It wouldn't be right. That's to do in private." Carrie Ann wasn't going to do that in front of Jamie Lee. No way!!!!!

"Oh, little girl. You have so much to learn. Of course you can do that in front of me. Just like I can do this in front of you."

With that, he reached down and took a hold of his cock and started to stroke it. Carrie Ann started to turn her head but he reached out and turned her head back by her chin.

"Watch me baby. It feels good." So she watched.

"Now touch me sweetheart. Put your hand on me…feel me. It's okay." Jamie Lee took her hand and placed it on his stiff cock. It was soft to the touch. Hard…but soft. Erect. The bulbous head was a purplish color. He took her hand and guided it up and down his shaft. She looked up at him. Awe was on her face.

"Does it feel good, little girl?"

"Yes, it does. So soft, yet so hard. What is that coming out of the top of it? You're not peeing on me, are you?" Carrie Ann had seen pictures of a male penis in her father's books but this was the first real live one she had ever seen. She had no idea what was going on.

"No, baby girl, it isn't pee. It is called precum. It's a form of lubricant to help when we are having intercourse. When I put my cock inside of you. So that it doesn't hurt you. There are other ways to make sure he is wet enough too. Would you like me to show you?" Jamie Lee was almost out of his skin with anticipation of her putting her lips upon him.

Oh, yes please. I want to learn all I can from you. You are so patient with me." Carrie Ann was excited to learn what Jamie Lee had to show her.

"Okay sweetheart, you know how good it felt when I kissed you down there on your private area?" Carrie Ann shook her head yes. "Well, it would feel just as good if you were to put a kiss on the top of my cock. Would you do that for me?" Jamie Lee looked at her with beseeching eyes.

"You want me to kiss where you pee from? But you just had that thing inside of me. I can't touch it with my mouth. That just isn't nice." Carrie Ann couldn't believe he was asking her to do this.

"Baby girl, do you not have a pee hole down there? Did I not just have my mouth down there? Did I complain or say that it tasted bad? Oh, no little girl. You tasted wonderful. So sweet and nice. Did you not kiss me after I had been down there? Did my mouth taste bad to you? Taste me baby. It is only you and I that you will taste. Not any pee. Just us. I promise. Do you trust me? Have I told you wrong yet?" Jamie Lee was on the edge. He wanted her mouth so bad he was aching for her. God, please, just let her try.

Carrie Ann wavered between what he was saying and what her mind was trying to intercede with. But soon, Jamie Lee's words won out and she lowered her head and lightly kissed the tip of his engorged, purple head. His cock jumped and a moan escaped his lips. Carrie Ann jumped back.

"It's alright baby girl. He just liked it, that's all. It felt really good. You can do it again." He waited. And waited.

Carrie Ann reached with her lips and kissed him again. This time she didn't jump back. She touched her lips to him again and lingered a minute or two. This wasn't too bad. She licked her lips. Didn't taste too bad either. Wow. So, she did it again, then she licked the end of his cock. Jamie Lee let out a groan. Carrie Ann got the message. He likes this. He really does.

Then she took her tongue and circled around the tip of his cock and Jamie Lee took a hold of her head on either side. He held her head steady. Then he slowly pushed the tip up and in until she opened her mouth and let his cock start to go into her mouth. She stopped just short of letting it go all the way in.

"Relax your mouth and lips baby. Open your mouth and let my cock go into your mouth. I won't hurt you." Carrie Ann opened her mouth a little wider and he pushed in a little more.

"That's it, little girl. Aah yes. That feels so good. Your little mouth is so hot. So warm. Hum. Oh, yes, darling...open up for me. Suck my cock. Run your tongue along it." Jamie Lee was giving her lessons and she was trying her best to please him.

Carrie Ann was trying to relax her mouth and run her tongue along his dick as he was instructing but she kept getting confused. But she tried and tried again. Soon she was getting the hang of it. As he pushed further into her mouth she started to gag and he backed off. He held her head still as he moved back and forth into her mouth. He was proud of her for how fast and how well she was grasping how to love on his cock.

But he didn't want to cum in her mouth. Not yet anyway. He didn't want to scare her. There would be plenty of time to teach her that. For now, he wanted to cum again inside of her. Gently he pulled himself out of her mouth. She looked up at him quizzically.

"You did a great job, baby girl, for your first time. I am so close to coming and I don't want to do it in your mouth. I want to make love to you again. Please, lay with me in the hay and let me enter your body. Let me give of myself to you, from a man who desperately loves you."

Jamie Lee was so hard and wanted nothing more than to be inside her and pumping his cum deep into her cunt.

Carrie Ann sheepishly smiled and turned to lay on the mat of hay where they had first made love. Yes, she wanted him to enter her again. Yes, she wanted to feel him empty his seed into her again. Yes, she needed him to hold her as he gave of himself to her and her to him. Jamie Lee covered her with his body and entered her with no resistance. She was already wet from their previous joining and his cock slid all the way in, up until he hit her cervix. He wanted to completely bury himself in her this time. He wanted her deep and hard. He had been easy for her first time. Now he really needed her, wanted her, would take her as he had never taken a woman before.

Putting his hands under her buttocks he had her wrap her legs around his back and lifted her to him and pushed hard and deep. Carrie Ann moaned and rolled her head to the side. Again, he pulled out to the tip and pushed hard. He felt her cervix. He felt her womb. Her moan was deeper this time. She reached for him. Grasping his upper arms, she held on to him. As Jamie Lee started pumping her hips started moving along with his rhythm. Her clit was hitting his pelvic bone and soon she was on the edge of another super climax.

Jamie Lee couldn't hold out much longer. He wanted to cum in her so badly. She had to cum and cum now. So, he took one hand and reached around and touched her little puckered hole. Carrie Ann jerked in astonishment. He continued to rub and worked the juices from her cunt to her puckered hole and rubbed it in little circles. When she relaxed just a little bit and he was pumping her for all he was worth, he felt her orgasm coming, as was his, and pushed his pinky finger into her ass hole. Both of them came with a fury of passion and emotion.

"Holy sweet Lord Jesus. Damn it little girl. You drive me crazy. Oh, My God." Jamie Lee buried his head in her shoulder, kissing her neck. "Oh, I love you so much." He lifted his head and looked into her eyes.

Carrie Ann heard herself scream. When Jamie Lee's finger entered her butt hole she had gone rigid but he held her tight and pumped her and pumped her right into the best orgasm she had ever had. It seemed to last forever. He was so deep inside her and she felt so full. Carrie Ann cried as her emotions got the better of her. God, how she loved this man. He was everything to her. Now, he was truly hers.

As Jamie Lee looked deep into Carrie Ann's eyes he declared his love to her again and again. His cock was still hard. He started pumping into her again. Moving slowly, sensuously.

"Carrie Ann. Now, you are my woman. Forever and ever. You are mine. Never will another man touch you. Never will another man know your body. You are my little girl...mine."

Jamie Lee took Carrie Ann and made love to her again and came in her again.

Yes, Carrie Ann was at last Jamie Lee's woman. A passion had awakened in him that he never knew he possessed. Now she was his and that passion would be awake for a very long time.

MY HEART'S DESIRE

Tricia and Guy had been dating for almost six months and had a fairly active love life. Both were open minded and were willing to try most anything if it didn't involve pain. They had tried vibrators and dildos, ticklers and different types of condoms. But there was one thing Guy wanted to do that he hadn't mentioned to Tricia. He wasn't even sure how to broach the subject.

You see, Tricia had been abused by her stepfather, physically and sexually. So, Guy normally treated her with extreme tenderness. But often, he wanted to push her limits. Not hard, just a little to see how she would react and to take her to higher pleasures.

He knew if he could get her past the trauma and to trust him, he could take her mind to places she never dreamed of. He could give her body such orgasms like she never knew existed. Far beyond anything he had ever done to her thus far.

Valentine's Day was approaching and he wanted to do something very special for her. So, he rented a room at a very prestigious hotel and asked them to have the works sent up. That meant the whole romantic package.... champagne, fruit plate, cheese and crackers and so forth. He also had some other surprises in store.

He went to the adult store and bought the items he would need and put them in the trunk of his car for safe keeping until that night. He hoped his plan would work and Tricia would overcome her fears. He wanted to give her her hearts desires and knew how to do it. She would just have to trust him.

February fourteenth came and Guy picked Tricia up at six thirty. They went to a glorious restaurant for a delightful dinner, then went out for drinks and some romantic dancing. At eleven o'clock he said he had a surprise for her and took her to the hotel.

When they entered the room, candles had been lit by the bed, on the dresser and in the bathroom. There was an Hors d' Oeuvres tray filled with cheeses, crackers and fruits. Champagne was on ice with crystal glasses. The bed was pulled down and red rose pedals were strewn upon it. It was breathtaking.

Guy looked toward the bathroom and saw that it had been set up per his request.

Tricia followed his eyes as she saw the flicker of candlelight from the bathroom.

"How had he set all this up without her knowing about it?" she wondered. But it was the most romantic thing she had ever seen. Excitement was bursting through her. This would be one of the most beautiful nights they had shared together.

Little did she know what Guy had in store for her. He had always treated her with gentleness and had been so concerned with her reactions. Tonight, he was about to bring out things in her that she didn't know existed. He had to get her beyond her past. There was only one way to do it and he intended to do just that. It was make or break time.

Guy set Tricia on her feet and turned her to look into his eyes as he spoke to her.

"Tricia, my love, this is all for you. Happy Valentine's my darling. Tonight, I want to make all your dreams come true. I want to spoil you. I want to make love to you and take you to places you never dreamed of. I want you to completely trust me with your mind and body. I will give you pleasure like you have never known. Just let me. That's all I ask of you." Guy searched her eyes. He needed her confirmation that he had her trust and that she would do as he asked.

"Of course I trust you Guy. I love you more than I have ever loved anyone. Yes, please make love to me. Take me to those places you speak of. I know you will never hurt me."

Tricia looked at him with tears brimming in her eyes.

He took her by the hand and led her into the bathroom.

"Then, let's start out with you taking a nice warm bubble bath. I'm going to bring you a glass of champagne to sip while you soak and relax."

With that he undressed her and helped her slip into the already prepared, scented tub of water. He opened the bottle of chilled bubbly and returned with a glass for both of them.

Guy sat on the edge of the bathtub watching Tricia as they both sipped their drinks. He loved looking at her body, but it was difficult through all the bubbles in the water. He told her how beautiful she was and what her body did to him. How much she turned him on. She smiled meekly. He knew how shy and timid she could be.

He watched her for as long as he could stand it. Finally, he reached and took her glass from her. He set them both on the counter, removed his clothing and slipped in the tub behind her. Tricia laid back against him with her head on his shoulder. Guy kissed the top of her head as he reached around and started massaging her breasts. Trisha moaned in pleasure.

His fingers played with her breasts and nipples. He rotated them, pinched them and tweaked them. Tricia squirmed around as the fire moved from her nipples to the center of her core. The water was cooling, but her body was becoming so hot. He started licking and kissing around her neck, her ears. Biting and nibbling on her earlobes. Still pulling, pinching and twisting on her nipples. She was going insane with want.

Slowly, he moved his left hand down her abdomen, teasing with his fingertips. He played with her belly button. He massaged her abs. He lowered his hand to her mound and teased. He rubbed her on the outside of her thigh to the inside and back out. Guy wanted her dancing with desire. And she was.

Tricia was moving her body in the water with his hand as he moved about her lower body. He played and toyed with her. He reached into her center with one finger and touched her. She jumped. Her body arched.

"Relax baby. Just enjoy my touch. Let me have your body baby." Guy cooed in her ear.

How was she supposed to relax when he was driving her deeper into desire? Her body was so hot. Her nipples were as hard as a nail head. When he touched her womanhood, she felt lightening go through her body. Her moans were getting louder. Her head was twisting as he kissed her neck.

Guy's hand cupped her and held her. He loved the feel of her as he moved her lips with his fingers. He slid his fingers between them and felt her wetness. As her desire built, he kept his movements going into a rhythm while her hips rose and lowered to meet his hand.

Her breathing increased and he knew she was getting close to her release. But he didn't want her to yet. He wanted to control her orgasms. He wanted her to learn to trust him. So he withdrew his hand. Tricia groaned and looked up at him. Frustration quickly set in.

She was so close to her orgasm. Why did he stop? He had never done that to her before.

"Let's get out baby, the water is getting too cold." Guy smiled down at her.

He stood up, stepped out of the tub, grabbed a towel and dried off. He turned around and helped Tricia out of the tub and quickly dried her off so she wouldn't get a chill. He had plans for them and didn't want her to come down too far from the desires he had already started. He lingered a bit at her feminine parts while drying her. He fingered her there, playing and teasing her clitoris and lips. He parted them and put his finger just inside of her. She was soaking wet and it went in easily. He fingered her for just a few strokes and then stopped.

Pulling his finger out, he licked it. His eyes meeting hers, he smiled.

"Baby, your juices are so good. I want more. Come with me. You are in for a real treat." With that, he leads her into the bedroom and laid her on the bed.

Guy looked into her eyes and spoke to her gently.

"I asked you before; I'm going to ask you again. Are you willing to give yourself to me totally and completely tonight? Are you willing to do as I ask you to do without question? I will not hurt you nor cause you harm. I only want to give you so much pleasure. Do you trust me Tricia?" Guy held his breath in anticipation of her answer.

"Yes. I am willing to trust you completely." answered Tricia with a smile.

Guy got off the bed and went to the left top corner. He reached for her arm and brought it back. He cuffed her wrist to the bed. He then went around to the other side and did the same thing. He leaned over and kissed her, then put a blind fold over her eyes.

Tricia gasped, then relaxed. She had to trust him. She knew he wouldn't hurt her but had no idea what he was going to do to her.

Guy kissed her neck on each side, down her shoulders to each breast. He suckled each one and nibbled and bit on each one. He got them hard and standing. He licked them, teased them. He massaged them and pulled on the nipples. Tricia squirmed beneath him.

Guy reached over to the table and got an ice cube and put it in his mouth. He turned back to Tricia and took her breast into his mouth. Tricia's hips came off the bed.

"Oh My God, that's so cold. What are you doing?" Tricia cried out. Guy didn't relent. He switched from one breast to the other, making her nipples so hard and taut. Tricia moaned and moaned.

Guy got a new ice cube, put it in his mouth and then trailed it down her abdomen. He heard her moans as he did. Her body moved about the bed. He reached and held her still.

Straddling her abdomen with his back to her head, Guy took another ice cube into his mouth. He leaned over and let the cool water drip from his mouth over her sex. Tricia moaned as her body tried to move away from him. He put a little more weight on her to keep her still. His hands lowered to her thighs to hold them apart and still. Then he dribbled more of the cool fluid directly into her lips. She moaned louder.

Leaning over, he sucked the ice cube until his tongue was cold, then touched it to her clit. Tricia gasped. He watched it as it rose and started to come out from its hood. He repeated the process again and again until her clit was hard. She was squirming beneath him and moaning relentlessly.

Having only a small piece of ice left, he quickly got off her and got between her legs. He put his head to her slit and pushed the piece of ice into her with his tongue. She screamed. He pinched her clit and pushed his tongue all the way inside of her and she exploded. Her juices ran from her onto his tongue and out, down to her pink puckered hole. She was soaked.

Tricia couldn't control her movements. Her body was quaking. Her legs quivered so bad that if Guy hadn't been holding them down they would have been all over the place. She had never cum that hard in her life. The things he was doing to her body had her mesmerized. Could she handle more? Did she want more? Before she could answer, he was licking her again and her body responded. Soon she was on fire, her clit hard and her slit begging for relief. More than that, she wanted him inside of her, now.

Guy teased and taunted her with his tongue and mouth. He licked and sucked her. He pushed his fingertips just inside of her sweet, juicy hole, wanting to feel her muscles squeeze him. She was begging and pleading for him to let her cum but he held her back while he tormented her. He wanted her to trust him. He wanted her to let him take her to the depths of enjoyment that he knew he could.

Without letting her cum he pulled his hands, mouth and tongue away from her. She squirmed and tried to manipulate her legs to rub herself. But she couldn't. Guy could see her frustration.

"Tricia, I am going to unlock the cuffs. I want you to roll over on your stomach. Then I am going to cuff your wrists again. Do you understand?" Guy asked as he moved to the head of the bed.

"Yes." She answered and did as he asked.

When Guy had her turned and the cuffs replaced on her, he had her lift her butt and put a pillow under her. He caressed her back, starting from her shoulders and working his way down to her butt cheeks. He loved the feel of her soft skin and the firmness of her ass. He spread her cheeks and admired her as he anticipated what awaited.

He got on his knees behind her and lamented kisses all around her lower back and cheeks as he felt inside her slit with his fingers. She was wet and getting wetter. Sliding his tongue between her crack he touched her pucker hole. She jumped, gasping.

Guy lightly smacked her butt as he told her to stay still. Her movements halted. Again, he licked down her crack and touched her little hole. She tried to remain still until his licks became more insistent. Her hips began to move, and she moaned. He reached up and smacked her again, a little harder and across both cheeks. She sniffled a whimper.

Guy smiled to himself as he knew he was now in control. He had her where he wanted her and he could do as he wished. She was trying to hold on, but he would have her at his mercy soon. She would learn that not all pain was bad. That there could be pleasure from pain. He was the one to show her that.

Getting directly behind her legs, he covered them with his thick thighs. He knew she couldn't move them. His hands rubbed over her already turning pink buttocks. Without warning he brought both hands down on each cheek. Not hard, but enough that she felt it. She held her breath for a second and then let it out. He ran his hands over her cheeks again and then spanked her again and again and again. He could hear her as she let out a slight sob. He knew there were tears behind that blindfold. Her cheeks were warm, a little red and looking so nice. He ran his finger down between her crack and into her slit. Damn...she was wet... so wet. His finger found her clit and he rubbed it slowly. She moaned with pleasure. As he kept rubbing it with one finger he brought his other hand down on her cheeks again, switching from one to the other. Guy brought up his soaked finger to her puckered hole and worked her juices around it, wetting it and slowly slipped his finger inside. Tricia moaned. Her hips came off the pillow as she pushed back into his hand. He slid his finger all the way into her.

"Tricia, I want you to cum for me baby." Guy told her as he fingered her hole. He reached with the other hand and pushed two fingers into her slit. Then he fingered both holes. Her body shook as she came on his hands. He reached up and hit her clit hard and she spasmed. Her body quivered. She was breathing so hard that she ached.

Guy quickly went into the bathroom and washed his hands with hot soapy water, rinsed and dried them. He went back into the room with a warm washcloth and wiped her down. He cleaned her completely. Soon she was breathing normally and was sound asleep.

He knew she needed to replenish fluids, so he got some ice water and set it on the nightstand. Taking off the restraints, he slowly rolled her over and removed the blindfold. The only conscious movement she made was a slight smile, turned on her side and passed back out... sound asleep.

This wasn't over by a long shot. Guy wanted inside of her where it was nice and warm. He was almost sure he now had her trust, but he had to make sure. Leaving it to another time wasn't an option. He had her primed and hot and he wanted her now. He was so hard for her it hurt.

Waking her up wasn't easy, but he told her she needed to drink the ice water he had brought her. She sat up long enough to drink it and laid back down on her side. Guy set the glass back down and crawled into bed with her, spooning up next to her. With her back tucked into his chest, he nuzzled her neck. He licked her earlobe, bit it, whispered how much he wanted her.

She moaned and curled tighter into him. His arms wrapped around her as his hand went to her breast and played with her nipples, first one and then the other. He lifted her leg with his and slipped his cock into her slit and rubbed it back and forth in her juices. She was so slick and wet, that when he entered her, he felt no resistance.

He left it there, just inside her, for a few moments feeling the warmth of her. God, she felt wonderful. He didn't want to move. He wanted to enjoy the feel of her silkiness and comfort. He needed her in a way she didn't understand yet, but she would soon learn.

Guy knew he had to have patience with her, so he started moving slowly inside of her. Her hips started moving with him. Soon they were bumping and grinding into each other. The rhythm they were setting was keeping him on the edge, but he didn't want to cum yet. He was far from finished with her lesson.

She still needed to give him her complete trust. Soon, he would know if she could do that. He rubbed her from her face to her torso. Up and down her body. Touching, feeling her. Letting her know that he had her. She relaxed and became so pliant in his hands and on his body. He sped up his plunges inside of her and she pushed back against him. He knew she was close, but he held her off. He wanted to control her climax. He would give it to her when he wanted her to cum.

Reaching down between them, he got his finger wet and played at her puckered hole. He teased it getting her to relax. Then he pushed and got her to let him enter her. She moaned as he fucked her with his cock and his finger. She was so hot and so turned on. He got a second finger wet and placed that finger in with the other one. She winced and tried to pull away. He held her to him.

"Relax baby. I have you." Guy said in her ear as he opened her up.

He continued to take her as he used her holes. She loosened up as he brought her closer again to her climax. But again, he held her off. She pulled her legs up against her chest as she stretched herself open to him. God, how he loved this woman.

Slowly, he pulled his fingers out and reached back to the nightstand, getting the lube he had set there earlier. He put the gel on his fingers and then rubbed it on her hole. He reinserted his fingers into her as he fucked her. She was opening more to him and he felt her clamping onto him. She was going to cum.

He pulled his fingers out of her as he pulled his cock from her pussy. Slowly, he rubbed his cock along her crack and positioned it to her little hot hole. It was already opened and he pushed gently. She pulled a little away and he held her.

"It's okay. I've got you. You can do this." He coaxed her as he continued to push into her.

Once his head was passed her opening, she seemed to relax a little bit. He held still and let her adjust to him being there. He held her close to him.

"Trust me Tricia. This will give us both so much pleasure. I love you so much baby. You are doing great sweetheart." Guy keep encouraging her.

Gradually he kept working himself into her until he was totally seated inside of her and her ass was up against him. He held her still. She was breathing hard. He played with her breasts...pinching her nipples and tweaking them to keep her mind occupied.

It also sent currents of want straight to her loins and she started moving against him. He returned her movements. Before long they were moving together in a synchronized rhythm that had him so close to orgasm that he reached down to rub her clit. She breathed in and moaned loudly. She was there. Her rectum squeezed him. He rubbed harder and he rammed her. She screamed. Her juices let go as she orgasmed.

"That's it baby. Take me. Let me have all of you. Fuck me baby." Just then he felt her as she rammed her ass into him. She fucked him for all she was worth. And he came.

"AHHHHHHHHHHHHH Fuckkkkkkkkk!!!!!!!!!!!" was all he could say.

When Guy could move again, he got up and went to the bathroom to clean up. He returned and cleaned her with a wet cloth, then got back into bed. He pulled her to him and held her to his chest.

Tricia sighed as she felt utter contentment. She had never known a man like Guy and had not known any of this existed. She had only known the pain of her past, the wicked things done to her. She did not know things could be done out of love and the result could be so beautiful.

"Guy, I love you so much. Thank you for showing me what I have been missing. What it means to really be able to trust someone and the joy that comes from that. You are truly what my heart has desired. You are my heart's desire."

NEW KIND OF LOVE

Want a woman to text with any subject…it's your choice."

The ad stuck out at me like a sore thumb. This guy wants to talk to women about anything. Hum. So, I clicked on the ad and read it. Wow!!! This can't be real. A guy actually finds talking with women exciting. As I was having a lonely, quiet, boring evening I decided to answer his ad.

"Hi, this is Gigi. So, you want to do girl talk? Why? What is it you want to know about us?"

Curiosity was killing me about a guy who wanted to spend his time talking to women. What was he about? Well, let's see if he answers me. I hit the send button.

Within ten minutes I heard the ding that I had received an email. Sure enough it was from him.

"Hi, my name is Jake. Yes, I love talking to women. They are a most interesting species. I don't care what you look like or how old you are. Only that you truly are a female. No subject is taboo, and we can talk as often as you like. I do prefer to use text rather than email if that is acceptable with you. Here is my number…I hope to hear from you soon. Tell me what is on your mind right now baby."

Oh My God!!!! This guy is for real, I think. He wants to hear from me by text. Okay, let's give this a try, I said to Nikki my Maltese dog who was laying at the foot of my bed.

After I entered his name to my contact list, I hit message and text: "Hi Jake, it's Gigi. Now you have my number. Well, I'm sitting here on my bed with my little Maltese Nikki and writing to you. This is the first time I have ever answered an ad like this, so I'm not really sure where to start.

"Right now I'm bored out of my mind. I don't really like to watch tv, don't have a good book to read and no date."

"So, you're sitting or lying on your bed all alone?"

"Yeah, bummer, huh. What a way to spend a Friday night."

"You don't have a boyfriend or anyone special in your life?"

"No, we broke up about a month ago. Why are you home on a Friday night?"

"Actually, I'm at work. I watch monitors and it gets pretty boring, so I text."

"Do you have a girlfriend or significant other?"

"Nope...not anymore. Too many complications. Now I get to talk to you. Love it."

"Cool...so what do we talk about. Let's see, I'm sure you don't want to hear about my going shopping or what color I want to paint the kitchen."

"Well, do you like to cook...do you spend much time in the kitchen? It should be a color you feel comfortable in... warm… relaxing. Do you have a glass of wine while you cook? What do you wear while you are in there?"

"Why is all of that important?"

"Because, my dear, a kitchen can be just as romantic as the bedroom. Think about it. What and how you cook sets the mood for the rest of the evening. What you wear puts you in either a relaxed mood or in a hurry. If you wear short shorts and a halter top, drink a little wine and have on some really cool music your mind can conjure up some mighty fine dishes. You've also set the ambiance for your guest or mate to satisfy his pallet as well as his eyes. Loving is not done just in the bedroom."

"I suppose next you're going to tell me to cook with a negligee on."

"If that suits the situation, by all means yes. wow what a turn on."

"Hum...never thought of it that way. Well, it's late and I have to work in the morning so am going to go. Nice talking to you, Jake."

"Yeah, you too Gigi. Hope we can talk again. You seem like a really nice person."

I thought about Jake all day. I couldn't get him off my mind. I had only talked with him for a few minutes, yet he intrigued me. What was it about him? Why did he want to talk to me of all people? And his ideas of the kitchen were kind of a turn on. Yep...I wanted to talk with Jake some more. I definitely wanted to know more about this guy and what made him tick.

Quickly I changed my clothes, grabbed my cell and made sure it was fully charged, called to Nikki and climbed onto my bed. Sitting there cross legged I pulled up Jake and hit message on my cell.

I waited and waited and waited. Nothing. Damn it, I knew it was too good to be true. I threw the phone on the bed and headed for the bathroom to take a shower.

As I reached for the faucet, I heard the phone beep. message from Jake...

I ran for the bed and picked up the phone.

"Hi Gigi, how was your day? I thought about you and wondered if I would hear from you again."

"Yeah, I wondered if I was going to hear from you too. So, are you at work now?"

"No, not yet. Go in at ten thirty tonight. What are you doing right now?"

"I was fixing to get into the shower, but I heard there was a message from you, so I decided to read it first."

"What do you have on right now?"

Wow!!!! This guy is wasting no time is he I said to Nikki.

"A t-shirt and a pair of cutoffs. Why?"

"Aww babe that is sooo sexy bet you look really cute."

"It's comfortable."

"How are you wearing your hair? Is it long or short?"

"It's long and I wear it down. Mousy brown."

"Nice. I bet you are a sexy little thing. Have you ever done sex on the phone or by text?"

"No. I've never even talked about sex with someone I don't know. Why are you asking me about this? I must be crazy to be doing this."

"You're not crazy Hun. We all need a release in one way or another. Why not this way? Try it... you might like it. If not, we will stop. You are in control, ok?"

Well, it seemed harmless enough. What could it hurt? "Nikki, what do you think?" She licked my hand as I petted her back as if to tell me it would be fine.

"Alright Jake, but you're going to have to help me with this as it's all new to me. So how do we begin?"

":) Ok baby… relax…let whatever happens come naturally. We just start talking. What are you doing?"

"I'm lying on my bed texting you."

"Are you comfortable?"

"Yes."

"Have you ever played with your breasts?"

"Yeah."

"Okay, rub your breasts honey. Massage them, one at a time. Oh, how does that feel?"

"Feels good."

"You still have your t-shirt on?"

"Yes. Is that okay?"

"Oh yes baby…that is just fine. Pinch your nipples and get them hard honey."

"Ahh, yeah, that does feel good. What else do you want me to do?"

"Do you feel like you're getting wet?"

"Kinda."

"That's good. When you feel the need, put your hand down on your crotch and rub it. I bet that feels really good doesn't it sweetheart?"

"Yeah, but it's hard to do that and text you too."

"It's ok, you're doing just fine. How does your pussy feel honey?"

"Wet and hot and excited. She is so horny. Wow, I can't believe this feels so great."

"You like this huh…not so bad is it? You think you can get yourself off?"

"No problem there. How about you? What are you doing?"

"Baby, my cock is so hard just thinking of you playing with your pussy. I want to cum so bad."

"OMG, I'm going to cum. oh yeah I'm cummmmmming."

"Squeeze those titties and rub that pussy baby…make yourself cum oh yeah girl, go with it Gigi. enjoy it."

"Oh yes…it was great. OMG. I can't believe I just did that. I can't believe it."

Gigi laid on her bed in stunned disbelief. What the hell had she just done? And why had she done this with a man she didn't know and by text on the phone? Was she that hard up? All kinds of thoughts were going rampantly through her mind.

"Gigi, are you there? Are you okay?" asked Jake. OMG, I can't talk to him now what can I say?

"Yes, I'm here."

"Well, how was that for your first experience in text phone sex? What do you think?"

"It was great. I've never done anything like this before and it was mind blowing. You are a very good teacher. Did you cum too?"

"Oh yea baby...I came a lot I need to go clean up and go to work. Can I text you later?"

"I'm really kind of tired and I have to go into work early in the morning. How bout I text you after I get home in the evening?"

"Sure, whatever works best for you."

"Okay Jake, have a good night at work later."

After I hung up the phone I sat there and stared at the phone. 'What the hell am I doing? But I do feel so relaxed and sleepy.

"Come on Nikki, let's get some sleep."

The next morning Gigi showered and went into the kitchen to have her morning coffee. She didn't function without her caffeine. As she looked at the kitchen walls, she remembered her conversation with Jake the night before. What color should she paint them? That had led to the best climax she had had in weeks. Was this a fluke or could this lead into something fantastic? What else could Jake teach her about the joys of text sex? Hum. guess I'll have to wait until this evening to find out now won't I.

Where do Jake and Gigi take their newfound relationship from here...

"Hi Gigi. Are you there, baby?"

"Yeah, I'm here Jake." send.

"So, how did you feel today?"

"Okay. I sat in the kitchen this morning drinking my coffee and thought about what you said. It started to make sense." send.

"Baby, the imagination has no limits. Sex can be and happen whenever and wherever. Did you not discover that last night?"

"Yeah, I sure did...with your help of course."

"What do you think...want to do it again?"

"Um, yeah."

"Alright. Where are you?"

"Sitting on the couch in the living room."

"Tell me about the room."

"Well, its small cuz it's only an apartment."

"What color are the walls."

"Kind of a sandy tan with light brown baseboards and trim."

"Nice and warm…I like that. What color is your couch?"

"Chocolate brown."

"Oh yeah…really warm…nice to make love on too…any pillows?"

"Yep. Several throw pillows…flower prints."

"Ah…very feminine. I can picture putting one under your ass and fucking your pussy. What other furniture do you have?"

"A love seat, light brown with floral print, and a sage colored recliner."

"Any tables?"

"A small coffee table and two end tables between the love seat and recliner."

"Cool…what kind of lamps?"

"Have two…a stand-up floor and one on the end table… medium size."

"Do you have a television in there?"

"No. Just my stereo system. TV is in the bedroom."

"So you have an entertainment stand of some sort?"

"Yeah, a small one."

"Okay, I think I have a pretty good idea of what it looks like. I bet you have a throw rug in front of your recliner, huh?"

"How did you know that?"

"Just a good guess. Sounds like something you would do."

"Wow…you're good."

"You know it baby. What do you have on sweetheart?"

"A pink sweatshirt and jeans."

"Is that what you wore to work?"

"No way…I have to wear suits all the time…hate it…just want to get comfortable when I get home."

"So, why do you get dressed again?"

"What do you mean"

"Why do you come home and take off all that stuffy stuff and get redressed again? Why not relax in something more comfortable.. looser.. not so confining?"

My eyeballs popped out of my head. What was he saying? It was only six o'clock in the evening…not bedtime.

"Umm…cuz it's early yet, haven't taken a shower and gotten ready for bed yet."

"OHHH BABY!!!!! You've got to loosen up honey. Relax!!!"

"What do you have on?"

"Nothing."

"You mean as in nude?"

"Yup. I like feeling free. No inhibitions. No pretenses."

OMG.Nikki…this guy is something else. Look at me…dressed and not going anywhere and no one coming over. But what if…

"What if someone comes over?"

"There is such a thing as a robe or a pair of sweatpants to throw on. Baby…lighten up…it's okay…it's natural. Do you not like your body?"

"Yeah, I guess so."

"Gigi, I want you to go take a shower and put on something VERY comfortable and then text me, okay baby?"

"Okay."

As I closed the text I wondered what Jake was up to. Why did he want me to take a shower now? It's still early. I haven't even eaten dinner yet. Oh well... It would feel good just to relax and unwind. Come on Nikki. let's go in and do this.

After I took a hot soothing shower I poured myself a glass of Lancer wine, made a ham salad sandwich and curled up on the couch with Nikki, who was waiting to eat the crust which I peeled off for her. Jake had said to put on something comfortable. Just what did he have in mind I wondered? I had put on my favorite nightshirt and had love songs by Alabama playing on the CD player. When my sandwich was gone, I picked up the phone and text Jake.

"Hi Jake."

It seemed like forever before he answered back and I was so relaxed I was almost asleep when I heard the buzz of my phone. "Hey babe. Glad you're back. How do you feel now?"

"Better. The shower felt great and Nikki and I ate a sandwich and I had a glass of wine."

"Wonderful. What do you have on now?"

"A pink nightshirt."

"Do you have on a bra and panties?"

"No to bra yes to panties."

"Good. Now take off the panties and night shirt and put on a light, silky robe. Where are you and what are you doing?"

"I'm sitting on the couch with Nikki. listening to Alabama."

"Do you have any candles?"

"Yes. let me get them."

"Okay, I lit them and set them on the coffee table."

"Good. Now, use your throw pillows, lay down and get comfy."

Nikki, you're gonna have to go lay on the bed for a while. go in the bedroom like a good girl.

"Okay, now what?"

"Did you turn off the lights? Are you in a romantic setting?"

"Yeah."

"Here we go baby.. you ready for me?"

"Ummmm yeah, I think so."

"We're going to do this together, okay?"

"Yup.. let's do it."

"Is your phone fully charged?"

"Yes."

"Honey, let your body go limp... close your eyes for a minute and put yourself in a peaceful place. Then open your eyes.. pull your feet upwards from the ankles. Hold them.. now slowly let them back down. Do this a few times on each foot. Good. now tighten your calf muscles.. hold them.. now relax them slowly. do this several times each side. Do the same with your thigh muscles; continue to your buttocks.. up your back, to your shoulders, your arms and neck. You should now feel very relaxed."

Jake waited for a few moments.. waiting for her to complete the process.

"Gigi. How are you doing?"

"MMM.. I feel really good.. soooo relaxed. How did you learn to do that?"

"A woman taught me a long time ago."

"Well, she knew what she was doing."

"Yep, she sure did."

"So what do we do now?"

"Okay, take a drink of your wine, take off your robe and lay back down. Take your left hand and caress the left side of your neck gently with your fingertips. Run them back and forth. Then switch and do the same with the right."

"Umm.. that feels good."

"Now use your right hand and run your fingertips along your right side of your chest. Then up and over your breast. gently. barely touching.. but enough to feel the sensations."

"Ohhhh. that really feels good."

"Now do the same with your left hand… gently… feeling the sensations… feel your nipples getting hard. Let your hands play with your nipples… squeeze them a little… pull on them a bit.. go with the feelings."

"Jake. this feels so wonderful. much better than when I use to do it before."

"Take your time, baby, we have all the time you need."

"I want more. this is so awesome."

"Okay. Now run your fingers down your stomach toward your pubic area. But don't touch it yet."

"Why not… I want to so bad."

"I know. But be patient love… in time."

"Damn… my phones ringing and it's my sister.. hold on okay?"

"I'll be here."

Hello Jessica… just sitting here reading my cases for tomorrow. No, please don't come over now. I'm really tired and am going to turn in early. Big day ahead ya know. Okay, we'll have lunch Wednesday. Yeah, I love you too… bye.

"OMG. I thought she would hear my heavy breathing or something."

"And what would happen if she did? LOL."

"Well she didn't, thank God."

Jake had to laugh. This girl was really uptight. Let me see if I can get her over this phobia of hers and release her into the world of erotic relaxation.

"Okay sweetheart. lets pick up where we left off. but first take a drink of wine. now take a deep breath. let it out. lay back down and concentrate on my voice. You can hear me by how I'm talking to you."

He's right, I really can hear him. God, he sounds so gentle and easy going. And so romantic. This man is getting me to feel things I didn't know I could feel just by texting with him. Cool.

"I'm with you now baby."

"Great..now start stroking your fingers down your stomach and back up to your nipples. Rub your breasts and pull and squeeze your nipples. Get those pussy juices running honey."

"Ahhh, I feel so wet…so ready…so hot."

"Are you wet baby? Are you hot for me darling. Do you want me?"

"Ohhhh yes!!! I'm wet and hot and I want you so bad."

"Ahhh baby, my cock is sooo hard…I'm rubbing it and playing with my balls. It feels so good."

"My clit is getting harder and when I touch it, it makes me jump."

"Honey, rub my cock all over your clit…feel my precum on the head of my cock making you so slick, running down your slit. Run your fingers up and down your slit baby."

"Jake, you feel so good. Please, I want you so bad… take me…put your cock inside me…oh God, yes. I can feel you I need you…now."

"Are you cumming baby, cum for me…my dick is inside you and I'm fucking you. Take me baby. Oh yeah, I'm close too sweetheart."

"OMG Jake..I'm cumming with you. Ahhh, yeesss…Lord God. OMG…ummmmmm."

"Keep it going baby, don't stop rubbing your clit…put three fingers into your pussy. My cock is still hard for you darlin'. Oh God, Gigi, let me hear you cum again girl."

"Jake, I'm cumming again, baby… oh yeaaaaaaaa."

Gigi arches her back off the couch as her fingers fuck her pussy hard. Her clit is like a rock protruding out of its hood.

"Fuck my cock baby. Take it all the way into that hot pussy. Pinch your nipples hard. Feel that pain of pleasure all the way to your cunt and explode into another realm of pleasure."

"Oh sweet Lord..what you do to me..I can't take anymore…I..can't.. aaahhhhh Goooodddddd!!!!"

"Good God Almighty..here it comes sweetheart.. take it all of it you got it…I'm stroking him so fast…he's so hard.

"Jesusssssssssss..aaaawwwwwwwwwwww"

"Oh My God, I blew a big load.. biggest in a long-time baby." Jake was breathing sooo hard he couldn't type for a few seconds.

"Ahhh baby…you are fantastic."

"No, you are…wow…awesome, incredible…I am overwhelmed."

"Gigi, I think you are one hot woman. Gotta clean up and get ready for work. You okay?"

"Yeah…I just want to go to sleep now. Good night Jake. Talk tomorrow?"

"You bet we will. Sleep tight my baby."

With that I fell into a deep sleep and barely heard the phone ringing about three hours later.

"Gigi? I had to talk to you. After what we had earlier this evening I haven't been able to concentrate on anything at work or think of anything else but you. I am hard as a rock right now and it hurts so bad. I want you baby. I need you. Please don't be mad that I took the liberty of calling you."

"Jake, oh no honey. Of course I'm not mad. You made me crazy tonight…and I loved it. I need you too."

"Do you sleep in the buff?"

"Not usually. But I did tonight. I fell asleep right after we finished."

"So you're naked now.. oh I love it baby. Touch yourself. Are you wet?"

"Oh yeah, she's wet."

"Honey, I'm stroking my prick. I love your voice. You sound so sexy and sweet. You really turn me on baby."

"I like your voice too. You sound so gentle and kind."

"What are you doing Gigi?"

"I'm rubbing my clit with my thumb and have a finger in my pussy, stroking in and out imagining it's your cock in me."

"Awww honey, I wish it was really me in your nice, warm, snug cunt. Do I feel good inside you?"

"Oh My God…you feel awesome. I can feel your long, thick dick stretching my pussy and going in so deep."

"Put in another finger baby. Work that pussy. Make it all wet and squishy. That's it. Now take out your fingers and put them in your mouth and suck your succulent juices from them. Tell me how you taste, baby."

"It tastes good. Sweet. I wish you could taste me. If only you could put your lips on my cunt and suck my juices out of me."

"Wow, what a little slut girl you are. Love it sweetheart."

"Oh, I want to cum... I want you so bad.. fuck me Jake."

"Okay darlin.. here it comes…put your fingers back in and fuck that pretty pussy of yours. Oh, baby, I want to fuck you so bad right now."

"What are you doing?"

"I'm stroking him baby. I see and feel him in you and my prick is fucking you so good..ahhhhh, you feel so good. Okay I'm picking up the pace a little.. you feel it baby?"

"Yeah, it feels soooo good..I'm gonna cum Jake..oh baby..I can't stand it..make me cum..."

"Pinch your clit baby, hard.... push your fingers in deep and wiggle them till you find your gspot and push up on it."

"AHHHHHHHH…OOOHHMYYYGGODDDDD.. JAKEEEEEE.."

"That's it baby…go with it.. let it last…keep your fingers moving and rub your clit...don't stop.. bring it back up..let it go again."

"I… I… here it goes.. ooohhhh...aaahhhhh.."

"Are you still there baby..are you cumming again?"

"Almost there...oh God…I never thought..aaahhh yeah, I'm cumming.. again. oh Lord…eeeeGGGooooooddddddd."

"Yeah baby, here I cum aaahhhhh yeah…oh you feel soooo good.. squeeze my cock...make me cum in your sweet pussy...AAAAAhhhhhhhhhhh. oooohhhhhhhhhhhhh."

Silence

Heavy breathing on both ends of the line. "Gigi?"

"Yeah."

"You, my sweet angel are fucking awesome. I will never get enough of you."

Twice more that night Jake had to beat off, cuz every time he thought about Gigi he got so hard it was painful, as well as every day since. Several times a day. God how he missed her.

Jake had been trying to text Gigi for the next two days with no response. In the afternoon of the third day he finally heard the beep signaling a message from her.

"Finally. I've been trying to reach you for the last two days. I was getting worried. I was ready to send out the militia or something."

"I'm so sorry Jake. My sister hurt her back and we spent thirteen hours in the emergency room and then they decided to admit her. She didn't want me to leave her alone, so I spent the night in her room with her. Then they did a bunch of tests and I wanted to know the results so I had to wait around the hospital for the doctor to come to her room. It's been a long two days."

"I'm sorry to hear about your sister honey. Is she going to be okay?"

"Yeah, I think so. She'll be in there a few more days. I just came home to take a shower, change clothes and see about Nikki. Thankfully my neighbor, Samantha, has a key and came over to take her out and feed her for me."

"Wow, well at least she's where she'll be well taken care of."

"Yeah, I just worry about her a lot. She gets to be such a baby when she's in pain. She depends on me a lot. Anyway, how are you?"

"Great and horny for you."

"Awww honey.... I would love to play but I really need to go to the hospital and be with my sister. Maybe I can slip out later and we can play, ok?"

"Sure baby, I understand. Text me when you can. Let me know how things are going."

"Okay, later."

I really wanted to spend some time with Jake, but I knew my sister was expecting me back soon. As I took a shower I couldn't stop thinking about Jake. He aroused me just by knowing that he cared and was worried about me. How sweet that was of him, yet he hardly knew me. Well, then again, he did know me in a most intimate way. Hum..I was getting so hot thinking about the last time we had made love on the phone. That was so freaking hot. God, I would feel so much better if I could get off right now.

As I was thinking this, Nikki was standing patiently by the shower door waiting for me to finish my shower and take her out. "Okay girl, I'll be done in a minute. You're such a good girl."

I quickly finished getting myself off, dried off, dressed, took Nikki out and returned to the hospital to my sister Jessica's room. She was sound asleep. After sitting there for about half an hour I tiptoed out, went down to the cafeteria to get a cup of coffee and went outside for some fresh air. I thought about Jake again. How could I miss someone I barely knew? But I did! I took out my phone and hit his name.

"Jake?"

"Hey babe. How's your sister?"

"She's sleeping so I came outside for some fresh air."

"Oh, how far are you from your car?"

"Not far. Why?"

"Go sit in the car and lock the doors, okay?"

"Okay. I'm in the car."

"Answer your phone. It's me."

"Hello."

"Hi Gigi."

"Hi Jake."

"Thought you could use someone to talk to right now."

"You are so sweet, thank you."

OMG, he has the sexiest voice. Not soft but not harsh. Kind of gentle yet masculine at the same time. I missed hearing his voice more than I knew.

"Your voice sounds nice honey." Jake said. "So does yours. So, how are you?"

'I'm fine. Better now that I've heard your voice. You sound so sweet and tender."

"Awww, thanks." said Gigi.

"Baby, you want to relax some before you go back in with your sister?"

"UM...and how do we do that out here in the parking lot?"

"I'll help you if you want me to." Jake suggested.

"I don't know, there are so many people around, coming and going to their cars. Somebody would notice what I'm doing wouldn't they?"

"Only if you let on to what's happening." answered Jake.

"Oh, and just how do you suggest that I don't?" asked Gigi with a giggle.

"You'll have to be careful of your facial expressions. Just relax and let it happen…but keep your composure. Act like you're just resting. You could be having a great dream. Can you do that honey?" Jake asked suggestively.

"Yeah, I can try. I sure would like to let go of some of this tension." Gigi replied.

"Good, now just listen to my voice. Close your eyes, let yourself go limp and then reach under your top and touch your breasts one at a time."

"Thank God it's nighttime and no one can really see into the car."

"Are you touching them baby?" Jake asked her.

"Yes, mmm feels good. My nipples are getting hard."

"Oh yeah baby...get them real hard.... pull on them and pinch them."

"AHH."

"Now keep one hand on a breast and put your other one on your crotch. Push on your clit area and move your hand around. Rub your clit and breast at the same time. OH, honey you are getting so wet, aren't you?"

"Oh Jake, it feels so good. Your voice sounds so great talking to me. Keep telling me what you want me to do. I like hearing that." said Gigi.

"Sweetheart. Do you have on a skirt or pants?" Jake asked. "Pants." answered Gigi.

"Okay, Slide your pants down and your panties. You ok? Now rub your clit. Rub it lightly at first and then increase the pressure."

Gigi could hear Jake's breathing changing as he was guiding her through her incline toward climaxing.

"Jake, are you stroking him?"

"Oh yeah baby. I'm stroking my dick up and down. The head is so purple. He's crying out for you baby."

"Awww..God I want you so much Jake..my fingers are inside me and working on my g-spot. It could only feel better if your prick were really in there instead of my fingers."

"You keep talking like that and I will blow my load right now."

"No..wait for me…I'm so close..please, baby.. take me with you."

"I want to cum with you. Are you getting close?"

"Yes, I'm very close."

"Is she getting real wet sweetie? I want you to cum. I want to hear you cum, baby."

Ahh, Jake, I'm almost there honey…talk to me…bring me there."

"I want you so bad, I want to fuck you with my hard cock. OH baby… cum for me."

"OH MY GOD, OOHH MMYY GGOODD." Yes…Yes. AAAAHHHH..UUUMMM," cried Gigi.

"OH YEAH BABY..AAHHH…so gooodddd..," exclaimed Jake.

"You ok darling. Feel better?" asked Jake.

"You are so good. Thank you, baby," said Gigi.

"You are most welcome. So, what are you doing now?"

"Still messing with her a little. Feels good just touching her."

"Oh yeah? You're a little minx. Are you still horny baby?"

"Yup...you do that to me...you and that sexy voice of yours."

"Is she still wet?"

"Oh yeah."

"Keep playing with your clit honey. Rub it gently back and forth."

"Mmmm...feels sooo good."

"Oh Gigi, you get me so hot honey. What are you doing now?"

"I've got one finger inside me. Mmmm I like this...with you."

"Me too baby, me too."

"Jake, are you horny again, too? Is your dick hard?"

"Oh, you bet it is. Hard just for you love. I can't remember when a woman has gotten and kept me this alive."

"I feel the same way Jake. You keep me so horny. I think about you and she develops a mind of her own. She gets so wet and an ache between my legs that won't go away until you are with me."

"I know, I know. I'm the same way. My concentration level seems to be in my pants all the time since I met you."

"Please make me cum again. Take me and do what you will with me."

"That could be dangerous, babe."

"Yeah, but I bet it would be fun."

"That it would be. Do you have two fingers in yet?"

"Glory be yes...and working on a third."

"You are horny today...damn...I wish I was there right now. I'd fuck you and eat you and fuck you again till you couldn't move a muscle."

"Ooh baby.. that sounds so wonderful and you made her squeeze my fingers so hard. I love making love with you. It feels heavenly."

"Oh my God...if only we could."

"Yeah, I know...but this feels so good..I want to cum again Jake."

"I'm with you honey. Work those precious fingers faster and rub your clit. With your other hand reach up and grab a hold of your nipple and pinch the hell out of it. Now switch to the other one."

"Keep doing that baby while you are stroking your vagina and rubbing your clit."

"AAAHHHH....I'm cumming.... I'M Cumming!!!!"

"Let it go sweet thing.. cum for me baby...let your juices flow and run all over my cock. I'm fucking you so hard and so deep I am touching your cervix with my dick. I'm going to fill you with my love juice baby. Feel it coming. Feel my sperm flooding your cavity, sitting in and along the walls of your sweet pussy."

Both at the same time yelled into their phones.

"AAAAHHHHH..YES.. Oh, My God.."

"So, tell me about your sister. What's her name?"

"Actually, she is my twin, born 5 minutes after me. Her name is Jessica."

"Really..wow!!!!!! Is she as sexual as you are?"

"Um, I don't know...could be I guess."

"Well, does she play?"

"How do you mean? Like we do?"

"Yeah, do you think she would join us sometime?"

"Are you saying the three of us.. together?"

"What do you think of that?"

"Hum, I'm not sure."

"Would you think about it?"

"Yep...I have to go and get her now. She just text me that she is being released. Who knows...you just might get a phone call tonight."

NO NAME

Oh, baby, you feel so good! I love having my cock buried so deep in your pussy," the stranger said as he pumped his dick in and then slowly out of me.

I laid there not knowing why my body was reacting to his cock stroking me. I was getting so wet and I could feel a climax nearing the more he pushed. He went so deep, clear to my womb. His body was slippery from the sweat he was causing to build up between us. He nibbled on my neck and ear, kissed my neck. Then he reached between us and took hold of my clitoris and pinched it between his fingers.

"Ohhhh Gooodddd...nnnooooo, please," I cried.

He was bringing me to the most intense climax I could remember ever having. I tried to move away from him, but his weight was too much. I couldn't move my arms, they were tied and held above my head my legs were held out to the sides and I

couldn't move them either. What the hell was going on? And who was this man lying on top of me?

Suddenly I felt him grow bigger inside of me and he started pulsing. I felt a warm liquid deep in my cunt. He moaned as he spurted over and over again, seeming never to end.

Finally, he rolled over to his side with one leg and arm still across me. He cuddled me and held me as if I was his only love.

I lay there in total confusion. Who was he, why was he in my house and why was he having sex with me? He raped me...yet he was so gentle and caring. He made sure that I reached my climax before he did. It's so dark in here I can't see him. He had made sure all the lights were off and the shades were all pulled. Not a hint of light was shining in my bedroom.

When I woke up there was light shining through the shaded bedroom window. My arms and legs were still tied and in the same position as they were before I went to sleep. I was really wet between my legs in my private area and the stranger was asleep beside me. And I really had to go use the bathroom.

The stranger looked over at me, smiled, pulled his hand through his thick black hair and sat up putting his legs over the side of the bed.

"Good morning sweet thing," he said with a grin on his face.

He had the most beautiful smile and the whitest set of teeth I had ever seen. As he stood up his lean body was taut with muscles that bulged from his wide chest and thick thighs. He had washboard abs and arms that would rival any body builder. As he turned to walk toward the bathroom he stopped and looked at me.

"Do you have to use the bathroom darlin'? I bet you do after all that lovin' last night."

He came back to the bed and started untying the ropes on my arms one at a time. As they came down, I rubbed them trying to get the circulation going again. He then went to the bottom of the bed and undid the ties on my ankles. Slowly I sat up in bed and rubbed my legs to the ankles. I felt so stiff and sore from being in that position for so long. I looked around me to see if there was any way I could get away from him, but he knew what I was thinking. "Don't try to go anywhere but to the bathroom over there babe."

The stranger had a firm look in his deep brown eyes that told me not to take any risks or I would truly be sorry. So, I walked carefully to the bathroom and closed the door behind me. Letting out a deep breath, I just wanted to sit there and cry.

"Just do your little potty thing sweetie and be quick about it." he said through the door.

As soon as I was finished, I opened the door to him standing there waiting for me. I looked up into his eyes and he stared back into mine. Then a slight grin formed across his face. He turned me around and led me back into the bathroom.

"Why are you bringing me back in here?" I asked not sure what he was up to.

"Well, I can't very well leave you out there by yourself, now can I? So, you'll have to sit in here with me while I relieve myself and then we are going to take a shower together. We're both pretty messy after such good lovin' last night. And oh baby, it was great."

"Who are you and why are you doing this to me?" I asked him as I sat on the edge of the bathtub while he urinated.

As he finished, he turned to me, pulled me up by my shoulders and looked at me softly and answered.

"Because you are the most beautiful, sensual woman I have ever seen. I have watched you for a very long time and couldn't wait any longer to make you totally mine. Your body is so soft and supple. Your breasts are so pert, and your nipples peak so well at my touch. I like to suck on them and bite on them like this." He bent down and put his lips to her right breast and took her nipple into his mouth and suckled it gently, lovingly, worshiping her.

My hands reached into his hair and held his head as he loved on my breast...then he moved to the other one and continued the same treatment. I felt myself getting wet as his hands roamed over my back and down my hips. God, he felt so good. How can I let this man whom, I don't even know do these things to my body?

We both let out low moans at the same time. He then raised his head and kissed me, gently at first then pushing his tongue into my mouth and devouring me. I returned his kiss with as much as he gave. We warred each other with our tongues, teasing and tasting one another. The sensations I was feeling were overwhelming and I wanted more. My body was craving him needing him. God, I'm losing it how can I want someone who is taking me against my will, by force... or is he?

Suddenly he stopped, pulled up and just stood there. He looked confused, like he didn't know what he wanted to do next. Then he slowly looked at me and pointed to the shower. my eyes followed, and I knew what he wanted.

So, I went to the walk-in shower and opened the glass door. I stepped inside and turned and looked back at him. He was right behind me. As he stepped in, he grabbed me around my waist and turned me around so that my back was to his chest. He turned the water on and adjusted the temperature to make it nice and warm. He held me close as the water cascaded down from my breasts, down my stomach and over my patch of pubic hair.

The stranger reached up and grasped both breasts in his hands and started massaging them and tweaking my nipples. I could feel his hardness against my ass cheeks and my lower back.

His hands slowly traveled down over my stomach and splayed over my mons, barely reaching into my vaginal area. He played there for a short time while I kept feeling his manhood growing and pulsing behind me. I knew I was getting really wet. He then stopped and turned me around and put my head under the water and wet my hair. Taking the shampoo, he put some into his hand and worked it into my hair, massaging my scalp. Oh Lord, it felt so good. I relaxed at his ministrations. He rinsed out the soap and put in the cream rinse.

With some of the cream rinse still on his hands he reached down and started working his fingers back and forth over my pussy lips, inserting first one and then two fingers into me. My legs started to wobble with the intensity of how hot he was getting me. He grabbed hold of me around my waist with one arm and I leaned into him to keep my balance. I was coming unglued. It seemed like every part of my body was on fire.

How could this be happening to me. I don't even know this man, yet he has managed to turn me to putty in his hands. I couldn't resist any longer.

As I neared my climax I reached for his cock, which was so hard, and stroked it with my fist tight around it. He moaned loudly as I screamed with my release.

My knees buckled, and he grabbed me tighter, holding me up and closer to his body.

"Ohhhh mmmyyyyy Gooodddd please stop I can't take any more." I reached for his hand, trying to slow down the motion of his fingers in my cunt but he kept up the pace, not relenting.

His thumb on my clit kept circling and circling. I felt like I was going to faint and then everything started to go hazy

When I came to, he had carried me and laid me on the bed. He was looking down at my face while he brushed my hair and rubbed my neck. "What happened and how did I get here on the bed?" I asked as I tried to get my vision back.

"You, my dear, had one gigantic orgasm. I would venture to say the best one you have ever had in your entire life and you passed out." explained the stranger.

I started to cry. The tears flowed down my face as he looked at me frowning.

"Why are you crying my sweet pet? You just had one fantastic orgasm and your crying. I don't get it." He had a forlorn look on his face. He really didn't understand.

"Look," I started explaining. "I haven't had sex in almost two years. Then I wake up to you being on top of me giving me the best sex I've ever had. I don't know who you are and why you are here. Yet, we have clicked so well, and you have made my body do things that my late husband never could. He didn't take the time to try." By then I was crying uncontrollably.

The stranger reached out and took me in his arms and held me close to his body. I tried to push away but he just held me that much tighter. I cried until I couldn't cry any longer. He then gently laid me down, went to the bathroom and came back with a warm wet washcloth and washed off my face.

"Do you feel better now?" he asked. "You seem to have had a lot of feelings built up inside that needed to come out."

"I'm sorry. You didn't deserve that. It's not your problem." I said back to him with a sigh.

"It seems to me that it became my problem when I came into this room. You are one hell of a woman. You are sensitive, responsive beyond belief, one of the most desirable women I have ever known."

"And do you meet all your women by appearing in their bedrooms and raping them?" I asked not daring to look at him.

"No, I do not. Someday, I will tell you why I am here, but not now. Because, right now, I want only to make you forget everything you have ever known about pain, sorrow, grief, sadness, and men who didn't know how to make you feel like a completed woman."

I slowly raised my eyes to look into his. He had the most honest looking eyes I had ever seen.

He took my hand and put it on his chest as he lowered his lips to mine. Tenderly our lips met. Neither of us moved. As he held my head his tongue licked at my lower lip, going back and forth until I opened my mouth and let his tongue in to explore every inch, along my teeth, over my gums, deeper in as if he was trying to push all the way down my throat. His kiss went from gentle to firm, hard to devouring. He wanted every inch of my mouth. He explored me, memorizing my mouth.

Finally, he broke away and looked into my eyes. We didn't have to say anything. No words were needed. He reached up and touched my breast as his head bent to kiss along my neck. My body was igniting with intense desire. He bit my ear and then licked it. Oh, God he was driving me wild. He leaned back again and looked at me intently.

Taking both breasts in his hands he massaged them and played with the nipples, pulling on them making them hard and pointing straight out. Each time he pulled I could feel tingles going straight into my cunt. Oh, I was getting so wet.

"Aaahhhhh, please," I moaned as he manipulated and played with my breasts. He lowered his head and took my right breast in his mouth.

"OOOOHHHH that feels soooo good. " I cried.

He continued from one breast to the other for what seemed like forever. He moved and kissed down over my belly all the way down over my pubic hair to my pussy. He pulled my lips apart and licked between them from my puckered little hole to my clit in one slow move.

"Oh Lord Jesus you are killing me aaahhhhh." I couldn't contain the feelings he was causing in my body.

My hips raised to meet him as if they had a mind all their own. My body couldn't stay still. I reached and took hold of his head with both hands, pulling on his hair. Pushing his face into my cunt as I couldn't get enough. He licked me over and over again staying away from my clit.

His tongue stiffened, and he inserted it into my vagina. Each time he went in he went a little deeper...sucking me, drinking me, loving me. when his thumb hit my clit, I exploded. My juices ran all over his tongue and face. He lapped at my pussy fast and furiously getting every drop of my succulent body fluid that he could get.

He eased up off my clit but kept his tongue in my hole as he started fingering my little cherry butt hole. Wow. this was a totally new feeling. It felt so good...

My hips gyrated, pushed up to meet his face and buried him in deeper. Then as his thumb hit my clit his little finger went inside my little hole.

"Holy Mother Mary GGGOOOOOOODDDDDDDD!!!!" I screamed!!!!!

Blast after blast hit me and I just kept cumming and cumming. I soaked him, me and the sheet. It took forever for me to come down from the high he had put me on. When he finally lifted his head and looked up at me, he had a big grin on his face.

"Did you like that baby? Are you ready for round two?"

"Please, let me rest. That was overwhelmingly fantastic." I said as I smiled back down at him.

"Oh, no baby, that was only the beginning."

I tried to wiggle away from him, but he grabbed a hold of my thighs and pulled me tighter to him.

"No way madame, you still have a lot to learn and we are far from through." He then lowered his head and started licking on my pussy lips again. He went for my pucker hole and swirled his tongue around and around it. I squirmed and moved my hips around. God he was good. He knew just where to go to get my body to respond to him. He then inserted two fingers into my other hole and moved them in and out at a slow pace. My hips started moving with him, up and down to his in and out. The pace went steady for a while and then he started curling his fingers upward and pressing on something inside me. His fingers started moving faster and faster. It started to feel like I had to pee. All of the sudden I felt a warm liquid running out of me and down his hand and my leg. My hips were out of control I couldn't stop, I didn't want him to stop...I pulled his hair, I yelled like I wanted everyone to hear me.

"Don't stop don't stop yesses uuuuuuuuuhhhhhhhh!!

The stranger grabbed my thighs and held on to me, but never once let off. He kept me going and going and going. His pinky was working its way in and out of my rectum as his middle and index fingers were pumping in and out of my cunt.

And his tongue was going wild over my clit. He was driving me into another realm of reality. My lips were so swollen from his ministrations and the blood flowing into them. I was in utopia and never wanted to come back.

When he finally moved, I didn't realize it until he was sitting on my chest with his cock in his hand. Slowly, he was stroking it back and forth.

As I looked up at him, I knew what he wanted. I had never been one to like sucking on a man's penis. Now, here it was, right in my face and he wanted me to suck on him. After what he just did for me, I did owe him that much, didn't I?

As he leaned closer, I stuck out my tongue and licked the tip. He already had pre-cum dripping from it, so I licked at it several times. It didn't taste so bad. I got a little braver and licked all around the engorged head. He jerked a little. I took notice that I had caused that. So, I did it again. And again, it jumped.

Damn, I thought, I do have some control of what happens with his cock, don't I? As I stuck my tongue out again, he reached out and touched my chin. So, I opened my mouth and he pushed forward until the tip of his penis was starting to enter my mouth. I closed my lips around his tip and sucked a little. He let out a low moan. We kept our eyes on each other as I opened my mouth again and took a little bit more of him. His groan was a little bit louder this time.

God, I never knew I could have this effect on a man. My husband was not this gentle and all he wanted was to jam it in my mouth and get off quick. This stranger wanted to savor the feeling. He was definitely enjoying himself.

"Well then, let's let him really enjoy it," I thought.

So, I kept opening my mouth and taking a little more of him each time. Finally, I had him to right at the beginning of my throat. I gagged a little and he backed off some. He kept slowly inching deeper until I was able to take all of his 8 inches. Then he pumped his hips back and forth while holding my head still. I had a couple of gag moments and he would stop until I had it back under control and then he would start out slowly again and build up the pace.

"Ah baby, your mouth feels like heaven. You are a great cock sucker darlin," he said as he kept a steady pace. "But I'm gonna cum in your mouth if we keep this up and I don't want to do that. I'm not finished with you yet."

So, he pulled out of my mouth, backed down my body and leaned over and kissed me hard. He was devouring me. As he was, he positioned himself between my legs and put his cock up to my pussy lips and pushed in all the way to the hilt. We both let out a deep moan at the same time.

God, he felt so good filling me all the way up my cunt. He was so big so hard. I wanted him more than I had ever wanted any man.

"Baby fuck me please. fuck me hard. Make me cum!!!!!!!! I want you so much. You feel soooo goood. " I couldn't get enough of him.

The stranger reached down and pulled up my legs and held them by my calves bending me almost in half and he pounded me. He gave me all that he had. Our eyes were focused only on each other.

We knew nothing but what we were at that moment. I felt his cock get huge inside me and then he came and I came all over him him deep inside of me pulse after pulse. hot semen into my womb we were one together.

We slept for hours wrapped in each other's arms. The stranger woke before me and was already showered and dressed. I asked him why he was dressed, and he said it was time for him to leave.

"Why? Can't you stay a while longer? I've gotten kinda use to you being here."

"No, my dearest. My time here is over. I've done what I was sent here to do. You will be fine now."

"What are you talking about? Who sent you?" none of this was making any sense.

"I'm an Angel and God knew how much difficulty you've been having adjusting since the death of your husband. I was sent here to let you know that you are a great and wonderful woman who can be happy again. All you need is to believe in yourself. I think you can now do that. So, it is now time for me to go back to my Heavenly home. But I will miss you. You are one hot, sexy lady."

With that the Stranger was gone. I blinked my eyes and thought to myself,,,,,,,,,,

"I didn't even know his name!!!!!!!!!!!!"

PLAYING ROULETTE

There he was, laying on the couch as usual. I was so sick of it. Nothing ever got done. The garage was a total disaster and I had been after him for two years to go through everything and clean it up. I guess this was just another task I was going to have to do myself. Why was I even married???

My good for nothing husband did nothing around the house, didn't even take out the garbage anymore. And sex. What was that? I hadn't had any in so long I forgot what it felt like!! I stood and took another look at him as he laid there watching television and it make me sick inside. This was not what I had in mind the day I walked down the aisle and said, "I do".

The next morning, Saturday, I got up early. I went down to the kitchen, made myself a hot cup of coffee and sat on the stool at the counter. The more I thought about the picture in my mind of last night and Dennis laying on the couch and the image of the garage the madder I became.

The kids had already moved from the house, going on with their lives. Jimmy was in college and Dani (her name is Danica) was married. "God, I hope she doesn't go through this too." I thought. So, there was no one to help me but Me, Myself and I.

I picked up my cup of coffee and headed for the garage, putting my hand on the doorknob and sighed. I turned the knob and walked into the garage. I let out a deeper sigh. There lay my work in front of me. Might as well get started. This was going to be a very long day.

I opened the garage door and started moving things out so I could sort out what was what. What I could get rid of and what needed to be kept. Then I started making piles of what needed to be put back and where to store it. It was in one of the corners that I found something that I hadn't seen in a very long time.

Many years ago, we use to hold casino parties. All our friends would come over and we would have a great time. Then it would be one of their turns to hold one. Every New Year's Eve we would hold one at the Community Center for the whole town with prizes and dinner.

In the corner, stashed under some other stuff was our tabletop roulette wheel. It was dusty as all get out...but it was still beautiful. What was I going to do with it?

I pulled it out and took it outside. I set it up and put a spin to it. Yup, it still worked. Amazing. But, we were never going to have parties like that again. So, what in the world was I going to do with it?

I left it sitting there while I straightened out the rest of the garage and put things away as I wanted them. Then, I loaded up the van with the things I was going to donate to the local charities. I looked at the wheel again. It held so many great memories that I couldn't just give it away. Besides that, it had cost us a pretty penny. No, I was going to hang on to it and figure out what to do with it later. So, I stuck it back into the garage and covered it with a quilt to keep it from harm.

Several days later I had been thinking about how mad I was at my husband and his good for nothing attitude when an idea struck me. I had that roulette wheel sitting in the garage doing nothing. What if I brought it in the house and set it up in the family room? He's sure to see and ask what it's doing there. But instead of numbers showing. there are little pieces of paper in each space. Maybe I can get him to play along...and off the damn couch. Hummmmm!!!!!!

When Dennis came home from work that night he took his shower as usual and went straight for the couch.

"Janice, what is this thing doing in here?" he yelled.

"Oh, you mean the roulette wheel?" I asked as I walked into the family room.

"Ah, yeah. What the hell is it doing here? And what are those things on there?" Dennis took a slug of his beer from the bottle he had in his hand.

"Well, you see dear, I found this way in the back of the garage. Buried under a bunch of stuff when I was cleaning it out. Like I asked you to help me with. I didn't want to throw it out...it had cost way too much money. And I didn't want to give it away. So, I think I have found another use for it." I saw a curious look come across his face. At least I had gotten his interest.

"Oh you have. And what pray tell might that be?" Again, Dennis took another drink of his beer as he sprawled out on the couch. I went and sat on the edge of the cushion beside him.

"On the wheel, in each of the slots is a piece of paper. You can't see what is written on it. When you spin and the ball lands, you have to do whatever is written on the paper." I said to him with a grin on my face. "And just what is written on these little pieces of paper? More jobs you want me to do? No thank you. Nice try babe." Dennis turned his face away from me and switched on the television to his favorite show, the damn football game.

"Ok, if you don't want a blow job, that's fine with me." I said as I got off the couch and started to walk out of the room.

"WHAT!!!! You put that on the wheel? Really?" I never thought Dennis could move so fast from the couch, but guess I was wrong. He was standing over the roulette wheel faster than I could turn around.

"Well, yeah. And some other stuff too." I answered back.

"Yeah, like what?" he asked. The beer bottle had been left on the coffee table and he was staring at the wheel.

"AHHH..well, let me think. Oh yeah…eat me.. take out the trash.. shower together.. fill dishwasher.. fuck me.. sweep floor.. sit on me.. mop floor.. suck me.. want me to go on?" His face was stoic…his mouth wide open yet he couldn't speak.

I looked at him and smiled. My nipples were already hard. This was really turning me on. I had him right where I wanted him and he knew it. But would he play along? I didn't know for sure. I held my breath.

"Damn. Oh My God. This is unreal. How in the world did you ever come up with something like this? So, if I spin this and it lands on a sexy thing...we get to do it? And if it lands on something to do that is work…I have to do that? Is that right?" He was still stunned…but he got the idea.

"That's it baby. But I get to play too. It's not just for you. We both get to play. We both get to enjoy this together. Do you like my idea?" I was so hoping he was in for this.

"Hell yeah!! I love it. This was brilliant. Can we try it out now? I can't wait to give this thing a whirl. How many times a day…night do we get to spin it?" Dennis was full of excitement. He was eager to try his luck with it.

"Well, we'll each take a turn tonight. So how do we decide who goes first?" I looked at him.

"Hum. Good question. I guess we'll flip a quarter. Which do you want, heads or tails baby. Oh, I can't wait for this!" I hadn't seen him so excited about anything in years.

As he flipped the quarter I called tails. It landed heads up. He had won. A huge grin crossed his face. Dennis stepped up and spun the wheel. The ball landed and he took off the piece of paper. Slowly he unfolded it. He looked up at me.

"Well, what does it say?" I asked him with anticipation.

"It says..'Eat Me' then he grinned and I grinned back at him. "So, where would you like to do this?" I asked him. "Um..where would you prefer? I want you to be comfortable baby." he said as he finished off his beer.

"How about right here on the couch?" I wanted him to know his couch could be used for something besides him laying on it all night long watching TV.

"Fine." He took me by the hand and led me over to it and laid me down. He unbuttoned my jeans and pulled them off, then removed my panties.

Dennis started at my feet and kissed his way up to my thighs, alternating from one leg to the other. He spread my legs wider as his head went between them and he tenderly kissed my love bud. Then his tongue circled and flicked it back and forth. He sucked it into his mouth and loved on it until I was moaning and my hips were rising to meet him.

My hands went into his hair to hold his head closer to me as his tongue worked its way down through my lips and into my love channel. His mouth felt so good. It had been way too long since he had done this to me. I moaned as he devoured me. I was so close and he continued to assault my wet and erupting vaginal chamber.

Just as I was ready to cum, Dennis slipped his finger inside of me and started pumping me. I clamped down on it with my inner muscles and came so hard I couldn't catch my breath. My head was going back and forth as my hips rose and fell. His finger kept on working in and out as his mouth sucked until I started coming down from my utopia.

"Damn baby.... that was awesome.... mmmmmmmmmmmmm" I said as he lifted his head and looked at me. He had the most loving look in his eyes. I hadn't seen that look in a very long time. It brought tears to my eyes.

Dennis crawled up and kissed me, then kissed me again as our tongues met. We kissed passionately.

"I love you babe. That was a hot idea you had. I kinda like this little game of yours." Dennis smiled.

Janice had to turn away from him as she grinned. "I wonder just how much he will like it when he has to do something that entails a little bit of work?" She thought to herself.

It was now my turn to spin the wheel. I gave it a huge spin, waited for it to stop and the ball to land. Pulling off the slip of paper, I opened it slowly. The agony on his face was making me wet. I loved this. I read the slip and grinned.

"Well, what does it say? Are you lucky or not?" Dennis was beside himself. He couldn't stand still.

"Well, I guess we are both lucky tonight. It says.." and I twirled my hair around my finger as I smiled up at his waiting face.

"Yes, come on Janice…what the hell does it say?" Dennis was dying here. I was absolutely loving this.

"It says that.."

"Give me that damn piece of paper. You are killing me, you know that, right?" Dennis reached for the paper but I jerked my hand back.

"Oh, no you don't. This is my turn." I grinned at him.

"So, come on already. Stop messing around and tell me what the hell it says." I knew he was getting really agitated.

"Okay, it says 'Shower Together.' So, turn off the TV and let's go. Now!!!" I turned and started for our bedroom.

"Wait a minute. Right now? It's still early. And my game isn't over with." Dennis started to protest.

"Dennis Rayburn. Don't you even dare do this. You agreed to the rules. You had your turn and now it's mine. So, yes, right now. Move your butt. Now!!!." I turned again and went into our bedroom.

Amazingly he did follow me. He threw off his clothes and was in the shower, water on, waiting for me before I got all of my clothes off. Well, this wasn't how I had intended for it to be, but it wasn't how it was going to end up if I had anything to say about it.

Dennis turned around as I got into the shower. With my back to him, he took the soap and started washing my neck and shoulders. His hands felt wonderful and relaxing as he worked the muscles loose. He worked his way down my back to my buttocks, over my hips and down my legs. Then he turned me around. He started at my neck and worked his way down my chest, over my breasts, down my tummy, around my waist to over my hips. He went down my legs and washed my feet. I wondered why he never touched my private area, front or back. Disappointment enveloped me and my eyes started to well up with tears. He rinsed me off and I thought he was finished.

Dennis took the soap and lathered his hands again. He worked his way from my mid thighs upward to my nether region. He spread my legs and put his rather large fingers between my lips and started playing and rubbing on my quickly hardening nub. While doing that, he cleaned me from my little hole frontwards and rinsed me, never missing a rotation, keeping me on the edge.

When I was totally rinsed, he brought his head to my lips and licked me, little by little easing back further and further until he was licking me from my little pucker hole to my hard nub. He then took that hardness into his mouth and sucked it. I gasped and moaned at the same time.

I grabbed his shoulders and hung on. My knees were so weak I felt like I would sink down to the shower floor. I knew he sensed this because he grabbed my right leg and put it over his shoulder. This gave him open access to me and he went to town. As he chewed and nibbled and sucked on my little nub he inserted a finger into my soaking wet vaginal home.

"Oh God Dennis. Yes, Baby. Please don't stop. That feels so good." I couldn't help it.... I wanted him to do this to me forever.

Dennis stopped and looked up at me. I hadn't seen that look on his face in a very long time. It almost put me over the edge. My body shook. The look of pure lust and desire he had was more than I could take.

As his finger moved inside of me, he lowered his mouth to me again and as he sucked my clitoris back into his mouth I came with a vengeance. My juices flowed all over his face, his finger and his hand. He slowed his movements until my climax passed, then stood and held me tightly to him. God, how I loved this man.

As I came in control of myself, I knew that I wanted to bring him the same pleasure, so I turned him around and washed him. Starting from his neck, down his shoulders and back. Worked my way across his buttocks, between his cheeks, and down his legs.

Then I turned him around, repeating the process, dropping to my knees to wash his thighs, legs and feet. I knew he was watching me and I looked up and smiled at him. I then took the nozzle and totally rinsed his body off. I had purposely not touched his already hard manhood.

Dropping to my knees again I held his hard shaft in my hand as I stroked him slowly up and down. His skin was soft and smooth and he felt wonderful. As I stroked him I lightly kissed his balls then licked them… first one side and then the other. I could hear him moaning as I did.

Coming back up with my tongue, I licked up his hard piece of manhood all the way to the top. Seeing his drops of fluid, I licked it up and spread it around his head and the upper part of him. His staff jerked in my hand. My lips wanted to take him and surround him in my love. He tasted so good.

Dennis put his hands on my head and held me still as he centered his rod to my mouth. I opened for him and he entered me. I sucked him in and he gasped. His breath caught. My hand stroked him as I sucked him in deeper and deeper. He thrust. His meat hit the back of my throat. He groaned.

Then he pulled out.

He didn't say a word.... he pulled me up...turned me around... spread my legs and thrust into my very wet hole and bottomed out inside of me. He grabbed my breasts and played with my nibbles, pinching them, then massaging them, then pinching them again.

"Oh..God.." Was all I could say.

"Take me baby. Take all of this hard man meat I have for you."

Dennis was pumping me hard and fast. He reached around and played with my little nub, rubbing it. I was going to cum and cum hard. My hands were holding on the wall in front of me, my head down and I was moaning so loud I thought the world could hear me.

Faster and faster he gave it to me. Then he grabbed my hair and pulled my head back as he groaned loudly. I came all over him as he came inside of me. Pulse after pulse of his hot, sticky jism filled me. So much that it ran down my legs.

Both of us were breathing so hard we were panting. Dennis held onto my hips to hold me up. Gradually we gained our breath and he pulled me back against him. As I stood to lean on him, his magic wand fell out. I say magic because he just gave me what he hadn't in years. It felt magical. It felt wonderful.

We showered off again, dried off and he resumed his spot…watching the rest of the football game. I stood there smiling.

I looked at the roulette wheel and wondered what tomorrow would bring when we spun the wheel again. There would be two more times. Would it be a fun time or a chore? Who knows. Only the wheel knows for sure!

SEXUALITY

Time seems to catch up with the best of us. I mean our bodies aren't what they use to be. Titties get a little saggy, belly sags a little too…and a few other sags here and there. Hair changes color…either naturally or by a box…but it still isn't what it was in our youth. Nothing is as it was in our youth. Neither is our sexuality. Really???

Really!!! Let me demonstrate for you..

Sybil had been the horniest bitch in high school. Mitchell Harrison had been her steady fuck for most of tenth through twelfth grade. But he knew she was getting it on the side too. She would blow just about anybody who asked her to, including the worst, ugliest nerd. She just loved cock and didn't care whose it was.

But the one thing she was very particular about was who put it up her cunt. That privilege was saved for only Mitchell. And absolutely no one got her little pucker hole. NO WAY!!!!

After graduation from high school Sybil worked a couple of odd jobs until she met Julia Anderson. Julia worked at the local massage parlor and told Sybil how easy the money was. Not just giving the massage, but the fringe benefits. When asked what she meant by that, Julia explained that a good massage always had a "happy ending." Sybil still didn't understand so Julia told her to come by for a free massage and find out.

Several days later, Sybil arrived at the parlor at a little after two pm. She was greeted by Marissa, who had long, black hair pulled up into a ponytail. Her smile was infectious and Sybil smiled back. She was led into a booth and told to take off all her clothes and wrap a towel over her breasts and groin area and to lay on her stomach. Julia was finishing up with a client and would be in shortly. Soft music played in the background as she laid there and relaxed.

Julia came in the room wearing a robe of lavender, both in color and scent. It was short, just under her butt cheeks and hid very little in the front. She had never been turned on by a woman...but her pussy was telling her something different. The top was open enough to show quite a bit of cleavage. Her nipples were hard and pressed against the robe provocatively. Julia smiled and asked Sybil if she was comfortable. Then told her just to relax and enjoy the massage.

Julia undid the towels and laid them to the sides. She told Sybil to lay still and relax.

Julia's hands were gentle as she applied the oil onto Sybil's upper back and started to rub up and down and around her shoulders and neck. She could feel herself loosening up. Julia proceeded down her back, working her stiff fingers into the tissue of Sybil's muscles. Next, she pinched and rotated the skin, working and working her whole back repeatedly.

"God, this felt so good," was Sybil's thinking. She felt like she could drift right off to sleep.

Julia applied more oil and started rubbing her butt cheeks. One side at a time she massaged and pinched and rotated until all stress was relieved.

As she applied more oil Sybil felt some run between the cheeks and down the crack of her ass. Julia took her finger and went down to retrieve it. Sybil jumped a little at the feel of her being down there. No one had ever touched her there. No one had ever been allowed. Nope. that was off limits. Sybil's butt cheeks tightened automatically. Julia rubbed and moved them apart and continued to rub her finger in and out of the crack of Sybil's ass. This actually started to feel good and she soon relaxed.

Julia went to the bottom of the table. Applying oil to Sybil's feet, she started with the soles and bottom, then worked to Sybil's toes, doing each one at a time. She then worked up the calves. First massaging one, then the other, relieving all the tension.

Using more oil, she worked up Sybil's thighs. Working and kneading the muscles into submission as she inched her way up until she was at the Y. Lightly, she would brush against Sybil's pussy as she worked her fingers on her.

Slowly, she would spread out her fingers and touch more and more with each passing of her hands. At first Sybil felt uncomfortable...but then it started to feel nice.

Having Sybil turn over, Julia started on her arms, wrists, hands, fingers and palms. Working the oils in, massaging. This girl was talented. Julia put her fingers on Sybil's face and applied the oil and massaged it in gently, going from the bottom of her chin to the top of her forehead.

After that Julia put oil on her shoulders and upper chest, working it into her skin and then went lower, down to her breasts. As Julia massaged them, one at a time, Sybil's nipples hardened and stood straight out.

She hopped up on the table and straddled Sybil at her waist. Julia played with Sybil's breasts, rolling the nipples and pinching them in between her fingers. Sybil let out a soft moan. Julia gave a small smile as she inched further down onto Sybil's legs.

As she sat there, she rubbed oil onto Sybil's stomach and down to her navel. Julia played with her belly button. Then continued down to her hips. Julia knew she was reaching the start of the point of no return. Slowly she maneuvered her hands to go across Sybil's low abdomen to the lush bush of pubic hair on her mound.

She rubbed oil into her hair and on down and to the insides of Sybil's groin, careful not to touch the labia lips. Julia watched Sybil's face as she massaged in between her legs, back up to her mound, then back over her clit and down through the slit in her labia. Sybil's hips lifted off the table. Julia knew this was the normal reaction of a woman not used to being touched by another woman, yet her clit was being so stimulated. Gently Julia pushed Sybil's hips back down and her other hand continued working back and forth along her slit. Being totally oiled and slippery, Julia had no trouble finding Sybil's entry place and pushed one finger inside of her.

Again, Sybil's hips started to rise but Julia held her in place. She told Sybil to relax and just enjoy the feelings going through her body. She would be coming to a climax very shortly.

Julia pushed another finger in with the one already inside Sybil's delicious, wet cunt. Sybil jumped again, thrusting her hips up and into Julia's hand. As she did, Julia's fingers went deeper into Sybil's soaking wet pussy. Swirling her fingers around, Julia found Sybil's walnut...her g-spot and pushed on it. Sybil came like a lightning bolt. Her juices ran down Julia's fingers, down her hand and onto the sheet. Slowly, Julia kept her fingers moving in and out of Sybil's cunt until her hips quieted and her breathing returned to normal.

She opened her eyes and looked up at Julia. Sybil let out a huge sigh. They both smiled at each other. Sybil raised up and gave Julia a hug and thanked her for making her body feel so great. Julia hugged her back and told her, "That's what a Happy Ending is."

That was almost forty years ago. A lot has changed since then. Are there still massage parlors? Sure, there are. Are there sill "Happy Endings"? Depends on where you go. My husband, Mitchell, has had many of them. His favorite one is at a local parlor. Mitch leaves the house on a Saturday afternoon and says he will be back in a few hours. I say fine, see you later. Of course, I know where he is going. So, I go down into the basement and make myself comfortable.

MITCH

Mitch walked in the door and was greeted with the usual smile and was taken into a room and told to take off all his clothes, lay on his stomach and his masseuse will be right in. As soft music plays, he hears the door open and the soft footsteps of his masseuse as she approaches the table. "How are you today?" she asks as she begins to rub oil on his upper back and neck.

"I'm a bit tight today, Angel…would you mind a little extra pressure on my back?" Mitch replied.

"Oh, I can feel it darling. Just relax and I'll have you feeling better in no time."

"That's why I come here to you sweetheart. You know how to release all my tensions."

So, she started working on my back, neck, arms, all the way down to my buttocks. She kneaded my cheeks, one and then the other. Then she worked on my feet, calves, thighs, up to the crack of my ass and back down again. She worked her finger in between the crack of my ass to my tight little butt hole and massaged it gently.

"OH GOD!!! Baby, you do that too well. Rub my little shit hole… put your finger inside and make me squirm." Mitch was thoroughly enjoying this massage.

As she did this, she grabbed my sack and massaged my balls. Rubbing them lightly back and forth in her hand as she pushes her finger into my puckered hole I cry out, "AHHH, Baby…yes, yes…Ahhh." I say it as I push my butt into her finger, pushing her finger deeper into me. "That feels so wonderful." She pulls her finger out and tells me to turn over.

Missing her finger inside of me, I roll over quickly and my rod is standing straight up at attention. All nine inches if it. She doesn't even bat an eyelash as she reaches for the oil and totally ignores my staff. She begins rubbing my chest, hairy as it is, with the warm oil, all over my breasts and hard nipples. She pinches them just a bit. Enough to let me know that she is still the boss.

Then she hops up on the table and sitting right at the base of my hard, throbbing cock. She takes off her robe, puts oil on her tits and leans over my body and rubs them on my chest. Oh my God, what this woman does to me. She has me on fire!! My cock throbs hard against her abdomen. She rocks and rolls against it and drives me insane.

She sits back up, takes my cock in her hands and begins to stroke my hard on. Up and down her hands slide, slickened by the oil and my precum. She leans down and licks my thick, purple head with her tongue.. Oh, Sweet, Jesus…she is so awesome…as she strokes me and puts the head of my cock in her mouth and swallows. "Lord have mercy. That feels so incredible." I speak, barely audible.

She eases me down her throat until my dick reaches all the way to the back. How does she do it I wonder. How can she swallow all nine inches of me??? Her tongue wiggles back and forth as she moves her head up and down my shaft. My hips rise up to meet her.

I take hold of her head and guide her as my hips move up and down. I build a faster rhythm. I'm going to cum any second. She knows it and reaches down…puts a finger to my pucker hole and pushes in steadily….and low and behold…I feel my jism rise and leave my cock as rope after rope hits the back of her throat and she swallows…all of it…all of me.

All of the tension…every bit…has left my body. I am so relaxed; I don't think I can move a muscle. My cock deflates and she raises her head. She looks deep into my eyes and says.

"Welcome to my parlor, sweetheart."

After being married to Sybil for forty years, she has a few sags here and there, but she can still suck a mean cock.

Does sexuality change? Hell yeah. It only gets better with age, baby!!!!

SHE'S MINE

She was going to a conference in Illinois in two days. The timing couldn't be more perfect for what I had in mind. I have watched her for many years, as she is my wife's best friend. Her husband has been ill for several years and isn't going with her so it was now or never.

We have been working together for a little over twelve years and my fascination with her has only grown stronger. Yes, I got married. Yes, I have two children whom I love very much. But there is just something about this woman that I can't let go of and want much more of. Oh, so much more.

As she has gone up the corporate ladder, her allure has become so rampant with me that I have had to take the situation in hand way too many times. I've had to leave my office for the men's room to relieve the agony before I could continue with my day's assignments.

Well, soon, that is going to change. I have made arrangements to be on that trip right along with her. She just doesn't know it yet and won't until we are at the same hotel. Correction. When she is laying on her bed, being totally satisfied by me, then she'll know.

Silently, I made all the preparations at work to clear my schedule and told my wife that I was attending a different conference in another city. My hotel room was reserved and guaranteed. My flight was scheduled, making sure it was at a different part of the airport. Everything was set and ready for my departure.

The day of travel arrived and it was rather tricky getting through the check in counter at the airport without running into her. But I did and boarded my plane. The flight was smooth and I arrived at the hotel before her. I asked what floor she would be on and asked to be put on the same one, as we were working on a project together for the conference. The hotel clerk was very gracious and accommodating.

Room service brought me dinner, and then I showered and settled in for the night. My mind started to formulate my plan to make my fantasy come true at last. I fell into the best night's sleep I'd had in a long time.

During the day, I knew that she would be in meetings. That gave me ample time to wander around and work out my nervousness. Toward evening, I went to the front desk and told the clerk that she was in a meeting and needed some important information and that she had forgotten to give me the key to her room. The clerk said she wasn't supposed to give it to me and would have to call her. I explained that she was on stage and that would be impossible, but that this was most important to her presentation. Finally, she agreed and gave me a key card.

Smiling, I got on the elevator, went to my room and got what I would need for the evening I had in store. I then proceeded from my room to hers and let myself in.

She had left all the lights on and the television. So, I turned off all but the dim one over in the corner that stood behind the tall back armchair. I turned the television down. Walking to the night stand I placed the items I was going to use later. I also prepared the bed by pulling down the spread and top sheet, spreading rose pedals along the middle and pillows. Then I took off all my clothes, folded them and put them in the top of the closet.

Knowing when the meeting was to be over, I sat on the end of the bed and watched television until I knew she would be coming to her room. Turning the volume down very low, I got up and stood at the wall, being right behind the door when it opened.

Waiting.... Waiting...Waiting....

The key card went into the slot.... back out...and the doorknob turned. She opened the door and stepped inside. As the door started to close I reached out and covered her mouth with my hand and wrapped my other arm around her waist. I held her back to my chest. I held her still. Now I had her. She's mine.

She started to pull, turn, twist trying to get away but I held her tightly against me. I pulled her head back and whispered in her ear to calm down, that I wasn't there to hurt her. I asked her if she understood and she shook her head to affirm.

I moved her further into the room as I wanted her closer to the king size bed. She was breathing hard and I wanted to calm her down some but knew that wasn't going to happen right now. Both of us were running on adrenaline so I just held her to me. God, her body felt so good next to mine. Soft, supple, sexy. I had waited so long to feel her next to me. I felt my member wanting to grow but tried to hold him at bay. I wanted to go slow and savor each and every moment with her.

I told her I was going to take my hand from her mouth, but not to make a sound. If she agreed, to shake her head. She did. Slowly, I removed my hand. I reached down to the nightstand and brought up the scarf that I then inserted into her mouth and tied around her head. She tried to turn around but I held her still. I then reached and grabbed the blindfold and slipped it over her eyes and around her head. She whimpered.

Again, I told her I wasn't going to hurt her, but for her to enjoy this experience. It would be the best one she probably had ever had. I explained that I only wanted to give her pleasure but it was her choice if it went that way. Did she understand? She shook her head that she did. She felt so good in my arms but I knew that I had to get her hands secured so that I could move her down onto the bed. I reached over to the nightstand and took the hand cuffs, placing one on each wrist, securing her hands behind her back. Running my hand down her back sent shivers over her skin and goose bumps formed along her arms.

I put my hand on the back of her neck and told her to climb up on the bed and to lay on her stomach. I guided her, laying her head on the pillow. Trying to be as thoughtful to her comfort as I could, I removed her shoes and gently rubbed her feet. Working my way up, I rubbed her ankles, calves and on up to her thighs. Continuing up was such a temptation, but I had to have patience. This was a work in progress and it had to go slowly.

Soft moans started to escape from her as I reached the top of her thighs toward her center. But I didn't want her that warm yet. So, I stopped and went to the head of the bed. Sitting down, I turned her over. She had on a purple button down, short sleeved blouse. Slowly, my fingers released each button until the blouse was completely open. Lightly I ran my fingertips across the very top of her breasts that were riding at the top of her bra. Her skin was so soft and supple. She felt heavenly.

Noticing that she was uncomfortable with her hands cuffed behind her back, I told her to keep very still and I would remove the cuffs from her hands and move them for her. I said to nod if she agreed. She did.

Having prepared the bed already, knowing she would probably try something the moment I released her hands, I took her right hand and released it, keeping her left one underneath her. I took it and moved it quickly to the silk rope I had attached to the bed and tied it. She tried to roll into me and move her left hand and arm but I moved over her fast and held her down while I took her left hand and tied it to the bed. She tried to buck and move me off of her but I wasn't going anywhere.

She twisted again but it was of no consequence. As I slid down her legs to her ankles, I took first one and then the other and secured them to the corners of the bed. I stood up at the foot of the bed and admired the lady lying before me.

She was a treasure I was going to enjoy unwrapping, slowly. Very, very slowly. I was going to savor every part of her. She would know that she had been thoroughly and completely ravished. Her head went back onto the pillow and a deep sigh escaped her lips. Yes, she's mine!

Going to the head of the bed I pushed the rose pedals away from her hair. Some stands of hair had stuck to her face and I gently brushed them aside, letting my fingertips travel along her cheek. She shivered in response.

Her lips, with that bright red lipstick, looked so soft and inviting. Leaning down I lightly touched them with mine. She hesitated for a moment before returning with a slight kiss of her own. It was very slight, her lips barely moving. That was alright. They would be put to better use later.

Kissing and licking down her neck to her ear and sucking on her earlobe, then continuing down to her shoulders made her squirm and wriggle. Her body wanted the attention. Her nipples were getting harder. They were poking through the fabric of her black lace bra.

Reaching over to the nightstand I retrieved the scissors and placed the blades on her chest. She shivered at the touch of the cold metal. I snipped first one strap and then the other and watched them slip off her shoulders. Dragging the blades downward I centered them over her breastbone and slid them into position and cut her bra in half, letting the cups fall to the sides. Her glorious globes settled a little to each side as I beheld such amazing breasts.

My eyes worshiped her. She was all I had envisioned in my mind. Putting the scissors back, I reached out with both hands and my fingertips grazed her breasts. Her nipples hardened more. Goosebumps formed on her flesh. I could almost see her breasts enlarge before my eyes. I leaned over taking one breast in my hand and licked it all over. Tasting her, savoring her flavor.

Leaning over I switched to the other breast, taking it in my hand and massaging it. I could hear her low moans as I lightly licked it.

"God, she tasted so good." I thought.

I took a nipple into my mouth and toyed with it, nibbled it with my teeth. Her moans grew louder. Her hips started to wiggle back and forth. She couldn't lay still. I knew my ministrations were having the desired effect on her.

While my mouth, tongue and teeth were working her breasts, from one to the other, I moved my hand down over her tummy from side to side and up and down avoiding her clean-shaven mound. Her hips rose, wanting the contact with my hand but I held her at bay. I wanted her hot, so hot that she needed me. Desired me.

My engorged manhood lay nestled beside her outer thigh. As I slid down her further, trailing kisses and licks down her abdomen I rubbed myself against her leg. I knew she could feel me there. What was she thinking? Did she want me yet? Was she wet yet? Her body said she wanted me. Did her mind?

As I kissed down her tummy, I lifted myself over her to be between her legs. I could smell her scent. Her female pheromones were strong. She was so much of a woman and I wanted her so much.

Watching her face, I took my index finger and moved it to her outer labia and touched it. She squirmed. My finger moved gently up and down and over her lips. She moved more. Her face flushed as she gave a slight gasp.

My breath caught in my throat. She was so beautiful, so sensitive and so responsive.

Deeper I moved my finger into her lips feeling her wetness. She was so turned on. She wanted this. She wanted me.

"Oh My God!!! Yes." My thoughts were bursting in my head. My finger moved back and forth in her slit as I played with her, getting her hotter still. Her hips rose up wanting more. Needing more. Desire building. I avoided her little bud as I reached for her opening and slid my finger in. She jumped and cried out. Her moans were loud. Her head twisted on the pillow from side to side.

"Ahhhh...." She cried.

Keeping silent, I kept my finger inside of her, moving it back and forth, watching as pleasure washed across her face. Her hips were moving in rhythm with my fingers and I knew she was getting close to her orgasm. But I wanted to hold her off just a little bit more. I wanted her to want me. To desperately need me. I wanted her to be mine.

Slowly I took my finger out and ran it up and down her slit. Then ran it over her little puckered hole. I used her juices to make her wet and kept running my finger back and forth. Her whole body was wreathing and I knew she wanted to cum so much. Her body ached for it, needed it, wanted it.

I pushed my finger back inside of her and started the back-and-forth movement again. After a few times, I inserted a second finger. She felt so tight inside. She squeezed my fingers with her inner muscles. I knew it was time to let her reach her pinnacle of joy. I took my thumb and pressed on her little nub and she exploded all over my fingers. She squeezed them so hard they wouldn't move inside of her. Her legs grabbed me as best they could and held on. And then she screamed. I gave her a few minutes to calm back down from her orgasm, gently rubbing her tummy while still slowly moving my fingers inside of her. We had only just gotten started. I had a long night planned for this lovely, sexy beauty. She had many more orgasms left to be had.

Turning my hand, I stroked her working her gspot with the "come hither" movement. I knew this would bring her to the brink again. I rubbed her nub with circular motions and just enough pressure to make it harden. Being already sensitive I knew it wouldn't take her too long to get worked up again.

Her brow was showing signs of sweat and her breathing was beginning to increase, showing she was getting close. Her hips started to move with my hand. She was starting to pull and twist. Oh yeah, she wanted this. She was so hot and needy. And I was just the one to take her where she wanted to be.

While using my fingers and thumb of my right hand in her love canal and on her little button, I took my other hand and reached for her nipple and teased it. She moaned. Using her juices, I took my little finger and placed it at her little pucker hole and pushed just slightly. Her hips bucked.

As I kept the movements of my fingers in her love hole working fast, my thumb on her love button rubbing harder, I pushed the pinky finger into her pucker hole and pinched her nipple hard.

She let go with a howl I have never heard before. Her back arched. Her head jerked back as her body went rigid. I felt a flood of liquid flow out of her and all over my legs, hers and the bed.

"My God. This woman just squirted!!" I had never seen that happen before and sat in utter amazement; a huge grin plastered on my face. I pulled my hands out of her, went to the bathroom and got a washcloth with warm water and went back to bathe her. I washed her thighs, buttocks and womanhood until she was clean. She only moaned.

Then I lay down beside her and held her close. Her body was still so sensitive that if I even touched her she quivered.

My shaft was so hard that it hurt. I wanted inside her so badly, but I knew I had to give her a few minutes to calm down. I had never seen a woman with that much passion and desire before. This woman was beyond my expectations. I knew in that moment that she would always be mine.

I needed something to drink so I went to the refrigerator and got a bottle of water. Pouring some in a glass, I took it over to her, removed the scarf from her mouth, lifted her head and held it to her lips. She took several sips. Still I held it to her lips and she understood that she needed to drink more and drank the glassful. Then I finished what was left from the bottle.

Feeling rested and refreshed, I lay down beside her again and traced my hand over her body. Her skin was so soft and she smelled heavenly. I nestled my head in her hair, down her neck kissing her, licking her, playing and toying with her. She knew now that I only cared about her pleasure and she seemed to be more receptive to my touch. I had so much more to give to her. And she was mine to give it to.

As I touched her now her body responded faster. Her nipples got harder sooner and her skin flushed. I leaned over and kissed her lightly and she kissed me back. This was progress.

I deepened my kiss, inserting my tongue, this time with no resistance. I played in her hair and ran my hand down her cheek until I was holding her face in my hand. I wanted to look into her eyes so much. I wanted to see her passion and desire. I could feel it in her body and her kisses. Her tongue was now toying with mine. She was actually kissing me back with feelings and emotion. But would she if she knew who was giving her all this pleasure? I couldn't take that chance yet.

My hands moved along her skin, from her chest down to her thighs. She quivered at my touch. Her nipples hardened as I circled them each with my fingertips. I leaned down and licked them each, savoring her scent.

Sliding lower with my tongue I licked my way to her clitoris. It hardened quickly at my touch. Still being sensitive, she moaned as I flicked it and played with it. I licked around it, kissed and pulled on her lips with my teeth. They were still swollen and bright pink. I could still smell her essence from her precious climaxes and wanted to bring her there again.

Slowly my tongue played at her opening, inching its way in and out. She squirmed and moved trying to make me go inside her more. I licked her up and down, stopping to take her little button into my mouth and suck on it for a moment then go back down to her slit and push my tongue back inside of her. She was bouncing her hips off the bed wanting and needing more. Her hands were in fists.

Finally, she was begging. "Please, let me cum."

A smile crossed my face. I hummed across her vagina. She was so wet; she was so much in need of what only I was able to give her. I stopped, then started. Stopped, then started. Over and over again.

She was crying, pleading, begging.

"Stop, please. I can't do this anymore. Please let me cum. Please." She would beg me as I would lick her, suck on her button. Then I would stop.

"Please, fuck me. I need you to fuck me. I need to feel you inside of me." Now she was crying in earnest. Tears were soaked through the blindfold scarf and rolling down her cheeks.

Lifting my face from her I saw the tears and I knew she was totally mine. I knew that it was time to fill her with what she truly desired.

As I rose to move over her, I lifted her legs as much as possible. I moved between them and held myself before her beautiful entrance. It was so hot, wet and ready for me. She was open and waiting to receive me. I took hold of my hardness and held him to her. She moaned as she felt him start to enter her. I pushed him gently and slowly just until the head passed her inner lips. She felt so warm and wonderful. We both groaned at the same time.

I lay down over her and held her to me. We just stayed that way for a few moments. I wanted to savor the feeling of being inside of her. I wanted her to feel me. I wanted her to know that I was the one to give her what she needed. I held very still, not flinching, not moving.

He decided he had a mind of his own though. My manhood loved the warmth and wanted more. Inch by inch I slid further into her. Her muscles contracted around me, welcoming me. When I was all the way in I held still again, letting her know that I had her. She was mine.

My hips moved at a slow pace back and forth as I took her to another realm of ecstasy. I wanted each of us to enjoy this, bringing her to as many orgasms as possible. I worked my hips taking my rod in and out, in and out. Twisting it side to side…up and down. I grabbed her under her hips and lifted her so I could rub her special spot with him and soon she was moaning loudly.

"Yes. Please, do that again." she said as I took my shaft and started to go harder and deeper.

She started grunting as I felt her muscles closing around him. I knew she was going to cum. She started pumping back with me. I sped up and pumped her hard and fast. My juices were rising from my back; my sack was so tight. I was going to cum with her.

I held her butt tight as I took her hard. She was breathing as hard as I was as her breasts bounced and her skin flushed bright pink. Sweat was on our brows, mine dripping onto her chest. I pushed hard, felt her cervix open to receive my sperm. I pushed again. We both screamed as I let loose and jets of cum erupted into her. She milked me with her orgasm. Our spasms meeting, keeping each other's climaxes going. As they receded we both lay there as our bodies melted into each other. We became as one.

Time stood still. The only sound was our mixed heavy breathing. We felt the beats of our hearts from one to the other. We felt the pulse of our bodies, still bound from the inside. Neither one wanting it to end. Both feeling the enormity of what had just happened.

Leaning up onto my elbows I put my hands on each side of her face and kissed her. She kissed me back. It started as a gentle, slow kiss but moved into a hard, desperate need. My tongue licked her lips, entered her mouth and tasted and explored. She did the same to me.

My hand traveled down and played with her breast and nipple which instantly became hard. She became more and more aroused the more I played with her.

Never had my shaft not gone completely limp after I had unloaded, but it was still hard, and I started moving inside of her again. I felt like I could go on for hours pleasuring this hot, sensual woman.

"Please, let my legs free. I want them to be around you." She asked me quietly.

Pulling out, I untied her legs, crawled back up on the bed, but instead of reentering her, I flipped her over on her stomach. I lifted her up and put a pillow underneath her. Damn, she looked good. As I pulled her ass cheeks apart, I could see all of her. She was so shiny wet that I had to taste her again. I buried my tongue inside her and licked her from top to bottom, not leaving out her little hole. She moaned in pleasure.

With my soaking wet face, I rose on my knees and scooted up until my shaft was pushing on her slit. Then I entered her. She was so wet he slid right in and I buried him. My balls slapped her button and she moaned. I didn't waste any time as I started in a steady rhythm taking her from behind. I loved watching my stiff rod going in and out of her. So slick with her juices. So hot. She moaned more.

As I rocked her harder and harder, I reached from in front of her and rubbed her button. Her juices flowed more as she squeezed me. I knew she was close, so I reached up and smacked her butt cheek. She moaned, I smacked her again, a little harder. She groaned. I gave each side a few more then grabbed her hair and pulled her head back as I ground into her. She gave it back to me. She started pumping back. Her body was rocking. I wanted to cum with her, so I gave her all I had. As I pinched her nub, she screamed and came all over me and I let out a yell. "Pamela!!!!!!" I screamed her name as I came harder than I had in my whole life. I shot rope after rope into her. Five, six, seven times. It seemed like it would never stop. My leg cramped and I fell on top of her, pushing us both down onto the bed.

"Bronson?" she cried as her head went up. "Is that you?" Oh, shit. Did I really say her name? I'm fucked now. I thought. What the hell do I do now?

"Yeah. It is me." I said as I reached down and removed her blindfold. I wasn't stupid enough to untie her hands yet. I had no idea what she would do.

"What in the hell were you thinking? Why?" She was looking at me like I had two heads. Yet there was another look that I wasn't sure about. Was it lust, desire, I wasn't sure. But she didn't look mad.

"Pam, I have wanted you for years. I kept my desires to myself and never made a move on you. I respected your friendship with my wife and my marriage. But I just couldn't stop myself anymore. You are one hot and desirable woman. If you never speak to me again, I'll understand."

She didn't say anything for a very long time. She just stared at me. Then a smile started across her face.

"Would you please untie my hands? I promise I'm not going to harm you." She looked sincere.

So, I untied her and sat there for whatever was to come.

God, she was so beautiful. So sexed, satisfied, that lust filled look. Her body just gleamed.

"You know I could cause you some real trouble for this. First, you break into my room, basically kidnapping me. Then you tie me up and technically rape me. Oh, yes, you made damn sure I had my pleasures. But it is what it is babe. Then, you scream out my name in your moment of ecstasy." Then she smiled.

"To be honest, that was the best sex I have had in a very, very long time. I've wanted you for so long. But I too respected my friendship with your wife and you were off limits. So, thank you for taking the first step." She then got this look in her eye that I had no idea what she was up to.

She crawled up next to me, lay me on my back and started kissing me. She worked her way down my body until she was between my legs. Taking my already very stiff member into her hand, she licked it. Then she smacked her lips. Damn, this woman drives me crazy.

She licked me like a lollipop all over, then slid me into her mouth. She sucked and licked, sucked me deep into her mouth and back out. She was loving the control she had over me. Guess it served me right. I grabbed her hair and pushed my rod deep into her mouth and she swallowed all of me. I felt her nose on my public hair. I held her there for a moment and then let her up for air. Back down I pushed her as she took me again. I pushed my hips up and down as I had her take me. Soon I was unloading my cum deep into her throat. God, this woman was awesome! Now, she's mine!!

STRANGER IN THE NIGHT

Walking along a dark road, late at night isn't the smartest thing to do, especially if you are a young woman. Neither does it help if you are an attractive, well-built, sexy-looking woman. They say that such a combination is asking for trouble.

Did I ever listen to well-intended advice? Not usually. I was the very independent type. Being five-foot-nine, one-hundred thirty pounds, all well-proportioned, I believed I could take care of myself in any given situation. My long brown hair was always in a ponytail and my green eyes were constantly on alert to my surroundings. So what was there to be afraid of?

Finishing up my shift at the local grocery store, which I had been working at since I was eighteen, just after I graduated from high school, I figured having walked this same route for the last four years if no one had messed with me by now, no one would.

Just as I passed the house that belonged to the Adelson family, I saw someone walking on the other side of the road. They seemed to be walking rather slowly and aimlessly. Caution took over me and I walked a little faster. The person seemed to notice but went on past me. Taking a breath of relief, I slowed back down and continued toward home.

Being halfway between the Adelson's and my parent's home, there is an open field. The roadway is long and dark, but it's never bothered me before. Tonight, I have a strange feeling and there are little hairs standing up at the nape of my neck. I don't know what it is or what's bothering me, but I just have this weird feeling.

Slowly I turn around to see if anyone is watching me or following me. Maybe that creepy guy didn't keep on going when he passed me. Or maybe I'm just being paranoid. Nothing seems to be unusual though. No shadows, no noises out of the normal. Guess I'm just being jumpy tonight.

My brain couldn't stop thinking about the strange man who had passed by me. I've walked this same route for four years and never have seen anyone this late at night. Once in a while, a car might pass by but that was it. No one ever walked. Just me.

Yes, I was offered rides home from co-workers, and yes mom or dad had offered to pick me up. But I'm an adult and stubborn as hell and wanted to be on my own, so I declined all offers. I didn't own a car as I was saving enough money to move out and be on my own. Besides, it helped me unwind before I got home. Walking in the fresh air was good medicine for the mind and soul.

"Ummmppp." I tried to yell or scream as I was grabbed from behind and dragged into the field. My mouth was covered and an arm was around my waist with my body held tight against a massive hard body.

He took me down to the ground and lay on top of me. I struggled with everything I had in me until I wore myself out. He just lay there until I stopped.

"Are you done now?" The man asked.

He still had his hand over my mouth so all I could do was nod my head yes.

"Good, then listen and listen well. I'm only going to explain things once. Do you understand?" He asked as he took his other hand and rubbed it along my face.

Again I could only nod my head yes.

I tried to look into his face and eyes but it was so dark I couldn't see him very well. He had on dark clothing, but I could tell he had a beard and mustache from feeling them brush along my cheek. I couldn't see the color of his eyes.

"You are not to scream when I take my hand away from your mouth. You are to do everything I tell you to do, with no questions and without hesitation. Is that understood?" He waited for me to answer.

I nodded my head in the affirmative.

"One more thing. If you hit me, bite me, or misbehave in any way, I will punish you and you will not like what I will do to you. If you behave, this could be most pleasant for both of us. Do you understand?" He said as he slowly took his hand off my mouth. "You may answer me now." He said.

"Yeesss. Yess I do understand." I answered him..scared to death. "Good, now, I'm going to stand up and I want you to do the same, slowly." The man said as he got up off of me and got to his feet. He was tall...very tall. Must have been around six-foot-three or four. He seemed to be pretty well built too, from what I could tell.

"What are you going to do to me? Please don't hurt me, mister." I pleaded with him.

"That's another rule, no talking unless I ask you to." The man said. I nodded that I understood.

"Now, I want to see what you look like under all that clothing. We can do this the easy way or the hard way. You can make the choice. But make it quickly." He said as he stared at me.

Looking around I saw no way out of this. I knew what he wanted. Although I certainly didn't want this, there seemed to be nothing I could do but do as he asked. I'd worn the uniform I wore every day, so it wasn't anything special. Still, I needed it for work and didn't want it destroyed. So I didn't have any choice but to remove my clothing myself.

Unbuttoning my white shirt, I opened it up and slipped it off over my shoulders and down my arms till it was off. I lay it on the ground. After slipping out of my black sneakers, I then opened the button, unzipped my black slacks and lowered them down my legs, and stepped out of them. I put them with the blouse. My breathing had increased as I stood there in my underwear and socks looking at the stranger.

"Very nice, but please continue. There's more to go baby." He said with a hunger in his voice.

Reaching around I unhooked my bra and let the straps go down my arms. I was shaking so badly that I almost lost my balance. The man reached for my shoulders and held me steady and told me to remove the bra. I did as he asked.

No man had ever seen me like this. I was petrified.

He reached up and took hold of my ponytail and released the band to let my hair fall around my back and shoulders. He ran his hands and fingers through it, then let it fall.

"Your hair is so soft and beautiful. Why do you keep it up and hidden?" He asked.

"I have to wear it that way for work," I answered him.

"Well, you're not at work now and I prefer it much better like this baby." He said as he kept touching it.

The stranger took my face in both of his hands and looked at me for several seconds, then lowered his lips to mine and kissed me. Gently and tenderly. His lips were so warm and tender. He kissed me several times like that...off then on again. He ran his tongue over my lips, tasting me. It felt so good, I didn't want him to stop, but stop he did.

He stood back and looked at me again, almost in admiration. Like he'd never seen a woman before. I stood still and let him. I'd never been in this position before so I didn't know what to do. What did he want me to do?

He reached up and took both of my breasts in his big hands. His hands covered them completely. They were warm and felt good to me. He rubbed and massaged them, played with the nipples. He tweaked them, teased them. His groan was deep from his throat.

Taking a deep breath, my body started tingling, sending vibrations through it. A warmth started going down to where my panties were. I didn't know what was happening. Why was this happening?

"What are you doing to me? Why, why me?" I asked the stranger. "What did I tell you. Do Not Talk. Now I will have to punish you." He said as he got a little angry with me.

Now I got scared. What was he going to do to me? Would he hurt me now? Oh God, I don't understand this but I damn sure don't like it. I turned and tried to get away from him but that was the biggest mistake I could have made. That really fired up his anger. He grabbed me by my hair and pulled me back into his body and held me tight to him.

"Thought you could run away from me little girl? Not a chance. I'm going to have you one way or the other. But you disobeyed me and I will punish you for that. Then we will proceed into the pleasantries of lovemaking." He said without breaking a sweat or raising his voice.

What the hell? Who the hell did he think he was?

"You call rape lovemaking? I didn't agree to make love with you, you're taking what you want. That's rape!!!!" I yelled at him.

"Oh, my sweet girl. By the time we get to that part, you will be begging me for it. You will want what only I can give you, pure bliss." The stranger said with complete confidence.

"In your dreams. I'll never beg you to rape me. You're sick." I said as I fought to get away from him again.

"Oh sweetheart, you will. But before we begin that journey, let's get your punishment over with shall we?"

He grabbed me by the hair again and threw me to the ground face down. I landed so hard that I knew I'd skinned my knees and hands trying to break the fall.

I tried to raise up, but he reached down and put one hand on my back pushing me back down. Then I felt the first smack to my backside.

"Oww," I yelled as he hit me.

"That's the first one. Ready for the second?" Smack Smack Smack

"You son of a bitch..." was all I got out before another one came. Smack Smack

"You have four more to go unless you want to add more. I suggest you count them and say thank you. Ready?" he asked, still in that calm, annoying voice.

Smack

"One." Silence

"Did you forget something?"

"What?"

"What are you supposed to say after you count?" he asked.

"Thank you?"

"Correct. Now we will start over."

Smack

"One. Thank you." I said.

"Very good, you learn well." He said as he chuckled.

Smack

"Two. Thank you"

Smack

"Three. Thank you."

Smack

"Four. Thank you. May I get up now?"

"Seems you didn't learn a thing did you? DO NOT TALK!!!" Smack, Smack, Smack, Smack, Smack

Then the stranger reached down and pulled her panties aside and put his finger between her nether lips. There were soaked. She squirmed all over trying to get away from him but to no avail. He wanted her good and wet and open for him. Slowly he worked his finger into her and then hit her barrier. He stopped instantly.

"Baby. Have you never been with a man before? And tell me the truth." He asked her.

"No, and I don't want to start now," I yelled back at him as he slowly continued to use his finger inside of me.

"Well, your body says otherwise. You're very wet down here. You don't get that way unless you are enjoying what I'm doing to your body." The man stated.

"That's a lie. How can I know what I like if I've never done it before?" She knew he had to be lying.

"Baby girl, your body reacts to stimulation from what I'm doing to you. It's a natural thing that happens. It means your body wants to make love." He said, still working his finger in and out of her.

"I want no such thing. You're making it happen. Just stop, ok. I'm done with this. All I want is to go home." She cried at him.

"Oh, no honey. We're just getting started. You're going to enjoy what happens when we finally get to the good part. But since you're so new to this, I promise to be very gentle with you." The man said as he rubbed her back with his other hand.

Slowly he rolled her over onto her back without removing his finger from inside her. As his thumb moved to start rubbing her clit in little circles he reached up and started playing with her breast.

Her moans reached his ears and he smiled down at her and moved his fingers and thumb a bit more aggressively. Her moans deepened as her body started moving with him.

"What's your name, little girl?" He asked while still working with her.

She debated whether to tell him her real name or not but if he found out she lied to him she would be in more trouble so she told him. "Clara."

"Hello, Clara. My name is Mike. So nice to meet you." He said as he leaned down and pressed his lips to hers. The kiss was gentle. He kissed her again as his tongue slipped into her mouth. He worked his tongue around her mouth fully tasting her. He moved it in and out, the same as he was doing with his finger.

Clara's body started moving up and down with his movements. Her body was on fire, doing things she didn't understand but felt so good. She wrapped her arms around his neck and held him to her as she kissed him back.

Suddenly Clara realized what she was doing and dropped her hands from around his neck and tried to push him away. Mike chuckled as he continued with his fingers inside of her.

Mike was extremely engorged by this time but wanted Clara to feel what an orgasm was like and wanted to be the person to give her the first one. He also wanted to taste her juices before he took her virginity. He licked and kissed down her body until he reached her lower abdomen. He stood at her feet and slowly pulled off her socks and panties. Then got down between her legs and pushed them open to get at her sweet spot.

Clara wondered what he was doing down on his stomach as he reached his head in between her legs and touched her with his tongue right where his fingers had been.

"Oh nnnooooo. What are you doing down there? That's nasty!!" She cried trying to get away from him….

"Shhhh.. Just lay back and relax. You will enjoy this, I promise." Mike cooed to her as he pulled her toward his face.

"NOOOO…NOOO… get the hell out of there…" Clara started yelling as she tried desperately to scoot away from Mike. "Don't you dare put your tongue on me there. That's just plain nasty and disgusting. I pee out of there!"

Mike backed away as he was laughing. He didn't let her get far as he grabbed her legs and held her still.

"Clara. This is going to happen whether you want it to or not. But let me tell you something. So shut the hell up and listen to me."

Mike knew she was scared and had never had this done to her before, just by her reactions. He had a choice to make. He could either just take what he wanted or he could be patient with her and get her to understand what he was doing and get her to enjoy it. He much preferred the latter.

"Baby, I know you've never done anything like this before. I want you to enjoy this as much as I'm going to. If I thought for one minute that you were dirty and nasty, do you honestly think I would put my mouth done there? I guess your momma never taught you about the joys of sex, did she?"

He stared at her as his finger played with her nether lips. Drawing her attention back to what he wanted from her was his intention. The last thing he expected was for her to start fighting with him again.

"You are sick if you think I'm going to let you do that to me. And no, my momma never said one word about doing THAT." She said as she tried to push off of him again.

"Just what has your momma told you about sex little girl?" he asked out of curiosity. Surely she couldn't be that naive.

"That's none of your business. I didn't want any of this in the first place. You're the one who grabbed me and brought me into this field and decided I had to have sex with you against my will. So get the hell away from me and let me go." She tried with much more force to get away from him again.

"That's it. I tried to do this the nice way. I wanted you to enjoy this as much as I did But now I can see there's only one way to do this." Mike said as he tackled Clara to the ground and held her on her stomach. He reached over and grabbed her bra, pulled her arms behind her back, and tied her hands together with the bra. Standing up he found her panties. As she opened her mouth to continue screaming, he stuffed her mouth with them.

Kneeling down beside her, he let her wear out her frustration. When she quieted down he moved her hair away from her face. Looking into her eyes Mike smiled and said, "Now that I have you where I want you, shall we commence on what I started to begin with?"

He couldn't decide whether to roll her over or just leave her laying like she was. Either way, he would be able to accomplish his goal. Mike wanted to show her that despite her denial she could learn to have pleasure by receiving his mouth upon her lips. Her lower lips that is.

First, she needed to know that her behavior wasn't acceptable. He reached down and sat her up. She had this notion that oral sex was totally disgusting and nasty. Well, he would show her otherwise, just not how she expected. Not yet anyway.

"If I take your panties out of your mouth, will you stop screaming?" Mike asked her.

Clara nodded her head yes.

He reached down and took them out of her mouth. He paced in front of her for a couple of minutes and let her wonder what he would do next. Her eyes followed him as he moved.

He walked over to her and knelt down in front of her. Looking into her face he again noticed how beautiful she was. The clouds had moved and let in enough moonlight to show her to him. He loved looking at her. But time was moving on and he wanted pleasure from her.

"Since you haven't been taught the pleasures between a man and a woman, I'm going to show you. I'm going to show you that there is nothing nasty or disgusting about pleasing your partner with your mouth." Clara shivered as he spoke.

Mike stood up and pulled his hoodie up over his neck and off of his body. Clara knew he was strong but MY GOD. This man was built. He had tight abs and big biceps. His shoulders were broad and he looks strong as hell. But she already knew that the way he manhandled her. He reached down and untied and kicked off his sneakers and took off his socks. Unbuckling his belt he slid it through the loops until it came loose from his jeans. He dropped it to the ground. As his eyes watched Clara, he unbuttoned and unzipped his jeans. Hooking his fingers in the waistband he pulled them down over his hips and lower to his knees. He stopped for a moment to let her see the bulge in his skivvies.

Clara's eyes grew as she watched him lower his jeans. What showed in his underwear seemed to be bigger than it felt when it was rubbing up against her earlier. 'Lord, Lord. This man is huge all over,' she thought to herself. 'What the hell am I supposed to do with that?'

After taking his jeans completely off he stepped up to Clara. His hand went to her cheek but she flinched away from him. She was scared of what he was going to do to her.

"Babe, look at me." He said sternly.

Clara looked up to him as he stepped even closer. His loins were right near her face. She trembled harder now.

"Don't be scared, little girl. This won't hurt you." He said as he grabbed his package through his skivvies. "It will give you so much pleasure if you will let it. But you have to learn to trust me. Let me teach you. Obviously, your parents haven't." He said as he reached out and untied her hands.

Mike took her right hand in his left and held it for a moment. "How old are you baby?" he asked her as he slowly led her hand towards himself.

"I'm twenty-two. What difference does that make?" She asked as she kept trying to pull her hand back but he wouldn't let her.

"It's just hard to believe that in this day and age that you don't know a thing about sex, that's all. But we're going to change that right here and now. You have so much to learn. Sadly we can't do it all tonight, but we'll do the best we can." Mike said as he pried her fingers open to put her flat palm against him.

"Feel that honey. It's nice and warm. Soft. Yeah, it gets hard but that's because of you." He watched as she looked up at him like he was stupid.

"How the hell is it because of me? I haven't done anything to you." She asked.

"It's because you are a very beautiful and sexy woman sweetheart. When a man gets turned on, his meat gets hard. It means he wants her... you." He smiled down at her.

This wasn't exactly what he'd had in mind when he had grabbed her and led her into the field. He'd wanted to grab a quick piece of ass and get the hell out of there. He only cared about his pleasure. He didn't give a rips ass about her or whether or not she enjoyed it. Usually.

But when he saw how scared she was. How she had no idea what was about to happen to her, he just couldn't be that cruel. Now he wanted to be the one who gave her the best pleasure she could know. Could ever have in her young life. Hell, why should he care? Why should it matter? He had no idea, it just did.

Mike wrapped her fingers around his shaft along with his and slowly started an up and down movement. Her eyes got bigger as she felt him start to swell in her hand. He seethed through his teeth from the feeling going through him. Her eyes fell from his as she looked down to where her hand was.

Clara felt him guide her hand as he held her hand tighter around him. Up and down their hands went. She felt the wetness at the top of the head, wetting his underwear.

"Did you just pee in my hand? EWE!!!" Clara cried as she tried to move her hand off of him.

"No baby, that isn't pee. That's called precum. It happens when a man gets turned on. It's lubrication to help when having sex." He explained to her.

Pondering this, she went there again, feeling more. Mike let out a groan this time and she jumped, thinking she had hurt him. He chuckled but let her move away.

"See darlin', that's what happens when you touch him. He likes it…a lot." He was grinning at her.

Kneeling down in front of her, he kissed her lightly, then more passionately. Leaving her lips he kissed down her neck, to her breast, taking the right one in his mouth. God, she tasted so good. He laved one and then the other and back again. Laying her down onto her back, he half-covered her with his near-naked body relishing in the feeling of her skin on his. She was so soft and warm.

Kissing and licking his way down over her abdomen, circling around her belly button, he stopped at the top of her mound. Mike looked up to see her looking down at him.

Clara watched as Mike worked his way down her body. She really wanted to trust him to know what he was doing, but she was scared at the same time. What if he hurt her? What if all he wanted was to do that thing with his tongue again? Could she let him do it this time?

"Little girl, have you ever touched yourself down there? Have you ever made yourself feel good?" He needed to know just how much she knew about her own body.

"Nnnooooo…I never have except to bathe myself. My momma said that good girls don't do that. Only their husbands touch them there." She explained as she turned her head away from my gaze.

After taking a deep breath Mike started moving his index finger down toward her inner mound, running his fingers through her hair.

"Okay, let me explain this to you. I'm not going to hurt you in any way. I'm going to give you the best pleasure a woman can ever know. It's called a climax or orgasm. It makes a woman wet from inside her vagina to the outside of her succulent lips. Her moisture tastes awesome to most men. They crave a woman's smell and taste. I know I do. You will learn to crave this too. All I ask is that you lay back, relax and let me give this to you."

Without waiting for an acknowledgment he scooted down between her legs and pushed them open wide.

"Wait. Does that mean you're going to use your mouth down there again?" she asked.

"Yeah, honey I am." And he dove his head in.

Mike kissed and licked her slowly at first. He wanted her to get used to the feeling. Little whimpers soon turned into light moans. She seemed to be getting into the idea.

'Well, this does feel kinda good. I still think it's nasty though." Clara thought to herself.

Just as she thought that Mike put a little more pressure on her clit, which had started to get a bit harder. The little nub was trying to peek out of its hood and he was more than willing to help it get out. Her hips started moving as he was building up a rhythm with his tongue.

Louder moans escaped her lips as she was enjoying his tongue and mouth upon her. 'What the hell is he doing to me. Whatever it is, I'm starting to like this…a lot.' Clara was now starting to mumble.

Harder and harder, faster and faster his tongue moved over her lips and clit as her hips moved more. He reached over her legs and held her still on her stomach with one hand as he slipped a finger into her with the other. She gasped. Her hips rose off the ground. His finger went deeper and he felt her squeeze it. He knew she was close. He also felt her barrier. He knew for sure she was pure. He was indeed her first.

Mike was trying to make a decision in his mind. He'd started out only wanting a fast piece of ass. Now he was here teaching this young lady the facts of life. And he actually was enjoying it. Who'd have thought? But where was he going to go from here? He knew he was going to break her in, but then what? Was he just going to walk away?

Shaking those thoughts away, he continued to take her higher with his tongue and finger, working both in rhythm toward what he knew would be her first orgasm.

Clara's body shook with feelings she'd never experienced before. Something was going on in her lower region that felt hot, quivering, and overwhelming. The more Mike licked her the more she wanted. The more his finger moved inside of her the more she needed. The harder he pumped her the closer she felt like she would burst at the seams. Then she felt him touch something inside of her and she let out a howl.

"That's it, girl. Let it go. Give me all of your hot juice. I love the taste of you coming on my mouth and finger." He coaxed her.

'What the hell is he talking about?' Clara thought as she started to calm down. She didn't know what had just happened…but she did feel very wet down there.

"How can I taste good when that's where I pee from…and did I just pee in your mouth? I'm so wet." She asked him as her face turned a shade of red.

"Baby girl. You just had an orgasm. That's what happens when your body responds to sexual desire. When you do, your vagina expels liquid, not pee. It lubricates you. Just like I do from my rod." Mike took his finger and covered it with her wetness and rose to put it on her lips.

Quickly she turned her head away as he reached to touch her. "Taste yourself. It's not harmful. You might just like it." Mike encouraged her.

Timidly she touched her tongue to his finger and took a tiny taste. She grimaced. Mike rubbed his finger over her lips and toyed with them enough to work his finger into her mouth.

"Suck on my finger love." He said as he watched her fight with herself.

"See, it isn't that bad, is it? And it don't taste like pee." He said as he grinned at her.

Sliding back down between her legs he went back to work, sucking her clit back into his mouth. This time he had no mercy on her as he went for the kill. Mike slid one finger back into her to get her nice and wet, then slid a second one in, preparing her for his large, stiff, hard rod. He was more than ready to make her into a woman.

Working her up to another orgasm didn't take long and her hips worked along with his fingers and mouth. She was riding his face as he got her to the point of going over the edge. Then he backed off a little. He wanted to hear her beg him. He wanted to hear her ask him for what she wanted. He knew this was all new to her but he needed to know that she needed this as much as he wanted to give it to her.

'Ohhhh..please don't stop…it feels so good." Clara said as she rolled her head from side to side and pushed her hips up higher. She wanted to feel as good as he made her feel the first time.

Mike raised his head, seeing her distress. "What do you want little girl?"

"Please, make me feel like you did before. I liked it. Do it again.. please!!" Clara cried.

"Oh, you liked it did you? Well, let's see if we can do that then." Mike smiled up at her. But she didn't see as her eyes were closed.

Mike went back down to her clit and licked it hard as he turned his fingers over and hit her G-spot. Clara jumped, raising her hips, almost smashing his nose. He held her tighter with his hand on her stomach and bit her clit hard.

"OHHHHHHHHH....OH MY GOD.AYYYAAA"

Clara screamed into the night air as she came harder than before. It kept going and going as Mike kept the pressure going in and out of her.

Clara wreathed around on the ground as she came and came all over Mike's mouth and hand.

He gently coaxed her down and then held her body until she stilled. By this time he was rock solid hard. So hard that he was in pain. He wanted her as he had never wanted a woman before. Realizing that the ground was going to hurt her when he entered her, he reached over and put his hoodie underneath her bottom. He stood and removed his skivvies then knelt back down between her legs once more.

Clara had opened her eyes just as Mike had removed his underwear and her eyes grew huge.

'Please God, don't let him try to put that thing inside of me. It's Huge!!!' she thought to herself.

Mike started working his boner up and down her slick lips, getting her and himself wet enough for him to enter her. He wanted to cause her the least amount of pain necessary.

"Baby, look at me. I want you to watch as I put myself into you. This might hurt for a bit, but then you are going to enjoy me being inside of you. Do you understand? Are you ready?" He asked her as he started to inch his way in.

Clara looked at him in bewilderment as he kept pushing in. Little by little he worked his way in, stretching her until he reached her barrier. Then he stopped.

"You doing ok love?" he asked as he reached up and massaged her breast. Then he pinched her nipple. Clara let out a gasp.

"This is the hard part babe. I'm going to break through your barrier then you will be a woman. You will be my woman." Did I just say that he thought?

Grabbing her legs and holding them up Mike reared back, after pulling out some, and pushed into her as hard and fast as he could. A second later he heard her scream and tears were running down her face. He stilled, leaned over, and held her body tightly to his.

"Shhhh, it's ok love, I have you. The pain will stop in just a minute. Your body will get used to me being inside of you. When I move in you again, the pain will turn into pleasure like you've never known my sweet girl." Mike held her for a few seconds longer till her whimpering quieted.

Very slowly he started to move and rotate his hips. Back a little and in a little, then a bit further. Clara groaned as he worked her until he heard those groans turn into moans. He did this until he was able to go almost all the way out and then slide back in. He took it slow and easy for quite a few strokes, then increased his speed. Gradually he got into a rhythm, put his hands under her bottom, and filled her with his rod to the hilt. Back out and back in again...over and over again. Tilting his hips he hit her G-spot and she moaned louder. He knew he could make her cum and was trying to get her there before he came.

Reaching between them he massaged her clit, lightly at first as he pumped into her. As he increased his speed, so did his finger. Clara was moaning louder, her head moving constantly from side to side. He could feel her muscles inside tighten and knew she was very close. He took two fingers and pinched her clit and she exploded. She gripped his pecker with her inner muscles, squeezing him as she came all over him. Mike removed his hand from between them, He lay over her and increased his speed going in and out of her. He was so close. He took her mouth in his, his tongue into her mouth, and kissed her fervently. He fucked her mouth as he fucked her love hole. He raised his head and howled at the sky as he let loose with all he had stored up inside his sack.

Rope after rope of his seed filled her.

Clara felt as Mike got faster and faster, his rod getting bigger...if that was even possible and felt when he stiffened and let his seed fill her.

He lay there, arms held so as not to hurt her with his weight and caught his breath. Then leaned down and kissed her slowly and passionately.

Thinking to himself, 'I've had a lot of sex, but this has to be the best I've ever had.'

Rolling over onto his back, he pulled Clara with him so she was tucked into his arm, her head on his chest. He played with her soft pretty hair with his fingertips. For once he felt content, satisfied, didn't want to be away from her.

"Clara, I need to talk to you. Will you hear me out before you say anything, please?" He asked as he leaned his head over and kissed her on her forehead.

She nodded her head that she would.

"I have not been a nice guy. Correct that. I'm not a nice guy. I usually go out looking for a woman I can take, rape, make have sex with me. I don't want to hurt them but I will if they don't give me what I want. I've been doing it for quite a while." He could feel her stiffen in his arm.

"That was my intention with you tonight. I saw you walking. When I went past you I thought to myself, she looks hot. Why not. Just another piece of ass I get quickly and get the hell away."

Mike takes a deep breath, kisses her again on the forehead, and continues.

"That's how it started out to be with you. That's all I wanted from you. But I saw how scared you were. Then I realized that you knew absolutely nothing about sex. I was amazed and shocked, to say the least. But I was also honored that I would be the one to teach you. It did something inside of me. I wanted to be the one who gave you that pleasure. I wanted to see the way you came and how you looked. I wanted to be the first man to ever be inside of you. It meant something to me."

Mike stopped again and sat up, having her sit up with him. He took her hands in his and held them. He looked at her and smiled as he saw the contented, soft look on her face.

"I loved how it felt when you came with me inside of you. Damn woman, it felt so amazing. I guess I never gave a shit before, so I never took the time to really feel it. Now that I know, I want that feeling again and again and again. I loved how it felt to cum inside of you. You are so warm, soft, and tight. God, if you only knew."

Clara was staring at him. She didn't know what to think. Yes, he had opened up a whole new world for her. She couldn't imagine why he picked her to change how he behaved. How he made love. What he made her feel was so good...no it was awesome. And she wanted to feel it again. But with him?? She just didn't know.

"I need to get home. My parents must be worried sick about me. I should have been home a long time ago." Clara stated...not knowing what else to say to him.

"Clara, wait. I know it's my fault you're late. But I promise I'll make it up to you."

"And how do you plan on doing that?" Asked Clara as she started to get up to get dressed.

"Let me take you out. Let me prove to you that I can be a good guy for you. I want so much to see you again. I want to be with you again." Mike was close to begging her as he was trying to get back into his clothes too.

"Hum...well. I don't know. You did kidnap me and drag me here. You did have bad intentions from the start. But I'm so glad that you changed your mind and took good care of me. Let me think it over for a day or two and I'll let you know. Please? This is a lot for one girl to digest." Clara needed time to deal with this.

"Sure. We can do that. Just please, don't make me sweat too long. I really do like you." Mike kissed her again and started to walk her back to the road.

"Wait, how will I know what you've decided?" Mike asked.

"Be here in the field two days from now. On my way home from work I'll either keep walking or I'll turn and walk into the field and join you." She answered back.

On the designated night Mike went to the field and waited and waited and waited. Just as he was about to leave he saw Clara walking. Maybe she had to work late tonight. His hopes were high but he stayed rooted to the spot they had agreed on. He kept his eyes on her as she started to approach the area he was in. She kept her head looking straight ahead. She didn't even glance toward the field. Mike started to panic.

As she got to the spot on the side of the road, she stopped, bent down, and acted like she was tying her shoe. Then she glanced over at him, stood up, and started walking again. His heart broke.

"Well, are you going to stand there all night or are you coming with me?" Clara asked him as she kept walking.

'What the fuck??' Mike asked himself as he ran after her.

"Okay, I'll bite. What are we doing?" Mike asked after he'd caught up to her.

"Oh, I thought it might be nice to be a little bit more comfortable rather than that itchy grass and dirt," Clara said with a smirk on her face.

Mike wasn't going to complain about that but still wasn't sure where she was taking him.

A mile down the road they turned down a long driveway and walked up to a huge farmhouse with a wraparound porch.

With the light coming from above the door, Clara could finally see the face of her lover. But she wanted to see more, so she reached up and pulled his hoodie back from his face and over his head. He had reddish-brown hair that hung down below his ears and over his forehead.

It was thick and she ran her fingers through it. His skin appeared to be an olive color and his eyes were a bright emerald green. God, she loved his eyes.

"You'll have to be quiet. My parents are sleeping. We're going up to my room." Clara said as she led him into the house.

"Are you sure this is ok? I don't want you to get into any trouble with them." Mike wasn't too sure about this but it did beat being out in the field.

"Yes, it's cool. I told my parents I have a boyfriend and I wanted to bring him home to meet them. So, they'll meet you in the morning." Clara said matter of factly.

Just as they were getting ready to climb up the stairs, her parents walked out of their bedroom.

"Clara is this your boyfriend?" her father asked her.

"Yes sir. This is Mike. Mike, this is my father Anthony Genovese." She said with a grin.

Mike went pale as a ghost. He knew of them and their family. They were one of the biggest mob families in the area. And here he stood in their home dressed in a hoodie, jeans, and boots. He must be making a great first impression.

"Well, son, nice to meet you. Since you took it upon yourself to already have sex with my daughter, when is the wedding?" My dad asked. "Well sir, we actually haven't discussed it. Yet." I answered as the sweat was running off my forehead.

"Then I suggest you set the date soon. See you two in the morning." Dad went back to his bedroom, mom right behind him. After we got in her bedroom I unleashed on her.

"You never told me you were the daughter of a mob boss. What the hell? Now he says I have to marry you? Oh My God. What have I gotten into?" Mike was panicking now.

"Well. You didn't ask me if I was a mob boss's daughter. You just wanted to rape me. Although you did change your mind about that and it was good. But when I told papa what happened he went ballistic. And now you know the rest. He told me I had to bring you here." Clara was totally unfazed by the whole thing.

Now Mike was in a panic like he'd never known. What the hell had he gotten himself into? Here he was in the house of a mobster with his daughter, whom he had taken her virginity. Fathers don't look down lightly on that shit. What was he going to do now?

When they got into Clara's room they lay on the bed and talked. While talking he lightly rubbed her arm and her skin felt as good as it had that night in the field. Within a few minutes, they were completely unclothed. Seeing her in the light, he appreciated her more. She was beautiful. Her raven hair, her lean and slightly tanned body. But her eyes were her best asset. She smothered him with the look she gave him with those big brown orbs.

They explored each other's bodies: her admiring his hairy chest, muscular abs, his large biceps, his tight and strong thighs. Mike played with her breasts, suckled each one until her nipples were hard. He fingered her and teased her clit.

"Please make me feel as good as you did the other night Mike," Clara asked as she reached down and touched him.

"Baby I will but there's something I want you to do for me first. You know how I kissed and licked you down here." He said as he touched her nether part.

"Well, I want you to kiss and lick what you're holding in your hand right now. It would feel just as good as I made you feel." He waited for her to see what she would do.

Clara's eyes got big as she looked down at him. It was the first time she had seen him and he wasn't small. He had a big prick. It must have been at least eight to nine inches long and it was wide with bulging veins. 'God,' she thought. 'I know he fit inside of me down below. But will that fit into my mouth? And will it taste nasty? He pees from there.' After debating for a minute, she sat up and leaned over him and stuck her tongue out, and took a lick. Then she took a couple more.

"That's it, baby. Lick all around it. Make it good and wet then put your lips over it. Damn that feels so good." Mike was enjoying her tongue as she was slowly getting the hang of it.

Getting a little more daring, Clara started licking and playing around the head of his penis and then decided it was time to wrap her lips around the crown. As she did so Mike let out a groan. At first, she thought she had hurt him, but he reached up and held her head gently and pushed her down so she would take a little bit more.

"Yeah, honey...I love how you're doing that. Damn your mouth feels so damn good. Keep doing that. Roll your tongue around...that's it."

Taking a deep breath Clara tried to go a little bit deeper. She gagged and backed up. Then tried again.

"Take it, slow baby. You'll get there. No rush. Take it as you can. I'm loving what you are doing." Mike wanted to give her all the encouragement he could. She was doing an awesome job for her first time.

"Wrap your hand around me and move it up and down at the same time you are going up and down with your mouth. That's it...like that. Yeah...oh "God yes."

Clara started to taste something different than her own spit and realized that was what she had seen on his underwear. So that was what he had been talking about. It tasted good.

"Okay baby, now speed up some...go faster with your hand and your mouth. You're getting the hang of this well. When I cum it will shoot out of my hole there. But it isn't pee. It's my seed. It's what helps make babies. I want you to try to swallow it, ok.?"

Clara pulled off of him and stared at him. He had to be kidding, right. He was going to shoot stuff into her mouth. Then he wanted her to swallow it!!!!!

She started to shake her head no. She couldn't do this. It wasn't right. "Clara, stop and listen to me. When I was down on you I made you cum. I took your juices from you and drank them. They were good. I made you taste yourself. Well, I need you to do the same thing for me. It won't taste exactly the same, maybe a little salty, but I really need this baby. At least try for me. Please."

Slowly she nodded her head and took him back into her mouth. He had softened some so she had to work and got him hard again. He took her head in his hands and guided her as she moved up and down and worked her tongue along his shaft. Over and over, up and down. He was so close now. He wanted to come but didn't want to scare her. "I'm close baby, I'm going to come very soon. Stay with me.

Keep sucking…hard. Take as much of me in as you can. Work your hand up and down..fast. Go baby…oh yeah..come on honey…you got me....yeah...yeah...ooohhhh....yeah....CLARA AAAAAhhhhhhhhhhh.."

He gripped her head and raised his hips as he shot rope after rope into her mouth. She tried to pull up but he held her tight.

"Swallow babe..swallow fast."

And she did…once…twice…three times. Mike pulled back and let some shoot onto her tongue and held her still. She could taste him. He pulled out, pulled her down to him and kissed her, put his tongue into her mouth, and tasted them together. Glorious!!

"Clara baby. You are so hot. And a fast learner. You did an awesome blowjob for the very first time. I loved it. Thank you." Mike said as he held her close.

"I'm glad. Now it's my turn?" she asked him.

"Yeah, baby. Just give me a minute to recoup. That takes a lot out of a man.

"How…I did all the work?" Little did she understand the workings, but she would learn. Such innocence. Oh to be that way again Mike thought.

They made love several times that night and in the morning they went down to the kitchen for breakfast, which was a ritual in her household.

"Well, seems you survived the night with my daughter." Her father said as a greeting when they entered the kitchen.

"Yes sir." Answered Mike as he took the chair he was shown to sit in.

"Normally I would ask you what your intentions are toward Clara, but I think I already have a pretty good idea from the sounds coming from her room all night." Both Clara and Mike looked at each other meekly.

"So all I'm going to say to you is this. Don't you even think about hurting my little girl. If you do, I will find you. Is that understood?" Her father looked at Mike sternly.

"Yes sir, perfectly," Mike answered him.

"Daddy, thank you. May we be excused from the table? I have to get ready to go to work." Clara asked her father.

"Sure baby. And don't be too late getting home unless you phone and let us know. I'll still worry about you, ya know." He said as they rose from the table.

Mike rose and shook her father's hand. When they had left the house and were walking toward her work, Mike stopped.

"So where do we go from here? What do you want out of this?" He was scared to ask and really wasn't too sure what he actually wanted either.

"Mike, I love what we are doing, but I'm not going to force you to do anything. Why don't we date for a while and see if this is what we both want? We don't really know much about each other, do we?

"No, but I do know I like being with you. Sex isn't everything though. But damn it sure is good with you." He said with a smirky grin. They dated for seven months, and during that time they spent most nights either at her house or his apartment. They found that they liked most of the same things and their interests were similar for future endeavors.

Ten months later they announced their engagement and had a lavish wedding at her parents' home.

Twelve months later their little girl arrived into the world. "Mike. How do we tell our little girl that our love started as a rape, that turned into love? How do we tell her to watch out for strangers in the night?

SWEET MOUNTAIN LOVING

Somewhere in the mountains of Colorado there was a cabin that housed a family of eight. There was the mom and pop, three daughters and three sons. The kids ranged in age from twenty to six. One of the daughters, being the oldest, had the most responsibility in helping her mother with running the household.

She had been helping her mother for so many years, she felt like she was a mother herself. All except for the pleasurable parts, which she had heard many times at night when her parents had gone to bed.

She knew what they were doing, as she had seen the animals perform, and after a time there had been an offspring. So, it made sense that her mom and pop had to be doing the same thing for that to happen. After all, she had seen her last two siblings being born. But Lord have mercy. She had watched her mother suffer so much baring those children, she didn't know if it was worth all that much pain coming from all that much enjoyment.

Yet, every time she heard them; she had this feeling down in her region where she tinkled that made her feel funny. And whenever she touched it, it made her jump with fright. Oh, what was she supposed to do?

Her brother, who was a year younger than her, had tried many times to see her without her clothes on but her mom or pop always chased him away. So she was very careful whenever he was around.

One day, it was so hot out that she needed a way to cool off. Water was scarce, as there hadn't been much rain and it was used for cooking, bathing and the animals. None was wasted. All she wanted was to take the edge off.

She couldn't strip down. It wouldn't be proper. Her brothers had roving eyes. Pop had told her that a woman kept herself covered except when she was with her man. Well, there were no men around in these parts for her to even be with. And Lord knows, she knew nothing about even being with a man. Only what she heard at night.

She decided to take a walk into the woods to the cooler, shaded parts of the mountain. She knew not to venture too far because of the wild animals and varmints. Lord have mercy, all she needed was to meet up with a bear or a mountain lion.

As she wandered up the path, winding her way beside the large rocks, she spotted a hidden place that she thought no one could see her. She climbed up and sat there for a few minutes. No sun had hit the rock and it felt cool to her hand. She wondered how cool it would feel against her hot skin. She lifted her skirt and placed her legs against it.

Oh, what relief she felt. It felt like her body temperature went down ten degrees. She sat there a few minutes until she started feeling warmer again. She lifted her dress skirt a little higher and moved over to another part of the rock. Coolness. Again, she sat there and enjoyed the relief.

She could tell the sun was starting to go down, as it was getting darker in the forest, so she headed home. But now she had found a way to cool herself down on these hot days and promised herself that she would return.

For the next couple of days there was so much housework to do and things to do for her siblings, that she was kept very busy. But on the third day, the heat was overbearing. She couldn't take it anymore. She told her mom that she needed to take a break and a short walk.

Going the same way she had gone a few days before; she followed the path up the mountainside. Finding her hiding spot, she once again raised her skirt and sat upon the cool rock and immediately felt the relief. Wanting to feel even more, she raised her dress up past her bum and sat back down. She was in heaven.

She sat there for a long time, watching nature at its best and reveling in the quiet. The coolness of the rock was relieving her body and she was content. She soon sensed the darkness coming and headed back for home.

Little did she know that on her little excursions, a woodsman, who had been traveling through, had seen her. He had seen her beauty and watched her while she sat upon the rock. Then he watched her leave. He followed her to see where she went. He wondered if she was coming back to the rock and how often.

He saw as she had lifted her skirt up her legs. They were long and slim. Then the second time, she had lifted her shirt all the way up and over her bum. He felt a rise in his britches. Oh, dear God. This woman was gorgeous. But who was she? Why does she hide on these rocks? He had to know more about her. He wanted to know more about her. He wanted her.

These hot days were getting to be worse and she wanted to get to her hideaway more and more often, but the household chores kept her from going every day. Today, she was going to make a point of getting away and go. She could almost hear the rocks calling her. The coolness beckoned to her. Yes, she was going somehow.

The woodsman had been there every day for the last three days. Still the beautiful woman had not been there. Why? Was he chasing a dream? Was he wasting his time on something he couldn't have? As he was about to get up and leave he heard a noise coming up the path.

There she was, in a light blue dress, her brown hair put up tight on top of her head. But her face was of such beauty. Large eyes, like a doe, a petite little nose and a mouth with light pink lips. Her cheeks were a little rosy, probably from the heat.

He watched her walk with ease to the rocks and sit down. Again, she lifted her skirt all the way up above her bum and sat down. He saw the relief wash across her face. As he watched her, he felt the tightening in his groin. He groaned in silence, not wanting to alert her that he was there.

Never once though did her skirt go above the middle of her thighs. Oh, how he would love to see more of her legs. But what she did next took his breath away.

She loved the relief that the coolness of the rocks gave her. There was a slight breeze today and she loved it blowing through the trees. She reached up and took out the band from her hair and let it blow free. It felt so good. But still she was so warm. She reached up and unbuttoned her dress front, all the way down and let it come open. She had never bothered with a slip, being in the mountains, so only her brazier showed. The coolness of the breeze felt wonderful on her chest. She put her hands behind her and stretched out...pushing her chest out and into the air.

The woodsman's breath caught and he held it. He didn't blink. He didn't move a muscle. His erection went from a tightening to a complete firmness in his britches. He was in awe.

He had lost his young wife and child ten years ago, during childbirth and had been a lonely man ever since. But to see this gift from heaven presented for his eyes to behold was breathtaking. He knew in his heart she was a gift from God and that she was meant to be his.

Just then, there was a noise in close proximity of the young woman and his eyes moved in time to see the mountain lion perched above her. He held his breath. He knew he couldn't reach her in time to save her and he didn't have a good enough shot to hit it and kill it. He also knew if she moved she would be done for.

Stealthily, he moved to the side opposite of where she was sitting. If he could avert the lion's attention, maybe she would forget about the woman. It worked. The lion watched him as he moved. But she didn't budge. She sat there listening. Watching.

The woman on the rock knew it was time for her to head back home and sat up to button up the top of her dress. She pulled her hair back up and stood to pull her dress back down. She had no idea that she was being watched by a woodsman and a mountain lion.

The woodsman watched both the woman and the mountain lion as she worked her way down the path. Both followed her, but neither blocked her way. Then they both turned and went their own ways. A catastrophe had been averted.

The woodsman knew that somehow he would meet this woman. He had waited a long time for God to send him another mate and he believed with all his heart that this was whom he was meant to be with. Time and patience is what he needed.

So, the woodsman began to watch from the edge of the forest hoping to get a glimpse of her every day. He saw her as she did the laundry outside and hung it up to dry. He watched her as she fed the chickens and chased after her little brothers and sisters. He saw that she was a good and gentle woman but also worked hard and was strong.

On her next trip to the rocks the woodsman had hidden a little closer so he could get a better look. He wanted to see her much closer. He wanted to reach out and touch her, but he didn't want to scare her. She sat upon the rock as usual and did her normal routine. Once settled, she relaxed to enjoy the breeze and the coolness of the rocks. She thought she heard a sound and looked around but saw nothing. She settled back down. Again, she heard something, sat up and looked around. Nothing. But she stayed sitting up. Her hearing was keen and she listened. Then she saw him.

The woodsman had stayed squatted down a short distance from her, watching her. She was so beautiful it took his breath away. She made him hard with want. His heart deepened with desire. He knew she saw him but he didn't, couldn't move.

She took a deep breath. A man. "Oh Lord. What do I do?? He's looking at me. I have half my clothes off and he's looking at me." she thought to herself. She reached to start buttoning up her dress top and she heard him speak.

"Don't....please." the woodsman whispered.

She stopped. Her hands froze. She looked at him. She didn't know what to do.

"Just let me look at you. You are so beautiful. Like an angel that God has sent." he said quietly, not wanting to scare her.

The woodsman moved a little bit closer and looked at her. She didn't move. She just watched him. She didn't seem afraid, so he moved a little bit closer still.

She watched him with interest. He seemed quite a bit older than her, but he didn't seem to want to hurt her. What did he want then? Why was he looking at her like that?

"Hello, my name is David. I don't want to hurt you or scare you. I saw you sitting here and saw how beautiful you are. Do you mind if I sit with you?" David had to move very slowly with her.

"No, I don't mind. My name is Charla." she answered him. "Well, hello Charla. It is so nice to meet you." he said to her.

"I really have to go back to my home now." Charla started to get up from the rock.

"Can't you stay and talk with me for just a minute more?" David asked her.

"No, I really have to get home. I have to help my mother." Charla got up, fastening her dress as she did.

"Well, okay, if you have to. Can I meet you again here and we can talk some more? I'd like to get to know you more. I like you a lot." David said.

"Yes, I'd like that. Maybe tomorrow if I can get away." Charla told the woodsman.

"Okay, I'll be here waiting for you. Let me walk you down the path to the edge of the forest, please." said David.

"Thank you, that would be very nice." Charla started down the path toward home.

That evening she thought about the woodsman. He was tall, taller than her pop. He had the same brown hair as hers and had brown eyes. His skin was tanned and a little rough, like he spent a lot of time outside. She liked him and looked forward to seeing him again tomorrow. They met several times at the rock on the mountainside and got to know each other a little bit. Their friendship grew and she began to feel more and more at ease with him. Then he didn't come for a few days.

She wondered what had happened to him.

During the time they had been meeting she hadn't been doing her usual cooling off. She had been too interested in getting to know the woodsman. So, he decided to give her some space and see what she would do.

Today, she went to the mountain and to her usual rock. He wasn't there again. She waited for a while. Still not. So, she lifted her dress, only this time she took it off. It was stifling hot and she needed some serious relief. Since the woodsman wasn't around she felt she was safe. Being in her undies was okay. So, she laid back and relaxed.

The woodsman was watching. The tent in his pants was straining his self-will to remain where he was. His will didn't last long. Slowly he crept forward. Closer and closer he moved until he was an arm's length away.

He watched her as she slept. She was gorgeous. Her slim little body was the most precious thing he had seen in many years. He wanted to possess it...to have her. He needed her. He would have her.

Slowly her eyes opened and she saw the woodsman watching her. She smiled up at him. She wasn't afraid. He reached out his hand and touched her cheek. He leaned over and touched his lips to hers. It was like a lightning strike. Magic. The sparks flew between them. His lips kissed her more...and deeper. She kissed him back. Deeper.

She didn't know what was happening, but she liked it. It felt so good. It felt so right. He held her face as he kissed her and his tongue touched her lips. Her eyes popped open and she looked at him. He smiled on her lips. And he kissed her with his tongue probing her mouth. She opened to him. She didn't understand it.. but she liked it. She wrapped her arms around his neck and kissed him back, her tongue meeting his and they danced together. Tongue against tongue… playing and tasting. Loving each other.

Abruptly she stopped. The sun was starting to set and she knew she had to start for home. Charla looked into the woodsman's eyes and smiled.

"God, this woman was so sexy when she smiled at him like that." David thought to himself as he returned her smile. His lips twitched. He started to pull her back into his embrace to taste her again but she held him at bay. He studied her face.

"I'm sorry, but I have to head back. I enjoyed what you made my lips feel. It was wonderful. We must do that again David." Her face flushed as she smiled at him again.

David stood and pulled her to stand with him on the large rock. As much as he wanted to stand there and just hold her in his arms, smother her in kisses repeatedly, he knew he had to let her leave. Charla grabbed her dress and put it back on. The woodsman took her by the hand and led her down the path to the clearing.

Before he could let her leave him, he took her in his arms. Putting his right forefinger under her chin he lifted her head until her eyes looked into his. He saw the light, then the fire smoldering in them.

Heat was rising as he lowered his head to take her lips with his and he kissed her. Her lips were still warm and wet from their previous kisses. Swollen from their wanting of each other. Tongues collided in a heat of passion like he had never known. Her taste was branded in his mouth and he wanted more.

Heat was not only rising on his lips. His whole body was on fire. His loins were burning with desire. As he held her in his arms, he knew she could feel him as he rose in need of her. He felt her stir in his arms. He knew her desire was just as driven as his. Should he stoke it more or let her leave as he knew she needed to? Dilemmas… they we killing him.

But the woodsman knew she needed to return to her family before it got too late. Reluctantly, he pulled away from her. He looked deep into her eyes and saw the passion in them. Charla turned her head and looked in the direction of her home. Yes, he understood. He took her chin in his hand and turned her head back to him.

"I know you have to go. I don't want to let you, but I know. Please, come back to me." He spoke softly…almost a whisper.

"I'll come as soon as I can." She lowered her head in thought. Then she raised up and looked at him again, eye to eye.

They held each other with their eyes for what seemed like hours but was only a few seconds, then she turned and walked down to the house. He watched as she disappeared through the door.

Slowly, he turned and began the trek back into the woods to his cabin. He knew in that moment that he had to find a way to make her his completely. She was to become the completeness of him. He knew it in his head and knew it in his heart and soul. He just had to figure out how to make it happen.

Over the next several weeks they met many times on their rock on the side of the mountain. Slowly, the woodsman worked with her, coddled her into letting him kiss her neck, earlobes, down to the curve of her shoulders. He worked his way down to the top of her breasts. She would squirm and move her body in response to his caresses.

Charla would lay at night and listen as she heard her mom and pop make love and knew some of what they were doing. Her woodsman would come into her mind and she would picture him doing those things to her. Then her fingers would come into contact with her womanhood and she would jump. Slowly, she began to experiment. It felt good. She didn't understand why...it just did.

She felt her wetness...thought she had started to pee and stopped. Then started to touch herself again. She liked it. Needed it. She needed David.

Realization hit her square in the face. He had been trying to lead her to this all along. He had wanted to touch her there. She had stopped him. What would it feel like? Would it feel better if I let him, she wondered? Should I let him? She reached up and touched her breast as she touched her lower self. She felt the burn increase. Oh, Lord have mercy. She was on fire!

Charla knew what she wanted now and what she needed to do. She couldn't wait for the chance to get away and go back up to their secret meeting place on the rock. Fall had started to settle in and it was getting cooler so she couldn't use the excuse that she needed to cool off. "Why are you taking such long walks Charla? Where are you going to?" asked her brother.

"I just need to get away sometimes. It gets to be too much with all the work and taking care of the kids. Some peace and quiet means a lot, ya know." Answered Charla, looking her brother straight in the eyes.

"Okay, I just wondered. Where do you go? You aren't wandering up there in the mountain, are you? It isn't safe. Too many wild animals. Bears, mountain lions, you just never know. I don't want you to get hurt. I worry about you." Her brother was genuinely worried for her safety.

"Thank you for worrying about me, but I'm very careful. And no, I'm not crazy enough to go into the mountain. Just watch over the place and help poppa, I'm fine." Charla tried to convince him she was good on her own.

She knew she was tempting fate every time she wandered into the mountain, but she also knew that her woodsman wouldn't let anything happen to her. She trusted him with her life. She wasn't even the slightest bit scared.

Now she wondered if her brother would try to follow her to see where she went. Damn, that would ruin everything. She had to make sure that he didn't. She didn't want him to know about David yet. And she really didn't want him to tell mom and pop about the woodsman. She would do that herself when the time was right. But not just yet.

She needed more time alone with him. She wanted to know him better and wanted to understand what was happening to her. Charla liked what she was feeling and wanted more. Needed more. Even though she didn't know what it was she wanted...she did.

When she arrived at the rock, the woodsman was there waiting for her. Her grin lit up her face and she blushed a beautiful shade of pink. Her cheeks were flushed and she became the most appealing woman he had ever seen.

David took Charla in his arms and kissed her. Lightly, his lips touched hers as his tongue licked and tasted her. God, how he had missed her. He stepped back and looked into her eyes and saw the desire in them. He then drew her closer to him and took her mouth fully with his lips. He kissed her deeply, tongue pressed to her lips, probing, making her open for him.

As Charla wrapped her arms around David's neck and her fingers went into his hair, she opened her mouth to receive his kiss and his tongue. She was hungry for him. Desired him, needed him. She felt the burning from her neck to her womanhood. She pressed her body against him needing to feel his warmth and strength. She could feel his hardness against her belly and her heart leaped. Her breasts tingled as they touched his chest, even through her clothing.

These feelings were new to her, but she knew she liked them and wanted so much more. Their kisses deepened and their tongues explored each other's mouths. Tasting and teasing. Biting and nibbling at lips. David pulled away and lowered his head to the side of her neck. He kissed gently and lightly. He nibbled and bit. She giggled and moaned. They played, they laughed, they teased. His hands were moving, reaching, feeling. She didn't notice until he touched her breast.

She froze. Paralyzed. She pulled back, her eyes bulging.

"Relax Charla. I'm not going to hurt you. This is a natural way for me to show you how I feel about you. And it's natural for your body to respond to my touch. I want to make your body feel good. I know from the way you respond to me already that you want this…that your body does. Please let me show you how good I can make you feel. Just let me touch you a little bit. With your clothes on. I promise not to hurt you. Okay?" David knew he had to be very gentle and easy with Charla. But he wanted to teach her how much pleasure he could give her.

Her breasts were already aching. They felt bigger than they ever had. How was he going to make them feel any better? She had no idea, but she knew he would not hurt her, so slowly she shook her head that it was okay to touch her.

With relief and as passive a look as he could muster on his face, he took a step towards her. Then he took her in his arms and kissed her. While kissing her gently, he slowly lifted his left hand and ran it up the right side of her outer breast. Lightly, he caressed her letting her feel him. She moaned slightly. Gradually, he moved his hand to encompass her whole breast as he massaged it and held it in his hand. Her moans grew more intense. Then he did the same to the left breast. Her whole body was in motion to his stimulation.

Charla couldn't believe the feelings going through her body from his touch on her breasts. They were getting harder. Her nipples ached so much. She wanted more. They were starting to ache so much. And why was she starting to feel that tingling down below? No, it was more than a tingling. What was it? What was going on down there? She felt like she really wanted to be touched down there. Oh Lord! She didn't understand this at all. Was David causing all this to happen? Was he wanting this to happen? Is this what her pop did to her mom? Is this what they were doing at night that made her mom make those sounds?

As he released her from their passionate kiss and looked toward her eyes he saw her lowered lids and the pure expression of pleasure on her face. Her swollen lips, rosy cheeks, flushed skin and messy hair was a vision he adored. He knew in that moment that he couldn't live without her.

Her response to his touch was beautiful and he needed and wanted more. But he knew he couldn't push her to fast. She was just a little mountain girl and he had to take it slow with her. But he knew in the long run it would be very much worth it. He would have the most beautiful, gorgeous, loving woman in the world. He just had to be patient. And he would be. Yes, indeed. He would be.

It had been raining for over a week, nonstop. David knew the floods would be coming. He had been watching the water rising along the brook that ran along his cabin. It ran down alongside the outer ridges and into a larger creek which eventually ran into the main river. He also knew that Charla's parents farm was in direct line of a wash coming out of the mountain. If this rain kept up, the farm was in danger of flooding from the runoff from the creek beds above.

Charla had been cooped up while watching the rain each day. The children were growing restless as the activities were getting more and more boring. All the sewing had been caught up and the canning had been done and put away. Now there was nothing to do but read or sit and watch as the rain continued. She knew her pop was worried as he watched the creeks rise and she had listened to the conversations between him and her mom and brothers. Preparations were being made in case there was a flood.

Most of all she missed David. They hadn't seen each other in ten days. Her body craved him. She ached. She longed for his touch, his kisses, and his hands upon her.

As she stared out the window she wondered where he was and if he was okay. She had touched herself at night as David had touched her and it had only made her longing for him worse. Lord have mercy! This rain just had to stop. She needed him.

Just as Charla had taken the youngest child in to start her bath, she heard her pop shouting for her mother to gather the children and some food and run up the back side of the mountain. The flood waters were coming and they were coming fast. There was no time to waste. Go now.

Charla grabbed her sister and ran out into the main room. She saw the look on her pop's face and knew to move quickly. They had an emergency pack already made up for such an occasion and told her middle sister to grab it and one of the other child's hands and run as fast as she could.

Her pop told the boys to come with him to help with the animals. So, they headed to the barn. On the way there, they ran into a stranger. Pop looked at him quizzically.

"Who are you? What do you want? We are kinda busy right now, have a flood on its way." Pop said as he was running toward the barn.

"My name's David Jasper. I'm a woodsman. I have a cabin up in the mountain and I know what's about to happen. Please, let me help." said David as he ran with Charla's pop toward the barn.

"Well, I don't know who you are or why you came along...but yeah...I could use an extra hand. Come on...let's get these animals out of here." Pop hollered back at David.

So, for the next few hours they worked together getting the animals to safety. Just as the last were gone they heard the rush of the water and Pop turned to say thank you to the stranger who had come to help. Pop had sent the boys ahead of him so he knew they were safe.

As he turned to look when he heard the sound, he saw trees starting to snap. Water started rushing out from the forest. It seemed to be everywhere. He saw the barn being surrounded by water. Down it came. further and further. The cabin sat lower and was in direct line of the deepest water coming down from the mountain.

It hit hard and it hit fast. Just as the woodsman made it to the safety of the backside of the mountain he heard Charla's pop holler. He looked toward the cabin. There stood the oldest son with his head out the window. David's heart stopped. Pop hit the water and was trying to swim with all his might but was being pulled with the rapidness of the movement of the water.

Charla and her mother screamed simultaneously. They watched in horror as the man they both loved was being swept away with the flooding waters. It looked as if his body had gone limp. Like he was dead. Grief hit them at the same moment. Shock.

David sat and took off his boots, pants and shirt, leaving on his long johns, then dove into the water. He knew he had only a short time to get to Charla's pop to try to save him.

In the meantime, water was rising fast and was going into the cabin. Charla was trying to keep her eyes on both her father and her brother. Not knowing which way to look, her head going one way, then the other. Her brother was still hanging out the window, so at least he was sort of safe. She guessed.

David was swimming as fast as he could. He had pop in his view, but just couldn't reach him. The water was moving them too fast, but not in the same directions. He had to maneuver himself to get closer. Then, it seemed like out of nowhere, a huge tree branch appeared and caught Charla's pop and wrapped him like a glove and held him there.

David swam with all his strength to get to him. He pulled his head out of the water and felt his neck for a pulse. Thank the good Lord he had one. But how the hell was he going to get him out of there? The water was way to swift to try to move him. But if they stayed there, the cold temperature would put them into hypothermia.

Charla knew she needed to do something. David had made it to her pop, but they couldn't move. She had to help. She wasn't sure where David's cabin was but there had to be rope or something there that would help get them to safety. So, so grabbed her next to oldest brother and they took off to look for the cabin. Upon finding it they searched and found the rope and returned to the river of water.

Charla and her brother ran down to get as close to where David and her father were. David signaled for her to throw him the end of the rope and to tie it off on the nearest tree. She did. He then tied it around her father and told her to pull him to her. She and her brother did until they got him to where they were. She threw the rope back to David and pulled him to her.

Charla's mom was already working on her pop, covering him with blankets after she had stripped him of his wet clothing. He was very cold and needed to be warmed up. Her mom got into the covers with him and tightened her body with his.

Charla made David strip out of his wet clothing and wrapped him in dry blankets also. He shivered and she cuddled beside him and held him close. He had saved her father's life. How would she ever thank him.

David held Charla close. Her body warmth felt so good. He was so cold...chilled to the bone. He shook from the chill. He wrapped the blanket around both of them and pulled her closer to him. God, he loved this woman. She had saved his life.

David was still shivering and so cold even several hours later. It was nightfall. The sky had darkened and the little ones were all snuggled down and asleep. Charla had watched her mom take off her clothes and curl up in the blankets with her pop. She had said it would help warm his body up faster.

Knowing no one could see her and not knowing anything else to do to help David get warmer, Charla removed her clothing and got under the blankets next to David. If her mom did this to help her pop... then it must be the right thing to do. As she lay there, she wondered how just lying beside him would give him more body heat?

As Charla had her hand on David's arm she felt his skin start to warm a little. This was an interesting development. She scooted closer to him, putting her hip next to his. He was so cold. She aligned her leg with his and held her body closer. In a short time, his skin seemed to warm a little bit. But not nearly enough and he was still shivering. This was not good and she didn't want him to get sick. She had to do more.

Slowly, Charla turned over and wrapped herself around him. She put her leg over his and her arm around his chest. This might help a little bit more...she thought. She felt the strange sensations of her body touching his. Never had her body felt like this before. Never had her body touched another body in this way before. Her breasts tingled. And her womanhood ached as it touched his hard thigh. OH! Lord have mercy!! Charla lay very still for fear of what might happen if she moved too much. Before long she snuggled up closer...smiled...tucked her head into his shoulder and from pure exhaustion fell into a sound sleep. David woke up feeling very warm...cozy and had a tickle on his nose. He went to reach up and scratch it but his arm was pinned. He started to move and realized he couldn't. He looked down and saw...

CHARLA??

David was happily confused. How did she end up lying beside him? No.. curled up...almost on top of him? He smiled to himself. Oh yeah.

He liked this. He liked this a lot. He wasn't going to move a muscle and wake her up. Not just yet.

It wasn't quite dawn yet, but he could see well enough to know that there were bodies lying around in blankets sleeping. Then recollection started to seep into his memory of what had transpired and where he was. He remembered being so cold so he figured that Charla must have gotten into the blankets with him to warm him. Smart girl he thought.

Charla felt David's muscles move in his legs and arms as he adjusted himself on the ground. She shifted with him. She was so warm and comfortable; she didn't want to leave him. She also didn't want to lose the feelings going on inside of her body. She didn't know what they were, but she didn't want them to end either.

David started stroking her hair, slowly working it down her back and up again. Playing with it...twirling it in his fingers. As he played with her hair he would touch her back, running his fingers down her spine. Charla would move a little in response. Then he would do it again.

Slowly he started moving his hand around to her chest and neck as he kissed her head. He felt her move against him. Closer she clung as her body ached for more of his touch. He read her body movements and gave her more. Touching her breast, massaging it, grasping the nipple and rolling it in his fingers.

"David." Charla whispered. "Yeah." David answered.

Charla lifted her head and looked up at him. He lowered his head and kissed her lips, gently and sensuously. His tongue parted her lips and entered her mouth. God, she tasted heavenly. He wanted to devour her. David kissed her more deeply as his hands moved about her body.

The stimulation he was giving her was causing responses and he liked it. Her leg tightened around his and he felt her wetness against his thigh. He moved his leg so that the contact with her little nub kept her on edge as he continued to massage her breasts. He pinched and rotated her nipples and heard her groans and moans against his mouth as he kissed and tongued her.

Charla had no idea what was happening to her body but she liked it and wanted more, much more. David's hands and mouth were working wonders on her body. What she was feeling in between her thighs was wondrous and she needed him to keep it going. She rubbed herself up against his thigh. He moved his leg against her.

Slowly, David moved his hand down her body towards her mound and over to her nub. He touched her there. She held very still. She was startled, not knowing what he was doing to her.

"Relax darling. I won't hurt you. Enjoy this. I want to give you pleasure. I want to make you feel very good. Let me take you to a place of excitement. This is the best gift I can give to you." David whispered into her ear.

Charla looked deep into David's eyes as his fingers touched her again at her womanhood. She didn't jump this time but relaxed into his hand. He leaned down and kissed her as his fingers rubbed her gently, teasing her. Her body moved with him as he manipulated her.

He continued to move his fingers within her folds. Down into her inner parts where her wetness was flowing. Her breathing quickened, her nipples were very hard and he knew she was very close to reaching her first ever orgasm.

David grabbed her by the back of the head and held her mouth to his as he inserted first one finger into her while still rubbing her nub. Charla moaned into his mouth. He moved his finger in and out of her, stimulating her, bringing her closer. As she was about to reach her point of orgasm, he inserted another finger into her. Charla cried into his mouth. Her body spasmed, her leg grasped his thigh and held to him. Her hands clung to him.

Charla didn't know what was happening to her, but it felt heavenly. She felt her whole body reaching a pinnacle of release like she never had, even by her own hand. And he kept it going. He didn't stop. His fingers were working her over and over again...deeper and deeper. She felt herself leaking fluid that had released from herself down there. Oh, Lord have mercy!!

David brought her down gently, kissing her softly. He pulled back and looked into her eyes. Charla looked at him with a loving but confused look in her eyes.

"That, my darling, was your first orgasm. How do you feel?" David asked her, with a grin on his face.

"MMM. I feel wonderful. But how did you do that to me? I don't understand how all of this works." Charla had to admit that she didn't understand the ways of sexuality.

"My love, there is so much I want to teach you about how a man and a woman make love with each other. That is just the beginning. I will teach your body to beg for me to make love to you. You will crave it. Need it. Desire it. You will see." David was so in love with Charla, he wanted her to know everything but knew it would take time to teach her.

"Tell me David, how do you get to feel as good as I do right now?" Charla wanted to know.

"My dear. You will learn soon enough." He took her hand and had her touch his hardness. "With this is how I reach my pleasure. You will learn how to pleasure me and how we pleasure each other with him. All in good time my love." David grinned down at her and gave her a loving kiss.

Charla kept her grasp on him and moved her hand slightly up and down. David groaned.

"Oh, am I hurting you? I'm so sorry David." Charla quickly removed her hand from him.

"No, sweet girl, you did not hurt me. But if you had kept doing that we would have had very messy blankets to clean." David chuckled. Charla gave him a quizzical look.

"Soon I will show you and then you will understand. For now, just trust me. Okay?" David knew they couldn't go any further with this as the children had started to stir. He would have to wait until later to finish this.

Soon Charla's parents were up and moving around, as she was folding up their own bedding. Her mom didn't ask any questions but gave her a questioning look. Charla said nothing but went about getting the children their morning meal.

Later that morning, pop was feeling much better and was sitting up to eat when he asked Charla to bring David to come see him.

"Sir, you asked to see me." said David as he went to stand before Charla's pop.

"First I would like to thank you for saving my life young man. I wouldn't be here with my family if you hadn't come here to help us. I am much obliged." said my pop.

"It was my honor sir. I'm just grateful that I was here to help. I'm glad that I was able to get to you in that rushing water and pull you to safety. Your son and daughter helped too. They got the rope and helped pull us out of the water. Without them, we wouldn't have made it." I couldn't take all the credit David thought.

"Yes, well, I am most thankful. So, what is your interest in my daughter Charla? My wife tells me you are sweet on her. Is that true?" Pop didn't beat around the bush.

"Yes sir. I do indeed like your daughter. In fact, I love your daughter. I would like to marry her and make her my wife. I want to make her very happy." David answered.

"Well, sir. I know nothing of you. You come down here as a total stranger in the middle of a flood. Yes, you helped me and my family. But wanting my daughter is quite another matter. How do I know your intentions for her are honorable?" said my very protective pop.

"I respect that sir. I have lived in these mountains all my life. My parents own the property over the ridge on east side. I was married but my wife passed while giving birth and I lost my son. That was 10 years ago. I am a trapper by trade. I make a good living at it and also do wood carvings. I'm called the woodsman in these parts.

"Ah...yes, I've heard of you. You are very respected in these parts. Your reputation for your work is very good. But how do you know my daughter and how do you know you love her?" Pop wasn't going to let this go easily.

"Well, sir. We have been meeting for quite some time secretly. We have not been disrespectful. Just talking and getting to know one another. During this time, we have fallen in love. We had planned on talking to you soon, but the flood came and kinda forced this to happen now. Maybe fate has its reasons." David stood tall and sure of himself before her father.

"I see. And Charla, how do you feel about this young man?" her father looked at her.

"I love him pop. I want to be with him now and forever. He makes me happy. I laugh with him; he makes me feel good inside. It's hard to explain. I know when I saw you both in the water I didn't want him to die. It would have killed me inside." Charla didn't know how else to explain to her pop how she felt.

"I understand baby girl. I believe that you two do love each other. I can see it in your eyes. Well, David. Charla. You both have my blessing. If you want to be married, I will not stand in your way. David, you will be welcome into our family." Pop looked from David to Charla. Then took mom's hand and kissed her.

Mom smiled at us both, took my hand and said, "Little girl, we need to talk."

For the next month, David and Charla spent every free moment they could together. They explored each other's bodies. Charla's mom had explained the art of lovemaking to her. She told her about how babies were made and childbirth. Charla knew she wanted to wait until she and David were married before they consummated their love for each other completely. Then she wanted numerous children. She wanted a happy life like her parents.

The day of the wedding came. All of the mountain came. People from everywhere were there. It was a feast like no other. Food and dancing galore.

David came out to the barn, which had been decorated nicely. Two of Charla's brothers stood with David as witnesses. Two of her sisters came into the barn before her. Then she stood at the entrance. David was awestruck. Charla was gorgeous. She was in a homemade white gown, covered in lace. She had a bouquet of wildflowers in her hand and a broad smile on her face. She flowed down the makeshift aisle toward him like she was walking on clouds. As they stood, hands joined, taking their vows, love filled the air. Once pronounced husband and wife, they kissed passionately and the reception began.

There was eating, dancing, whooping and hollering for hours. It was a fantastic good old mountain party. But the time had come that David wanted to be alone with his new wife. It was time to leave. He went to get Charla and say their goodbyes and leave for his cabin.

Her mom wept as she realized that her little girl was now a grown woman with a husband and on her own. Her pop wished them the best and shooed them on their way. As they headed up the path, David took her hand. He led her to the rock that had been their secret meeting place. He placed her upon it, stepped up beside her and kissed her. He looked deep into her eyes and took her into his arms. She was now his. This was where his dream had started and now it was reality.

He then took her hand and turned toward the path and led her to his home.... their home.

Their haven. Where they would make love, make babies. Make a life for themselves.

While the reception had been in full swing, Charla's brothers had moved all of her belongings to David's cabin. His mother had been waiting there to set everything up for her so she would have nothing to do when she arrived. It was now time for her to do nothing but enjoy her new husband. Her mother had set up the bedroom for exactly that purpose. Candles had been lit, a warm bath had been drawn and Charla's dressing gown had been laid out. All was prepared for the newly married couple.

As they approached the cabin, they stopped at the door. David stooped, picked Charla up and held her close to him in his arms. He kissed her deeply, opened the door and carried her over the threshold. They had arrived into their home. Their life together.

While still in David's arms, Charla looked about the cabin. It was warm with color and furnished in abundance. There was a large sofa and an overstuffed chair with a foot stool near the fireplace. She saw a big rug covering a lot of the wooden flooring. The kitchen was off to the side. But David didn't stop nor set her down as he headed straight for the back of the house after kicking the front door closed.

He turned the doorknob and opened the door to a most beautiful site. Candles illuminated the bed from all sides. Curtains adorned the window and a beautiful patch work quilt was on the bed which had a brass headboard and foot board. They both looked with amazement. Then his eyes went toward the bathroom. He saw the candles glowing. David carried her into there and gently lowered her down.

Charla saw the tub full of water and let out a soft moan. It looked so inviting. She was tired after such a long day of celebration. David turned her around and started unbuttoning the numerous buttons of her dress. Slowly he slipped it down her shoulders as he kissed her from her neck downward, following his hands as he lowered the dress further.

Shivers and goosebumps traveled her body as he removed the dress from her. Then he removed her bra, and panties. Kissing her body as he did. Then he turned her toward the tub, picked her up and lowered her into the water. She sank into it like she had fallen into a cloud. It felt so wonderful. Charla laid back and absorbed the warmth. The calmness. The quiet.

David watched her for a moment. She looked so peaceful. Like an angel lying there. She was so beautiful. He undressed quickly and moved in behind her, moving her up where he could get in. He wrapped his legs around her as he sat down in the warm water. Charla giggled. She had never taken a bath with a man before. This was new to her. But he was her husband now. There were many new things she would have to learn. David kissed and licked along the back of her neck, up to her ears.

He nibbled on her earlobes and back down again. His hands rubbed along her arms, shoulders, down her sides. She squirmed and wiggled at his touch. She loved how he touched her. It made her body respond to him. He reached in and touched her breasts. He gently massaged them, working them. She leaned back into him making them fuller in his hands. He tweaked and pinched the nipples. She would squeal. They would play and play.

She could feel his hardness between them on her back. She loved to feel him, knowing she made him that way. She wiggled her buttocks and he would groan in pleasure. They teased and teased for a long time.

Then his hand moved between her legs and he found her hard nub. He circled it slowly. She gasped. He increased the pressure slightly and she moaned. He knew she enjoyed this as he moved his finger downward to her center and teased her opening. She groaned. Her hips rotated with his hand movements. He kept his fingers going in deeper and deeper as his thumb pushed on her nub and she shook with an uncontrollable orgasm. He kept her there for a few minutes...letting her enjoy her bliss.

Charla leaned her head back and kissed David passionately. She loved him with her whole heart and was so in tune with him. Her body craved him. She wanted so much more and wanted to learn all she could in the art of making love with him. She wanted to learn how to satisfy him as he had just done to her. She reached her hand between them and gave him a squeeze. David groaned. His hardened member moved at her touch. He wasted no time getting up from the tub, drying them off and taking them to the bedroom.

He wanted to fully make love to his new bride. She would be his tonight. She would be his completely. He needed to make her his. He needed her body like a hunger. It had been so many years since he had held a woman in his arms as he put his manhood into her. God, he need this so badly and now he had his woman. Charla. She was now his forever. He would love her, adore her and make mad passionate love to her. He would teach her how to pleasure him as he liked and how much rapture she could have. They would be happy.

David laid Charla on her back on the bed and laid next to her on his side. While looking into her eyes he stroked her from her shoulders downward with his fingertips. Then slowly back up again. He would trace around her breasts, around her nipples, then back to her neck. He would do this several times getting her relaxed and use to his touch.

He wanted to feel her body's responses. He wanted to know what made her react more than didn't. When he touched under her breast did her breathing increase? He needed to know everything that made her who she was.

David leaned over and took a nipple in his mouth and gently suckled it. He licked and teased it. He rotated it in his mouth and then gently bit it. Charla moaned in delight. Her hand went into his hair and push his head down for more. She wanted much more. He continued to tease and taunt her from one breast to the other, back and forth. Charla's body was on fire. The warmth was spreading down her tummy to her womanhood. She felt her wetness as he worked her with passion and love.

While sucking on her breast his hand moved to her mound and slid through the soft hair. He cupped her and pressed, holding her. Her hips moved into his hand. She moaned. She felt the warmth of his hand on her as well as the warmth he was sending through her body. She was going crazy with want. Charla didn't understand all that was happening to her, but she knew she wanted more....so much more.

As David sucked her breast and played with her nipple with his tongue and teeth, his fingers moved along her slit, making it moist with her wetness. He placed a finger inside of her as he pushed on her nub making her moan and her hips move in rhythm with his hand. Her moaning grew louder as she grabbed his arms. He could sense her peak was approaching. He drove her higher and higher. His finger moved inside of her faster, adding yet another finger. He rotated her nub and she exploded into pure bliss. Her juices flowed over his hand and down between her legs.

David slowed his hand movements as Charla's body calmed from her orgasm. He looked into her eyes, dazed with passion and hunger.

"This is only the beginning my love. I am going to show you all the ways of being loved, my beautiful wife. But for tonight, I must taste your sweet nectar. I will take you to another peak of delight your body will crave." David spoke to her as he caressed her, stroking her.

He kissed his way down her soft tummy, over her mound of hair and stopped to admire the place of her blessed womanhood as he knelt before her. She was beautiful. He ran his finger up and down her wet lips. She shivered at his touch. He leaned over and kissed her lips on each side. He let his tongue flicker over them slowly, tenderly. He licked her, from the bottom of her to the top. God, she was magnificent. A taste like no other.

Charla gasped as his tongue touched her nether region. She could never imagine a man's tongue down there. What was David doing to her? Her mom never told her about this. Lord Have Mercy!! But oh, it felt so wonderful. She did trust him and knew that he would not hurt her. How could he when this felt so good. Every time he moved his tongue back and forth it made her jump. It made her feel hotter inside. It made her belly get that funny feeling. Oh, yes, she wanted much more of this.

David licked her from one end to the other, several times, and then touched her hardened nub. Charla gasped and her hips jumped. He wrapped his arms around her legs and held her down as he attacked her nub. He sucked it into his mouth and licked and sucked it with want and need. Charla's moans grew louder. David reached down and inserted a finger into her as he continued to suck her love button and she cried out in passion and desire. He inserted a second finger and pumped her as he sucked her button. Charla came in his mouth as he covered her hole and sucked her fluids from her. He inserted his tongue into her and lapped up her juices. She wreathed and moaned as she came and came all over his face. Her body arched.

Slowly, David licked her until she quieted, avoiding her sensitive and swollen knob. He knew she had had an explosive orgasm and needed time to calm down. Then he was going to take her back up again. He wanted her ready for him when he entered her for the first time. He watched her face. He saw her expression of bliss and knew she was ready. He felt her body relax.

He lowered his head again and licked slowly. Separating the lips... playing with them and teasing them. He tickled her hole. He moved his tongue in and out of it. Her hips moved in rhythm with his movements. He let his tongue go down to her little pucker hole and he licked it lightly. She froze. He tapped her leg. She relaxed. He did it again. Then he went all the way back up to her button and all the way back down to her little hole. Up and down he went…Teasing and taunting her. She was moaning. Her head was moving back and forth. Her body was tensing. He knew she was getting close again. He raised up. He was ready to make her his wife completely.

David moved his body close to her and rubbed his manhood along her womanhood. She was so wet and ready for him. He was very hard and so in need of her. He touched her nub with his penis and she felt his warmth and hardness.

"Look at me my love. I want to see your eyes when I make you mine." David said to Charla.

Charla opened her eyes, so hot and full of passion and looked at David. At that moment, David leaned forward and pushed himself into her, hard. He saw her pained expression. Tears filled her eyes.

David held very still. He leaned over and held her. He kissed her tears away.

"It's Okay. It will only hurt for a moment. I promise to make it better. Then we will only have joy and happiness." David whispered into her ear. He held her for what seemed like a long time.

Charla knew about the pain from what her mom had told her. She was ready for it. But, Lord Have Mercy..it hurt!!!!

David started moving in and out in very small strokes. He did this for a little while to make sure she wasn't in any pain. Slowly, he increased the tempo and took larger strokes. Gradually, Charla started moving her hips along with him and they were making their own music together. David leaned up on his arms and looked at her as he stroked in and out of her. She looked back at him with eyes of love only for him.

They increased their pace and were soon in a hard tempo. Charla now knew what the noise from her mom and pop's room what all about. This was wonderful. She was loving it. She was close to another climax and wanted nothing more than to give that to her husband.

"How can I make you feel as good as you make me feel?" She asked David.

"Oh, baby. You do. And there are other ways you will also. And you will learn in time. But I am loving what we are doing now. I am going to cum inside you in a little bit and maybe we are going to make our first little one." David smiled down at her.

Charla smiled back up at him. She would like that. She had always wanted children of her own. Now she could do that and enjoy the process as well.

David leaned down and held her tightly as he unleashed his powerful thrusts upon her. They were both able to cum at the same time. It was a strong, long and hard orgasm for both. They clung to each other. Their breathing was erratic. It took time for them to come down from the high that they had traveled on.

"Oh My God!! That was awesome. David? Can we do that again? Charla asked with a huge smile on her face.

"Yes, my darling, as often as you like. But I think you might be a little bit sore as this is your first time. So, I think we'll wait for a few hours before we do it again. But there are other things we can do instead." He said with a wink.

"Oh yeah! Tell me." Said a hungry Charla.

THE BEACH

An older lady is walking along the beach one evening. She's had a hard day and is wanting some time to just unwind. The water and sand feels good working its way through her toes as she gazes out on the horizon. She isn't paying attention to the people around her.

A young man walks close to her... his head down....and almost runs into her. She has to move over to avoid a collision. He looks up; starts to say pardon me and freezes on the spot.

She is clad in denim cut offs and a pink tank top. Her short red hair is blowing in the breeze. She has the face on an angel and her light brown eyes are mesmerizing. But there is a sadness about her that he can't help but wonder what could possibly be so bad to make her look off into the distance like she is.

She turns to look at this young man who has intruded on her space. He is tall, tanned, weight proportioned and has dark hair. His broad shoulders look strong and she wishes she could fall into them to hold her up. What is she thinking? She's way too old to be having these thoughts. She starts to walk away but he turns and watches her.

He feels a tug. Is it in his heart…his body…down where it shouldn't be? She's too old for him to desire her. Isn't she?

But there was something about her that he wanted to know more about…or needed to know more about. His body was responding to something about her, as if it had a power of its own. He felt his cock stir as he stood there watching her. He didn't know whether to go after her, but if he didn't, how would he find her again? So rather than take a chance of losing out, he started walking in her direction.

He stayed a safe distance behind her, still not sure what he wanted to do or should do. In this day and age, you just didn't accost a woman.

That could cause a guy to get into some real trouble. You know...the sexual harassment thing. But he just couldn't and wouldn't let her walk out of his life. He had to know more about this woman. His dick was getting harder with each step and his mind was having all kinds of erotic thoughts. What the hell was wrong with him?

As I kept walking along the beach, the water massaging my feet and toes, I could feel someone behind me. I turned my head slightly and saw that young man following me. What the hell was he doing? Why would he be following me? I hadn't encouraged him in any way. I hadn't spoken to him. I don't think I looked at him to give him any impression of anything.

So, what was he doing coming up behind me?

Should I be afraid of him? For some reason, I'm not. He didn't seem like he wanted to harm me. He stayed a good distance away. So, what did he want? I guess there was only one way to find out.

I did feel a longing inside of me that I couldn't explain. Why had I wanted to fall into those big, strong arms the way I did? He looked so warm and had a strength that I didn't seem to have right now.

So, I stopped and played in the water with my toes. I looked out into the ocean and then looked to my left, then to my right. He slowed down. I saw him to my right. He also played in the water with his toes. He looked at me and smiled. I smiled back.

His smile was broad and made his whole face glow. I felt a warmth travel through my body...from my breasts down to my womanhood. This was unreal. I haven't felt this way since my husband last looked at me a few years ago. How can this young man be doing this to me?

He turned his head and looked back over the water again, but I saw him look coyly at me from the side. He looked so hot in his speedo type suit that allowed every curve and muscle to ripple. His back was taut as he bent over, picked up a shell and skimmed it over the water. Damn, the heat was flowing.

Slowly, he worked his way toward me. I stood there wiggling my toes in the water watching him approach. He seemed harmless enough and to be honest, my hormones were going into overdrive. My nipples were becoming inflamed and the heat was moving downward at warped speed. Damn.

She stood there watching me as I ambled toward her. I eyed her carefully, not knowing if she would be afraid of me or not. But judging from the look in her eyes and the flush of her face, I saw only desire. That was a very good thing. And my cock appreciated it.

It was getting very difficult to hide my desires in this tiny suit as I neared her. I know if her eyes lowered she would have no doubts. I held her eyes with mine as I stood in front of her.

"Hello. My name is Eric." I greeted her.

"Hi. I'm Jessie." She said as I extended my hand to her and she took it.

"It's nice to meet you." She nodded her head in agreement.

"May I say you are a very beautiful woman? But you also looked so sad. I felt I had to ask you why? I hope you aren't offended by my being so forward." This was either make it or break it time.

As I still held her hand, she looked down at the sand, then back up into my eyes. Her lips went into a small smile.

"You are very observant. But really, I am fine. Thank you for your concern." she said as she started to pull her hand free.

Her hand felt so warm in mine. There was an energy between us that was unmistakable. As I looked into her eyes, I saw a mist in them and knew she wasn't as alright as she was pretending to be. She seemed lost and lonely.

"Forgive me for saying so, but you don't seem fine to me. What has you feeling so lost and alone? I saw you looking out into the water like you had lost your best friend." As she flinched, I knew I had hit something raw within her.

Her shoulders sagged and her head went down. The wind from the water was blowing through her hair. I lifter her chin with my finger and looked at her.

"Whatever it is, I'm sure it can be fixed. You're too beautiful to have the pain in your eyes. Let me help you feel better." I so wanted to help this woman. My whole body was on fire for her.

"You are a very sweet and kind young man, but you can't fix this. It is just life my friend. And life must go on." She took a deep sigh. Then she turned her head and looked out over the water again.

"Please, let me help you." I don't know why, but I wrapped my arms around her shoulders and she fell into me. I heard her quietly sob and I held her until her tears were spent.

"Did that help?" I asked her quietly.

"Yes, thank you. I'm sorry. I don't know why I did that." She said as she took her shirt and dried her face.

Pulling her shirt up to dry her face gave me a good view of her tiny abdomen and the top of her shorts. Damn, my rod started moving. She was so hot!

"You know what; let's go get something to drink. I know a place not far from here. We can sit on the deck and enjoy the water and talk. I'd like to get to know you better, and I think you could use a friend right about now. Okay?" I asked her as I started leading her down the beach.

"Yes, I'd like that. Thanks." She said as she walked with me.

We went to a little tiki type bar that sits right along the beach. After we got our drinks we sat along the decks edge and dangled our feet over, playing in the sand. She seemed to relax more as we drank and talked. She had been through the loss of her husband and had changed jobs, so life had been pretty rough.

I knew I could be of help to her, I just needed to get her to trust me. And believe me I was working on that. I just couldn't go too fast. But Damn...I wanted her bad!!!

Being a part time beach bum I had seen all types of women and had had my fun with quite a few. This woman was different. There was something very alluring about her. She had a quality and class about her that you don't see every day. I knew I would have to win her over and that wasn't going to be easy. But I also knew in the long run she was going to be well worth it. She was a one of a kind.

After we had our second round of drinks she said she had to get back home. I offered to walk her back, but she said she was fine and would make it home OK. I told her I had to go that way anyway, so I would walk her as far as I had to go. She said fine.

As we walked, we talked more, laughed, played in the water, and then I splashed her. She gave me that look like...: no, you didn't just do that. So, I did it again.

This time she threw water back at me. We ended up in a water throwing match until we were laughing so hard that she lost her balance and fell into the water. Now she was soaking wet and her shirt clung to her breasts with hardened nipples. Damn almighty.

I crawled over to her where she sat in the water. She watched me with a huge smile on her face. As I got to her, she threw a hand full of water in my face. I shook it off, grabbed her and hauled her out into the water, picked her up, carrying her deeper into the sea. She screamed and laughed at the same time.

Looking at her with pure evil on my face, she had no idea what I was going to do next. I knew what I wanted to do. As I held her in my arms, I leaned down and lightly kissed her on her soft lips. Then I lifted her up and threw her. She came up spitting. She lunged at me.

Putting my hand on her head, I could have dunked her under. Instead, I reached down and put my other hand around her waist and pulled her into me.

Her eyes met mine with a look of desire and want. But she held her body a little back from mine. She wasn't sure if she should let go. The water twirled around us as I held her still. I didn't push her too hard but wanted her to know that I desired her. As my eyes held hers I pulled her gently toward me. Her hands went to my shoulders as she tried to keep her body a little at bay.

I kept moving out a little deeper in the water so that her body was moving more with the water. Slowly her body came to meet mine and her arms circled my neck trying to keep her steady. Feeling her breasts through her shirt touching my bare chest was amazing and did things to my cock. I was trying my best to make him behave so as not to scare her.

Leaning into her I pushed her hair behind her ear and nibbled on her neck. She tasted like heaven. A mix of her and salt. Working my tongue up her neck to her ear I whispered that she smelled so good. I felt her take a deep breath and exhale slowly. Her body relaxed against me. I knew she was warming up to me. I knew she needed me too.

Feeling myself growing against her, I no longer tried to hide it from her. I knew she could feel me. She didn't seem to be moving away from me. In fact, she was holding herself closer to me. God, she felt amazing. So warm, tender, soft. Her body was so supple. Yes, she was older, but she was so desirable. I wanted her more than I had ever wanted any woman.

Wrapping my arms around her ass, I lifted her up as she put her legs around my waist. Carrying us even deeper into the water until it met us chest high, we moved and glided with the waves as they crashed against us.

This only succeeded in keeping us tight to each other. I was loving it. Her body felt so hot and good against me. She had her head to my neck and was kissing up and down. Then her tongue was licking up to my ear, along my jaw line, back to my ear and down my neck. Lord, Lord, I was so hard.

I reached up with my right hand and rubbed along her side and along her breast. She shivered. Working my hand toward the inside, I massaged her breast and played with her already hard nipple. I twisted and pinched it. Her body was moving and straining. Soon she was pushing on the tip of my very hard staff. God, this woman was driving me crazy. And I wanted her now!!

I leaned her back a little and put my hand under her shirt, going to her naked breast. Her body was cool, yet hot. She was cool from the water, yet her desire was hot. As she held on to my neck, I took both hands and played with both breasts. This woman was wild with want and need. Her hips were grinding against me now and I wanted to give her what she was demanding.

Reaching down I unbuttoned and unzipped her cutoffs. Laying them apart I took my hand and slid it down inside. I heard her moans over the roar of the waves. As my fingers reached inside, I could feel her wetness. Her clit was getting hard as I massaged it with my finger. Her moans grew louder. She let go of my neck and her hands grasped my arms. She lay back giving me greater access.

My fingers worked their way down into her shorts and panties to find her sleek, wet pussy. Damn. She was so wet and ready. I wanted to be inside of her so bad…but it would have to wait. Now was the time to take care of her.

I slid a finger into her wet pussy as I circled her clit. Her moaning increased and I knew she was close. I pulled her shorts down a little for better access. Sliding my hand in deeper, I was able to add another finger into her. Her hips moved faster as I pushed hard on her clit. She exploded. Her moans turned into a yell. Her eyes opened and looked at me. Her passion was deep.

She pushed her hips right over my cock and ground on him. I groaned. I had to have her now. There was no more waiting. I was ready to burst. I pulled her shorts off and told her to hold on to them. I then pulled her panties to the side. Taking my cock out of my lowered suit, I entered her slowly. We both groaned. Oh, this was the best feeling in the world.

Gradually working my cock into her hot, wet pussy I finally felt my public bone hit hers. I was all the way in, and I stood still, absorbing her warmth. Feeling her pulsing around him. Damn, but she felt wonderful.

Then she squeezed him. Christ Almighty! She did it again and smiled up at me. I reached out and lifted her up so that she was sitting on me. I held her close to my chest. Nuzzling my nose into her neck I smelled her essence and it drove me nuts. But I didn't want to cum yet. I wanted this to last for as long as possible.

We stayed there in the water, joined together, just feeling and enjoying each other for quite a while. Then Mother Nature interfered. A thunderstorm was rolling in. I knew we wouldn't be able to stay in the water for much longer.

Rocking her back and forth over my hard cock she started moaning. I told her to wrap her arms around my neck and to hold on. I grabbed her around her waist and started moving her up and down on me. Then I rocked her hard.. once…twice…three times and she exploded. She bit my neck and I came deep inside of her. Rope after rope of my sperm went deep into her welcoming canal. She squeezed and sucked me dry.

We kissed long and deeply. She tasted like rum and salt and her. Damn…so good.

I heard the thunder and told her we had to get out of the water. She groaned but said she knew. I helped her get her shorts back on and we walked back in to shore hand in hand.

I asked her if I could walk her home and this time she said I could. When we got to her house, she thanked me for a wonderful time.

I looked at her and wondered if I would get to see her again. Damn, I sure wanted to. I really didn't want this day to be over.

"I'd really like to see you again. I enjoyed being with you. You are an exceptional woman, Jessie." I was hoping she would see my sincerity. "Thank you, Eric. What we did was great. But I'm not so sure we should do it again." She had this lost look on her face again.

"Why, because I'm younger than you? Did you not enjoy what we did? Does age really make that much of a difference? Baby, you are only as old as you feel. You are as young as you want to be. We were awesome together. Don't throw something away out of fear. Or because society says you are supposed to be with someone your own age. Maturity doesn't come with age. It comes with life's experiences. There are 60-year-old men who don't have the maturity that I do. Please, give me a chance. I'm not asking for forever...at least not yet. I just want to be with you again." Wow, I was really pleading my case wasn't I?

She looked at me, a bit startled, a bit wary and a bit impressed. But she definitely had that look of desire and want again. She didn't say no. "I'll tell you what. Here is my phone number. Think about it and if you want to see me, call me and I'll come and see you wherever and whenever you say. Is that fair?" There, I took the pressure from her. That would give her time to think it over.

With that I left and went home.

For the next few days I thought about her often. The sex we had in the ocean had been the best I had had in a very long time. But I had told her to take her time and think it over. Damn, this waiting was hard. I was sitting watching TV when the phone rang eight days later.

Every time the phone rang I jumped, hoping it was her. But usually it was either work or one of my beach buddies.

"Hello." I answered.

"Hi." I heard her voice on the other end.

"Hey Jessie. How are you? How have you been?" I was breathless.

"I'm doing alright. Eric. I've been thinking about what you said when you were leaving the other day. Would you like to come over... maybe for a drink? I think we have some things to talk about." Her voice sounded so sexy over the phone. I was jumping out of my skin. And yes, he was jumping to attention too.

"Um, sure. When?" I asked her, trying not to sound too anxious. "Well, are you busy this evening? Maybe around nine?" She asked. "Ahhhh... yeah...that should be okay. Thanks. I'd like to see you." I was really trying to be as cool as I could be.

"Great. See you then. Bye." Then she was gone.

Oh, My God!! She really did call. She really does want to see me. She really did think about what I said. What the hell took her so long? This woman is killing me!!

It's now seven o'clock. I have time to take a shower, grab something to eat and make it over there on time. I'll wear something comfortable, yet presentable. She isn't just your ordinary beach girl.

Arriving in her driveway right at nine, I see there are very few lights on. Her house is small, and not far off the beach. It has a wraparound porch which is unique in these parts. The deck out back has a walk way that leads down to the beach. I go to the front door and knock.

"Hi Eric. Please, come in." She greets me with a small smile, then turns and walks into the living room. I turn and follow her after closing the door behind me.

Sitting in one of the wing chairs, Jessie takes a seat on the sofa. There are two glasses, an ice bucket, a liter of coke and a bottle of rum sitting on the coffee table.

"Would you like me to mix you a drink?" She looks at me as she asks,

"That sounds good. Thanks." I lean over to help her.

Holding up the glasses while she takes the tongs and places ice in each one, I watch her hands move with gracefulness. She pours rum and coke in each glass then stirs with a swizzle stick.

I move over to the couch, sitting at a comfortable distance, and hand her one of the glasses. We raise our glasses to each other and take a sip.

"So, what did you want to talk about Jessie?" I needed to get this conversation started.

Now she looks nervous. Her eyes divert from mine and look about the room. Then they come back to mine.

"I really did have a great time with you the other day on the beach. It was relaxing and I felt better than I have in a long time. But…" I put my finger to her lips.

"No negativity. There are no buts. There is nothing to feel bad about. You opened yourself up. You had a good time on an impulse. That is not a bad thing babe." I was looking directly into her eyes. They were glowing with desire.

"Let me ask you something. Do you know what I do for a living?"

"No, I don't." She let out a small smile.

"Do I just look like the run of the mill beach bum?" I asked with a smirk.

"Well, now that you said it, yeah, pretty much." She smiled again. "So, because of how I look, and because I'm young, you think I'm too young and immature for you. Do I have it about right?" I was still looking directly at her.

"Well, I try not to be judgmental, and I don't know exactly how old you are but you look young enough to almost be my son. So, yes, that could create issues." Her smile was gone and her face was serious.

"Well, let me fix this for you. I started as a floor boy for my father's company. I now am the CEO of that company. Have you ever heard of Everette Enterprises?" I still had my eyes on her face.

"You mean the largest investment firm in all of Alexanderville? Holy shit! Really? Just how old are you?" Now I had her undivided attention.

"I know I don't really look my age, but I am fifty-one. Yes, I still like to live life to the fullest, have fun and play. But believe me, I take life very seriously." Then I kissed her.

I kissed her softly for a little while, then I deepened it. I wanted her to know that I wasn't playing a game with her. I wanted her.

I put my glass down on the table, then reached for hers and placed it down next to mine.

I took her face in my hands and held her as I put my tongue to her lips pushing for entrance. She opened to me. I tasted her sweetness along with the rum and coke. I wanted more. So much more. I couldn't get enough of her.

Breaking the kiss, I looked at her. She was flushed and her eyes were clouded with desire and passion.

"Now do you understand that this is no game to me? Can you feel how much I desire and want you?" She was looking at me with sadness in her eyes.

"Yes, but you know nothing about me. My life is such a mess. All I have to offer..." I put my lips to hers to quiet her.

I didn't want to hear why she thought she couldn't be with me. I didn't want to give her time to think of all the reasons she could come up with. I wanted her to react naturally with her body. Then her mind would follow.

Moving my hand to hold the back of her head, I started kissing along her cheek, down her jaw line and around to her ear. I licked and sucked on her earlobe. Hearing her sighs, I moved down her neck, licking and kissing. Her hands went to my hair, playing in it and pulling gently.

"Eric, please, we can't be doing this." She was trying to fight her feelings.

"Shhh. Relax baby. Let me take all your cares away. Just let me give you the pleasure you deserve." While saying this, my other hand was working its way along her chest to reach her breast. I lightly massaged it through her blouse. Damn she felt so good.

My pants were getting so tight and uncomfortable, but I didn't dare move as I didn't want to distract her from the desires I was working to build up in her. She was breathing a little faster as I switched from one breast to the other, while still nibbling, licking and sucking on her neck and ear.

She had on a pull over blouse and I wanted it off her, so I worked my hands down her abdomen to the hem of her top. Slowly, I started pulling it up and put my hands under it. Her skin felt warm and smooth. Definitely, better than it had in the cool ocean water. I worked her top up and over her bra. Moving my head down I licked her nipple through her bra. She jumped as if startled.

"Eric, we can't do this out here." She started to pull her top back down.

"Fine, then lead me to your bedroom." I didn't want to wait for her passion to die down.

"Can we slow this down a little? Let's finish our drinks first, okay?" she spoke softly.

I know she saw the frustration on my face, but I nodded and picked up my drink and handed her hers.

Sitting back on the couch, I pulled her close to me and we cuddled. We talked some small talk as I played with her hair. I took an ice cube into my mouth and then attacked her neck. She squealed. As I let the cool liquid seep from my mouth, I let it travel down her neck, over her clavicle and into her blouse. Even though I couldn't get to her breasts, I could see the wet spots forming.

Taking another piece of ice, I grabbed her earlobe in my mouth and sucked. She jumped, and then giggled. I then said I could do amazing things with that ice cube.

Turning her head, I kissed her and slid the ice cube into her mouth. We played with it with our tongues until it melted. I was done with this type of playing around. It was time for some serious play.

Taking her hand, I pulled her up from the couch. Reaching for her top, it was my plan to either remove it right here, or we were headed for the bedroom. She got the hint.

Without uttering a word, she took my hand and led me down the hallway to the bedroom on the right. She set her drink down on the nightstand and lit a small candle. The room was furnished with a large bureau and a large triple mirror attached. There was a chest of drawers against a wall where a door led to the bathroom. The king size bed had a floral comforter of mostly purple flowers. There was a huge headboard and a smaller footboard, each having tall standing posts. There was a sitting chair in one of the corners by a door which led out to the back deck. All the furniture was made of mahogany, which stood out against the white walls.

Coming up behind her, I pulled her into me from around her waist. She laid her head against my shoulder. I wasn't about to waste any time as I reached for the hem of her top and pulled it up, over her breasts. She lifted her arms as I pulled it up her arms and off her. Reaching down her back I unhooked her bra, pushed the straps down and removed it quickly. My hands were on her breasts before she had caught her next breath.

Turning her around, I kissed her hard and deep. My tongue invaded her mouth as I demanded her to give me her passion. She reciprocated. Her arms went around my neck as her body pressed into mine. Realizing I had way too many clothes on, I couldn't feel her skin on mine. I broke away from her and pulled my shirt over my head. Pulling her back to me, the warmth of her breasts on my chest was awesome. But I needed more.

Stepping back from her, I bent my head and took a nipple into my mouth. Her moans were such a turn on that my cock stirred and my pants tightened. Taking the nipple between my teeth I nibbled and sucked. She moaned louder and her breathing increased.

Damn, this woman was so hot!!

While switching from one nipple to the other I reached down to her shorts and unbuttoned them, then slid down the zipper. I started kissing down, lower and lower as her pants were going down. As they hit the floor, she stepped out of them. Then I removed her purple lace panties.

I could smell her heat and it was driving me insane. My hardness was out of control and he needed out of his confinement. I stood up and quickly took off my pants. Taking her by the hand, I looked into her eyes and stepped toward the bed, bringing her with me. Turning her around, I laid her down, then lay down beside her. I curled her into my arms and held her for a few moments.

My thoughts went back to yesterday and how good it had felt to be inside her. I wanted back inside her again. This time I wanted to taste her first. I wanted to take it much slower and savor her. I wanted her to feel loved and wanted. Then I wanted to fuck her like she needed to be. Like she craved to be. Like she desired.

Kissing her, playing with her lips with my tongue, she opened to me. My tongue went into her mouth and I kissed her hard. My hand went to her breasts, massaging, squeezing, pinching her nipples, tweaking. She moaned through her filled mouth. Her hips started moving more into me. Her body was heating with want. She wrapped her leg around mine as her desire built.

My other hand had been rubbing down her back, going to her butt cheeks. The more I pulled her into me the more she wanted. Her breathing increased. Her moans became deeper. Ahhhhh yes, this was one hot woman.

Knowing she was ready, I turned her onto her back and kissed her breasts then worked my way down her tummy to her swollen mound. I bypassed her sensitive area and went to her thighs. Crawling between her legs, I kissed my way up both sides, taking nibbles here and there. She was moaning as I went.

As I reached her crossing, I stopped and just looked.

"God babe, you are so beautiful. I love that you are shaved and ready for me. You are so wet already. I can't wait to taste your sweetness."

I looked at her and saw her watching me with such passion.

When my tongue touched her clit, she gasped. I licked her from her taint to her clit and she moaned. She tasted as sweet as I thought she would. I wanted much, much more.

I laid down on my belly and went at her like a hungry man. My tongue went after her pussy slurping up every bit of juice she had. Then my tongue entered her hole digging for more. Her hips were grinding into me, begging, wanting. I knew she was close and I wanted her to squirt her juices all over my face.

I went for her clit, sucked it into my mouth as I pushed a finger into her sopping wet hole. I pushed up. Then I put in another finger and pushed the two fingers up hard to her gspot as I bit her clit. She came hard. Her juices poured out onto my hand. I kept moving my fingers in and out of her as I kept her orgasm going. She was moaning loudly. Her body was spasming. Her legs quivering.

Slowly, she receded, quieting. I pulled my fingers from her. Licking softly on her pussy, cleaning her. Damn, she tasted so wonderful. But I really wanted to be inside her now.

Getting off the bed, I took off my boxers, got back between her legs, and pressed my cock against her lips. Damn, that looked so hot.

Slowly I pushed into her, a little at a time. I wanted to relish this. I watched as I entered her. Then I looked at her face. She was so flushed. Her body was heated with desire. She certainly was a woman with passion and knew how to make love.

As my cock filled her to the hilt, I held still, enjoying the feeling. It felt so good to be inside of her. She was tight, and when she squeezed me, oh Lord. Then she did it again, with a small smirk on her face. She knew just what she was doing to me.

Oh, the joys of being with a woman who could control her body. She was going to drive me crazy!!

Starting to rock in and out of her, I moved slowly. I wanted this to last. I reached down and pulled her legs up so I could take her deeper. She groaned. Her eyes never left mine as I took her a little harder and deep. Her hips moved with mine. We had a great rhythm going and it felt awesome. As her climax was building, her breathing became faster. Bumping her clit with my pelvis, I knew she would cum soon. I reached down and pressed it hard. I moved my cock to hit right on her gspot and she shattered. Her screams where loud. I didn't stop. I kept pumping her hard. She came again.

"That's it baby. Take me. Let yourself go and enjoy it." I whispered softly to her in her ear.

Letting her legs go I lay between her and just let her rest as I gently pumped into her. I leaned on my elbows and looked into her eyes as I pushed her hair from her face. Then I kissed her. Our lips were sealed to each other as I continued to fuck her, picking up speed. She wrapped her legs around my waist and put her arms around my neck. God, this woman was awesome.

But I didn't want to cum yet, so I pulled out of her. I looked into her questioning eyes and smiled. I crawled over her and straddled her abdomen. I wanted her to taste both of us, so I tapped her lips with my very hard cock. She smiled up at me and opened her soft lips. She stuck out her tongue and licked me. Damn!!!

Pushing forward, the tip of my cock met her mouth and she opened for me. Her tongue received me, and her lips covered me. She stroked me with her mouth and sucked me in. "Ohhhh, she is good," I thought.

She took me and sucked and licked until I couldn't take it anymore. I didn't want to cum until I was back inside of her, so I pulled back from her.

I knew I wasn't going to last much longer. I wanted to cum inside her so bad. I told her to roll over on her stomach. As she did, I put a pillow under her. Getting behind her, I rubbed her pussy and then her clit. She moaned. She had her head down and her hands holding her pillow.

Lining my cock up with her, I entered her again. She was so warm and wet. I wanted her to cum with me. I laid over her and started pumping into her as I found her breast and pinched and played with her nipple. She started moving her hips back into me. She arched her back as she was getting close. I reached down a grabbed her hair, pulling her head up, arching her back more as I started pounding her. She took her hand and found her clit, rubbing it as she started cumming. This took me by surprise and made me so hard, that I came, shooting rope after rope of spunk into her. Three, four, five times. I fell over on her back as she fell to the bed. We were spent.

We laid there quite a while getting our breath back. I rolled off of her, laying on my side and pulling her into me.

Kissing her on the forehead, then her nose, then her mouth, I looked into her eyes.

"Is there still any doubt in that crazy head of yours that I want you?" I still had a death grip on her, letting her know I wasn't letting go of her.

"No, I guess there isn't. You proved your point very well." she said with a smile.

"Am I still too young for you? Are there still any questions in your mind about us that we need to settle?" I wanted this taken care of now, not to be brought up again.

"No sir, I don't believe there is. Ah, maybe one." She said with a smirk.

"And what might that be." I asked a little perplexed. "Are you ready to go again?" Then she kissed me.

THE TREASURE
OF DESIRE

Much time had passed since I had heard from him. What was wrong? It just wasn't like him not to call or text that he would be late. Our date was set for seven o'clock. Here I stood, dressed to the nines waiting for a date that might not show up.

Charles had promised me that he would never leave me standing waiting for him again. We had been in this place before. He had stood me up for the New Year's Eve party my boss had thrown and I was the laughingstock for months after. Now, here I stood, again. What the hell? Was I crazy to believe him? Things had been going so much better since then. We had even talked of moving in together. Well, if tonight was any indication, then I needed to rethink this relationship.

No, wait, there must be a good reason he is late. He just wouldn't do this to me again. I know it. We've worked too hard. Spent too much time getting things worked out for him to just throw it away.

Just then the red Chevy Colorado pick-up that I knew so well pulled up to the curb and Charles was out of the door and at my front door in a flash.

"Baby, I am so sorry. I had a flat tire about two miles from here. I went to call you, dropped my phone and it broke. Damn, I knew you were going to be mad." Charles couldn't talk fast enough as he tried explaining what had happened. He tipped his head, hiding his face with his black Stetson cowboy hat.

"Oh, Charles, I knew something was wrong. I just knew you wouldn't leave me waiting for no reason." Katrina exclaimed, throwing her arms around his neck.

"May I please use your bathroom to fix myself back up a little bit? Changing a tire is a little messy you know." he asked.

"Of course, you can. Just don't make a mess. Okay?" Katrina led him down the hall to the bathroom.

Charles knew the apartment like the back of his hand. They had been seeing each other for over a year and he had spent many a night here with Katrina.

After cleaning and straightening himself up he led Katrina to the truck and off they went into town for a night of dinner, dancing and pure relaxation.

Katrina looked every bit the cowgirl in her short, tight denim skirt, a pink rhinestone designed tank top and cowboy boots on her feet. Her long red hair hung loose over her shoulders, down over her breasts. Damn, Charles was getting a twinge in his pants just looking at her. This was going to be a long, hard night. How was he going to last, keep his hands where they belonged watching this little vixen all night? For a woman in her late fifty's, she was absolutely gorgeous.

Charles was every bit her counterpart. He was dressed in black jeans, a black cotton, snap down the front western shirt, black vest and a black Stetson hat. Black cowboy boots finished his attire. Katrina thought he was the most handsome man alive. His salt and pepper hair, mustache, and goatee set off his looks and she dared any other woman to look his way. He was her man.

They went to the Big Round Steak House and the hostess seated them at the back of the restaurant. It was a rounded booth, so they were able to scoot next to each other. The waiter came and Katrina ordered a frozen Margarita and Charles ordered a coke. They made small talk until the drinks were brought back. Then they ordered their dinner.

While sipping their drinks, and waiting for their food, Charles slipped his arm around Katrina's shoulder. She snuggled into him. MMMM...he smelled so good and felt so comforting. Charles looked down and could see into Katrina's shirt. He saw the tops of her breasts over her bra. Oh, God they looked so inviting, he thought.

His jeans became more uncomfortable and he had to do a little readjusting. So, he crossed his legs and turned a little toward Katrina as he eased himself, then put his arm more around her shoulder, going further down Katrina's chest. Charles's fingertips edged along the top of her shirt and over the tops of her breasts. She squirmed and moved about as she felt the tingle build between her legs. Damn. What this man could do to her.

Charles fingers traveled lower and had just started to enter her shirt as the waiter came to their table with their salads. Katrina's face turned a blush pink as she turned her head into Charles shoulder. The waiter said nothing...his smile said it all.... placed the salads down in front of each of them...turned and left.

Katrina gently removed Charles's arm from around her shoulder and proceeded to eat. Charles grinned, took his fork in hand and followed suit. His eyes never left her as he continued to eat...enjoying the fact that she felt uncomfortable but knew that she was turned on as well. Charles teased and played with Katrina off and on all through dinner. She wasn't sure what to make of it. He had never been this brazen before and she felt uncomfortable being this turned on in a restaurant. What were the other patrons thinking? Of course, they were somewhat secluded so maybe they couldn't really see what was going on.

When they had finished the main course, Charles ordered coffee and scooted over close to her again. Wrapping his arm around Katrina's shoulder, his hand went down her blouse. He wasted no time latching on to her breast and playing with the hard nipple. Katrina wriggled in her seat.

Charles leaned over and whispered in her ear to be still. With his other hand, he reached under the table and started rubbing Katrina's thigh. She could barely hold the coffee cup in her hand, let alone try to put it to her lips and drink it. But she put on a brave face, raised it to her lips and took a sip. As the coffee hit her mouth, Charles moved his hand up her leg and under her skirt. He went straight for her woman-hood and pushed his hand into her. Katrina moaned as she swallowed the liquid in her mouth.

Charles found her clit and started to rub it through her panties. Doing this made her cheeks turn a beautiful red and he was loving every moment of it. But his appendage was getting so hard he was in a lot of discomfort in the position he was in. He couldn't continue, as much as he really wanted to.

Knowing how wet she was and how much he had turned her on, Charles hated pulling his hand away. But he told her to finish her coffee because he had a surprise for her.

Katrina gave him a quizzical look. She had been on the receiving end of his surprises before and was a little leery of what he might have in store for her. If what had just transpired was any indication.... Lord... she was in deep trouble.

They got into Charles's truck and drove to the outskirts of town and on for another fifteen miles. Then turned down a dirt road and drove another few miles. Soon Katrina could smell smoke from a fire and heard singing. They pulled up to a ranch and around the gates toward a barn.

Just outside the barn was a wagon full of hay drawn by a team of two horses. Sitting on the driver's bench was an older man with a beat-up old cowboy hat and a well-worn jean jacket. Jeans and dusty cowboy boots finished his attire. He looked like a typical rancher. Katrina wondered what Charles had up his sleeve now.

Charles helped her out of the truck and walked her over to the wagon.

"Hi Jasper. You ready to take this buggy for a ride…nice and slow like?" Charles called up to the driver.

"Yup…ready to go Charlie. Just help your little lady up in there on that there hay and off we'll go." Jasper answered.

Charles reached down and lifted Katrina up by her waist and into the wagon. She was excited to see what he had in store for her. It had been a long time…since her teenage years to be exact…since she had been on a hayride. But a private one? Oh..this was going to be fun.

There were bales of hay lining both sides of the wagon and a matting of hay all along the floor. Katrina started to sit on one of the bales along the side but Charles pulled her down onto the floor. He sat with his back to the front boarding and pulled her to sit between his legs. He wrapped his arms around her and told Jasper they were ready to go.

As the wagon jerked slightly and rolled out…Katrina looked up to the sky. It was clear, showing beautiful stars aligned in their astrological designs and a moon that shown brightly. Though not quite full…she could see that the man in the moon was smiling down on them. Katrina felt like she was close to heaven.

Charles wrapped his arms tighter around Katrina. He could smell her hair. Smell her perfume. Smell her. God, how he loved this woman. Tonight, he would show her just how much he loved her. She would never doubt him again. It had taken all he could muster to get this arranged but she was worth every effort it had taken. Thank God for great friends. Jasper knew the score and would be discreet. Nothing would be said of what would transpire tonight. They had worked together for years and had helped each other before…so this was a no brainer. Tonight was going to be a night Katrina would never forget.

They rolled out through the gates and headed for the green pastures and beyond. It was rather bumpy but Katrina held on to Charles's thighs and balanced herself between his legs and leaning back on his chest. Charles moved his hands from around her waist up to her breasts and started massaging them through her clothing. His hands…so strong… yet soft…felt wonderful out in this open air. She leaned more against him and relaxed.

Charles massaged her and squeezed, working Katrina's breasts until her nipples hardened. He pinched them slightly…sending tingles through her. He worked his hands inside her shirt and pulled out a breast…working it and playing with it. He tweaked the nipple. Katrina moaned. Then he did the same with the other one. As they rode along her breasts bounced in his hands. Still he kept playing.

Katrina turned her head up to him and they kissed…lips touching. Her head was leaning on his shoulder as he kissed her harder. His tongue caressing her lips. Katrina moaned and her body moved against him. She could feel him hardening near her hips.

Charles loved having her breasts in his hands but wanted better access to them. He reached down and pulled Katrina's shirt over her head. He leaned her forward enough to unclasp her bra…then removed it. Ahhhh… so much better…he thought.

He took both her breasts in his large hands and held them… worked them…massaged them. Her nipples were so hard. Charles pinched her little nubs, pulled on them. He had to have them in his mouth. He needed to taste her. She intoxicated him.

Charles knew that Katrina, being in a skirt, would make it difficult for her to maneuver around, so he had to get it off her. But he also knew he had to take it slow…go easy with her. He took his left hand and started going down her tummy…down along the side of her thigh. He lifted the hem of her skirt and ran his hand under it. He heard her moan. He smiled to himself. Yes…this was going well he thought.

The bumpiness of the wagon, as it rolled on toward its destination, made moving his hand higher up Katrina's skirt a whole lot easier. Finally, he reaches her panty line. Yes, she was wet. Charles slid a finger inside her panties and felt her wetness as he worked his way around her to find her ultimate pleasure spot.

Katrina was wiggling around now. She couldn't sit still and the moving wagon had her bouncing up against Charles hard...rock hard manhood. She felt him hit her woman's button and jumped. Oh, God, his hand feels wonderful...she thought.

Charles played with her button and felt it becoming harder and harder. She was also getting wetter and wetter. Oh, yes. She was definitely enjoying this hayride.

He continued his playing as he leaned down and kissed her again. He pressed with his tongue on her lips and she opened her mouth for him. Charles pulled Katrina's skirt up more so he had better access to her mound and could continue manipulating her little love button. which was growing and getting so hard under his fingertips. Her moaning grew as well and he knew she was getting close to having a climax.

Charles worked his hand down a little more and pushed a fingertip into her woman's hole. Her hips bucked. Katrina ruptured into a climax as she pulled Charles's head down and kissed him hard. Their tongues mimicking what his finger has doing inside her. Her hips bucked, along with the bouncing from the moving wagon. Charles continued to move his finger inside of her as the palm of his hand hit her button. God. She was cumming so hard.. soaking his hand and her panties. Probably her skirt too.

When she was finished from that dynamite climax...she turned her face to Charles with a huge smile. Without saying a word...Katrina rose up, sat on her knees, unfastened her skirt and slid it off her hips. Slowly she lowered it...trying to keep her balance in the moving wagon. Not an easy task to do.

Charles had a perfect view of her back and then her buttocks as she lowered the skirt...teasing him as she lowered it slowly. She knew just what she was doing to him. He reached and held her by the waist so she wouldn't fall over.

"God. This is the most beautiful woman on the planet." Charles thought.

Once her skirt was lowered as far as it would go, Katrina sat back down, between Charles legs and continued taking her skirt the rest of the way off. She still had her panties on.

Then she realized that Charles was still fully clothed. So, Katrina got back up…turned around and was back on her knees. She leaned in and gave Charles a slow, lingering kiss. Then sat back up and unbuttoned his shirt. Button by button she worked her way down until she could open it up. She pulled the shirt out of his pants and then took it off his shoulders and helped him remove it completely.

She loved his hairy chest. MMMMM yes…loved to play in his hair, then play with his nipples.

But that wasn't what she really wanted. Katrina knew what her body needed. She wanted what had been pressing on her backside since this ride began. And she was going after what she needed and desperately wanted.

In the position Charles was sitting in, his manhood was pressing so hard in his pants, he was most uncomfortable. He also knew right where this was heading. Katrina's hands were wandering down from his chest to his abdomen to the button on his jeans. He knew he would have to move for her to have access. So, Charles slid down, allowing her enough room to get her hands where she could undo the button and then slide down the zipper. She then opened his jeans and saw what she had been looking for.

AHHHH. Yes indeed. There he was. Still covered in Charles's undershorts, Katrina pondered how to get her man out of his clothing. Bouncing around in a wagon was not the ideal place to get undressed.

Charles told Katrina to move over for a minute. He took off his boots, socks, jeans and undershorts. Now he was as open to her as she was to him. Katrina gazed at him in awe. She loved his body.

He wasn't perfect. Of course not. But he was perfect to her and that was all that mattered. This was the man she loved. Her man. With all his flaws and imperfections. And she wanted him. Now.

Katrina got down on her knees, lowered her head and kissed her man's love stick. He already had precum dripping from it and he tasted delicious. She licked him up and down and around. Stopping at his huge bulbous head..she opened her mouth and took him. Inch by inch she worked him into her mouth. Deeper until she started to gag. She stopped and held as still as she could. The bumping of the wagon only added to Charles's meat going so deep into her throat. But she tried to accommodate for that and kept her hand on him to control the depth.

Katrina would suck him for a while, then come off him and lick him from the top to his balls and back to the top. Finally, Charles could stand it no more. He reached for her head and pulled her off him. She looked up at him with those big brown doe eyes that killed him every time.

"Sit on me baby. Put my hard rod into you and ride me." Charles took her by the waist and guided her over him. As much as the wagon was moving, he had to take hold of himself and guide his stiffness to her opening. Once he felt her opening he slid into her easily.

Taking Katrina by the waist he guided her up and down on his staff and together they came to a steady rhythm. Katrina had been trying to hold on to Charles's shoulders but it wasn't working too well, so she reached up and grabbed hold of the backboards along the front of the wagon. This gave her the ability to control her movements along with the bumping of the wagon. Charles was guiding her and she wasn't far from having a climax again. Her inner muscles started closing in on his manhood and she could feel him stiffening even more. Charles knew Katrina was close and increased the speed of their movements. He wanted them to come together. He also knew he wasn't going to last much longer. Knowing she was holding on to the boards behind him, he reached up with one hand and started playing with one of her nipples. Then switched to the other.

As he heard her breathing become ragged and felt her muscles tighten around him, he pinched her nipple...Katrina exploded all over him. Right with her, he released his load. Rope after rope of semen went deep inside her. They both looked at each other at the same moment as they reached their release. Katrina bent her head and kissed Charles with such passion. This was a moment neither of them would ever forget.

They rode for a little while...still connected. Then they pulled apart. Katrina turned and sat between Charles legs as they continued to ride. A few minutes later the wagon came to a halt. Jasper jumped down and told them they would be staying here for a while.

Charles had a grin on his face as he moved Katrina forward and got up. He got down from the wagon and motioned for her to follow. Wondering what he was up to…she obliged him. They walked for a short distance. With just the light of the stars and moon she spotted the water in front of them.

Charles took her by the hand and led her out into the water. At first Katrina was a bit apprehensive. Where was she and what was this watering hole? Charles kept a firm grip on her hand and continued until they were waist deep. Then he wrapped his arms around her and kissed her. The water felt so good as it lapped between and around them.

Katrina was holding on to his arms, relishing in the feel of his body against hers when suddenly Charles reached down…took her by the waist and threw her into the water. Katrina was startled and came up out of the water sputtering. Charles was right behind her and grabbed her by the waist and pulled her back into him. He was laughing as she spit the water from her mouth and shook her hair from her face.

She spun so fast that Charles didn't feel her foot until she had wrapped her leg around his and pulled it out from under him. Down he went. Katrina was laughing so hard when he came up out of the water. Thus went the play time for the next half an hour. One after the other and then the reverse. They dunked, tripped, pushed and prodded until they were worn out.

Katrina called a truce. Charles agreed. He went to reach for her but she was wary that he was up to something again. He was so handsome and with that shitty grin all over his face she just didn't trust him. She knew he was up to something.

Yes, indeed he was, but not what she was thinking. Slowly he neared her. He reached out and took a small strand of her gorgeous red hair and played with it in his fist. He wrapped it around his hand and then pulled her toward him. When she was standing right in front of him, he let go of her hair, picked her up and had her put her legs around his waist.

Katrina felt his hardness the moment she wrapped her legs around Charles's waist. Damn, but this man is always having a hard on…she thought. But she liked it. She loved making love to her man no matter where it was. And what better place than here…in the water.. with the stars and the moon…nature at its best.

Katrina leaned down and kissed Charles. Softly at first and then deepened as her tongue licked his lips. Charles opened his mouth to receive her tongue. Damn, this woman made him so hard. He felt his hard, stiff rod poking at his beautiful woman's door and he wanted in bad. Katrina could feel his rod poking her and as she moved her body up and down her button would hit right on his pelvic bone.

Mmmmmmmmmmmmm..this was driving her crazy.

She wanted him…now. So, she squirmed around until he was in perfect alignment and then sat down on him. She let him enter her slowly, feeling the pressure of him opening her up.

Charles held her as he felt her lower herself onto him. He didn't want to go too fast. He wanted to relish this moment. Damn, she felt so good. This was an amazing woman. She knew how to please him. What he liked and didn't. What more could a man want? Katrina had her arms wrapped around his neck and was now moving up and down his shaft and moaning in his ear. He knew he wasn't going to last long if he didn't slow her down.

He let Katrina ride him for a few more minutes, feeling the water splashing up between his legs and onto where they were entwined. This felt so awesome he hated to stop it. But he wanted to make this one last longer so Charles pulled Katrina from him. She looked up at him in bewilderment. Why had he stopped.

Charles took her hand and led her out of the water to the grass covered edge. He laid her down and settled between her spread legs. In the moonlight her wet womanhood glistened. So inviting.

Charles looked in Katrina's eyes and then put his head to her mound. With his fingers, he spread her open and licked her from the tip of her button to her little pink hole. He heard her moans. God, he loved the sounds she made. He did it again. She moaned again. He licked her outer lips…paying special attention not to hit her button of love. She bucked her hips. He knew what she wanted. But she would wait. He licked her inner lips…all the way down to her little hole. And then back up.

Katrina knew he was playing with her. But she wanted him to take her. She needed to cum. She also knew he would hold her until he was ready to let her. She loved this torturous play because she knew where it would lead to in the end. It would be the best climax ever.

Charles licked and nipped at her labia and as she squirmed and whimpered, he loved it even more. Then he stuck his tongue into her love hole. Katrina's hips rose to meet his face. Oh, yes, he knew how much she loved this. He sucked and ran his tongue in and out of her until he was driving her to the edge. Then he went to her little love button and clamped down on it. He sucked it into his mouth. Katrina let go with a gush of her juices as she came all over his face.

He took his time loving her. There was all the time in the world to make this woman know how much he worshiped her and adored her. He wanted her to know that she was his for all eternity...to the end of time. As Katrina started to relax from her fantastic climax Charles pushed first one finger then two into her and started moving them back and forth. In and out, slowly imitating what he was going to do with the stiff rod he now had. As his fingertips found her gspot he pushed on it, stimulating it. Katrina started moving her hips into his hand. Charles started licking her button again as he kept his fingers moving on her spot and she reached another climax, coming all over his hand, dripping down between her butt cheeks.

Katrina knew that Charles could do to her what no other man had ever been able to. No man could stimulate her and give her such mind-blowing orgasms as Charles could. And she knew it wasn't over yet.

Charles was a caring and giving lover. He would make sure she was totally sated before he would seek his own release. She loved him for that.

Charles wanted her to have one more earth-shattering climax before he sought his own, so as he kept his fingers in her he stimulated her little button again. Licking and sucking it. Pulling on it, releasing it, then grabbing on to it with his teeth and nipping on it. As he did this, his fingers were working their magic inside her...moving back and forth...in and out... hitting her gspot....and as she reached the pinnacle of pleasure.. he inserted his little finger into her little pucker hole.

Katrina exploded. Her whole insides came apart. Her muscles clamped down on Charles's fingers, her rectal muscles grabbed ahold of his little finger and she screamed. The echoes of her scream delighted him. He didn't slow down...he didn't let up...and her climax continued.

As Katrina started her decent from the best climax she had ever had, Charles moved over her body and entered her. Her body responded. Her hips moved up to meet him. Their pelvic bones met. He held very still. He relished the feel of her still quivering vaginal muscles hugging his meat. He held her close, nestled his head in her neck, smelling her. Yes, she was his.

Katrina felt like everything in her had been turned inside out. She was totally relaxed and content. God what this man could do to her. He dominated her.. knew her body so well. He knew her so well. Knew what she needed and how to give it to her. Never could another man satisfy her the way Charles did.

Charles started moving slowly inside of Katrina. He felt her muscles slacken and tighten as he moved. He loved the feel of her. So warm, moist, wet from their lovemaking. She was always ready for him. He pulled out and teasingly went back in a little at a time. He watched her face as he moved. He loved her expressions. Then he pushed all the way in …hard… she moaned. God, he loved it.

He pulled out and pushed in hard several more times. She moaned each time. Then he slowed down and went gently…teasing her. She moaned even louder. The tip of him played with her, just inside her. She begged him to fill her…to give her what she wanted. "Want do you want baby." Charles asked her.

"I want you deep inside me." Katrina answered.

Charles pushed and slammed into her. He held still. He felt her tighten around him. He knew he was going to cum soon. He wanted them to cum together. He reached down between them and played with her button, rubbing it in circles. Pressing a little bit harder he heard her breathing get faster. Her head turned opening her neck to him. He licked it and then as he started to cum he bit down and they both came hard. Katrina's legs went around his waist and she pushed him into her deeper. He felt himself shooting deep into her womanhood.

Charles came the hardest he had in a long time. Six, seven, eight ropes of cum went inside of her.

Katrina felt him let go and her climax went right with him. She felt herself squeezing him…draining him of his juices and hers flowed around him and ran out of her. Just as she had felt him bite her neck she had heard him say:

"You are mine baby. No one else's. Mine.. for all eternity.. till the end of time."

Katrina opened her eyes and looked up to see Charles looking at her. He was smiling. His eyes were aglow. She smiled back at him. She put her arms around his neck and pulled his head to her and kissed him…tenderly.

"Yes, darling, I am yours. No one else. Just yours... until the end of time."

The wagon ride back was quiet as they had dressed and then just held each other. When they arrived at the barn Charles thanked Jasper and helped Katrina into the truck.

Charles had more plans for Karina before the night was over. He was going to show her the night of her life. She deserved it with all she had put up with from him. She had stood by him through his worst and his best. Now he was going to give back to her tenfold. Katrina would never forget this night for as long as she lived. Not if he could help it. She was his and he would make damn sure she knew it. Never would she have any doubts. Never would she wonder. Never would she look upon another man for anything. For any reason.

He headed the truck back towards the city. Once they were on the freeway he pulled her close and held her. He wanted her as close to him as possible. Needed her nearness. Needed her to be beside him always. There would never be a time they were not as one again.

Charles pulled into the Country World Apex, one of the best country western night clubs within a one-hundred-mile radius. He knew how much Katrina loved to dance, and tonight all her wishes were to come true. As he parked the truck he glanced at her and saw her eyes as they grew in size.

Katrina had always dreamed of coming to this place. She had heard how big the dance floor was and wanted to two step around its perimeter, over and over again. The line dancing was one of her favorites. Everyone moving in unison was so exhilarating and so much fun, everyone staying in step. She couldn't wait to get inside the door and watch. Better yet, get on that huge dance floor.

They walked in the door, paid the fee and found a table a couple rows back from the dance floor. The house band was fantastic and as they played, Katrina couldn't sit still in her seat. Charles ordered her a mixed drink and himself a coke. As she sipped her drink she got more antsy to get on the floor. A line dance came up and Charles finally asked her to dance. She was more than ready. They danced that one and the next two.

Returning to their seats, they were being watched from the bar. Charles's eyes rose as he sat down and caught sight of his friend Ross. But Ross wasn't looking at Charles. His eyes were fully on Katrina. He watched every move she made. Only when he felt he was being watched did he look over to Charles and see the stare of steel.

Katrina had barely sat down when "Watermelon Crawl" started playing and she loved to line dance to it. She started to pull on Charles's hand but he told her to go ahead. She jumped up and joined the others on the dance floor.

Charles was looking at Ross, watching his eyes on Katrina. He got up and walked over to the bar beside Ross.

"Hey Ross. How are ya tonight?" Charles asked his friend. "Great. How you doing?" Ross asked back.

"I'm doing good man." Charles answered.

"Man, that's some dish you have with you. She's hot." Ross said as he was watching Katrina dancing, her hips swaying.

"MMM, yes she is. That's why she's with me, man." Charles said back to Ross.

"Yeah, well, you're one lucky dude, man. You better hang on to that one. I'd be on her like a stud on a filly if she wasn't with you." Ross took a gulp from his beer.

"Oh, I intend to do everything it takes to keep her good and happy. So, keep your eyeballs in your sockets. She's all mine bud." Charles was leaving no doubts in Ross's mind whatsoever.

"I hear ya man. Can't blame a cowpoke from looking though. She's definitely good on the eyes. Best looking one I've seen in here all night." Ross indicated as he looked around the room. "And look how well she moves that ass man. I bet you get a lot of pleasure tumbling that."

"Well, that's for me to know and you'll never find out. Hands off big buddy." Charles warned.

"Yeah, I know. Say, haven't seen you in here in a long time. What gives? You getting hung up on this cowgirl or what?" Ross asked.

"Yeah. Stopped drinking. Straightened my life up. Working steady. Things are looking a whole lot better." Charles said with pride for the first time in his life.

"Wow. I'm impressed. They say it takes a good woman to straighten a man out. Guess you found one. Good for you." Ross took a chug on his beer again.

Ross and Charles had hung out for many years as drinking and carousing buddies. He missed the old days until he had gotten back together with Katrina. Now, he wouldn't go back for the world. She had filled every void he had had and then some. Charles told Ross good-bye and met Katrina as she was heading back to the table.

The band had broken into a nice slow song and Charles wanted nothing more than to hold Katrina in his arms....to show the whole world that she was his. He led her back out onto the dance floor and took her in his arms. She held her head back and looked into his eyes. They shone with all the love he had for her. She put her arms around his neck and buried her head on his chest. This was her man.

They danced with their bodies so close together. Her breasts were rubbing on his chest. He felt her nipples harden. He put his leg deeper in between her thighs. Charles was near to rubbing her throbbing button through her jeans. He could hear her breathing getting faster. He leaned down and licked her ear. Katrina moaned.

They danced that way through the rest of the song. By the time they headed for the table, Charles had to walk very close behind Katrina to conceal his raging harness. He leaned over and whispered in her ear that he was ready to leave. She reached and grabbed her purse and jacket as a reply.

Once outside Charles grabbed her from behind and rubbed his crotch right up to her backside. He was so hard he ached. Katrina gave a soft laugh and rubbed her hips back into him. He smacked her ass and said, "Let's get out of here. I want that ass baby."

Katrina grabbed his hand and headed for the truck. Once inside she took Charles's face in her hands, turned his face to her and kissed him passionately. Charles stuck his tongue in her mouth and moved it in and out like he wanted to do to her elsewhere. Damn he was so hard he hurt. He wanted her like he never had.

Charles started the truck, pulled out of the parking lot and pulled onto the freeway again, heading in the opposite direction of Katrina's place. She wasn't paying any attention, fortunately. She was busy trying to remove his manhood from his tight jeans. Succeeding, she licked the top of his engorged head, removing the precum that was now dripping freely. God, this woman was going to kill him yet.

Katrina licked up and down his hard shaft as Charles tried his best to concentrate on his driving. Difficult as it was, he had to keep his hands on the wheel and his foot steady on the gas. Her lips were now going over the top of his rod. As she lowered her head and took more of him into her mouth he groaned. Charles didn't know how much longer he could hold off the inevitable. He knew he would blow before long. But, damn, this felt so good.

Katrina worked her way up and down his long, firm meaty shaft. She held him steady with the movement of the truck with her hand, never missing a lick or a suck. Ten minutes down the road she felt his seed come up through his shaft and hit the back of her throat. She swallowed every drop. Sucked him dry…then licked him clean. Katrina sat up and smiled at him.

Just as she finished Charles pulled off the freeway onto the ramp. He slowed down and turned onto the frontage road. To the left was a huge hotel with bright lights and beautiful decor. He pulled up to the front door. Reaching down he put himself back into his pants and zipped them back up. Katrina had whipped her face clean and was sitting up, her eyes had grown huge in wonderment of where they were and why.

Charles got out and handed the keys to the valet, who had opened Katrina's door and helped her out. He went around and took her hand and led her inside.

The lobby was from a set in the movies. It was glitzy and beautiful. Katrina looked around in awe. Never had she seen anything so beautiful. She was in disbelief. She looked at Charles with questioning eyes.

He said nothing but led her to the elevators. Up they went to the fourteenth floor. Out to the hallway and down about two thirds and stopped at a door. Charles took a key card from his pants pocket and put it in the slot. With the green light…he opened the door.

Katrina walked in first. The lights were dim. The king size bed had been turned down…rose pedals were spread on it. On a side table was an iced down bottle of non-alcoholic champagne and two glasses. Some fruit on a platter with crackers was there too.

She looked at Charles in wonder. He took her in his arms and kissed her. Gently, lovingly. His hands went into her hair. He played in it. Then he held her head as he kissed her harder. Demanded more. Wanted more. She returned his kiss. He parted her lips with his tongue. It danced in her mouth. Her body swayed as she felt the passion emanating from him. He held her to him.

His hands went to her shoulders as he kissed his way to her neck. He felt her pulse. He sucked there. Felt her blood rushing. He moved to her ear. He whispered how hot she was. How hot she made him. Her body moved. Katrina grabbed his arms…holding on to him for support. Charles's passion was high. He had his woman in his arms. He wanted her to know how much she meant to him. How much he loved her. He would give her all he had. She would know that she was his.

Now, tonight and forever. For all time.

Charles moved his hands down Kristina's shoulders and across her collarbones. He went down her chest to the top of her shirt. He played with the top of her breasts. Running his fingertips along the edge of them. She moaned and rocked on her boots.

He put his hands over the top of her shirt and over her breasts. The nipples were already hard. He pinched them. Katrina's head went back and she moaned again.

Charles reached for the hem of her shirt and pulled it up over her head. He cupped her breasts through her bra and massaged and played with them. He took her in his arms and kissed her again while reaching around and unhooking her bra. He took each strap and slid them down her arms and off. Charles then backed up and let the bra drop away from her body. Her breasts, with the hard nipples, looked at him… aching to be touched.

Charles leaned down and licked around her left breast. Around the sides…under and back around. Finally, he took the hard nipple in his mouth. He sucked it in. he suckled it. He nipped it with his teeth. Katrina grabbed his hair…she pushed his head into her. She wanted more.

He switched sides and did the same to the right breast. Damn they tasted so good. He couldn't get enough of them. But it was time to move on. He wanted more of her. Charles stood back and unbuttoned her jeans. Then came down the zipper. Her heart missed a beat. She held her breath. Charles hooked his hands in her jeans and down they came…taking them down to the top of her boots.

Charles looked into Katrina's eyes as he put his hand down her panties. She was so smooth and nice. His finger went to her clit. Then down into her slit. Oh yeah. She was wet. He slicked his finger with her juices and went back to her clit. He rubbed it in little circles. Her knees went weak and he grabbed her by the waist to hold her up.

Katrina grabbed onto Charles shirt and held on. Her hips started moving with his finger. Then suddenly Charles pushed his finger into her. She jumped. Then pushed into his hand. His finger went deeper. The palm of his hand hit her clit at the same time. Katrina exploded. Her juices ran down Charles's finger and into his hand. His head came up and he kissed her hard. She was lost in the feelings going through her body. Charles put two fingers inside of her. She wreathed, gyrating her hips in time with his fingers. He didn't let up until she had come a second time.

Katrina was drained. Her knees buckled. She couldn't stand up. Charles pulled his fingers from her hot love nest and caught her as she started losing her footing. He picked her up and lay her on the bed. Quickly he removed her boots, socks, jeans and panties. She lay there naked before him.

"God, she is the most beautiful woman in all the universe." Charles thought to himself. "How lucky can one man be."

Charles left her and went into the bathroom. It was huge. It had a vast jacuzzi tub with candles all around it. He started the water to a nice temperature and lit the candles. There were mirrors all the way around, reflecting the soft light.

Charles stripped his clothes quickly and went back to get Katrina. She looked up at him with dreamy eyes. He picked her up and carried her to the bathroom. As they entered, she looked in disbelief.

He carried her over to the tub and gently lowered her into the water. Charles followed right behind her. He then reached and turned on the motor for the jacuzzi. The bubbles started moving around their bodies. Katina thought she had died and gone to heaven. She laid back against Charles, her back against his chest, her head on his shoulder. She closed her eyes and sighed.

Charles held her tight to him. He let their bodies absorb the warmth and motion of the water. He relaxed right along with her. They lay there for twenty or so minutes, just taking it all in.

Slowly, he started moving his hands along her body. Starting at her shoulders, massaging, rubbing. She moaned. He went down to her breasts, playing with them, bringing her peaks to hardness. He moved his hands down her belly toward her mound. But then went around it to her hips. He rubbed them.

Katrina could feel his rod getting harder against her buttocks and back. She moved slightly, rubbing herself against him. He groaned. She felt his hand as he started playing with her mound, down lower into her slit. He rubbed her, getting her wet. He stroked her clit. Making her squirm with want. Knowing she was ready, he lifted her by the waist and held her over his erection.

Katrina knew what Charles wanted. She reached between them and took hold of his erect staff and placed it between her wet lips and sat down on him. He slid in easily. They rocked back and forth. Water sloshed around in the tub... almost over the top as they moved. Charles lifted her up and down on his hard, engorged cock. She reached down and started rubbing her clit. She was moaning and he was groaning. Both in euphoria. He kept her moving on him, she rocked on him..it felt wonderful. They had started a rhythm.

Katrina reached her climax first. She came hard, she braced her feet on the tub and rocked as hard as she could on his cock. Charles took her by the waist and lifted her as much as he could and dropped her back down on him...hard.. fast.. he pumped his hips up into her..and he came…hard… pumping rope after rope into her hot pussy. Oh. God…she was so hot..

Charles grabbed her hair and pulled her head back to his face. He turned her head and kissed her hard. His lips burned hers. He broke the kiss and looked deep into her eyes.

"You're my woman, baby. Mine. Only mine." Charles told her.

"Yes, baby. Only yours." Katrina said back to him and smiled.

They cleaned up and got out of the tub. Dried each other and went back into the bedroom. They sat and had a drink, ate some fruit and made small talk.

Charles got up and took her hand, bringing her out of her chair. He held her in his arms and kissed her gently, with passion. He needed her again. Wanted her again. He could never get enough of her. He led her to the bed and laid her down. Pulling her to the edge, he held her legs up and over his shoulders. He then went to his knees in front of her. He pulled her love lips apart admiring how luscious they looked. Charles wanted to devour them but knew he was going to take his time and give her so much pleasure.

Slowly, he touched her lips. Rubbed them lightly. He pulled the outer lips apart and saw the beautiful pink of her inner self. He dropped his head and took his tongue to her. Lightly he licked her. Up from the bottom to the top. He stopped just shy of her clit. Then he went back down again, almost to her little puckered hole. Her hips moved and she moaned.

Again, he started at just below her clit and went all the way to her little hole. She jumped. He spread his tongue and went a little harder this time. God, she tasted so good. He had to have more.

He picked up the pace and licked her faster and harder. Then he hit her clit. Her hips came off the bed. Charles put his hand on her hip and pushed her back down. He held her there. He clamped onto her clit and started sucking. Katrina moaned and tried moving but couldn't. He held her tight and sucked her harder.

Katrina started to cum and as she did Charles inserted a finger into her pussy. She came like a rocket. Her cum ran down his finger into his hand. She was moaning. Her head was going back and forth. He kept his finger going in and out of her as he sucked her clit. Slowly she started to come down from her climax. Charles licked her cum from her clit and her slit. Then he entered her with his tongue and her hips tried to come up again.

Damn, he felt so good…she thought. She wanted so much more from him. He knew how and where to touch her to bring her to the best climaxes. Her orgasms were strong with him. No one had ever been better with her. She knew how good they were together and she wanted no other man. Ever!!!

Charles was just getting started with her. He started licking her again…from her little pucker hole to her clit. She started moaning again. She loved her ass licked. He knew just how to do it. Charles went back to her little hole as he put a finger into her pussy again. He pumped his finger into her as he licked and sucked on her little hole. then pushed his tongue inside of her. He still held her hips down and she was trying to press them harder into his face.

He left her ass and went back to suck her clit into his mouth. As he did this, his finger, then two in her pussy…he slid one into her ass. Katrina exploded. She came unglued. She came all over his face, hand, fingers. If she could squirt…this was the closest she had come. Her whole body had let go. She trembled. Still he didn't let up. He was going to bring her to another orgasm. And he did. She came again.

Charles got up off his knees, her legs still on his shoulders, and he entered her. Slowly. He teased her cunt with his cock. His tip played with her. In and out, little by little he inched into her. Just enough to hit her gspot and stopped. He held still for a minute. Let her catch her breath.

Katrina was breathing...no panting. Her hips were rising to meet his thrusts...but he wasn't thrusting. He was teasing her with his cock. He was in control. He had her where he wanted her. He could take her to the heights he wanted to...when he wanted to. She was his.

"Mine baby. This is mine. Only mine." Charles said to her.

Katrina's eyes met his and knew he was dominating her. But she didn't care. She was his and she knew it. Only this man could give her what she truly wanted. Only this man knew her body so well that he controlled her.

Charles started moving inside her again...inching in. backing out... inching in. backing out. Then when he was almost all the way out...just the head in, he slammed into her...hard. Katrina came in an instant. Her orgasm overwhelmed her. Her whole body broke lose into the most massive climatic overload she had ever known. Her juices flowed like never before. All over Charles's cock, out of her vagina and down between her thighs and buttocks. She was drenching the bed. Charles smiled to himself. Oh yes, her body and mind was his...for all time. Forever.

Charles remained still while inside of her, not wanting to reach his pleasure yet. He wanted her to cum one more time. Waiting for Katrina to come back to earth, he stroked her hair and then her face. He kissed her neck and ear. She moaned. He whispered how much he loved making her cum and that he was going to do it again. She moaned again.

Slowly, he started moving inside her again. He easily built her and built her until she was on the edge of cumming again. Now, she was pushing back into him as he picked up speed. Setting a steady rhythm, he kept hitting her deep inside, her gspot, her cervix, knowing it was driving her closer and closer. Her breathing was picking up, getting harder. Suddenly, she looked up into his eyes and he knew she was there. Charles grabbed her thighs...pushed them as far back toward her breasts as they would go and pounded into her. He got as deep as he had ever been inside of her. He branded her with his cock. Now he was going to brand her with his seed.

As he pushed with all his might, they both came together. Katrina let out a scream. Her body quaked. Charles threw his weight into her, leaning down and bit into her shoulder, as he claimed her as his own. His seed let go and ripped into her...stream after stream of hot jism, letting go inside of her. He pumped until there was no more left and pumped a couple more times. Then he slumped over her. Katrina wrapped her arms around his neck and held him to her.

No man would ever make her feel this way. No man would ever have what this man had. She was his forever. For all time.. For eternity. And all they had was TIME!!!!

TIME

As her eyes opened she already knew she was alone in the bed. Daryl had left for the day. Hers would be spent laying around the house, maybe doing a little bit of cleaning. Then she'd curl up on the couch and read one of her favorite romance novels. She hadn't read one of them in a long time.

She rolled over, just to see where he had laid beside her and she saw an envelope laying on his pillow. That was strange...she thought. She sat up and took it. She opened it up and took out the card that was inside. She read it and reread it.

"Good morning my sweet loving wife. I would like for you to take a nice leisurely bath, with your favorite bubbles. Then I want you to get dressed in the outfit I have put on your chair in our bedroom. There will be more instructions to come. You have one and a half hours to do this. I love you very much. Daryl."

Dee Anne sat there dumbfounded. What was he up to? He never left her cards. He never gave her instructions and he would absolutely never choose clothes for her. She had to admit though that her curiosity was piqued.

"Well, I guess the only way I'm going to find out is to do as he says." Dee Anne said out loud as she crawled out of bed.

Heading for the bathroom she stripped off her favorite football T-shirt that she always wore to bed and stepped out of her little lace panties. She put the stopper up in the tub and started the water, getting it at a nice warm temperature. She poured in some lavender and vanilla bubble bath and waited for it to fill up.

As she eased in, Dee Anne let out a sigh. Daryl sure knew how to make her feel good. She relaxed for a good twenty minutes, luxuriating in the warmth. When the water started to cool down she figured it was about time to get out and start getting dressed.

She got out of the tub and dried herself off with her favorite pink soft towel. Wrapping it around herself, she almost went to the kitchen to make herself some coffee before getting dressed. After looking at the clock she realized that she had been in the water too long and didn't have time.

When she walked to the chair and saw the outfit Daryl had left for her, her jaw dropped and she stood there unable to move.

Dee Anne spotted the black garter belt first. She had never worn one. Then she saw the black silk stockings.

"He has to be kidding, right?" she asked out loud. "These won't even go all the way up my thighs. What the hell is he thinking?"

Dee Ann had never worn anything but full pantyhose. She knew he must be making some kind of mistake. Surely, he knew she would never wear these.

As she picked through the rest of the clothes she came to what was supposed to be a bra. It was more like a corset. Wait a minute. That's exactly what it was. Or bustier. You know...that thing that looks like a corset but isn't. That holds the breasts up...way up...and your middle in. way in. OH LORD!!!!!

Then she saw the mini skirt. It was so short. So very short. And the top. It was a skimpy little thing.

"Daryl, what the fuck!!!!!" Dee Anne shouted.

She looked at the bedside clock again. She had a half hour to get dressed and be ready for whatever he had in store for her next. Although Dee Anne had no idea what he could possibly be up to, she figured he wouldn't do anything that would harm her so what the hell.

It took her almost the full half hour to get everything figured out and on properly. At exactly twelve o'clock noon the telephone rang.

The woman on the other end said that she was calling with a message from her husband.

You are to leave your house, drive to Jessica's Flower shop, go inside and ask for Rita. You are only to speak with her. You have fifteen minutes to get there. Then the phone went dead.

Dee Anne stared at the phone. What was her husband doing? Had he lost his last marbles?

But she knew she better get moving as it took almost the full fifteen minutes to get there. She put on the heels that Daryl had put with the clothing, making her feel like she was going to fall over when she walked. Thank God, her car was in the garage so no one would see her getting into it.

As she got out of the car at the florist she suddenly realized how exposed she was. Several men watched her while she climbed out of her car as she tried to hold her legs together. Her skirt was so short, and the stockings were only halfway up her legs. God, she felt so vulnerable. So on display. She would kill Daryl when she saw him.

As gracefully as she could she walked into the florist and asked for Rita. The gentleman behind the counter said that she had stepped out and would be back in about ten minutes. Was there anything he could do for her? She said no and that she would wait.

While she waited, she looked around the store. The flowers were beautiful, but she knew she was being watched. She felt his eyes, felt them like wet daggers drooling all over her. She was so self-conscious yet was getting turned on at the same time. She could feel herself getting a little more relaxed and comfortable with how she looked. He seemed to like it...a lot. So, why shouldn't she?

Rita came in the door, took one look at her and said, "You must be Dee Anne?"

"I am, and you must be Rita." answered Dee Anne.

"Yes I am. I have a package for you to deliver. You cannot look inside of it." said Rita. "Do you understand my instructions?"

"Yes ma'am. Where am I to take this package to and whom am I to give it to?" asked Dee Anne.

"There is a car waiting for you outside right now. Once I give you the package, you will get into the car and you will be given further instructions. Do you understand Dee Anne?" Rita was being most serious.

"Yes ma'am." Dee Anne was very puzzled but figured she better do as she was told.

Rita left the room and returned a short time later with a long narrow box. It was cold to the touch. It had a big red bow tied around it and a long red ribbon going down the length of it. "Wow.".... thought Dee Anne. "It must be flowers, but for whom?"

Dee Anne took the box and walked out the door knowing that both Rita and the clerk were watching her.

Sure enough, there was a black limousine parked in front of the florists with a young man dressed in a black suit standing with the back door open. He gestured for her to climb in.

She got into the car as gracefully as she could, considering what she was wearing, without letting too much being seen by the driver of her backside. The driver, trying to be as professional as possible, saw her plight and smirked just slightly.

Once in the seat, Dee Anne noticed an envelope beside her on the little refreshment table.

"Oh My God, not another note! Okay, let's see what this little game has me doing this time." Dee Anne was getting a little agitated by now. She opened the card and read it.

"Hello, I certainly do appreciate you're taking the time to do this little errand for me. And I really do hate to take up much more of your time, but I have one more little favor to ask of you. I need for you to enjoy your ride in this comfortable limo for about an hour to another little shop and pick up another package for me. I would be most grateful. Please, help yourself to the refreshments and sit back and relax. Thank you again."

Before Dee Anne could start to say anything or respond, the car was already pulling out and into traffic. What the hell was going on? And who the hell was she doing this for? Certainly, not her husband. But he was the one who had left the note in her bedroom this morning.. wasn't he? Now she wondered. Who else could have left her the note in her room? Who else would have her doing all of this crazy stuff and why on earth was she crazy enough to do it? But hell, it wasn't every day that she got a free ride in a limo.

So, Dee Anne helped herself to a glass of wine, some cheese and crackers and sat back for the next hour and enjoyed herself, immensely.

As the car rolled to a stop Dee Anne looked out the window to see a small little building among some other little shops. The driver got out, walked around and opened her door.

"Ma'am, I have been instructed to tell you to go inside and ask for a Mr. Whiteman. You are only to deal with him. Do you understand?" The driver looked directly at her.

"Yes sir. I understand." Dee Anne said.

She exited the car and walked to the shop. The door was opened for her by the driver and she entered the shop.

Dee Anne's eyes came out of her head. It was the most elegant store she had ever seen. It was lined in glass cases from floor to waist high with gems and stones of every conceivable type. She had never seen so many. Diamonds glittered, emeralds, rubies and more lined the cases. Necklaces, bracelets, earrings, and other bobbles were everywhere. Her eyes danced about the room.

A blonde headed lady approached her with a smile and asked, "May I help you miss?"

"Yes, please. I need to see Mr. Whiteman." said Dee Anne.

"Ah, yes. You must be Dee Ann. Please, have a seat. I'll get him for you." The lady indicated a seat near the cases.

Dee Anne took a seat and waited for about ten minutes before Mr. Whiteman came out from the door leading behind the cases.

"Dee Anne. I'm so sorry to keep you waiting." Looking her up and down he continued, "But I must say, you are worth waiting to see." Dee Anne blushed a nice pink at his blatant appraisal of her attire.

But he apparently liked what he saw. She then gave him a sly little smile. "Well, my dear. I see a beautiful lady was sent to do this task. I feel safe releasing this package into your care." Mr. Whiteman smiled at her just a little too long.

"So, Mr. Whiteman. Just what am I supposed to do with this package you have for me?" Dee Anne sidled up to him, playing along with this little flirtation he was obviously doing.

Mr. Whiteman was a fairly good-looking older gentleman. He had grayish hair, light brown eyes and a smile that would melt a woman's heart. He was about 5 foot eleven and around one hundred eighty pounds. He wore a brown suit with a white shirt and a paisley tie. All in all, he was every bit the businessman.

Dee Anne still felt a little like playing with this kindly gentleman so she tried to get as much information out of him as possible.

"Mr. Whiteman, I have been sent all over God's creation today picking up packages for God knows who. I have no idea what's in them or who they are going to. Can't you please give me even a little bit of a hint as to what is going on? I mean, could I get into some kind of trouble here? I am a married woman after all." She knew she was being a little coy, but damn, she wanted some kind of answer.

"Dee Anne, all I have been told is that this package is to be taken by you and to be delivered as directed. That's all I can tell you. I'm sorry I can't be of more assistance to you. I really am. You seem like such a... (he looked her over) sweet, nice young lady. Now if you'll excuse me, I'll get the item and you can be on your way."

With that Mr. Whiteman left and went through the door he had entered the room in and returned a couple minutes later. He handed her a box about three by four by eight inches. It was gift wrapped in a foil wrapping paper, with a small white bow on top.

"You are to go back to the car to receive further instructions. Have a good day Dee Anne." Mr. Whiteman said and she knew she had been dismissed.

She turned and opened the door and went outside. As she exited the shop, she saw the driver open the car door and wait for her. Again, she got into the car, careful to not show too much.

Once settled in the seat, Dee Anne saw another envelope sitting on the refreshment table.

"OH HELL NO!!!!!!" Dee Anne yelled at no one. Now she was pissed. Really pissed! Enough was enough already. This little game by whoever was playing it was done. She wasn't playing it anymore. She made her way up to the front and tapped on the window separating herself and the driver.

"Yes ma'am. May I help you?" the driver turned and asked her.

"This little shit party is over. Take me back home right now. I'm done with playing this game. You can deliver these packages yourself to whoever hired you to do this." Dee Anne was breathing hard and about ready to tear someone's head off.

"Ma'am. Did you read the card?" The driver asked her calmly. "No I did not and I don't intend to. This little whatever it is, is over. Take me home...NOW!!!!!."

"I'm very sorry, but I can't do that. Would you please read the card and settle down? I'm sure all will come to light soon." The driver remained calm.

With a huff, Dee Anne turned and went back to her seat and picked up the envelope. She tore it open and read it.

"Hello. I hope your little trip is going well. I would like to thank you for picking up the packages for me. You have been most helpful. Please enjoy your ride in my limo as you will continue the journey to your next destination to deliver the packages. Once you arrive, please meet the doorman. He will escort you. You will be most pleasantly surprised."

"Damn. Whoever this was...was going to a lot of trouble for some reason." Dee Anne thought.

The limo was well on its way by the time she had finished reading. Again, she poured herself a glass of wine and had some cheese and crackers. She put her feet up on the seat and remained there for the duration of the trip. Little did she realize she was giving the driver quite a view in his mirror.

As the limo came to a stop the door was opened and the doorman was there to assist her out. She was told to leave the packages in the limo. She stood and looked around her. The building was huge. The lights were brilliant. There was carpet on the steps leading up to the inside. Once in, she saw the gorgeous chandelier hanging from the ceiling that must have been near heaven. She had never seen such elegance. The doorman took her by the arm and led her toward an interior room. There another man dressed in a tuxedo guided her to a private room where there was a table set with dinnerware for two. A beautiful candle was in the center. Flowers and other decor made for a romantic and sensual ambiance. She was seated at the table and told to wait there.

After several minutes, Daryl came into the room. He was dressed in a suit and looked absolutely handsome. His smile was breathtaking. "Hello darling. You look fabulous. Stand up and let me look at you." Dee Anne stood up and turned around as Daryl filled his eyes with her. Damn she was beautiful! And that outfit was magnificent. He could sure make her look good. He took her in his arms and held her, kissed her deeply and then sat her back in her seat.

The waiter came with wine for them and they made a toast to each other and their love. Shortly a long white box was brought into the room. It had a long red ribbon down its length with a red bow in the middle. Dee Anne's eyes went wide. It was just like the one she had picked up.

"My darling Dee Anne. You are the love of my life. I wanted to do something very special for you. So, I got these for you today. But, as I could not leave the office to pick them up...I had you do it for me. I hope you didn't mind too much? Please, open the box dear.

Dee Anne gave him the evil eye but reached and opened the box and inside was two dozen long stemmed red roses. Tears filled her eyes. "Oh darling. It was well worth the trip to pick these up. Thank you so much. I love you more than words can ever say." With that she gave him a huge kiss.

They held hands and talked for a while and drank their wine.

A while later the waiter came in with another package. Dee Anne recognized it as the one she had picked up at the jewelry shop.

"My dearest Dee Anne. I know you got very upset today with the long limo ride. You were ready to quit. But I am so glad that you didn't. It actually proved your love for me even more. So, I would like for you to have this package. Go ahead and open it dear." Daryl gave her the package.

Dee Anne took it and opened it. Her eyes flew open wide. Sitting there, were three smaller boxes. In one was a gorgeous diamond heart necklace. The second was a matching bracelet and the third were the matching earrings. The tears flowed.

"Oh My God..Daryl!! You are the most wonderful husband in all the world. You are so thoughtful and loving. I love you so much." She was out of her chair and into his lap in an instant.

Daryl welcomed her with open arms. He held her tight to him as his mouth searched hers. His tongue found hers and he devoured her. Sucking hers into his mouth...tasting her. He couldn't get enough of her. She was indeed the love of his life and he wanted her to know just how much he treasured and desired her.

He had pushed her to the limit today and she had come through for him. He didn't know if she would actually wear the outfit he had laid out for her, but she looked stunning. And now he would prove to her how stunning she was.

Daryl held Dee Anne by her waist as she kissed him deeply. She had straddled his legs, her skirt making its way up her legs. She hadn't seemed to notice. She was so enraptured in her love for him that she had ignored what he was doing to her. His hands had moved down to her hips and were now rubbing her bare thighs and moving up to her buttocks.

Her skirt was now all the way up to her waist and her hips were moving with the rhythm of his hands moving along her backside. Dee Anne was so hot and getting so wet. She wanted Daryl so much. She felt him getting hard beneath her. She could feel him in her warmest place. She needed him.

His hands left her behind and moved to the front of her top. He moved the little blouse aside and saw the black corset. He told her to lift her arms over her head. As she did he took the blouse up and over her head. Off! She gasped. His hands went to her covered breasts. He groaned.

"Oh, my love. These are so beautiful. They look so gorgeous in there. But I have to see them. I want to taste them." Daryl was so hard he was in pain. He wanted her at that very moment. But he had to maintain. Patience.

Daryl reached around to her back and started undoing the corset and released it. He slowly took it off of her..looking as he did as her breasts came to life before his eyes.

"Oh My God. You are absolutely breathtaking. Oh, my darling." He reached out and touched her gently.. massaging each of her lovely globes.

Dee Anne arched her back as her breasts felt the touch of her husband. He massaged her tenderly at first. Then he grasped her harder and fondled her...taking her nipples and toyed with them.... pinching them. Daryl bent down and took one in his mouth and suckled gently. He loved the taste of her. She moaned.

He loved on her as her hips moved. She rotated on his hardening member. Her clit was enlarged and engorged. She wanted to cum so badly. He was driving her mad. Dee Anne knew she couldn't hold out much longer. She knew she was soaking wet and knew he could feel it through his slacks.

She reached down and grasped his hard cock through his pants. Damn. He felt so good in her hand. But she knew he would feel even better inside of her. She needed him.. wanted him. She tried to get off his lap but he held her firm.

"Not yet my little one. You're not quite ready yet." Daryl wouldn't let her go.

Dee Anne looked him in the eye and moaned loudly. She was ready to explode.

Daryl removed her hand from him and placed his hand between her legs. The other he put behind her butt. Holding her he started to rotate a finger around the outside of her clit. Dee Anne lifted herself a little to ease his hand in further. Daryl slid his middle finger into her slit as he found her clit. Dee Anne threw her head back and went into a climax as she had never had before. While in her rapture she felt his other hand meet her butt and a finger go to her little pucker hole. As he played with it her climax intensified. Her legs came up…she grabbed his neck and held on for dear life. Dee Anne squirted all over Daryl.

Dee Anne had never squirted in her life. It stunned her. She couldn't catch her breath. She gasped. Daryl removed his hand from her butt and massaged her clit slowly till she came back down. Then he put his arms around her and held her close. Her breathing slowly returned to normal and she rested against his chest.

"Oh My God. Daryl. I can't believe what you just did to me. That was awesome baby." Dee Anne was still in amazement.

"Nothing but the best for my beautiful wife." Daryl kissed her slowly and lovingly.

"Now I want to love you just as much." said Dee Anne as she slid from his lap and went to her knees before Daryl.

She didn't care that her bare ass was sticking out or that her pussy could be seen. Or that her breasts were open and on display. She reached up and undid Daryl's pants and pulled them over his hips along with his underwear. She ran her hands up his thighs as her eyes held his. Daryl watched as her tongue licked from the bottom of his manhood all the way to the top of his massive head.

"Oh yes, baby. That feels so good. I love how you do that." Daryl was beyond hard. He was aching for her mouth to take him.

Dee Anne loved the taste of his precum and licked it…moving it around the tip and down his shaft. Daryl groaned. She then took her lips and circled his head and kissed him.

"Oh God." said Daryl.

Dee Anne opened her mouth and took him inside.. sucking him in. down deeper. Daryl gasped. Her lips smiled up at him as she stroked him and took him even deeper. She went until she started to gag and then backed off. She continued this up and down motion as Daryl's hands went to hold her head. He loved how she sucked and stroked him. He could feel himself coming closer to cumming and didn't want to in her mouth this time. He wanted to be inside her. Daryl pulled her off of him and pulled her up.

"Sit on me baby.. take me inside of you. I want to feel myself inside that warm love nest." Daryl told her.

Dee Anne stood up and straddled Daryl. Slowly she sat down on him. She held his hard cock in her hand…stroking him as she lowered herself on him. Her womanhood opened to take him. Daryl watched as his cock entered her. He loved the site of seeing himself going into her. He watched as she parted and he went in..deeper and deeper.

"Ahhhhh. yeah.. baby.. that's it.. take me.. mmmmmmm" Daryl said to her.

"Oh God, you feel so good Daryl. I want you so deep inside me. I need you baby. Give me all you got honey." Dee Anne was rocking back and forth rubbing her clit against him. She was so ready to cum all over his cock.

Daryl grabbed her by the waist and moved her up and down on his hard shaft as he knew he couldn't hold out much longer.

"Cum with me baby. I'm going to fill you up with my hot sticky goo baby. I want to feel you squeeze me." Daryl kissed her deep with his tongue in her mouth doing what his cock was doing in her pussy.

They both came at the same moment.

"AAAAAhhhhhhhhh OH MY GOD!!!!!!!!!!!!!!" Dee Anne screamed. "Jesus. H. Christ....OII DEE ANNE." Daryl yelled.

Neither could stop the movement.. they both rocked together. him pumping…her still wreathing. Both trying to catch their breath. Daryl grabbed her and held her tight. Close to him.. near to him.. she was his. Is his. His life.. His lover.. His love.

WISTFUL PANDEMIC

Last night when I went to bed life was in an uproar. Things, as we had known them, had drastically changed.

Bars, restaurants, grocery stores, all closed. Schools were closed. No one was allowed into the hospital unless you were the patient. No one could visit loved ones in the nursing homes. You couldn't visit with friends and loved ones. In other words, you were confined to your house. Yeah, the dangerous disease known as Corona Virus 19 was declared a Pandemic. Highways were bare as no one could travel. Air travel was to a minimum. People were dying in vast numbers. Panic had set in all over the world.

Our apartment complex was no different. Rules had been established, even in this little town of Comet, Kansas. We hadn't been hit as hard as the larger cities, but it still wasn't safe.

Being a healthy twenty-eight-year-old female, five foot seven, one hundred thirty pounds, this was going to be hell. With long dirty blonde hair, blue eyes, and a medium complexion, I was pretty content with myself and got lots of leering looks from the guys when I went to the local pub.

Well, that abruptly changed in the blink of an eye. Now there would only be lonely nights stuck here in this apartment watching reruns or movies I had watched before. At least I wasn't the only one in this predicament. No one else in the complex could leave either. I knew several of my neighbors on my floor, and a couple of them use to come over once in a while to visit. That now ended.

One neighbor, in particular, seemed to ignore the stay-at-home order. He lived a couple of doors down from me. I didn't know him very well as he had moved in just a few months ago.

Not even knowing his name, I could tell he was into fitness as he was well built as well as handsome. We'd passed a few times in the hallway, nod at each other and enter our own apartments. Never once did either one of us even utter a "Hello". That seemed strange to me now.

He was quite a bit taller than me, so I would guess him to be about six foot three or four. He was well proportioned and had good firm muscles. His arms were bulky and very hard. He wore his light brown hair short on the sides, a little longer on top. He was always well-dressed. Usually jeans, a nice t-shirt or pullover shirt. He wore sneakers most of the time that I saw him.

The one thing that I found unusual was that he would be gone for days or weeks at a time. I did not know what kind of work he did, but I figured it must have something to do with his job. Well, not really my business anyway.

Fortunately, I wasn't affected by the job market as I worked from home as a medical billing specialist. I wasn't known as one of the "Essential Workers", so couldn't use that excuse to go out and about. Thankfully, I had enough groceries stored up for a couple of weeks. Lord knows how long we would be locked up for.

One night, about a week into the lockdown, I was laying in bed watching a boring movie when there was a knock on my door. Being in my pj's, which consisted of a purple tank top and matching panties, wasn't an ideal way to answer the door. So, I got up and put on my white terry cloth robe, and headed for the living room. I turned on the light on the end table.

Looking through the peephole I saw that it was the man down the hall.

'I wonder what he could want this time of night?' I asked myself. "Yes. What can I do for you?" I asked through the locked and chained door.

"I'm so sorry to bother you so late, but I seem to not have any coffee to make in the morning. I was wondering if you have any?" He asked me, with the door still closed.

"Um, sure. Hold on and I'll get you some." I answered.

"I have a container you can put some in if that would be alright." The man stated.

Since you have to go through a pretty hefty clearance to get an apartment here, I didn't think he would be much of a threat, so I unchained and unlocked the door to get the container.

"Hi, I'm Brody. Thank you so much. I don't do well without my morning coffee and with this pandemic, I can't seem to get any anywhere." He said with a smile.

Hi, I'm Morgan. I completely understand. Hold on and I'll get you some." I said as I reached for the container.

When I returned from the kitchen, Brody was sitting on my couch with one leg crossed over his knee, making himself comfortable.

I must admit, he looked hot sitting there. He had on jeans that hugged him well and a black t-shirt that wrapped around his chest and arms like a glove. Damn....

'Get your mind where it belongs, Morgan. He's just here for coffee.' I chided myself. I'd been cooped up for way too long.

"Here you go. I hope this will help you out until a store opens back up." I said as I handed him the container.

"Thanks, you're a lifesaver. I'm not the best person to be around if I haven't had at least one cup of joe to start the morning off." Brody said, still sitting on the couch.

"Well, we certainly can't have that. Then again, I guess it really doesn't matter much as you'd only be dealing with yourself right now with this lockdown." I said, trying to be a little friendly.

"Yeah, this shit sucks. Nothing is open, can't go anywhere. Sure cuts down on one's social life right?" He said as he put his foot back down on the floor and leaned forward.

Wondering where he's going with this and why he hasn't gotten up to leave yet I'm not sure how to respond to that question.

"Hopefully it won't last too long and then things can get back to normal." I tried to keep it simple.

"Hope you're right, but I have a feeling this will drag out longer than we think. Have a good night and thanks again for the coffee. Was nice to finally get acquainted." Brody said as he stood up and opened the door.

"Don't even say that. Things are bad enough. We don't need things to get worse. You have a good night too. And enjoy that coffee in the morning. Nice meeting you too. Night." I said as he left and I closed and relocked the door.

Wow, he didn't sound too optimistic did he? I headed back to my room and watched the rest of the movie and fell asleep.

I awoke to my phone ringing. Caller Id said it was my best friend Tina. Was I in the mood to talk to her before I even had my eyeballs opened? Hell yeah.

"Hey, what's got you calling this early in the morning?" I asked. "Are you just now getting that lazy ass out of bed? Guess you get to do that as you work at home." She said with a bit of sarcasm.

"Since I am lucky enough to work at home, and since we can't go anywhere anyway, why not sleep in a little bit later?" I answered back with just as much sarcasm.

"Now, now, take it easy. Just messing with ya girl. This shit sucks, ya know? It better not last too long. Jacob and I had plans for a really hot date for Saturday night. Guess that's off the table for now." She said, sounding a bit down.

"You and Jacob, really? What brought that about? I thought you couldn't stand that S.O.B. What changed your mind?" Now she had piqued my interest.

"You know he's been hounding me to death to go out with him. So, finally, I said yes, just to get him the hell off my back. So, go out with him then tell him I don't want to see him again. Done deal." She said.

"Oh, you're evil. But what else can I expect from you? So, what are you going to do today?" I wanted to change the subject.

"What the hell can I do. Can't go to work, the club is shut down. Don't know how I'm going to pay my bills if this thing lasts for very long." Tina complained.

"Yeah, at least I'll still have some income. People still have to see the doctor or go to the hospital. You know if you need help, all you have to do is ask." She knew I would always help her but I was reminding her.

"Yeah, thanks. Just hope it isn't too long. Besides, this cuts into our social life. We can't get it down for a while...cut the rug....get some booty." She says as she laughs.

"Yeah, well, I got one down the hall that's not too bad on the eyes. He came by for some coffee grounds so he can make some in the morning. Damn, girl…one hot dude." I said with a slight chuckle.

"Oh, do tell me more. Don't leave out a thing. Wait, you mean the elusive one down the hall from you? The one who disappears every now and then?" She asks with curiosity.

"Yeah, that would be the one. Not much to tell. He asked for some coffee…made himself at home on the couch while I got it. We chatted for a few minutes and he left. End of story." I said nonchalantly.

"That's it? Nothing hot, juicy, or anything?" Tina asked with total disbelief.

"Nope, that was it." I was jumping out of my skin to tell her how hot he looked and that it wouldn't take much for me to jump his bones in a heartbeat.

"Well on that note, I'm gonna find a hot movie to watch. You're no fun," she said with a laugh.

"Talk to ya later." And we hung up.

Getting out of bed, I went into the kitchen to make a cup of coffee in my little two-cup coffee maker. While it was brewing, I got two slices of bread and put them in the toaster, pushed down the lever, and left them to toast. I went to the refrigerator and got out the butter and my favorite strawberry jelly and put them on the small counter by the sink, where the coffee pot was also. I pulled out a coffee cup from the cupboard right above my head, placing it on the counter too.

This being only a small one-bedroom apartment, I only have room in the kitchen for a small table with two chairs. There is a small counter dividing the living room and the kitchen with two stools in front of it. I take a seat on one of the stools and look through my messages on my phone while waiting for my toast and coffee to finish.

One from my mom, one from my friend Charlene, and one from Brody.

'Brody? How did he get my number?' I ask myself. I click on the message to see what he wants.

"Hey Morgan, hope you're having a great morning. Was wondering if I could bring my coffee over and we could get to know each other better?"

"No, sorry, I have to start work in a half-hour. How did you get my number?" I know I didn't give it to him. Hell, I didn't even know him.

"You gave it to me last night when I got the coffee from you. You don't remember?" he texts back to me.

"Um, no, I don't." This was weird. I know I didn't.

"Ah, well, I guess with us talking so much you just forgot. Anyway, have a great day and don't work too hard. Later."

"Yeah, you too," I answered back.

My toast had popped up and was probably cold, but I got up and got it out of the toaster anyway, putting it on a small plate. I buttered it and put on the jelly, then cut the two slices in half. Coffee was next as I poured it in the cup, added a bit of sugar, stirred it, and placed the cup and plate on the counter in front of the stool.

I still couldn't get my head wrapped around that Brody had my phone number. I know I didn't give it to him. How the hell did he get it? Had my phone been in the living room when I went and got the coffee for him and he looked on it and took the number? No, I kept my phone in the bedroom with me. So how the fuck did he get it?

Not taking any more time to worry about it, I finished my breakfast, cleaned up the kitchen, and grabbed another cup of coffee. My computer is set up in the little office area in my bedroom. Having such a small apartment, there wasn't enough room to set up a desk, filing cabinet, printer, and little stuff I needed to do my job. I didn't need but one dresser in there, so there was plenty of room to set myself up a little space to work in.

Since I worked from home and didn't have to see anyone, I worked most of the time in comfort clothes or my pj's. Today I chose to put on a pair of gray sweatpants and a gray tank top with smiley faces all over it. I tied my hair back with a hairband, put my coffee on my desk, and sat down ready to get to it.

Having a desktop and a laptop that I work with, I turned them both on and waited for them to boot up. When they are up, I go to my email and check for messages. Seeing nothing important, I go to work doing invoices and EOBs.

It seems like I've been working for a while, especially when the last sip of coffee was cold. Looking at my watch, I realize I've been at it for about three hours. 'No wonder my back is aching' I say to myself as I stand up to stretch.

Since my coffee is stone-cold, I decide to get something else to drink, as well as a snack. As I reach the kitchen and set down my cup, there's a knock at the door.

'Who the hell can that be?' I wonder as I go to the door. Looking through the peephole I see that it's Brody. And he looks hot as ever.

'Get your head out of the gutter girl. Wonder what he wants now?' I ask myself.

"Hey Brody, what can I do for you?" I ask through the closed door. "Hey, Morgan, can I come in and talk to you rather than talking out here in the hall?" He asks.

Well, that does kinda make sense. We aren't strangers anymore. Sort of. Unlocking and unchaining the door, I open it and let Brody enter.

I catch a whiff of his aftershave and hot damn he smells so good.

Just past the entrance, before I get a chance to shut the door and turn around, Brody is right up to me. I can feel him up against my back.

"I hope I didn't interrupt anything important." He says.

I turn around slowly, look up into his face and his eyes are glued to mine.

"Well, actually, I was just taking a break from work." Why the hell did I just say that? He knows I work from home. I should have said I'm busy working.

"Well, sounds like I came at just the right time. I bet you're all tensed up from working so hard. How about I rub some of that tenseness away." With that, he reached up and started rubbing my shoulders and around my neck to the back of my shoulders. Damn, it did feel good.

But I couldn't just stand here like an idiot and let him rub me like that, even if it did feel good. I needed to escape his touch.

"Um, I was going to get something to eat and drink. Would you like to join me?" Was all I could think of to get out from under his hands. "Sure, I mean if it's not any trouble, I'd love to join you. I'd really like to get to know you better." His enthusiasm sure showed.

"Ok, follow me into the kitchen while I get it ready," I said, leading the way.

We sat at my little table while we ate and I drank a soda and he drank water. He said he was watching his figure. I laughed. He had no problem in that area from what I could see.

We chatted for about an hour, then I told him I had to get back to work. Even though I worked from home, I still had a quota I had to meet every day. If I didn't get back to it, I wouldn't make it today. He helped me clean up and then walked toward the door.

"Morgan, I like you a lot. I want to be with you more. Would it be alright if I bring something for dinner tonight and maybe we could watch a movie? I promise I won't stay too late." Damn, when he put on that sexy smile, who the hell could say no?

"That sounds nice. I'd like that." I said with a small smile. I didn't want to seem too eager.

"Great, how about I come over around six-thirty? Will that work for you?" he asked.

"Yeah, that would be fine. Now get out of here. I have to get back to work." I said as I opened the door to let him out.

Time flew by. The next time I looked at the clock, it was five. 'Oh shit, I have to get into the shower and get ready for Brody to come over.'

Just as I got up and turned off the computers and cleared up my desk, the phone rang.

"Hello Tina. And how did your day go?" I asked before she could start on whatever she was going to start ranting about.

"Well, if you must know, I talked with Jacob this afternoon. And guess what? Never mind, you'll never guess. He isn't who you think he is. I know, you think he's some nerd who just works all the time and has no time for anyone. Well, let me tell you that's the furthest thing from the truth. He is nothing like that." She stops and takes a deep breath.

"Oh yeah, so I'm sure you're going to enlighten me. But honestly, right now I don't have time. I have to get into the shower because I have company coming over shortly." I have to get her off the phone before she gets going again.

"Wow, wait, you can't have company. There's a pandemic going on in case you've forgotten." Tina sounds indignant. If she can't come to see me, how can anyone else?

"Like I'm not aware of that. It's just Brody, the neighbor guy. He's bringing dinner over. That's all. Nothing special." I say.

"You're kidding, right? The one you said had your phone number, that you didn't give to him. The one who's sexy as hell. The one you said you would jump his bones in a heartbeat...that one?" Then she started laughing harder and harder.

"Oh, come on. It's not like that. It's just dinner. For Pete's sake. Give me a break. I gotta go. Later babe..love ya." And I hung up the phone before she could start on me again. But she did have a point.. didn't she?

After taking a quick shower I dressed in a pair of stretch jeans and a purple-flowered tank top. I blow-dried my hair and put it up in a ponytail. 'Do I want to put on any make-up?' I asked myself as I looked in the mirror. Nah, I didn't want to go overboard.

Looking in the mirror for a final appraisal, I turned, walked out of the bedroom, and went into the kitchen. I set two plates and silverware on the table, along with napkins. Salt and pepper were already in the holder on it. Not wanting to make this romantic, I took off the candles and put them on the counter. This was, after all, just a get-together. I had just filled up two glasses with ice and set them on the table when there was a knock on the door. I looked at my watch. Six-thirty on the dot.

Making sure it was Brody, you never knew these days, I opened the door for him.

"Let me help you with some of that," I said as I grabbed one of the three bags he had in his hand.

"Thanks. They were getting a little awkward to carry." I kinda doubted that as strong as he looked to be.

We both carried the bags into the kitchen and placed them on the counter. I started taking the containers out of the bags. Damn, it looked like he had bought enough for a feast.

"Ahhh, do you think you are feeding an army here?" I asked with a giggle.

"Baby, it takes a lot to keep this body going. And I'm famished. I bet you haven't eaten since that little snack we had earlier, right?" he said while grinning at me.

"No, no I haven't. I was too busy trying to get all my work done for the day. Then I grabbed a quick shower and got the table ready before you got here. So, no, I didn't." I answered him while looking right back at him.

"So, I'm sure you will have quite the appetite too. Let's dig in and eat, then we'll find a good movie to watch. Sound good to you?" He asked as we put the food on the table.

Filling our glasses, mine with sweet iced tea and his with water, I put them on the table and we sat to eat. Chatting as we ate, it took us well over an hour before I cried uncle. I was so stuffed. I couldn't eat another bite. Brody helped me put the leftovers away and clean up the kitchen.

While I was putting the final dish away, Brody came up behind me and wrapped his arms around my waist. He leaned down, put his lips near my ear, and whispered, "Thanks for joining me for dinner. I enjoyed that a lot." Then he let me go and walked away.

I stood there for a moment not quite sure what to do. His body felt so warm and good. I didn't want him to move away from me, but he did. He was being a gentleman.

"Where's your TV babe? What kind of movie would you like to watch? Horror, drama, action, romance, you name it, I'll find it." He said looking at me from near the corner of the living room.

"My TV is in my bedroom. We'll have to watch it in there. Do you promise to behave yourself?" Why the hell did I just ask that? My face was getting warmer and I wondered if he noticed.

"Oh, hold on a second, I don't have movie channels, and I don't have many movies. Sorry. So have a look and pick out what you want to watch." I said.

"Do you have a smart tv?" he asked and I nodded that I did.

"Good, because I can upload my Netflix on it and we can get some pretty awesome movies on there. Is that ok with you?" He asked as he was heading for the bedroom.

As I followed him I said that it was fine with me.

Once he had it done, we looked over a lot of the movies and picked out a romance one.

"Really, you don't mind watching those?" I asked him as he sat on the bed beside me.

"Not at all. When you have four sisters, you get kind of used to that stuff. Sometimes I find it kind of amusing, actually." He said smiling rather smugly.

"Oh yeah, and why is that?" I wanted to be a little more of a smart ass but I didn't know him that well yet.

"Because most of life doesn't' happen that way. I just find a lot of it ironic." He said.

"Then we can watch something else if you'd like. Something more to entertain you better." I said to antagonize him a bit.

"Okay, how about a special ops movie? Have you ever watched one?" he asked while looking through the movie selection.

"No, can't say that I have. Was never really interested in it. All that war stuff. Yuck." I answered making a gross face.

Brody laughed but clicked on a movie he had found.

The movie was 'American Sniper' the story of Chris Kyle. By the end of it, I was in tears. I had been so engrossed that without knowing it I had slid into Brody's arm and my head was resting on his chest. It felt so natural to be held by him.

Just as the movie ended, his phone went off. He looked at it and jumped up off the bed.

"Sorry babe, but I have to go. It was great spending this evening with you and we are definitely doing it again soon." He leaned over and kissed me on the forehead and took off with the door shutting.

I lay there stunned. What the hell just happened? One phone call he's flying out the door. 'Well shit....shit, shit, shit....' I yelled as I pounded my fists on the bed.

Sleep didn't go well that night. It was fitful. I didn't understand why he left so abruptly.

Two days went by with no word from Brody. Tina had called but I wasn't in the mood to talk to her or listen to her ramblings, so I ignored the phone.

Work was a bitch, I couldn't concentrate. I mixed up numbers on invoices, data, and couldn't seem to get anything done. Food and my coffee just weren't getting it. What the hell was wrong with me? I only knew the man for one day or evening. Why was he getting to me so bad? My phone dinged with another message and I almost didn't look.

Tina had been bugging me all day and I didn't want to deal with her. This was day six and I was still annoyed. Why??? Who the hell knows.

"Hey. I'm sorry I left the way I did the other night. It's my job and I had to leave immediately. Come down to my place and I'll explain. Please." It was from the long-lost stranger. Well, I'll be damned.

How the hell did I know he was safe to be around. I didn't know where he had been, who he'd been around. There is a damn pandemic going on out there and it's killing people. Shit....what the hell do I do? But then again. He's been to my place. But he's been gone for six days. God knows where he's been.

"Um, there's a pandemic going on out there and I don't know where you've been. I don't really feel like getting sick…ya know. So I don't think that's such a good idea." He'd just have to get over it.

"Sweetheart, I swear to God that I'm safe. You'll understand when I explain things to you. I wouldn't want to make you sick for anything in the world. Please trust me. I want…no I have to see you. I've been going crazy just thinking about you. Please babe." Well, when he put it that way, how could I tell him no. "Alright, give me ten minutes," I answered back.

Another ding on my phone and it was Tina. I had ignored her long enough, and I would make this quick.

"Hi, Tina, what's up?" I asked.

"Oh, so finally you decide to answer me. Thanks…much. Where the hell have you been. And don't tell me you've been out because I know you can't with this damn pandemic." She sure was getting snippy. "I've been working my ass off. Seems with this pandemic and everyone at the doctors or in the hospital, the invoices and EOBs are flying in record time. I can't keep up with them. That's why I haven't answered you." I couldn't and wouldn't tell my best friend that I just didn't want to talk with her.

"So you seem to have time now. Good, call me. I have lots to tell you." She said.

"I'm right in the middle of something. Can I please call you tomorrow? I promise I will." I had to get rid of her. I only had five more minutes.

"Okay, I'm holding you to that. Talk to ya later."

I threw on a black t-shirt and a pair of black sweats, grabbed my keys, and went out the door. Making sure it was locked, I turned and went to the third apartment down from mine and knocked on the door. "Hey babe," Brody said as he stood in the doorway looking at me with nothing on but a pair of workout shorts. I know I didn't look my best but with the way he was starring at me, I wasn't sure if I was a total mess or if he liked how I appeared. I know I sure liked what I saw.

I barely got the word "Hey" out of my mouth and he was reaching for me around my waist and pulling me into him. God, he felt so good. His hard, hot body against mine made me melt and my knees started to go weak.

"Come on in and make yourself at home. It isn't much, just a usual bachelor pad. What would you like to drink? I have water, and umm water." He said as he ran his fingers through his hair.

"Water would be fine. Thank you." I said as I made my way to sit on the couch. It was up against the wall by the window and I had to be careful not to hit my head against the windowsill.

As he brought the glass of water in, with a few ice cubes, Brody reached out and took my hand.

"Morgan, please come with me. I have a movie I want to watch with you. I saw it the other day and I thought of you. I think you will enjoy it. But we have to watch it in the bedroom." He said with that slight crook of his lip.

As I let him lead me by the hand I asked him what kind of movie it was. He just said, "You'll see."

Brody's tv was high enough on the wall that I could lay down comfortably with my head propped up on the pillows. I put my hands behind my head and waited as he sat beside me and set it up. When it started to play, he turned the lights down very low, then curled up beside me. The opening scene was in a massage parlor lobby. The lady was escorted into a room, given a flute of champagne, and told to undress, get on the table, and put the cover over her. I looked over at Brody not believing he had put this type of movie on. He told me just to relax and enjoy.

Watching the lady getting a massage felt strange and a little uncomfortable. Yet it also made me wish it was me getting it from Brody. I wanted to feel his strong hands on my body making me relax like that lady was. He must have been reading my mind when he leaned his head next to my ear.

"Would you like to get a massage like that? Wouldn't it make you feel so good? Relaxing, feeling those muscles letting go." Then he started kissing my neck.

Oh, God. Was he seducing me? Yeah, he sure was, and I didn't want him to stop.

He kissed down my neck, across my chin, and stopped at my lips. His eyes met mine for a moment like he was asking for permission. My tongue came out and licked my bottom lip and that was all it took. His mouth covered mine with the most delicious kiss I had ever had.

Brody kissed me for a full minute or two before he pushed with his tongue for entrance. And I gave it to him. I wanted more from him and he gave it to me. His tongue explored and devoured me. I gave back as good as I got.

I moaned into his mouth, needing what he was giving, needing more. But he pulled away. My arms wrapped around his neck wanting to pull him back for more, but he chuckled.

"I'm not going anywhere little girl. There's plenty more to come." He said as he reached up and played with my hair.

He slid down on the bed and turned to lay partially over me. He worked my sweatshirt up slowly until he got it up above my bra.

"Please take your top off babe." He said as he started kissing along the top of the bra, along with my breasts. I did as he asked without thinking twice.

"Now the bra." I just did that too.

Brody got up on his knees and straddled my hips, reached up, and took both breasts in his hands. My thirty-six c's fit perfectly in his huge hands. He massaged them with practiced hands and had me moaning in no time. He worked his way inward to my nipples, playing with them until he had them peaking. Then he gave them little twists that had me moaning a bit louder. It hurt a bit but I felt it all the way toward my vagina.

When the tips were nice and hard he leaned over and took one into his mouth. Damn, it felt so good. I could deal with this all day long. Then he did the same thing to the other one. He kept it up, working each and then both at once until I was bucking my hips up into him. I was deep in need at this point. And I knew I was getting very wet.

"Something tells me you're liking this," Brody said with a grin on his face.

I could feel his hard-on through his shorts on my leg. My guess is that so was he. I also could tell that he was no small man down there either. Damn, what have I gotten myself into?

"Roll over babe." It wasn't a request. It was a demand. And I followed his directions.

He leaned over to his nightstand to get something, but I couldn't see what. When he was back over me, I felt something cool being rubbed into my back. He massaged it into my shoulders, back, and down to my buttocks. The more he did it the more I relaxed. It felt so damn good.

He leaned over and kissed my neck and whispered, "Are you liking this babe?" I shook my head yes.

Brody massaged my arms, all the way to my fingers and back up, down my back again to the crack of my ass. He worked my pants down and got them over my hips.

"Lift up sweetie so I can take these things off." He never asked, just told, but I did it.

He stood at the end of the bed and massaged me from my feet all the way to my upper thighs. He stopped at the apex of my sex and went back down again. He did this several times before he went for the gusto. When his finger went between my legs and touched my slit, I jumped. Even though I knew it was coming, at least I hoped it was, it still startled me. He put his other hand on my butt and worked the finger back in again. Back and forth he went for a few times, teasing, making me want more.

My butt started pushing up, trying to get more of his hand in there, wanting him to get closer to my little button to help me cum. I was getting so close.

"What's wrong babe? Is there something that you need?" he asked me, even though I know he already knew.

"Please Brody. I need to cum. Please help me get there." I was really moaning now.

"My my, you do have a problem, don't you? What do you think I should do about it?" He was really working me up now. I was starting to get a little irritated at him. He knew exactly what I needed.

"You know what I need, so please, be nice and play with my clit and make me cum." I asked him nicely.

"No, you're not quite ready yet sweetheart. I think you need a little bit more encouragement." He said as he flipped me over. I grunted as he did. What the hell was he up to?

Now I was flat on my back, looking straight up into Brody's eyes. They were so expressive, but I couldn't figure out what he meant when he said, 'NOT YET'. I know what edging is, but that wasn't what he was doing. Teasing, maybe, but what the hell was he up to?

I found out pretty quickly when he asked me how adventurous I was. I asked him why? What did that have to do with what we were doing? "Babe, I know how to make you cum like you haven't ever in your life. But I need you to take a chance with me and trust me. I promise not to hurt you. I would never do that. But I want to give you pleasure like you've never, ever known. Will you let me do that?" The look he gave me was serious, yet passionate.

"Look at the tv for a minute babe, watch what's going on." Brody's hand is touching me along my body as I'm watching. The lady has a blindfold on and her hands have been tied behind her head. She seems to be enjoying having the man touching her. He's gentle, caring.

"Imagine that being you. Me, touching you like that, as I am now, but with the blindfold on you won't know where or when I'm going to do it. There's no pain, just pleasure." He's explaining to me. It looks so good. I think I might enjoy trying this.

"Alright, I'll try. But what if I don't like it once we start?" I ask him just in case.

"Just tell me and I'll stop. Or you can pick out a word and if you say it, I'll stop. It's called a safe word." Brody said. "Morgan, I want you, very much. I want you to be pleasured so much that you will feel like your body has gone to heaven. All I ask is that you put yourself in my hands. Can you, will you do that?" Brody held very still, held his breath until I nodded my head yes.

"You have to say the words, my love." And he waited. "Yes, I want this. I want to try with you." I answered.

"First I want you to just lay back and close your eyes. Feel my touch. Go with it. Then keep them closed no matter what you feel or hear. Do you understand?" He waited for her to answer. She nodded her head.

"Always answer me with a verbal reply, so I don't misunderstand." He admonished her.

"Okay, sorry. Yes, I understand." Morgan answered.

I heard him get off the bed and move around the room. I didn't dare open my eyes as I'd been instructed not to. I lay there trying my best to relax.

Taking my right wrist in his hand, Brody tied something soft around it then took my left wrist and did the same thing. He took both my hands in his and lifted them to his mouth and kissed them. The next thing I knew he had moved them over my head to the headboard and tied them so I couldn't move them. It felt weird, but not too uncomfortable.

Still having my eyes closed, I felt a soft cloth being placed over them and being tied around my head to hold it secure. Now, I couldn't see nor move my hands.

I felt something warm like a lotion or oil being spread over my chest. He massaged it into my skin and it felt wonderful. Soon I was relaxing so much I almost fell asleep. He worked my breasts a little harder, putting more pressure toward the nipples. Tweaking them sent a kind of warmth down to my vagina like I hadn't felt since he had done it earlier. He did it several more times and I let out a few moans.

Brody poured more of the fluid on my abdomen and spread it around. He played around a little in my belly button and then moved his finger down toward my mound. His hand was gentle and it felt great. I was liking what he was doing a lot.

He pushed his finger down and into my lips, spreading them and working them as he worked the liquid in. It felt good and a little warm. Almost heated. Like he was using something different down there. As he moved his finger around the heat increased. My hips started moving with his hand as I was getting really turned on now. It was like I couldn't get enough. The more he gave, the more I wanted.

I felt him climb onto the bed and kneel in front of me. He spread my legs apart and I felt his warm breath upon me. The heat from the liquid and his mouth was like I was on fire. 'Holy shit,' I thought.

His hands spread my lips apart and his tongue touched my clit.

My hips raised off the bed in a jerk as my back arched. "Brody…My God." I cried as I almost came. I was so close.

His tongue came off my clit and worked all around my cunt as he brought me higher and higher, closer and closer. But he wouldn't let me reach that point yet. I begged and cried, but he denied me.

Brody played and licked some more, taking me to an abyss that I never knew before, yet he wouldn't let me get to the pinnacle of release. He finally inserted one finger inside of me. My hips rose to meet his thrust, but still, I needed more. I couldn't get there.

Then Brody put his left hand on my stomach, just above my pubic bone, and pushed down. At the same time, he pushed in a second finger and turned them upward to connect with my Gspot. As he did that he leaned down and sucked my clit into his mouth and bit it.

"Brodyyyyyy. " I yelled. My hips tried to buck but he held me down. I felt like I was exploding. My breath caught in my throat and I couldn't breathe. Yet he wouldn't let up.

The next thing I felt was his fingers pulling out and his tongue going inside of me, tasting me. He was like a ravenous man who hadn't ever tasted a woman. He couldn't get enough. He was getting as much of me as he could and damn if it didn't feel good. He brought me to another mind-blowing climax.

When he had satisfied his hunger Brody climbed up my body and kissed me fervently. I tasted myself on his tongue. His face was wet with my juices. But I didn't care. I loved what he had done to me. And I didn't taste too bad either.

At some point, he had slipped off his shorts, because I could feel his hard shaft sitting right at my opening. He was so hard and he was pulsing against me. I wanted him inside of me like a fish needs water to survive. I needed to feel him inside of me, filling me. Even though I hadn't seen him yet, I could tell by the feel of him, he had to be of pretty good size.

I was so wet now that he had very little trouble trying to work the head of his cock inside of me. But just barely.

"Damn babe, you're pretty tight. I'm a fairly big guy and I don't want to hurt you, so we'll go slow, ok?" Brody said as he pushed a little bit more inside.

I let out a slight wince and he stopped, letting me get used to him before he pushed again. It took us quite a few times of doing this before he was comfortably inside of me.

Well, I don't know if comfortable is the right word. Every time he tried to move back out a little and back in, it was difficult. For me. He filled me up so much there wasn't any room left to move around much. "You are a tiny thing. That's ok though, once we get you stretched out you'll love it. I promise." Brody was trying everything to encourage me.

He reached up and took the blindfold off. He said he wanted us to watch each other while we fucked.

Slowly and gently he kept working his shaft in and out of me. He played with my nipples, pinching them and it made my vaginal muscles squeeze him.

Smiling at me he said, " You seem to like it when I get a little rough with you. At least your cunt says so. It talks to me when I do this." He says as he pinches my nipple again. I let out a squeal.

Gradually we've gotten where we are able to move pretty easily with each other. In and out, deeper each time. I don't like it when he hits my cervix and I let him know it. He eases up for a bit, then goes harder again.

Brody reaches between us a plays with my clit until I'm so ready to cum. I tell him to please stop. I can't take it.

"Yes, you can." He says as he puts both hands under my ass, lifts it up, and starts to fuck me hard.

"I want you to cum with me, babe. Not before. Hold it as long as you can." He says while he's pounding the shit out of me.

'Is this guy for real?' I think to myself.

Brody knew he was getting close, but he wanted to get her there with him. He reached around and got his pinky wet from her juices. As he was ready to give the last few pumps into her he untied her hands, looked into her eyes, and told her to wrap her arms around his neck and hold on. He knew with what he was about to do to her, she was going to go wild.

I did as Brody told me to do, reaching up and wrapping my hands around his neck. He grabbed my legs and put them around his waist. He was holding me so tightly to him that my clit was being smashed into his pelvis every time he pushed into me. I was very close to cumming.

"Please Brody, I can't hold it any longer. Please, let me cum baby." I begged him.

"Almost honey, almost.. hold on just a couple of seconds more." Brody was banging her for all he was worth. He gave her his all.

Again, he got his finger good and wet and as he reached up to insert it he said,

"Now sweetheart, let it go. Cum for me." Then he pushed into her little star with his pinky as he pushed his cock a final time into her hard and he started pumping his cum into her, right up to her cervix.

I pounded on his back as I felt him slide his finger into my asshole. How dare he...but then I erupted into a massive orgasm. It was nothing compared to earlier, or ever in my life. What the fuck did he do to me?

I cried. I cursed. I wept. Then I passed out.

When I woke up I was curled up in Brody's arms. He was holding me tight to his body, cuddling me. I didn't know where I was for a moment, but then I remembered.

"Are you alright? Do you want some water?" Brody sounded concerned.

"Ahhh, yeah. I think so. And yes please, I'd like some water." I said as he released me long enough to reach behind him to get the glass off the nightstand.

I drank the whole glass before I looked back up at him. "What just happened?" I asked.

"I would say you had a super orgasm and passed out. Did you enjoy it?" He asked with a grin on his face.

"Well, I can't say I've ever done something like that before. I think it's the best sexual experience I've ever had." I grinned right back at him.

Just then my phone went crazy. It rang and rang, even though I let it go to voice mail, the caller called back again.

"Maybe you better see who that is. They seem pretty persistent." Brody said.

"It's probably my best friend Tina. She's been calling me all day. I told her I would call her tomorrow." I said as I again ignored the call. "Okay, how about we take a shower and clean up. Then you are welcome to stay the night if you want to. I'd really like it if you would."

Brody said as he headed for the bathroom.

As he was about to turn on the shower his phone went off. He walked out and looked at it.

"Fuck, not again. Already." He exclaimed as he hit the answer button.

"Yeah, this better be good." Brody wasn't in the mood to be called back in so soon.

He listened for a few minutes and then cut the call. Morgan was already in the shower. She didn't want to eavesdrop on the call.

He jumped in the shower with her. "Babe, I really hate to do this to you…and to me, but that call means I have to leave again for a while. But I need a favor from you. I need a ride to work. My truck is in the shop and I can't get it out at this hour. They did me a favor even working on it." He got it all out, holding his breath that she would understand.

"Sure, but what kind of work do you do that they call you out in the middle of the night? And that keeps you gone for days at a time?"

"You know that movie we watched that night at your house? Well, that's what I do." He waited for her reaction.

"Do what? No, you aren't serious. This is a joke, right?" I waited for him to deny it but he didn't.

"Holy shit. I'll be damned. You're a Seal? For real?" I still had my doubts. But I didn't think he would lie. Now it made sense why he was gone so much, and so long sometimes.

"Yeah honey, I am. And right now I have to go. But that doesn't mean this is over for you and me. Not by a long shot. You got me?" Brody said as he took her into a huge bear hug.

Oh My God, wait till Tina hears about this. She's going to have a cow.

They dressed quickly and got to where Brody had to be dropped off. He said he would call her when he got back to have her pick him up at the same place. No, he had no idea when that would be. But he'd stay in touch as he could. Then he kissed her and was gone.

Just as she was about to pull out of the parking lot she saw Tina's car. What was she doing here? She pulled up beside her and rolled down her car window.

"Hey Tina, what are you doing here?" Curiosity was killing her. "Well hello there, I could ask you the same thing."

"I just dropped Brody off. His truck is in the shop and he needed a ride. I just found out he is a Seal. Can you believe that?" She said with a sly grin on her face.

"That's strange, cuz I just dropped off Jacob. He got a call a little while ago to report in. I just found out a couple of days ago that he's a Seal too. That's what I was trying to tell you the day you cut me off on the phone." Tina said.

"Wow, this is so weird, two guys that we both like being Navy Seals. How crazy is that?" I said as I started to roll up my window.

"Wait, You like Brody? When did that happen? What the hell is going on with you two?" Tina made it her business to know everything. "Guess I found someone during a wistful pandemic." I rolled up my window and drove away.